SHAWN & MAC

PRESENT...

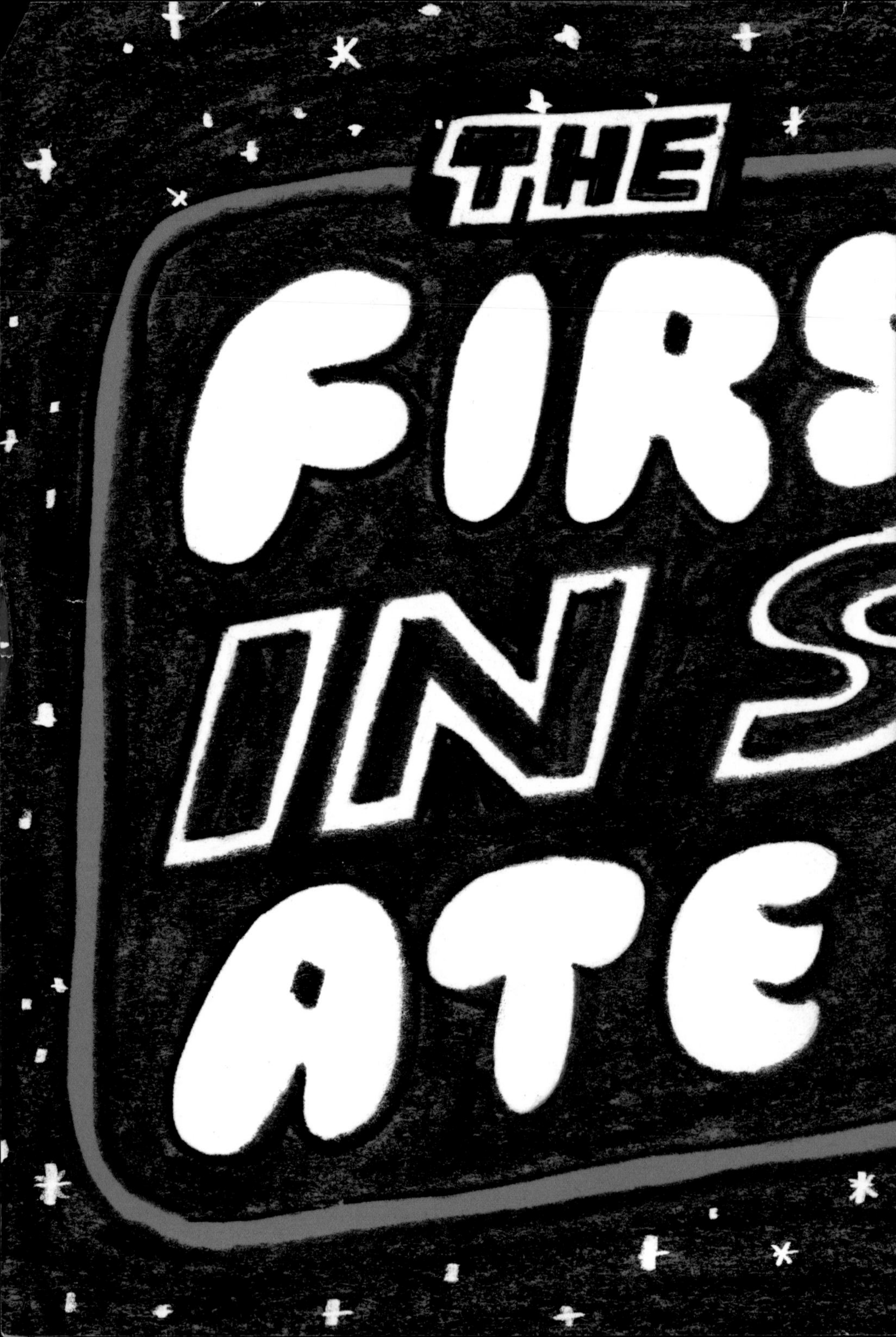
THE
FIR
IN
ATE

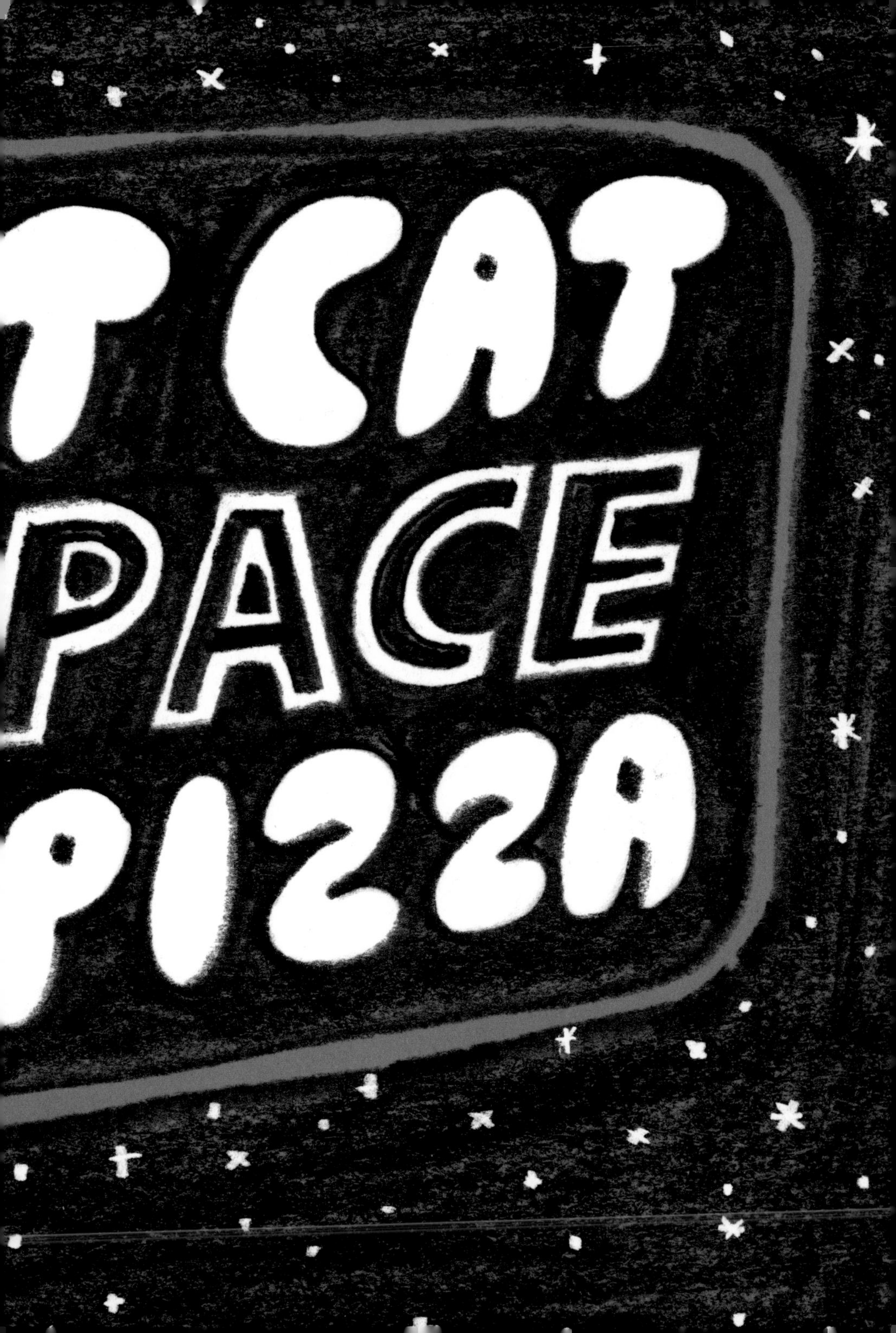
T CAT
PACE
PIZZA

For the Club Heads —M.B. & S.H.

Katherine Tegen Books
Imprints of HarperCollinsPublishers

HarperAlley is an imprint of HarperCollins Publishers.

Katherine Tegen Books is an imprint of HarperCollins Publishers.

The First Cat in Space Ate Pizza

For information address HarperCollins Children's Books, a division of HarperCollins Publishers, 195 Broadway, New York, NY 10007.
www.harpercollinschildrens.com

ISBN 978-0-06-308408-7 (trade bdg.) — ISBN 978-0-06-308409-4 (pbk.)

Typography by Shawn Harris
23 24 25 26 27 TC 14 13 12 11 10 9 8 7 6 5
First Edition

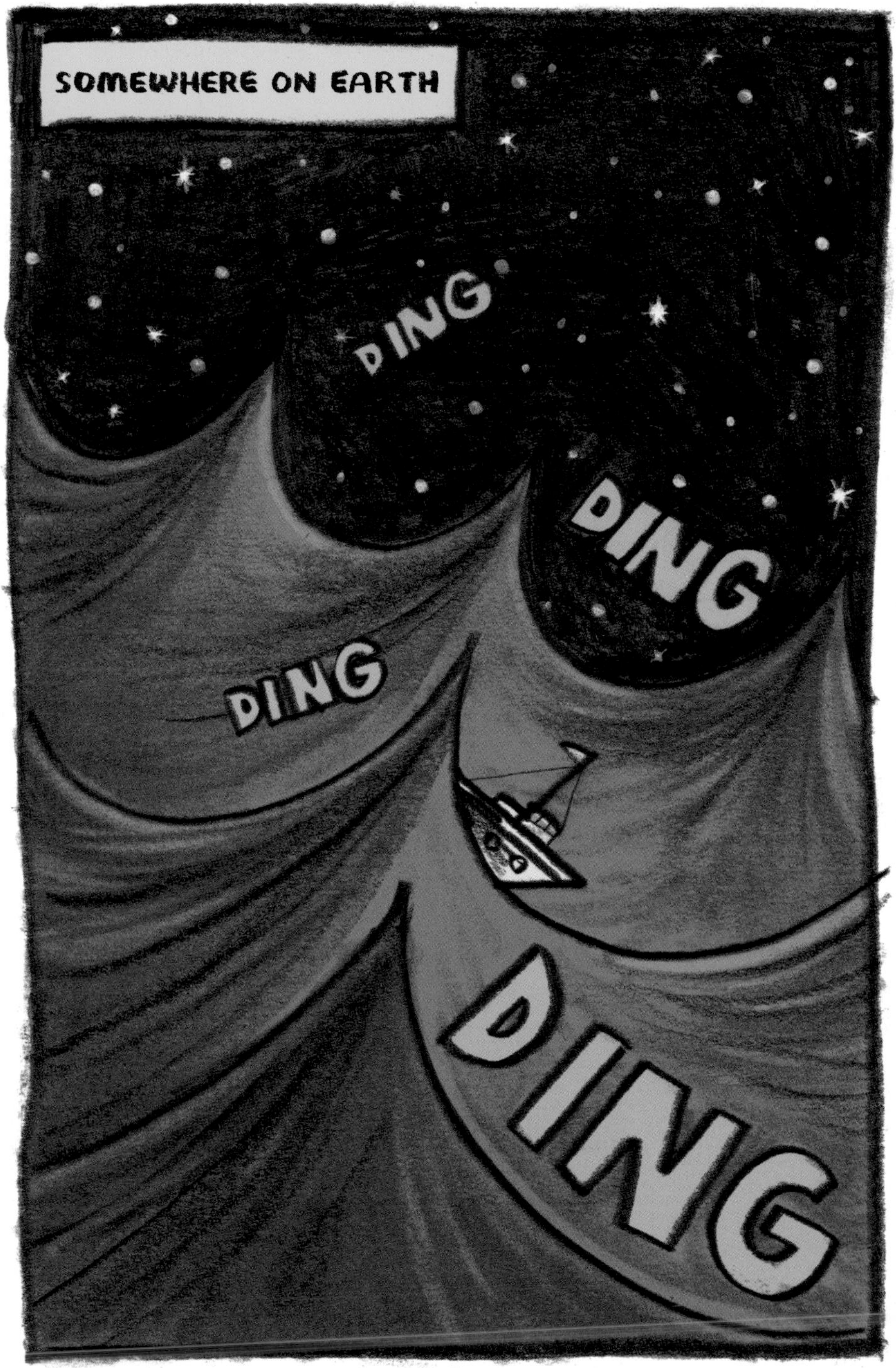
SOMEWHERE ON EARTH
DING
DING
DING
DING

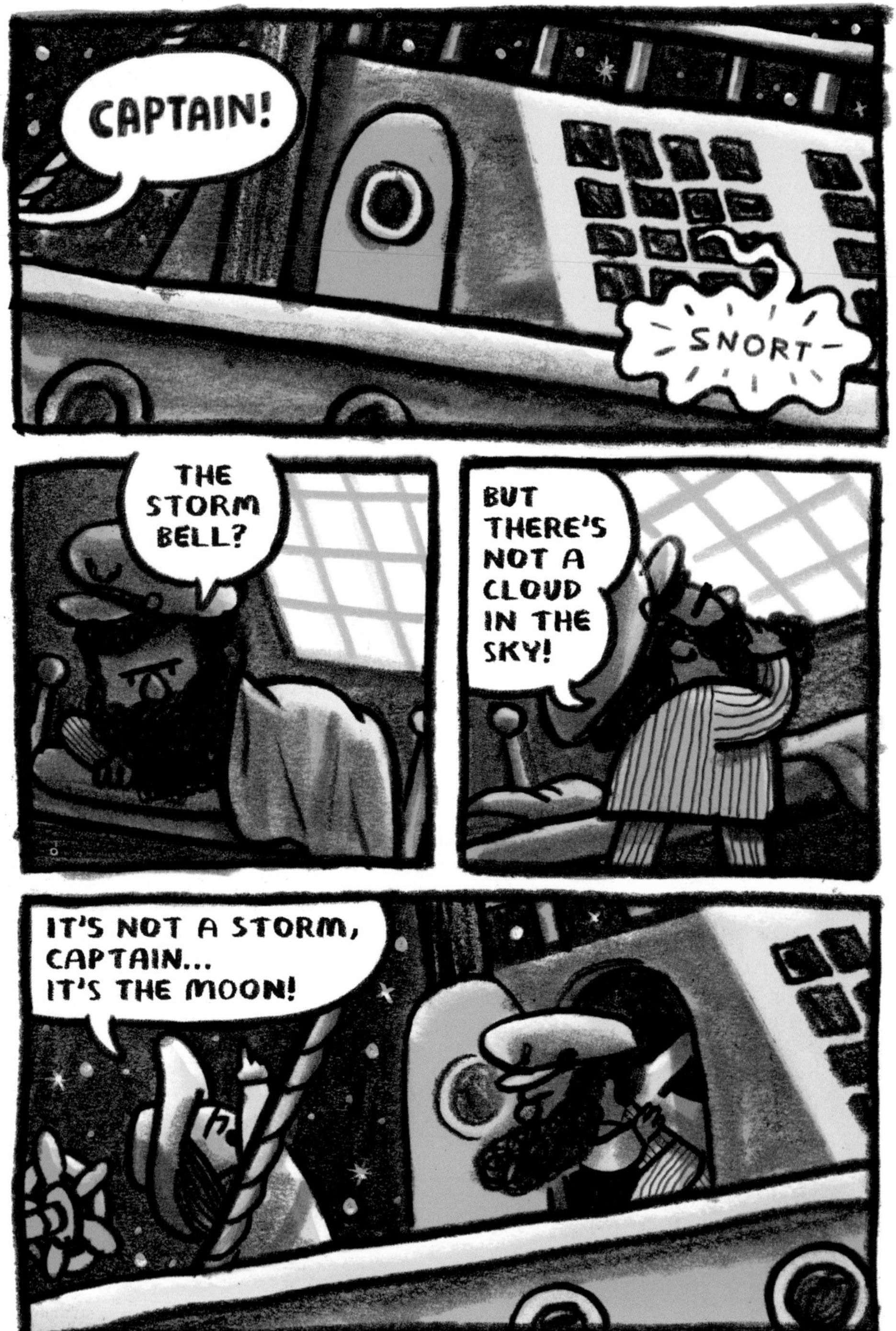
CAPTAIN!
SNORT
THE STORM BELL?
BUT THERE'S NOT A CLOUD IN THE SKY!
IT'S NOT A STORM, CAPTAIN... IT'S THE MOON!

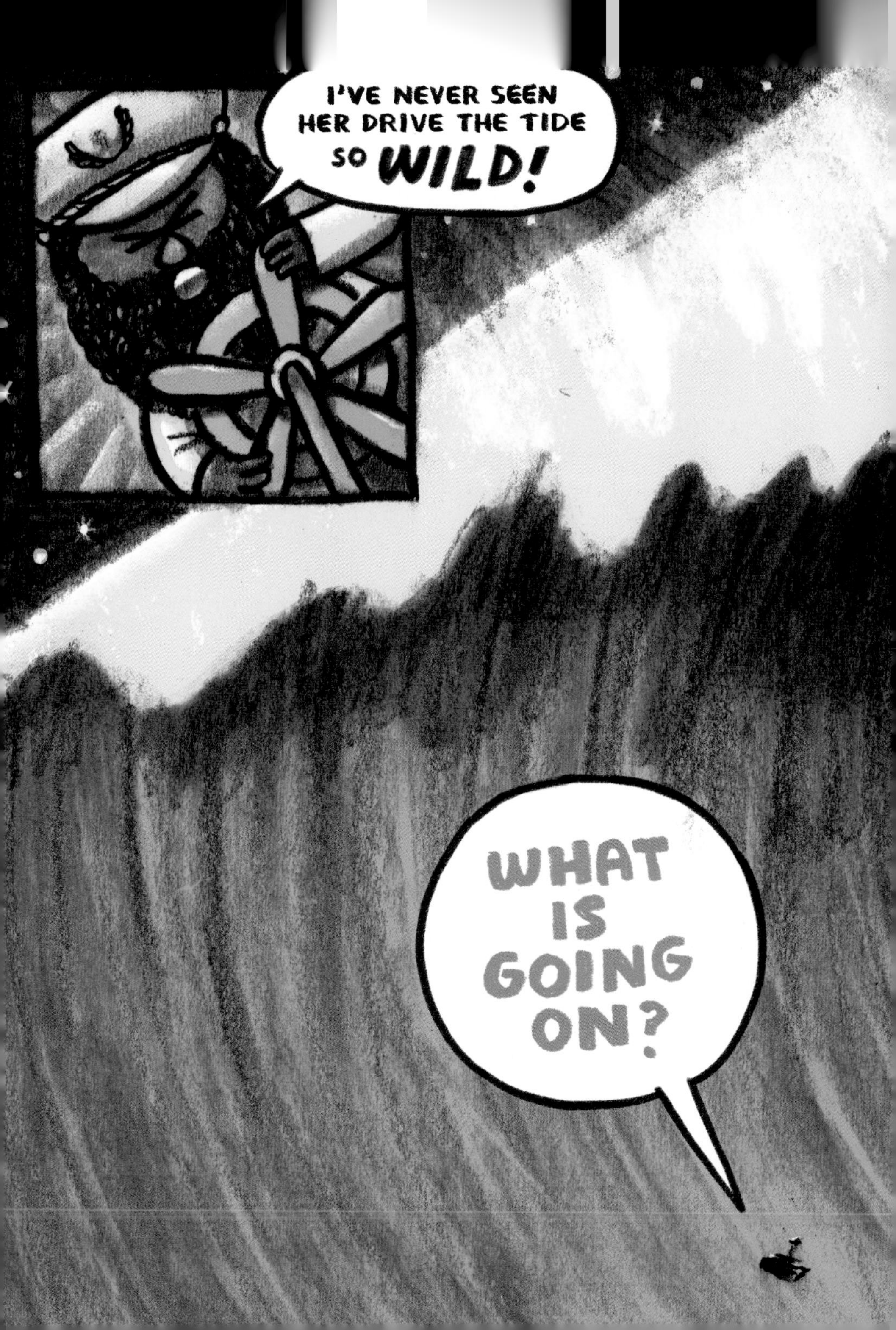
I'VE NEVER SEEN HER DRIVE THE TIDE SO WILD!
WHAT IS GOING ON?

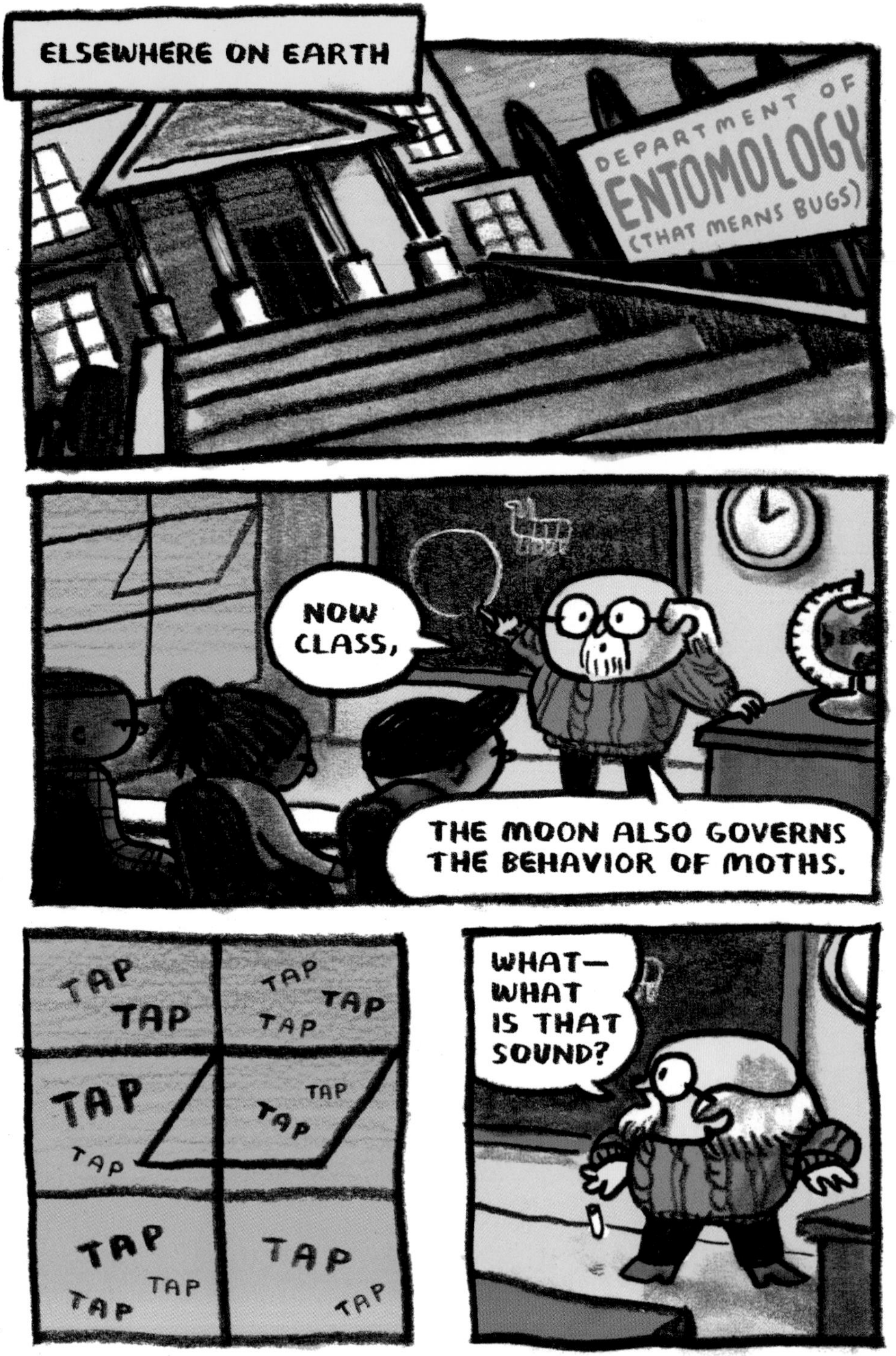
ELSEWHERE ON EARTH
DEPARTMENT OF ENTOMOLOGY (THAT MEANS BUGS)
NOW CLASS,
THE MOON ALSO GOVERNS THE BEHAVIOR OF MOTHS.
TAP TAP TAP TAP TAP TAP TAP TAP TAP TAP TAP TAP TAP TAP TAP
WHAT—WHAT IS THAT SOUND?

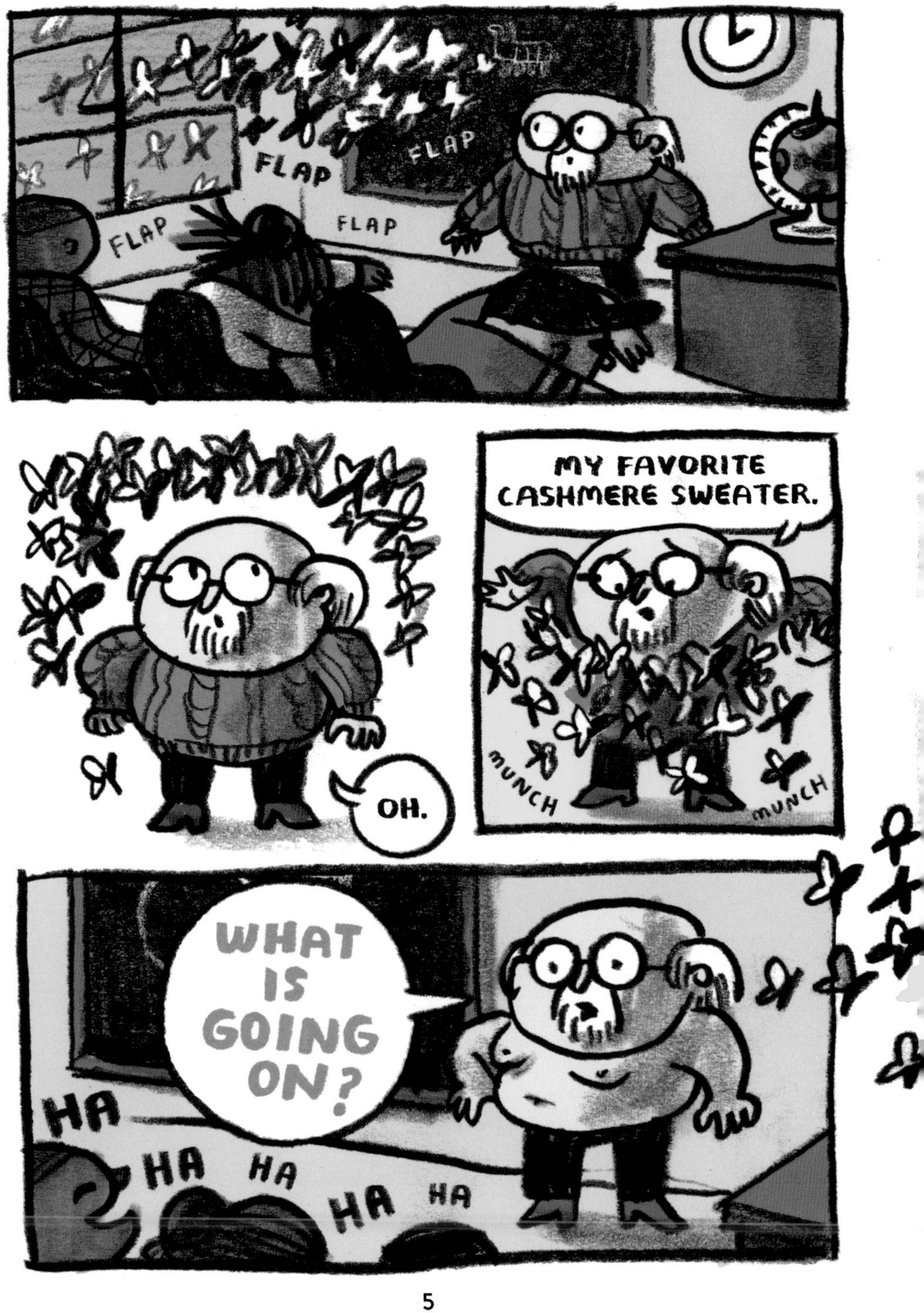
FLAP
FLAP
FLAP
FLAP
OH.
MY FAVORITE CASHMERE SWEATER.
MUNCH
MUNCH
WHAT IS GOING ON?
HA
HA
HA
HA
HA

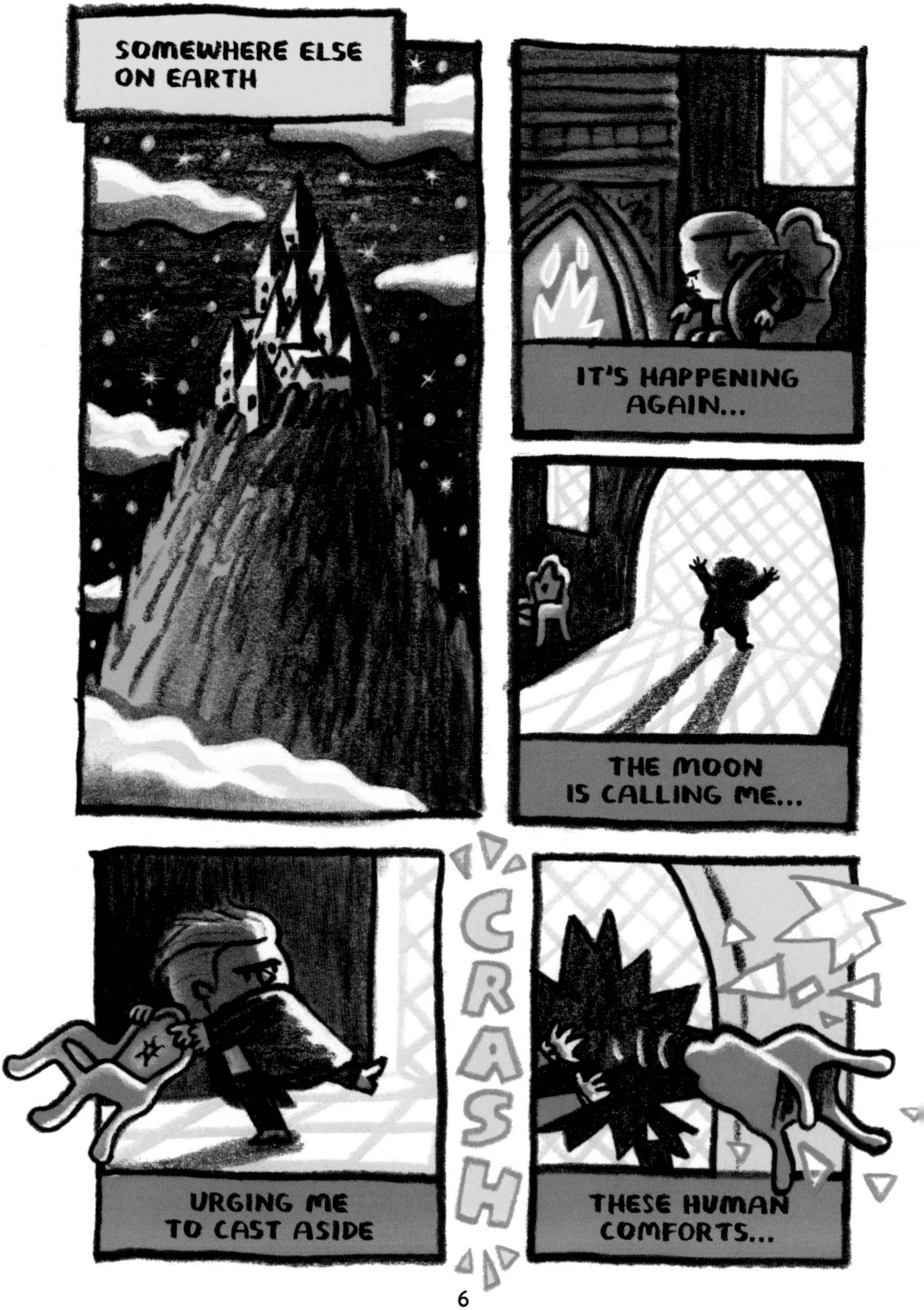
SOMEWHERE ELSE ON EARTH
IT'S HAPPENING AGAIN...
THE MOON IS CALLING ME...
URGING ME TO CAST ASIDE
CRASH
THESE HUMAN COMFORTS...

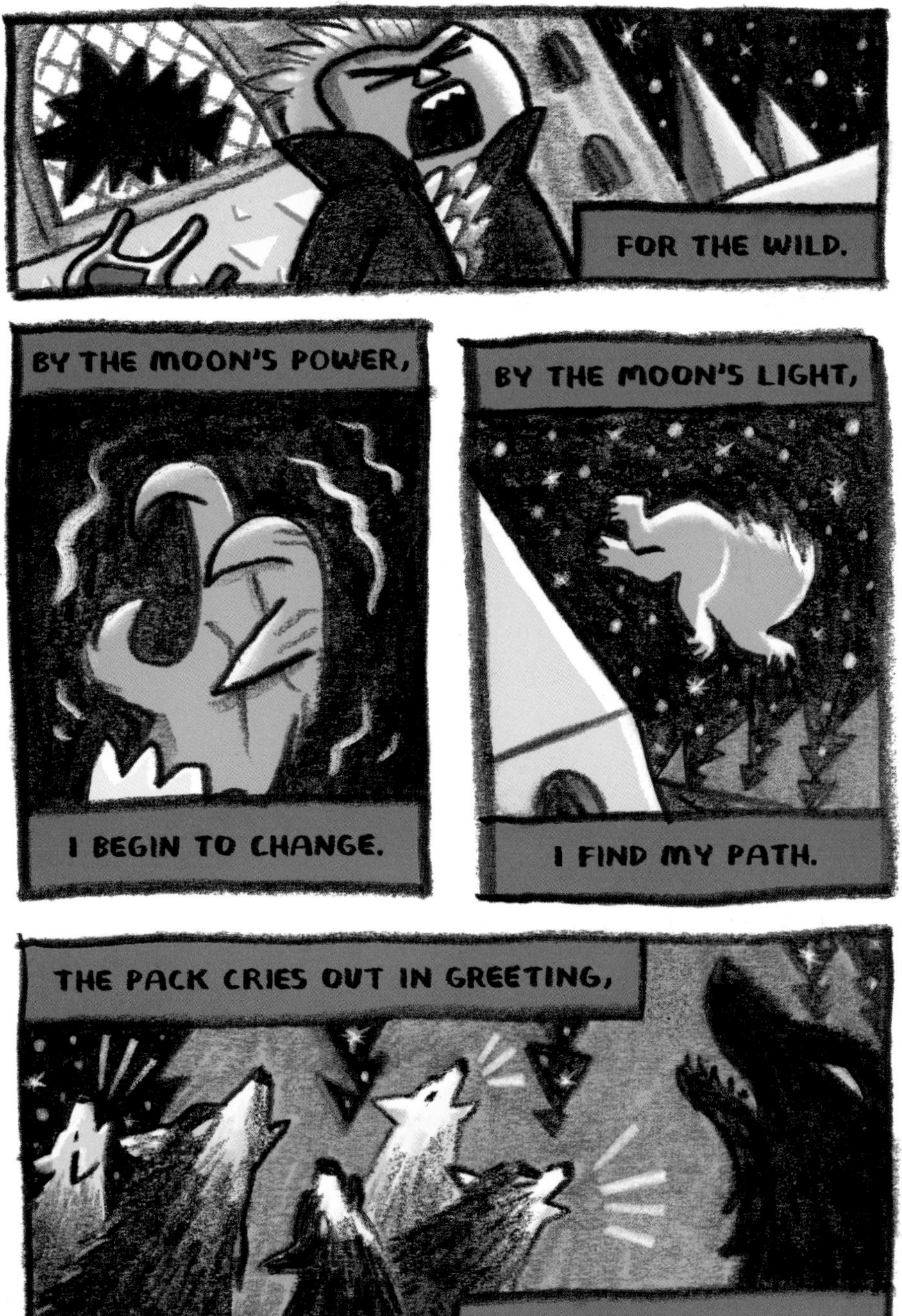
FOR THE WILD.
BY THE MOON'S POWER,
I BEGIN TO CHANGE.
BY THE MOON'S LIGHT,
I FIND MY PATH.
THE PACK CRIES OUT IN GREETING,
AND I ANSWER BACK...

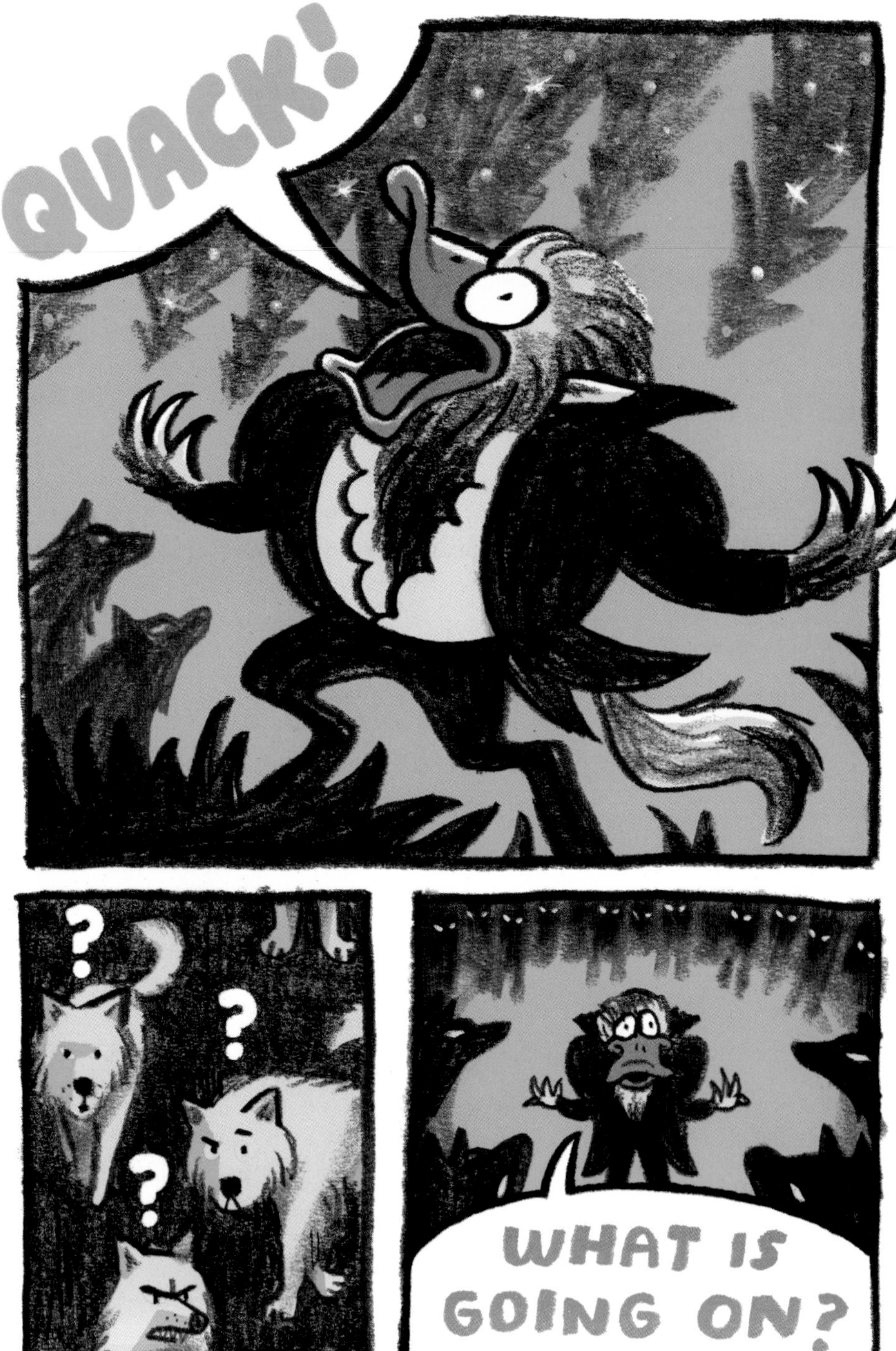
QUACK!
?
?
?
WHAT IS GOING ON?

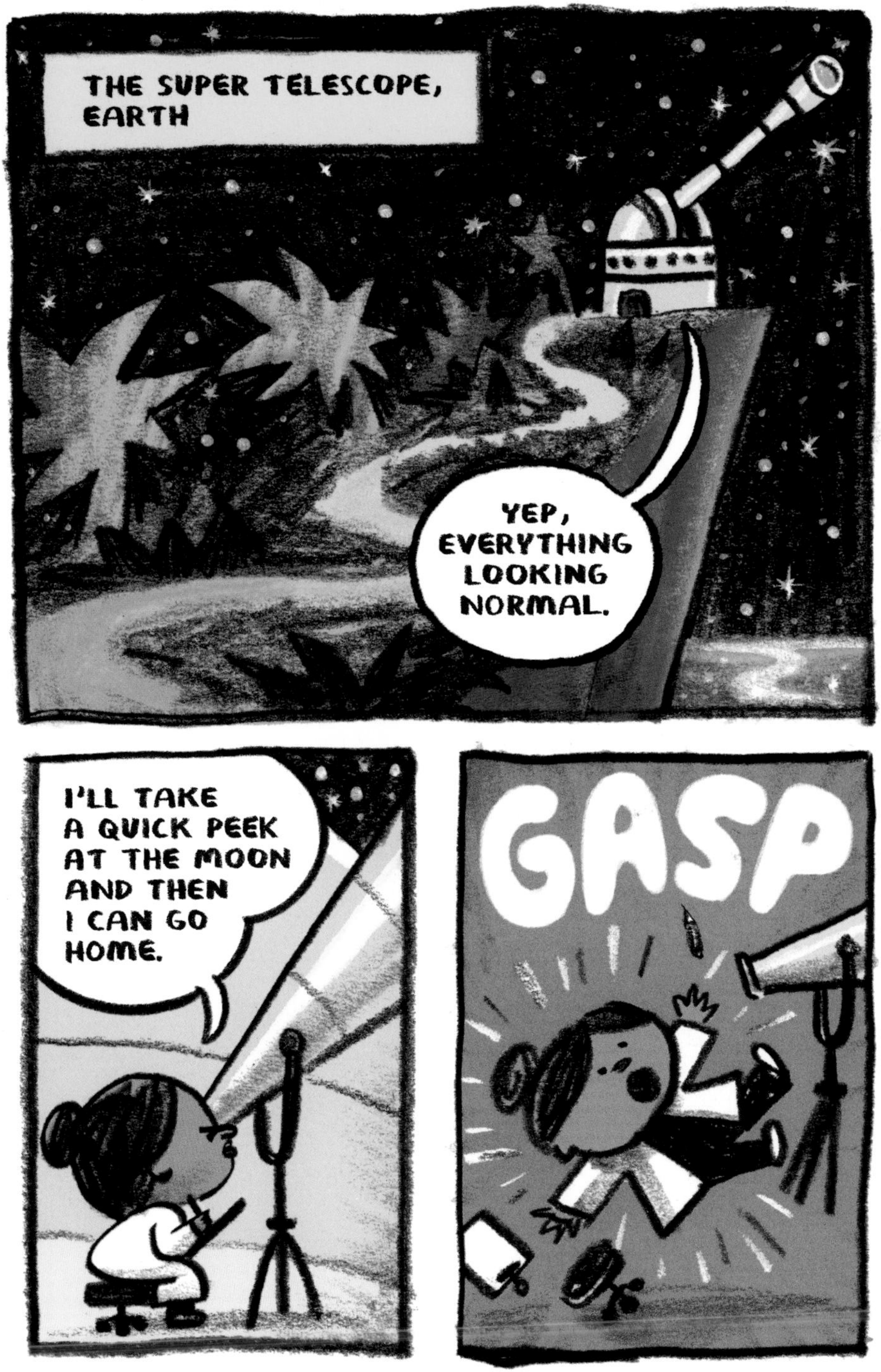
THE SUPER TELESCOPE, EARTH
YEP, EVERYTHING LOOKING NORMAL.
I'LL TAKE A QUICK PEEK AT THE MOON AND THEN I CAN GO HOME.
GASP

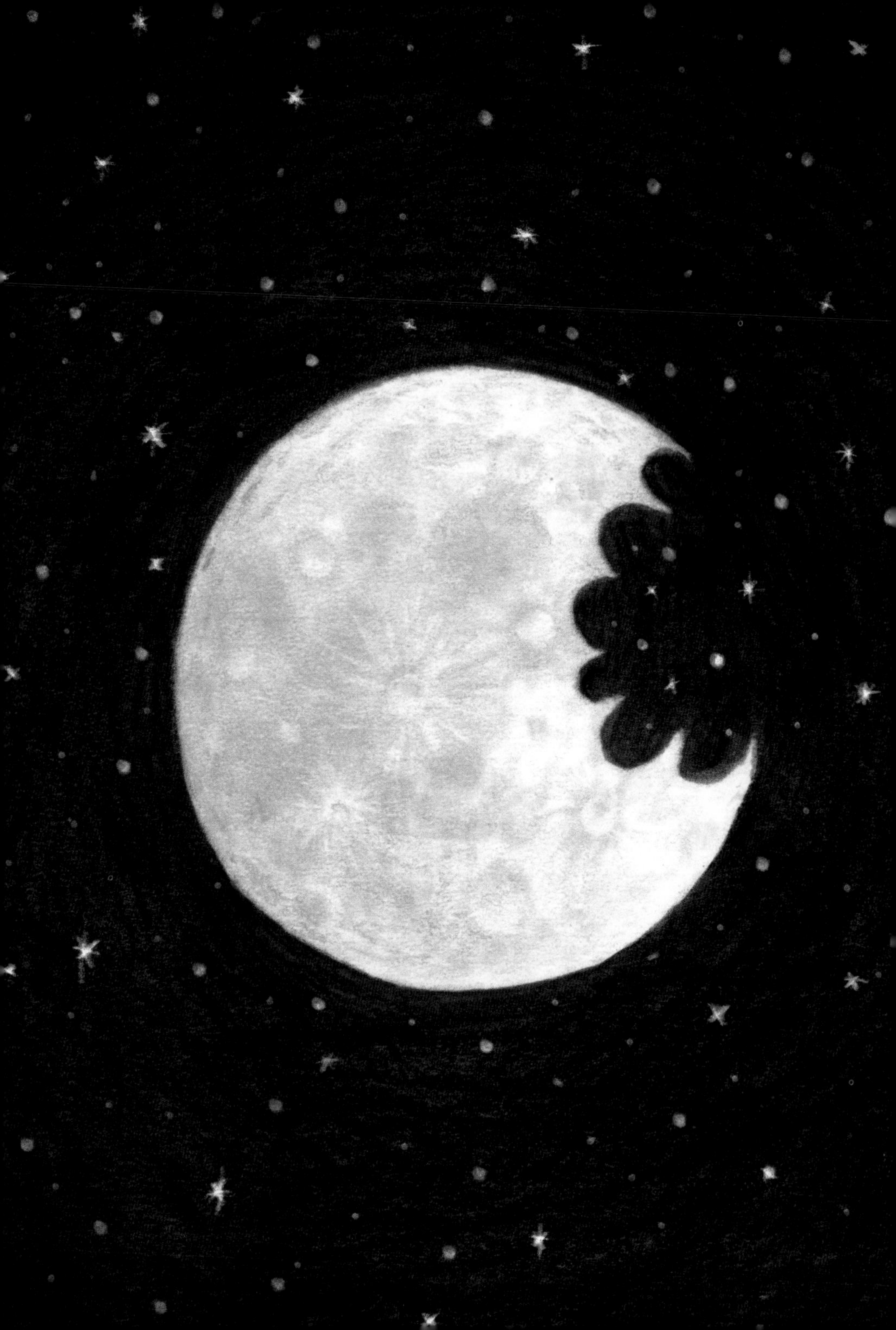

CHAPTER 1

MOON TROUBLE

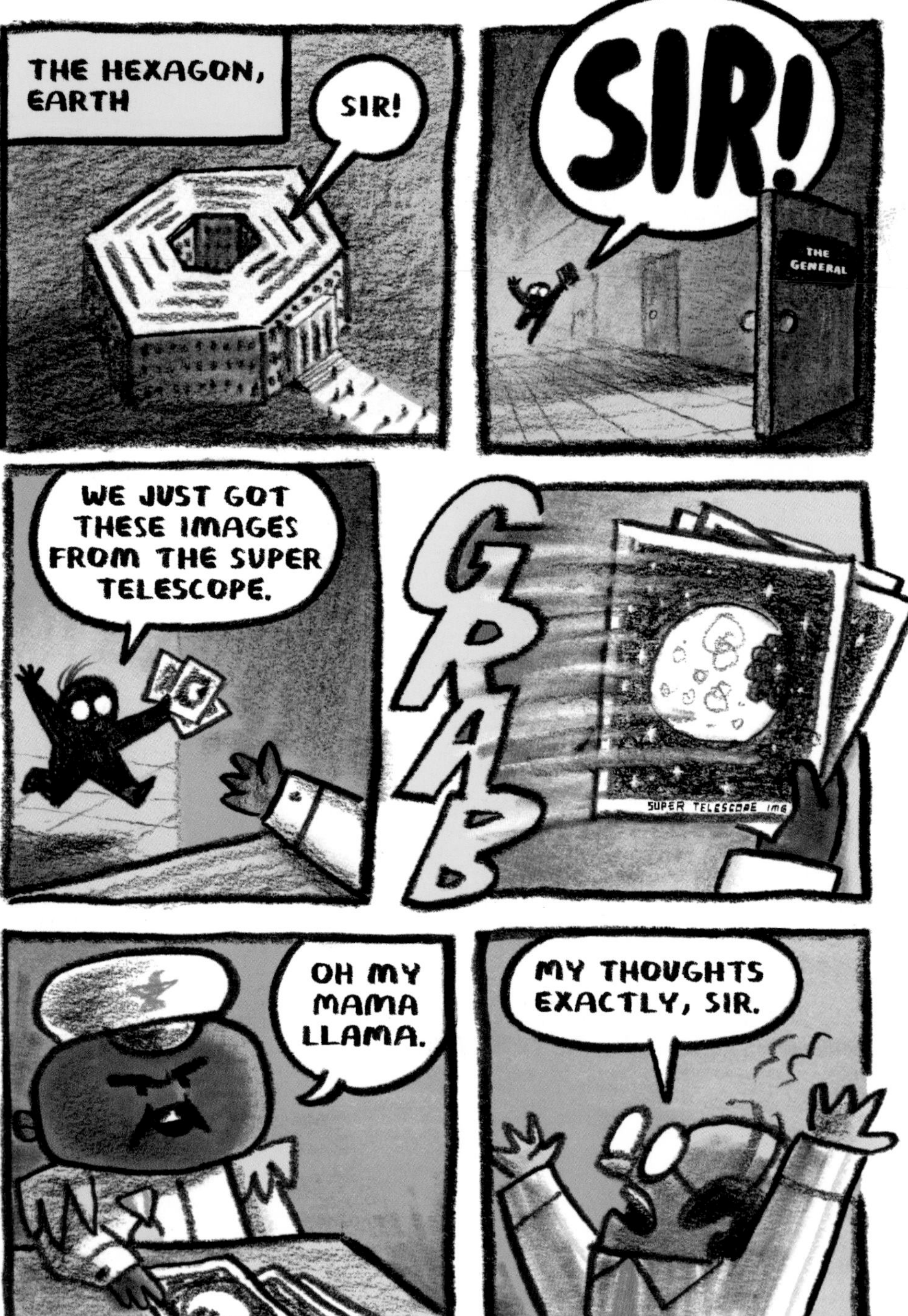
THE HEXAGON, EARTH
SIR!
SIR!
THE GENERAL
WE JUST GOT THESE IMAGES FROM THE SUPER TELESCOPE.
GRAB
SUPER TELESCOPE IMG
OH MY MAMA LLAMA.
MY THOUGHTS EXACTLY, SIR.

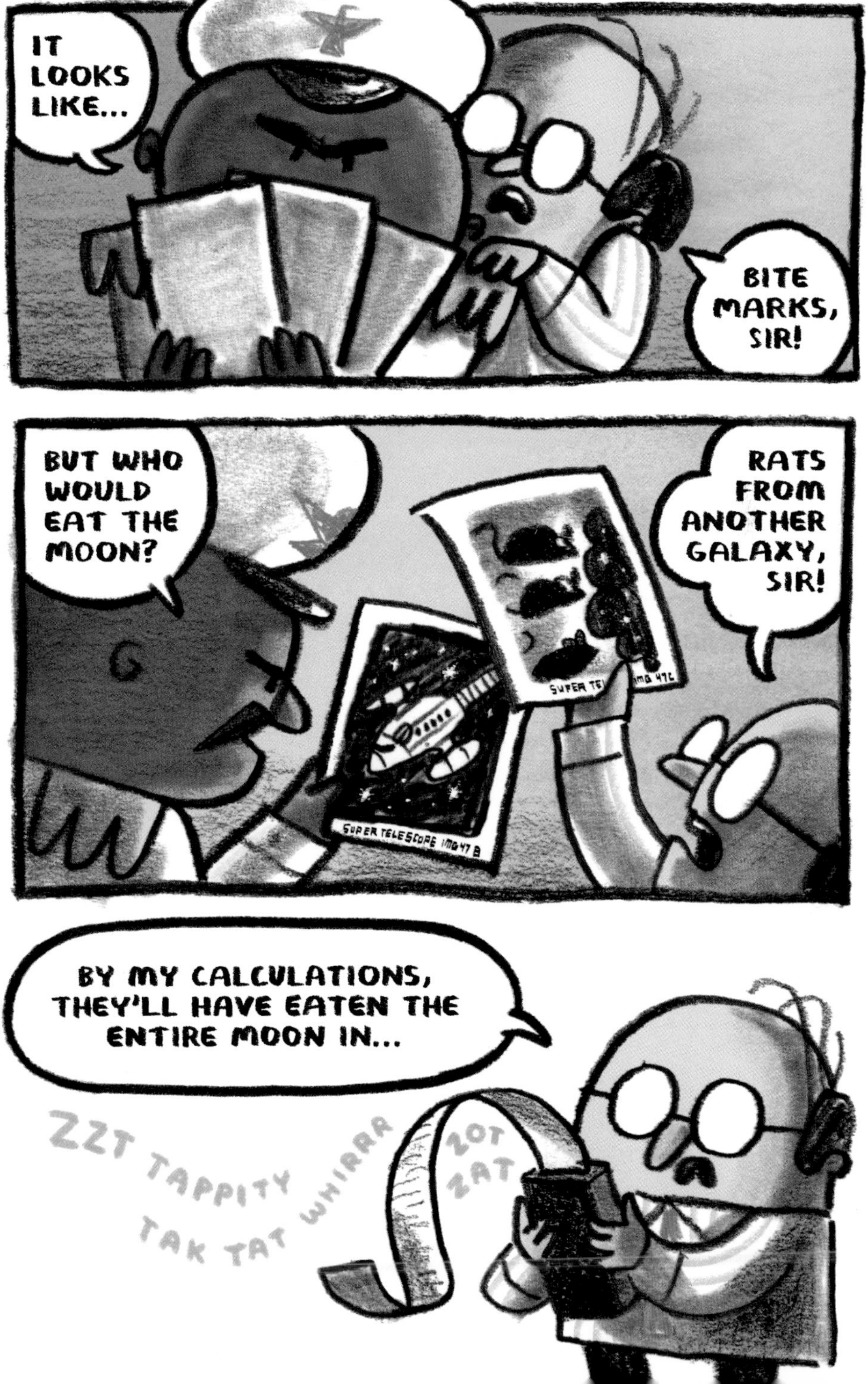
IT LOOKS LIKE...
BITE MARKS, SIR!
BUT WHO WOULD EAT THE MOON?
RATS FROM ANOTHER GALAXY, SIR!
SUPER TELESCOPE IMG47 B
BY MY CALCULATIONS, THEY'LL HAVE EATEN THE ENTIRE MOON IN...
ZZT TAPPITY WHIRRR
TAK TAT
ZOT ZAT

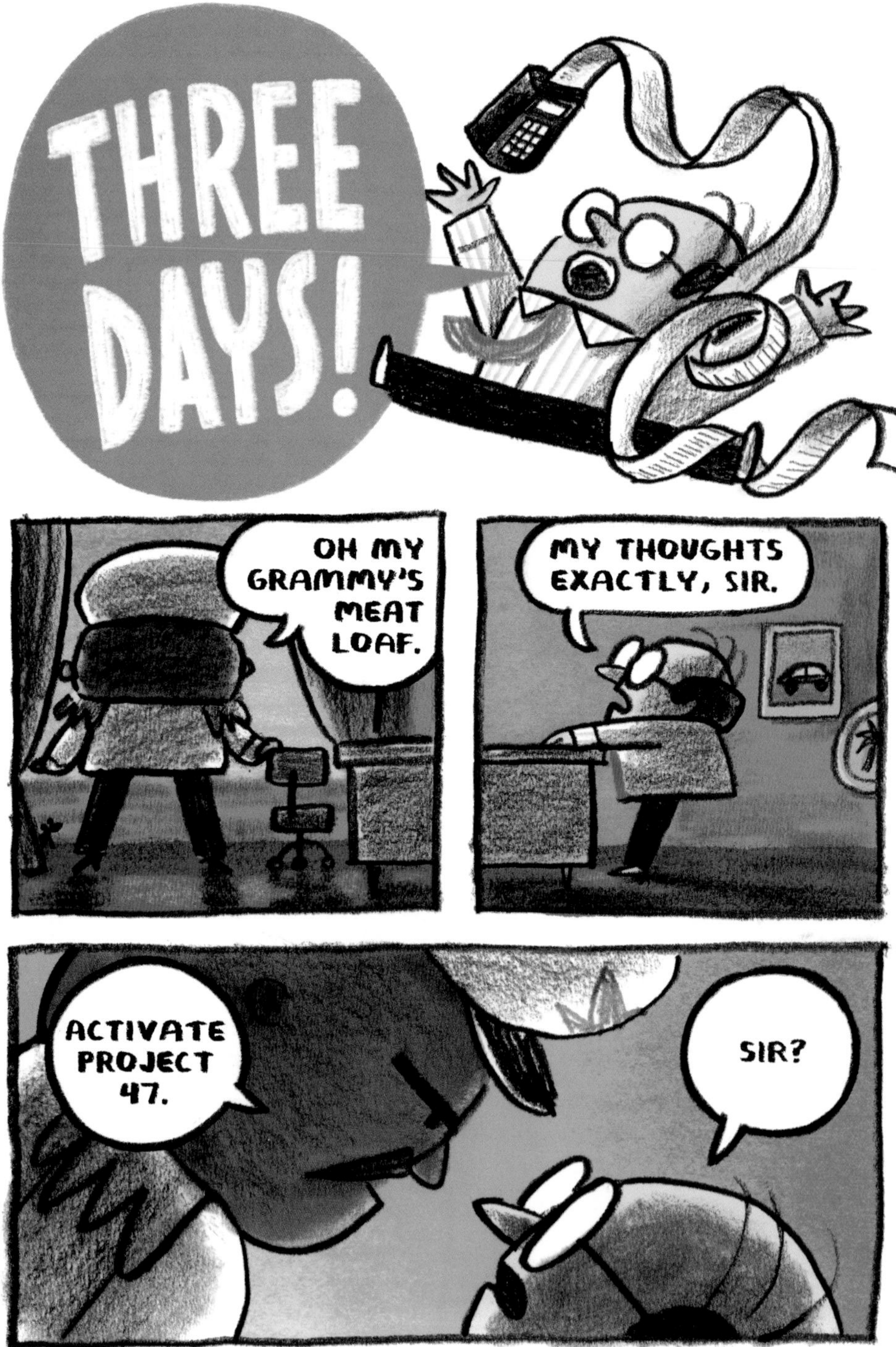
THREE DAYS!
OH MY GRAMMY'S MEAT LOAF.
MY THOUGHTS EXACTLY, SIR.
ACTIVATE PROJECT 47.
SIR?

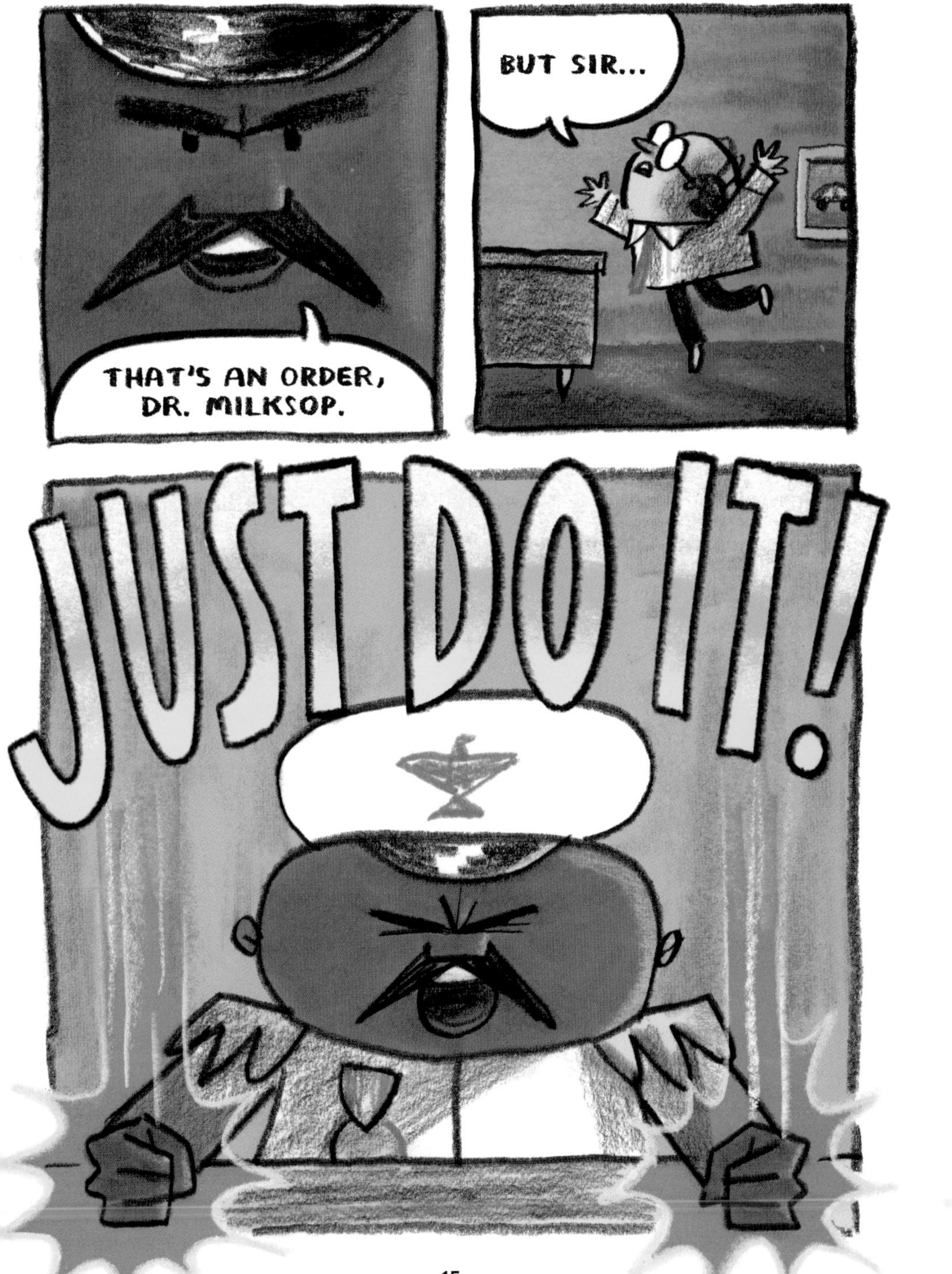
THAT'S AN ORDER, DR. MILKSOP.
BUT SIR...
JUST DO IT!

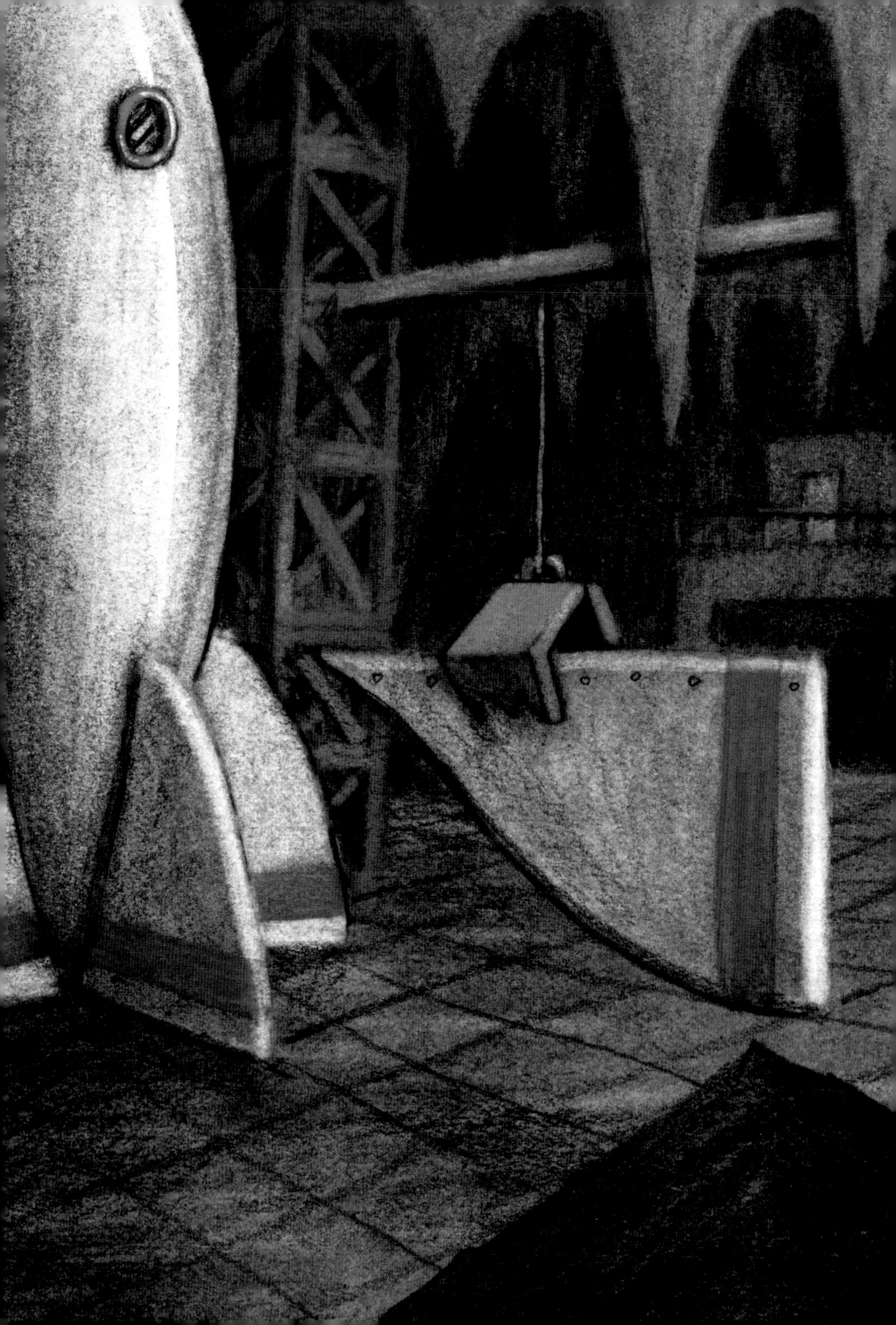

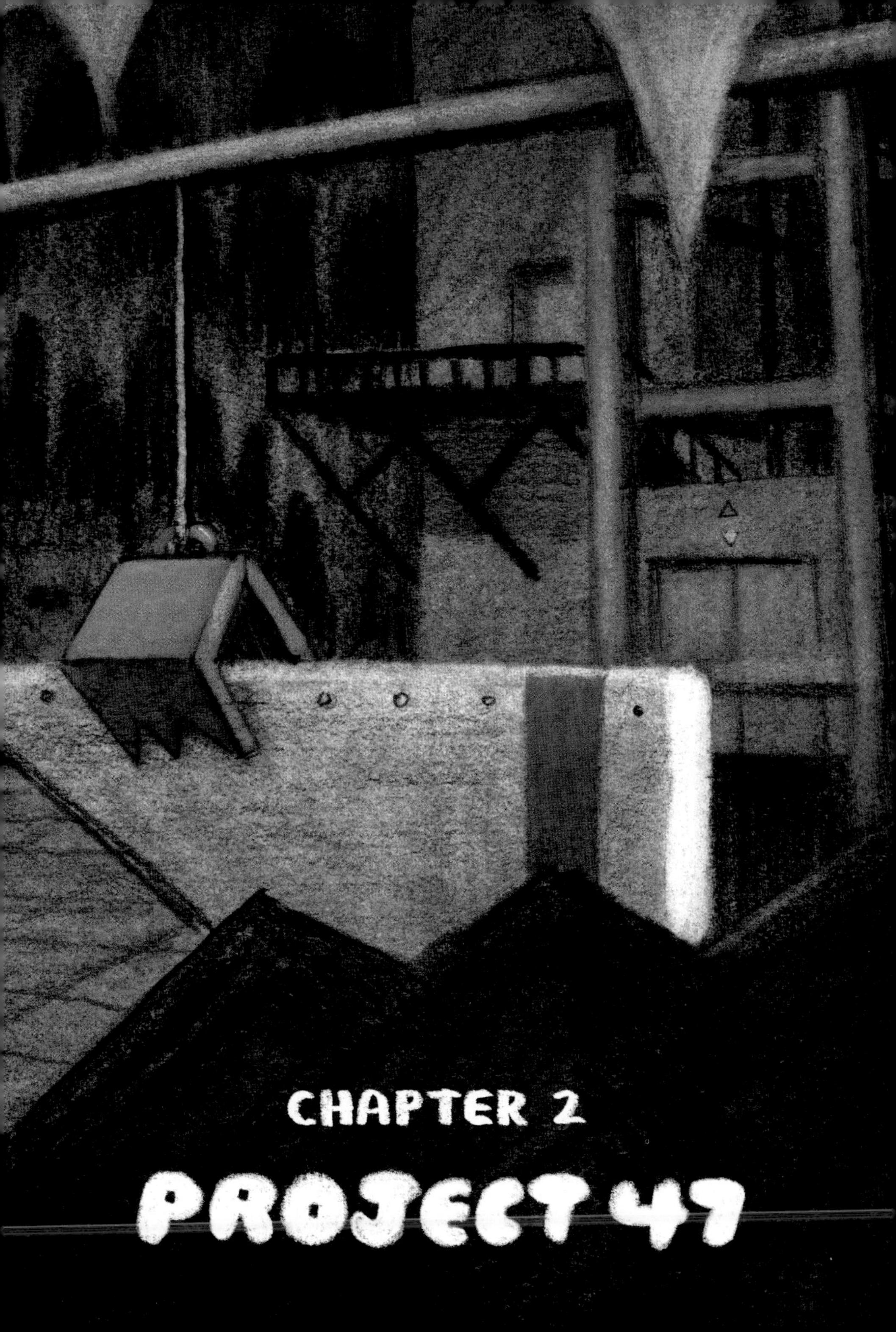

CHAPTER 2

PROJECT 47

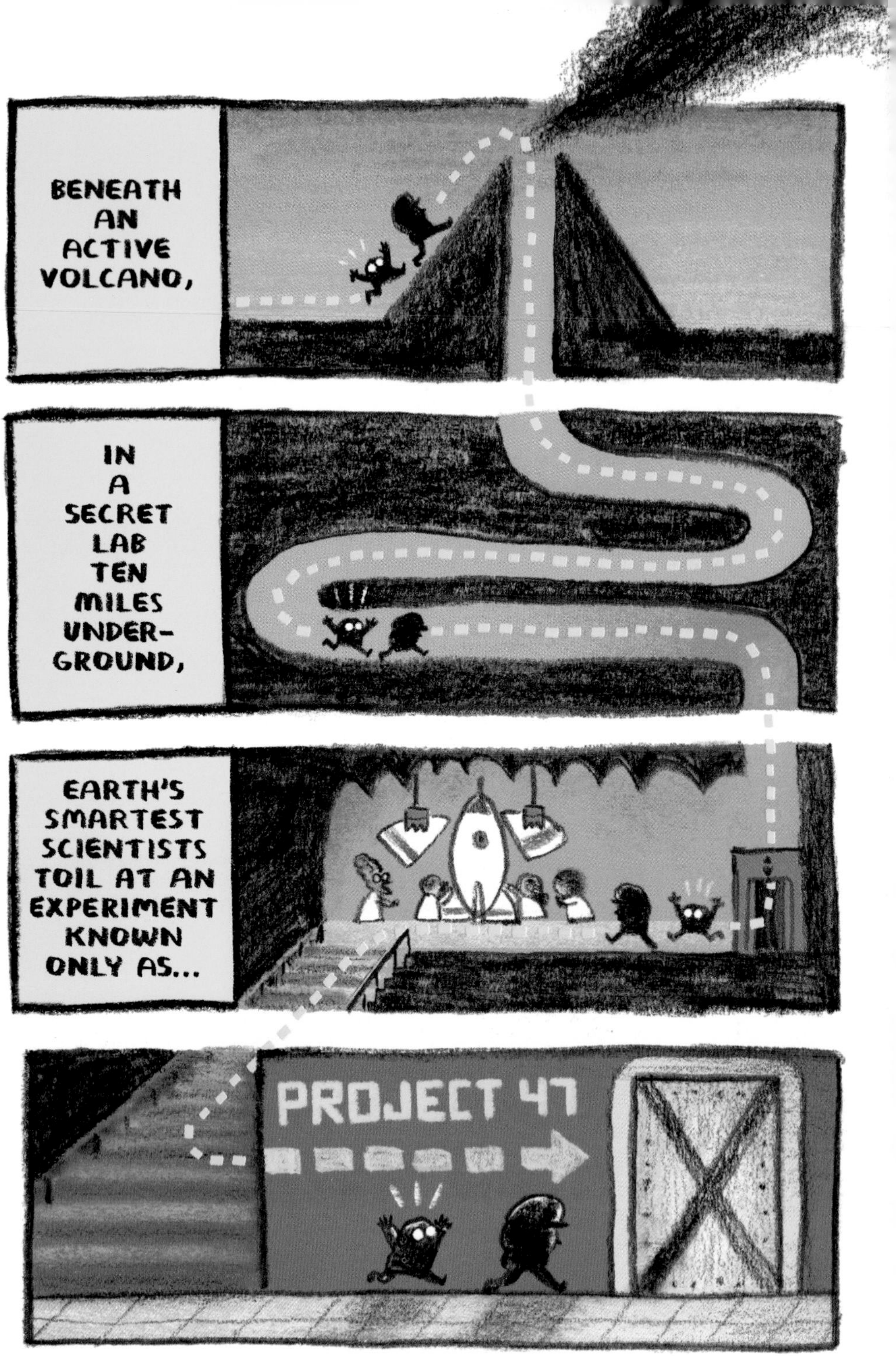

BENEATH AN ACTIVE VOLCANO,
IN A SECRET LAB TEN MILES UNDER-GROUND,
EARTH'S SMARTEST SCIENTISTS TOIL AT AN EXPERIMENT KNOWN ONLY AS...
PROJECT 47

BEHIND THIS BLAST-PROOF STEEL DOOR
LIES THE MOON'S SAVIOR
AND EARTH'S LAST HOPE...

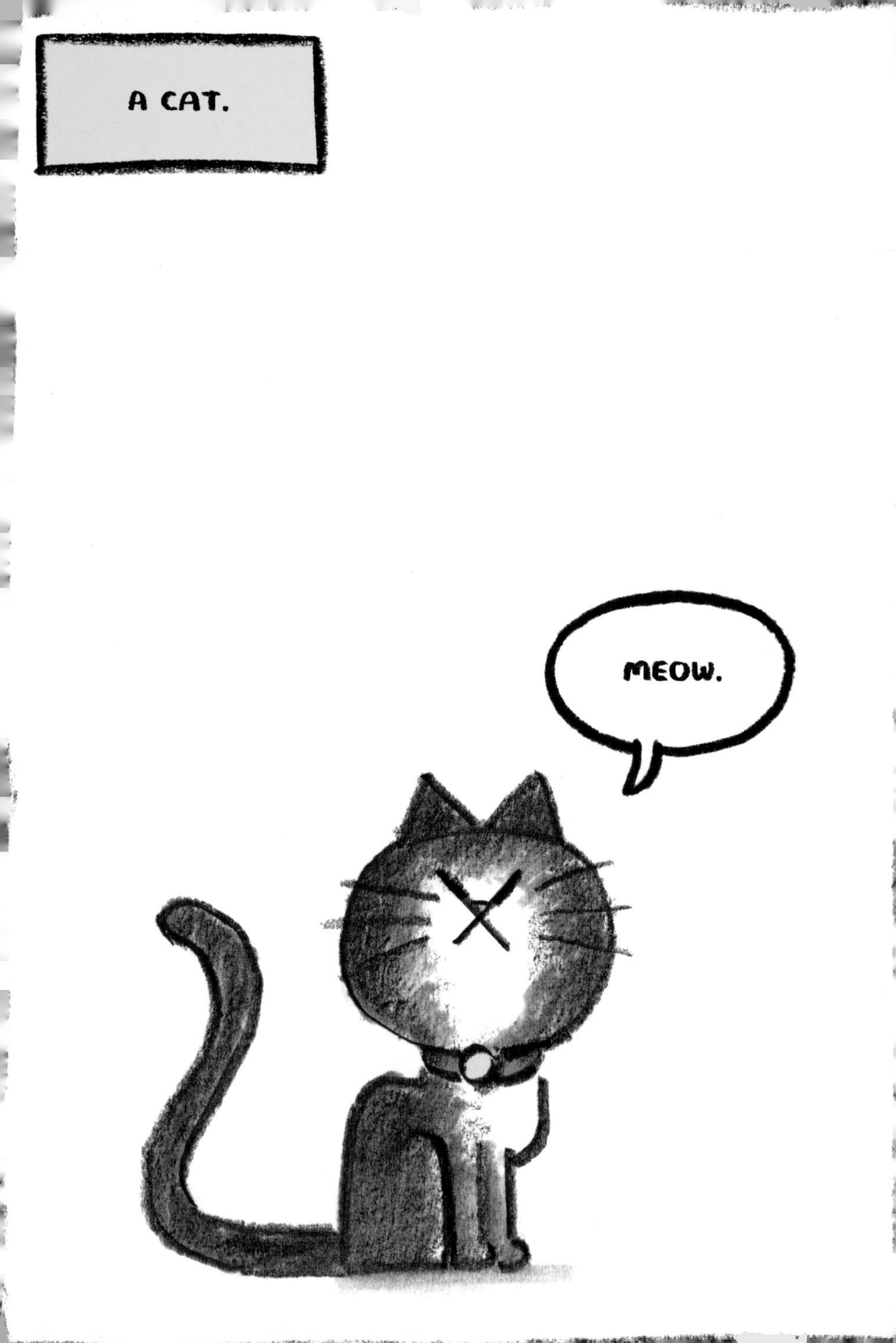
A CAT.
MEOW.

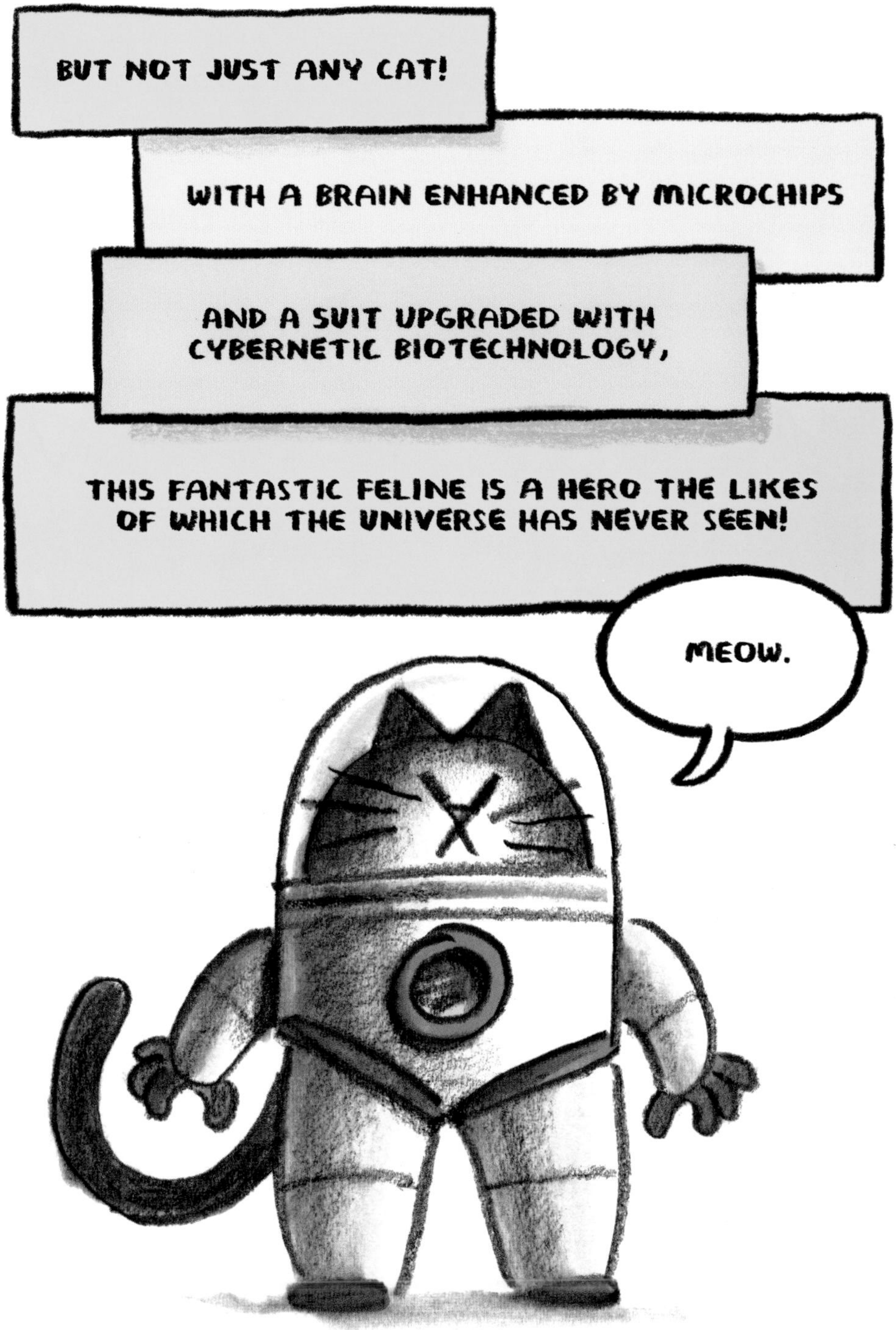
BUT NOT JUST ANY CAT!
WITH A BRAIN ENHANCED BY MICROCHIPS
AND A SUIT UPGRADED WITH CYBERNETIC BIOTECHNOLOGY,
THIS FANTASTIC FELINE IS A HERO THE LIKES OF WHICH THE UNIVERSE HAS NEVER SEEN!
MEOW.

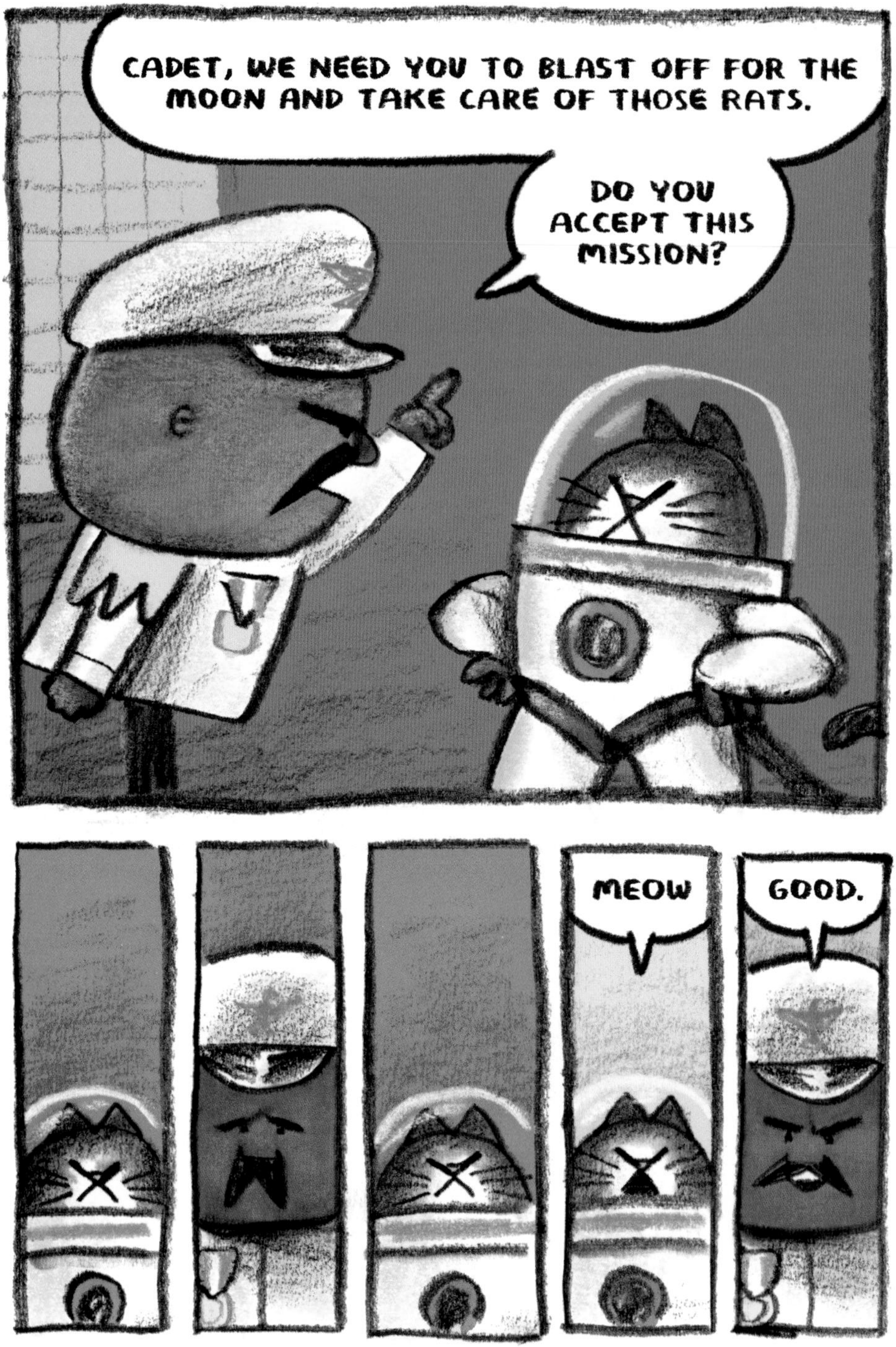
CADET, WE NEED YOU TO BLAST OFF FOR THE MOON AND TAKE CARE OF THOSE RATS.
DO YOU ACCEPT THIS MISSION?
MEOW
GOOD.

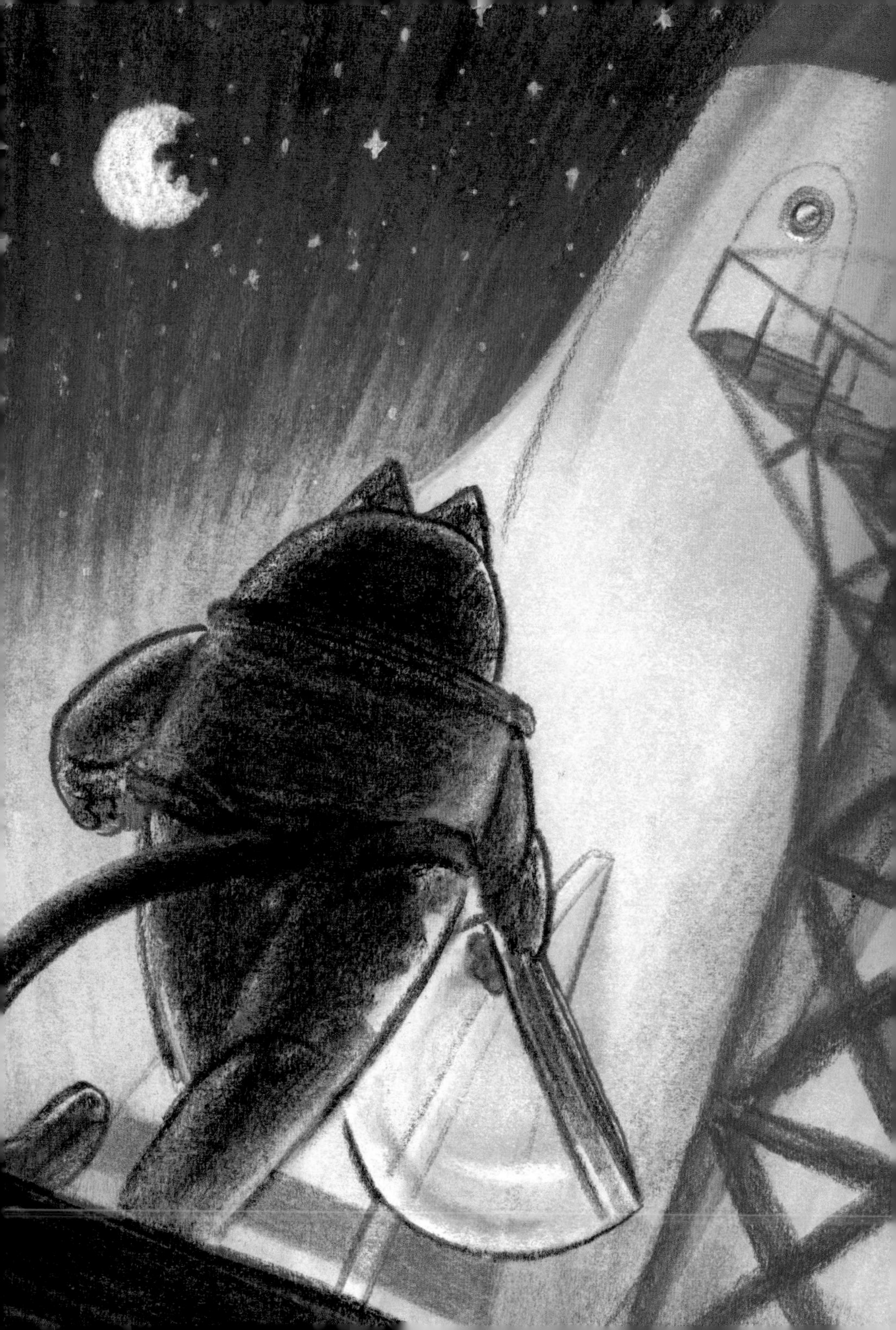

MISSION CONTROL

TAP TAP

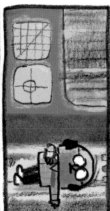

READY FOR LAUNCH, CADET?

BZZT

TEN

NINE

EIGHT

SEVEN SECONDS LATER ...

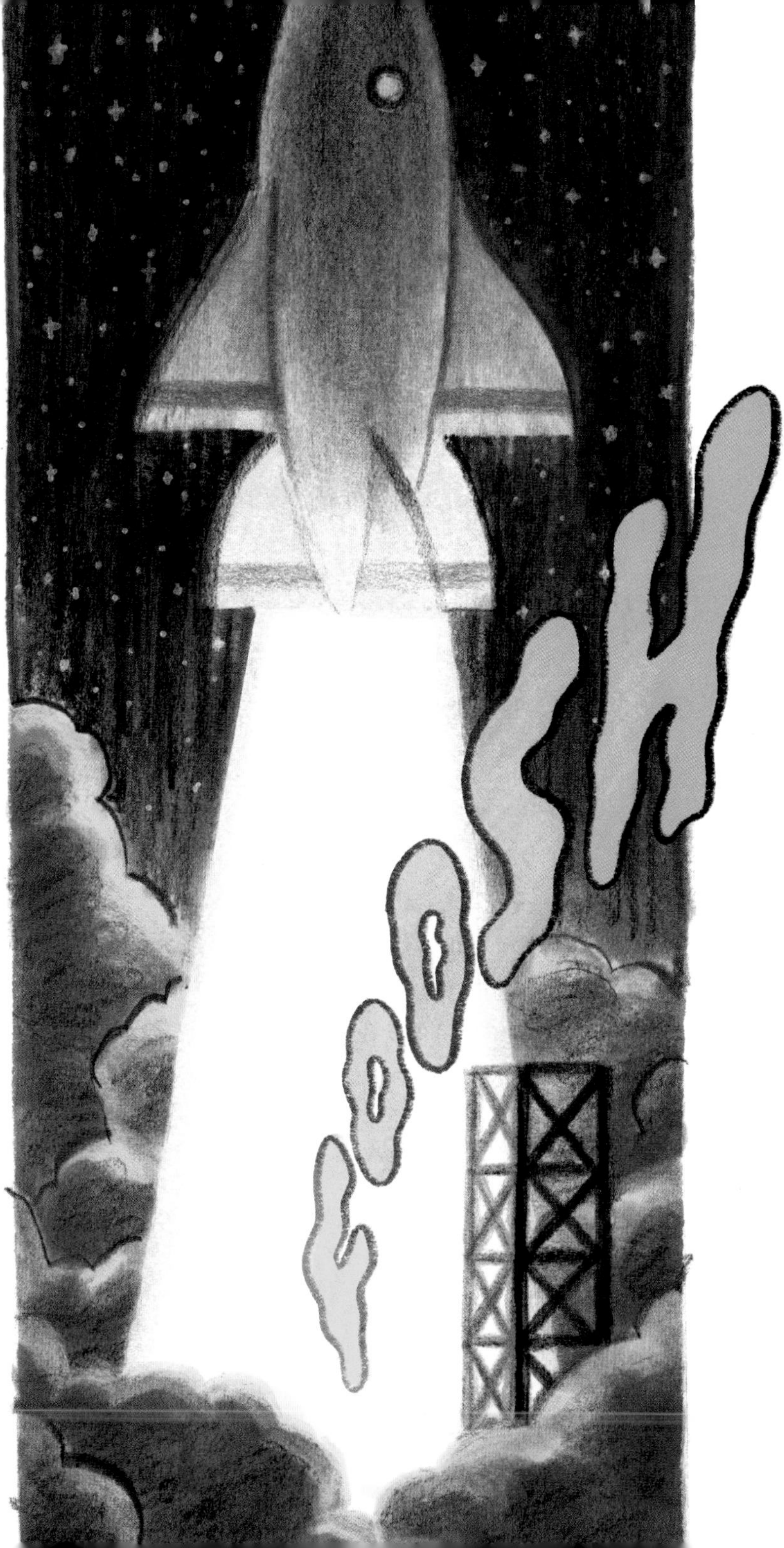
OOSH

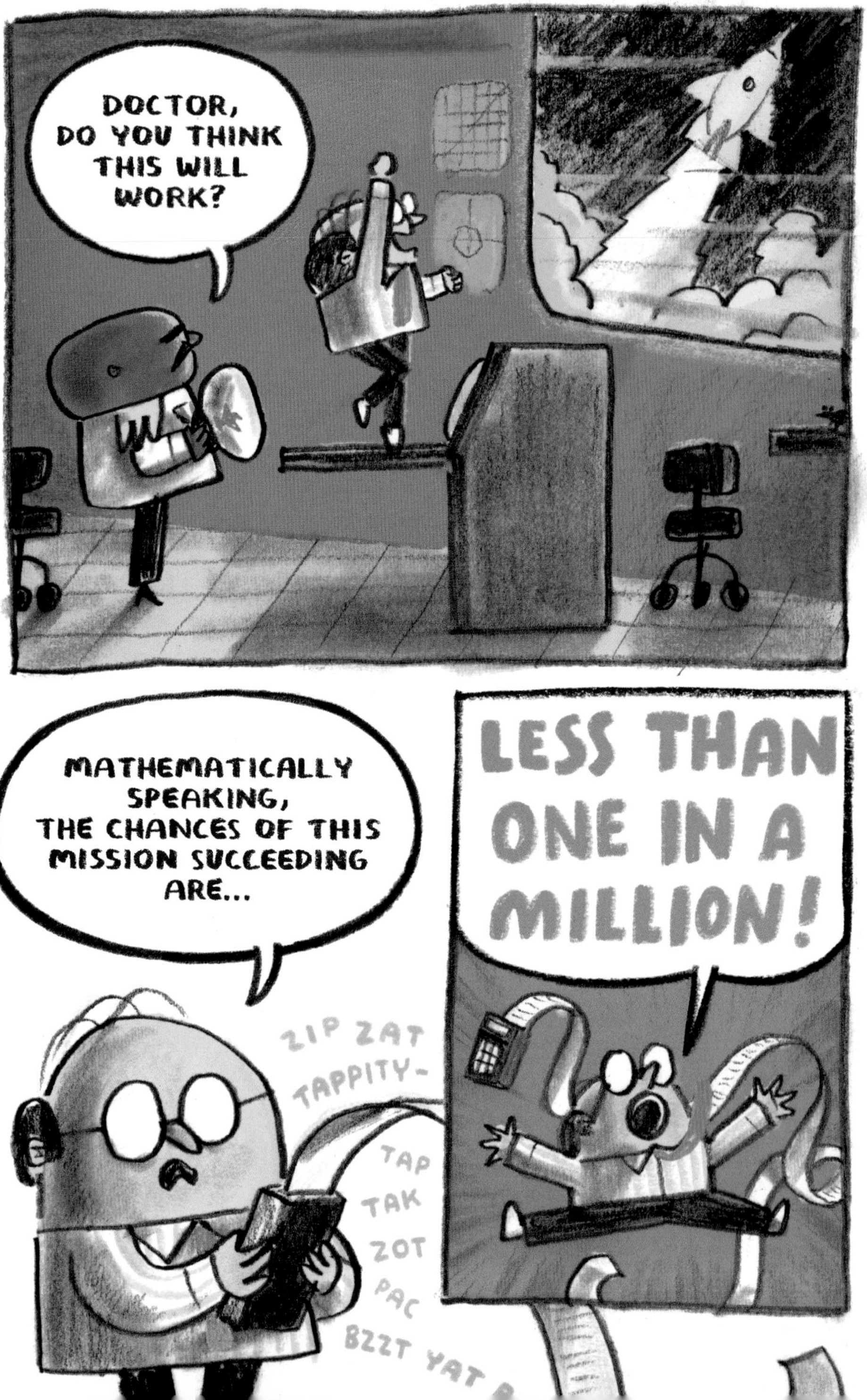
DOCTOR, DO YOU THINK THIS WILL WORK?
MATHEMATICALLY SPEAKING, THE CHANCES OF THIS MISSION SUCCEEDING ARE...
ZIP ZAT TAPPITY-
TAP
TAK
ZOT
PAC
BZZT YAT
LESS THAN ONE IN A MILLION!

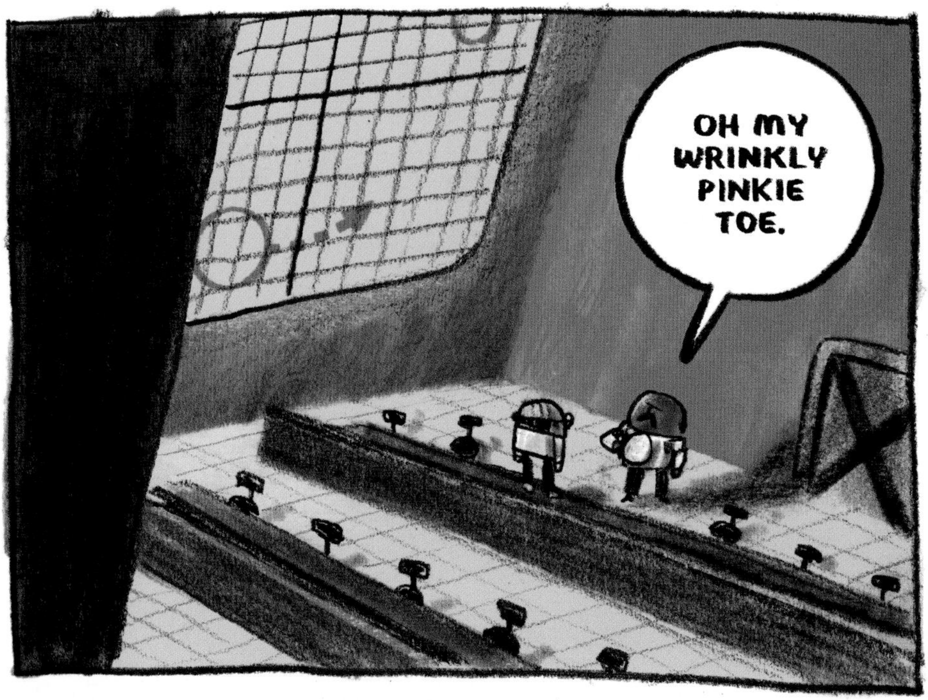
OH MY WRINKLY PINKIE TOE.

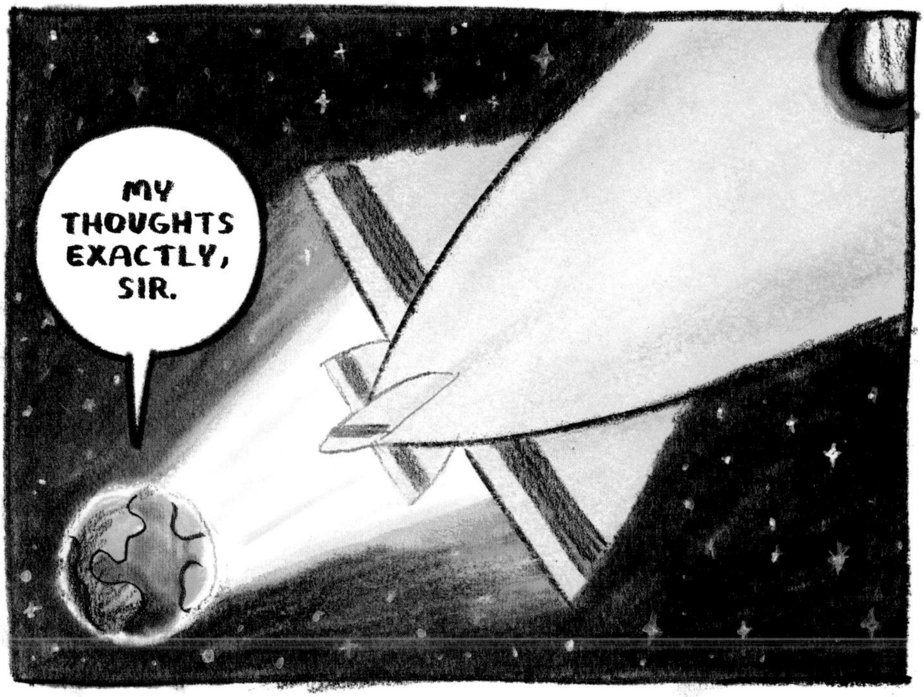
MY THOUGHTS EXACTLY, SIR.

CHAPTER 3

THE STOWAWAY

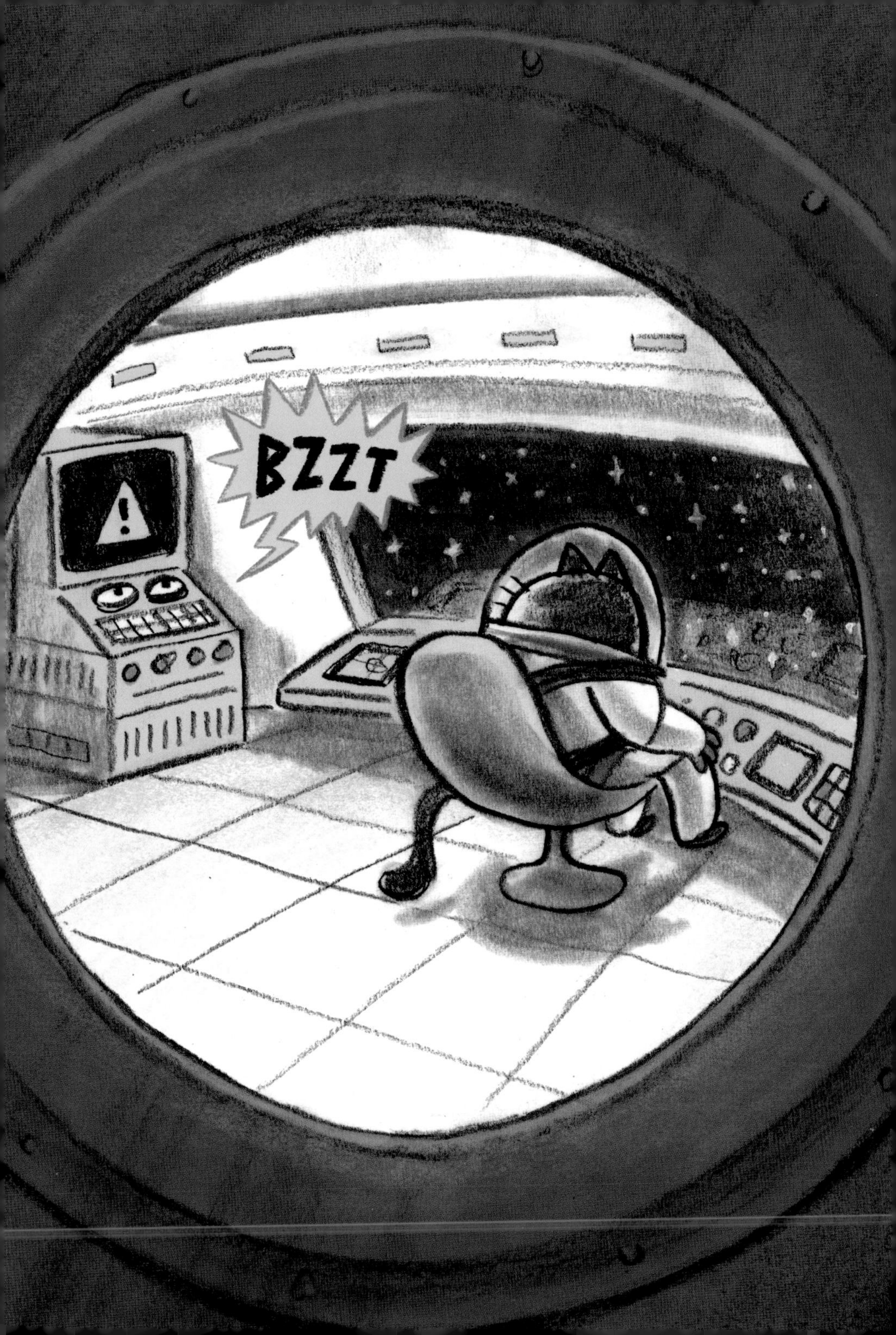
BZZT

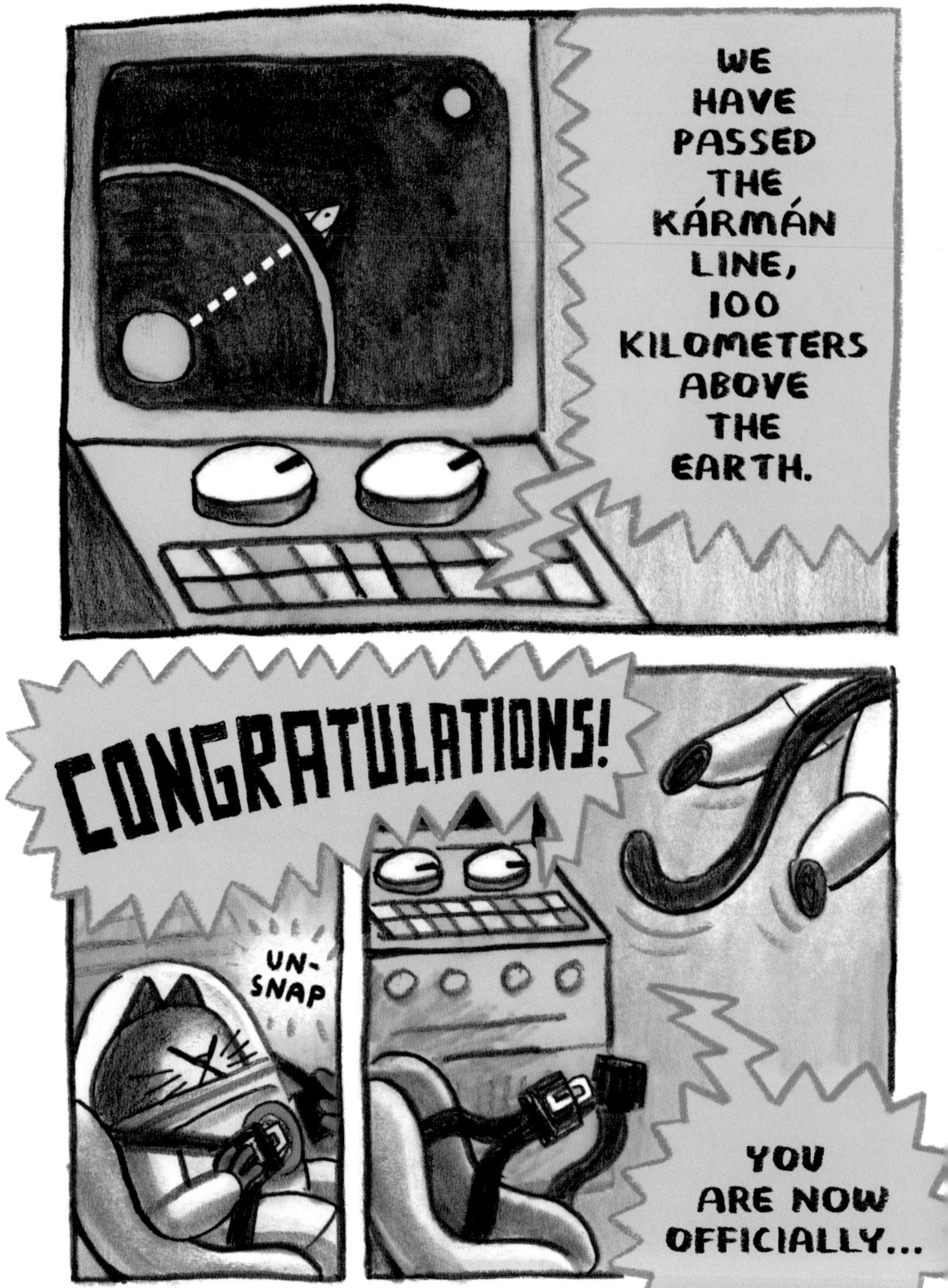
WE HAVE PASSED THE KÁRMÁN LINE, 100 KILOMETERS ABOVE THE EARTH.
CONGRATULATIONS!
UN-SNAP
YOU ARE NOW OFFICIALLY...

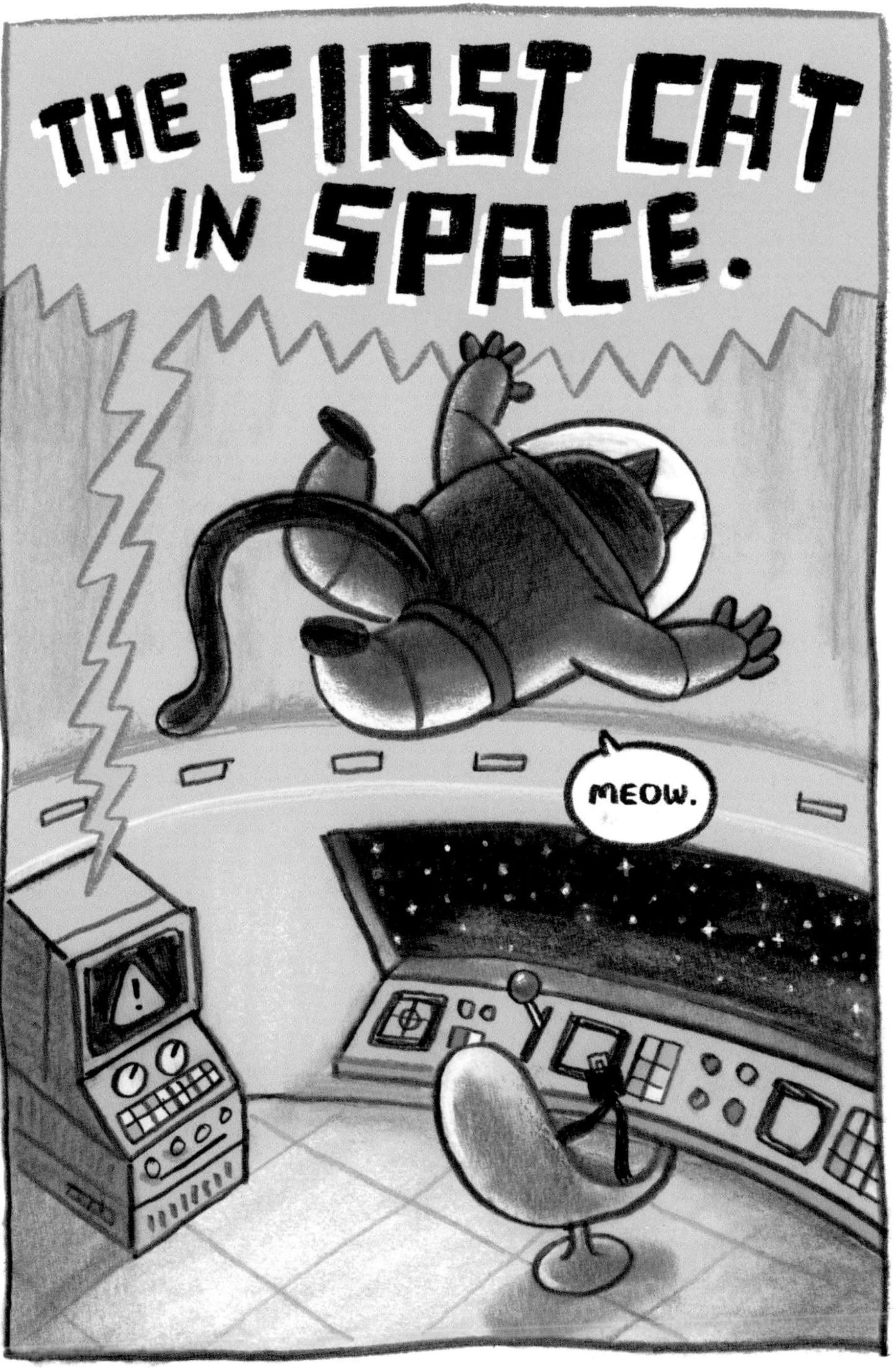
THE FIRST CAT IN SPACE.
MEOW.

ALLOW ME TO INTRODUCE YOU TO THE AMENITIES OF THIS SPACECRAFT.
HERE ARE YOUR LIVING QUARTERS.
HANGING GARDEN
PANORAMIC GALAXY VIEW
LIBRARY
ARCADE
SLEEP POD
THIS IS OUR TRAINING FACILITY.
STATIONARY BIKE
CENTRIFUGAL AXIS (to simulate Earth's gravity)
FREE WEIGHTS
INFINITY TRACK
SPORT FACILITIES
I HAVE SAVED THE BEST FOR LAST:
THE CANTEEN!
HERE, EVERY FOOD ON EARTH IS AVAILABLE...

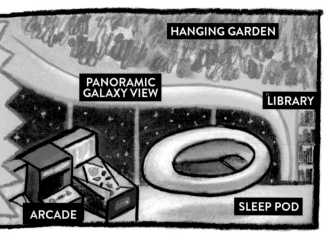

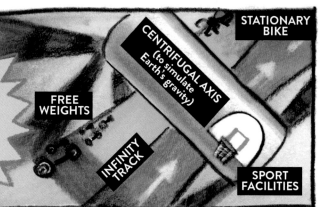

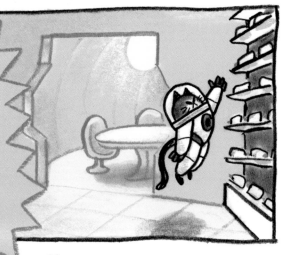

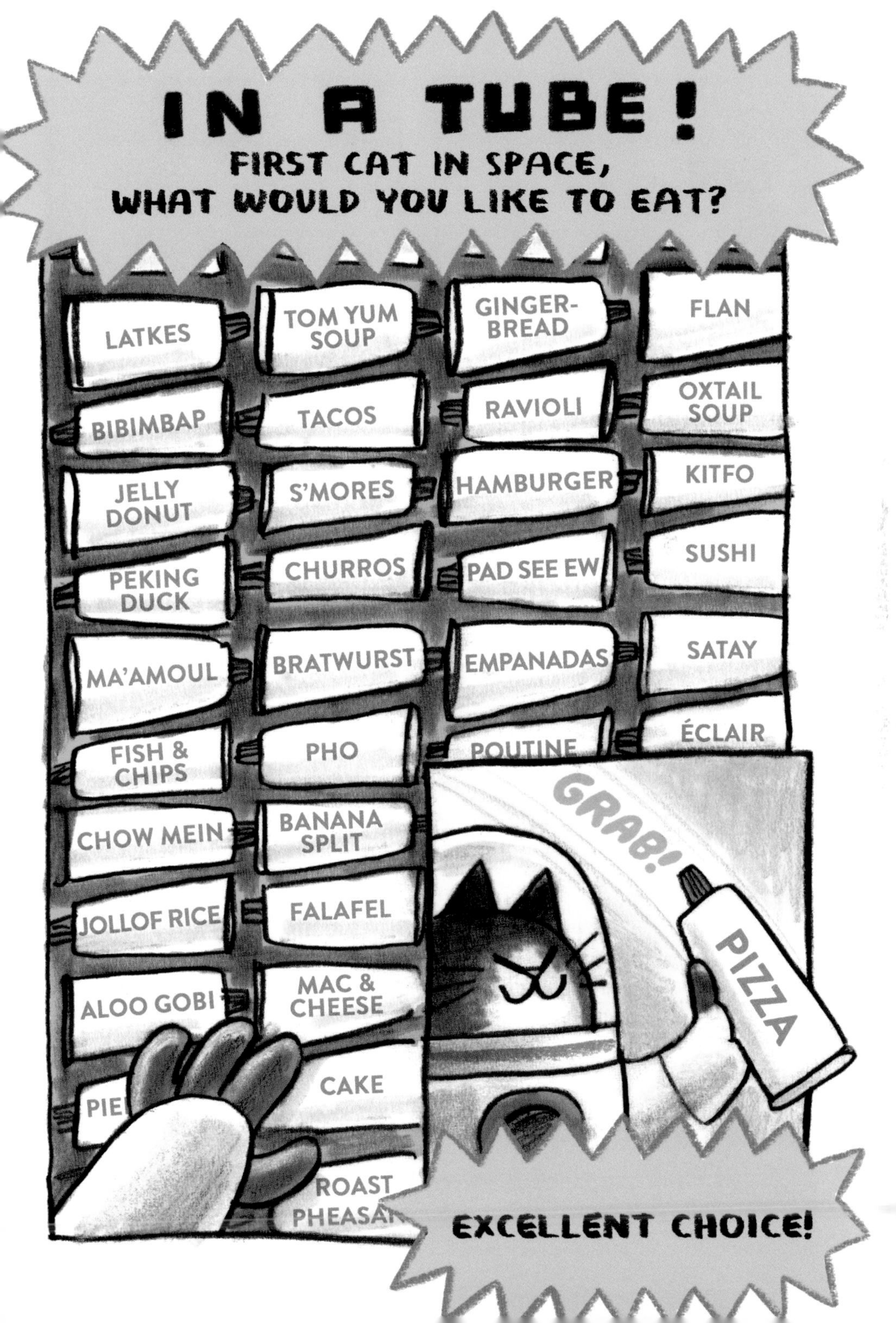
IN A TUBE!
FIRST CAT IN SPACE,
WHAT WOULD YOU LIKE TO EAT?
LATKES
TOM YUM SOUP
GINGER-BREAD
FLAN
BIBIMBAP
TACOS
RAVIOLI
OXTAIL SOUP
JELLY DONUT
S'MORES
HAMBURGER
KITFO
PEKING DUCK
CHURROS
PAD SEE EW
SUSHI
MA'AMOUL
BRATWURST
EMPANADAS
SATAY
FISH & CHIPS
PHO
POUTINE
ÉCLAIR
CHOW MEIN
BANANA SPLIT
JOLLOF RICE
FALAFEL
ALOO GOBI
MAC & CHEESE
CAKE
GRAB!
PIZZA
EXCELLENT CHOICE!

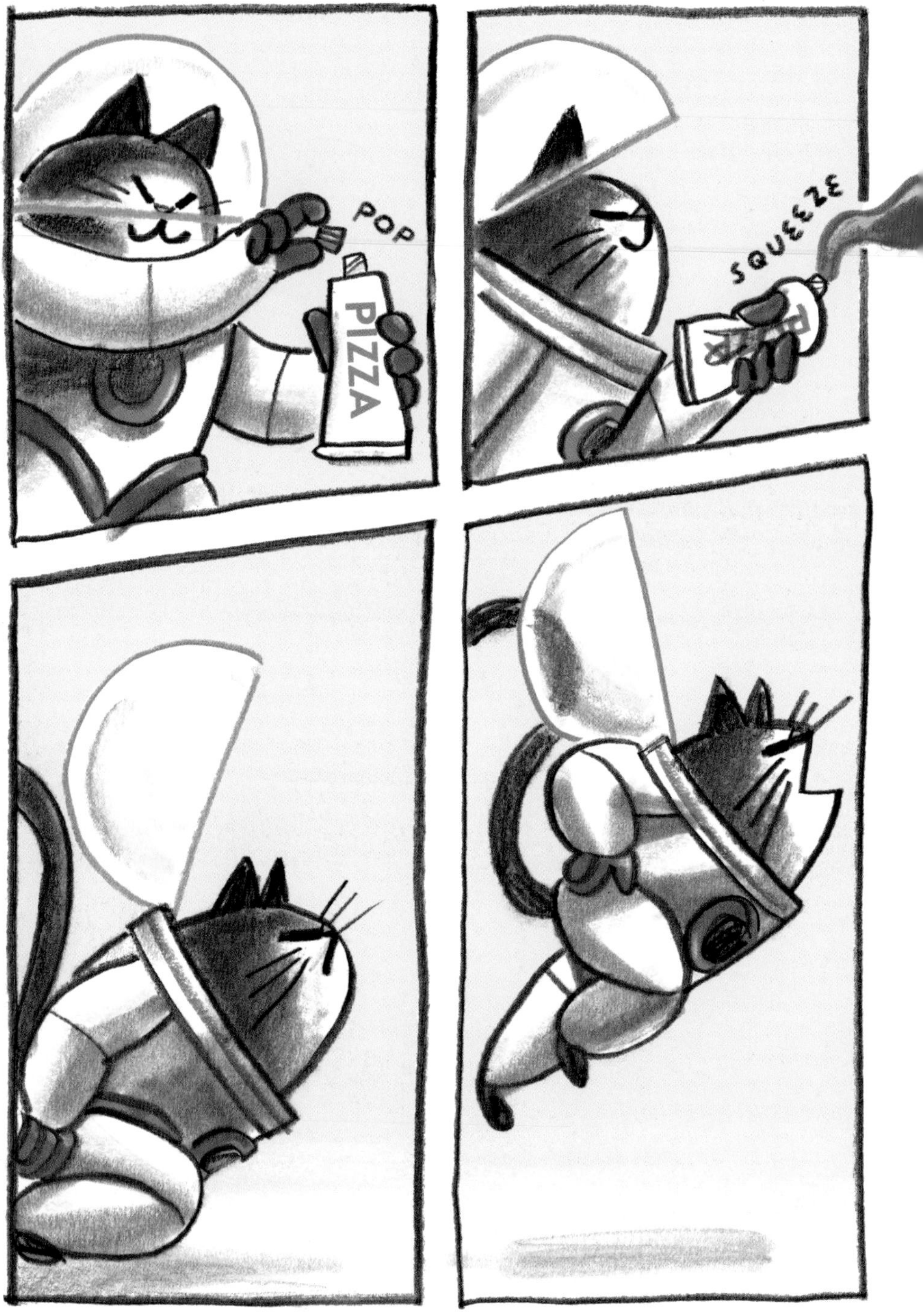
POP
PIZZA
SQUEEZE

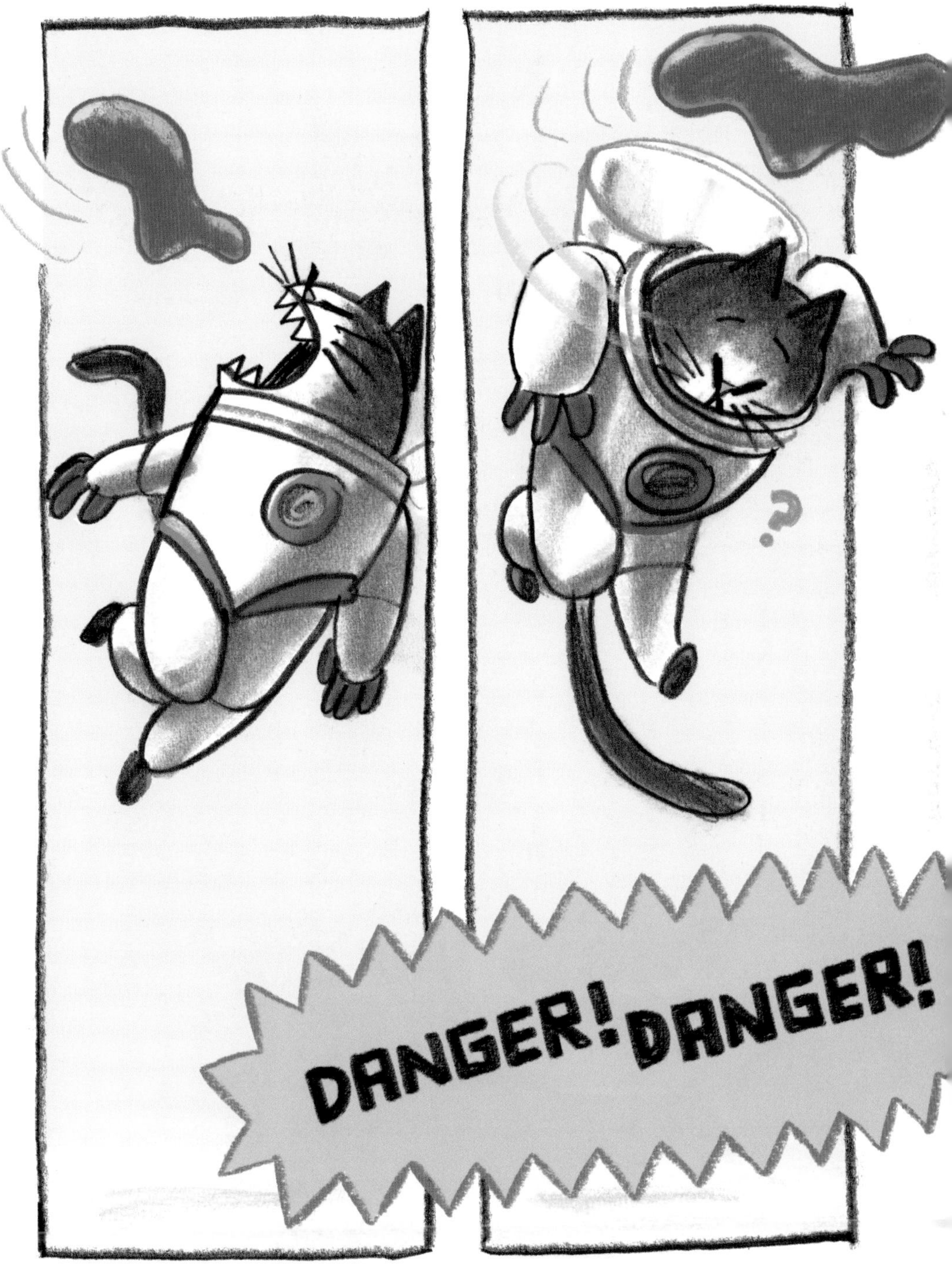
?
DANGER! DANGER!

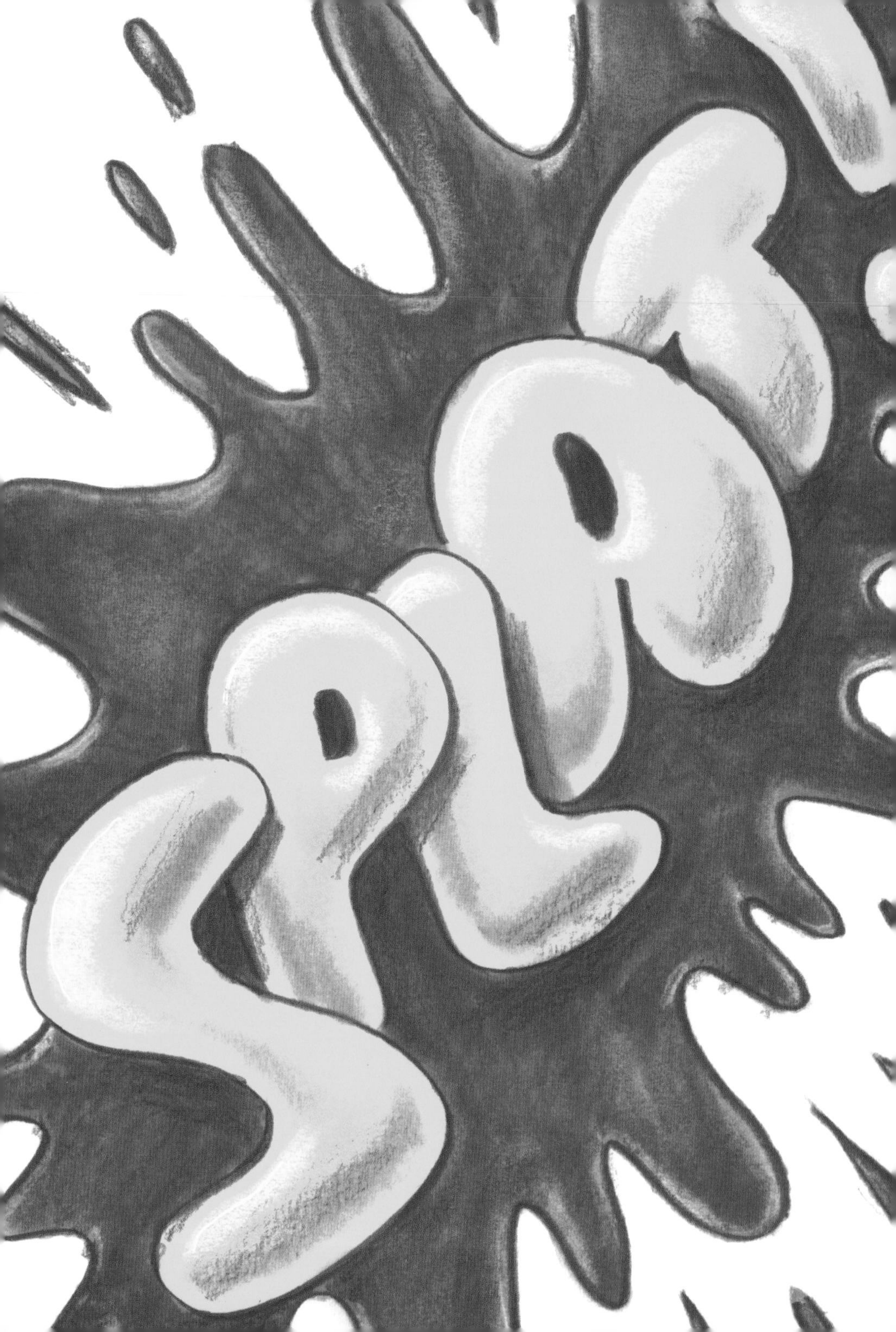
SPLAT!

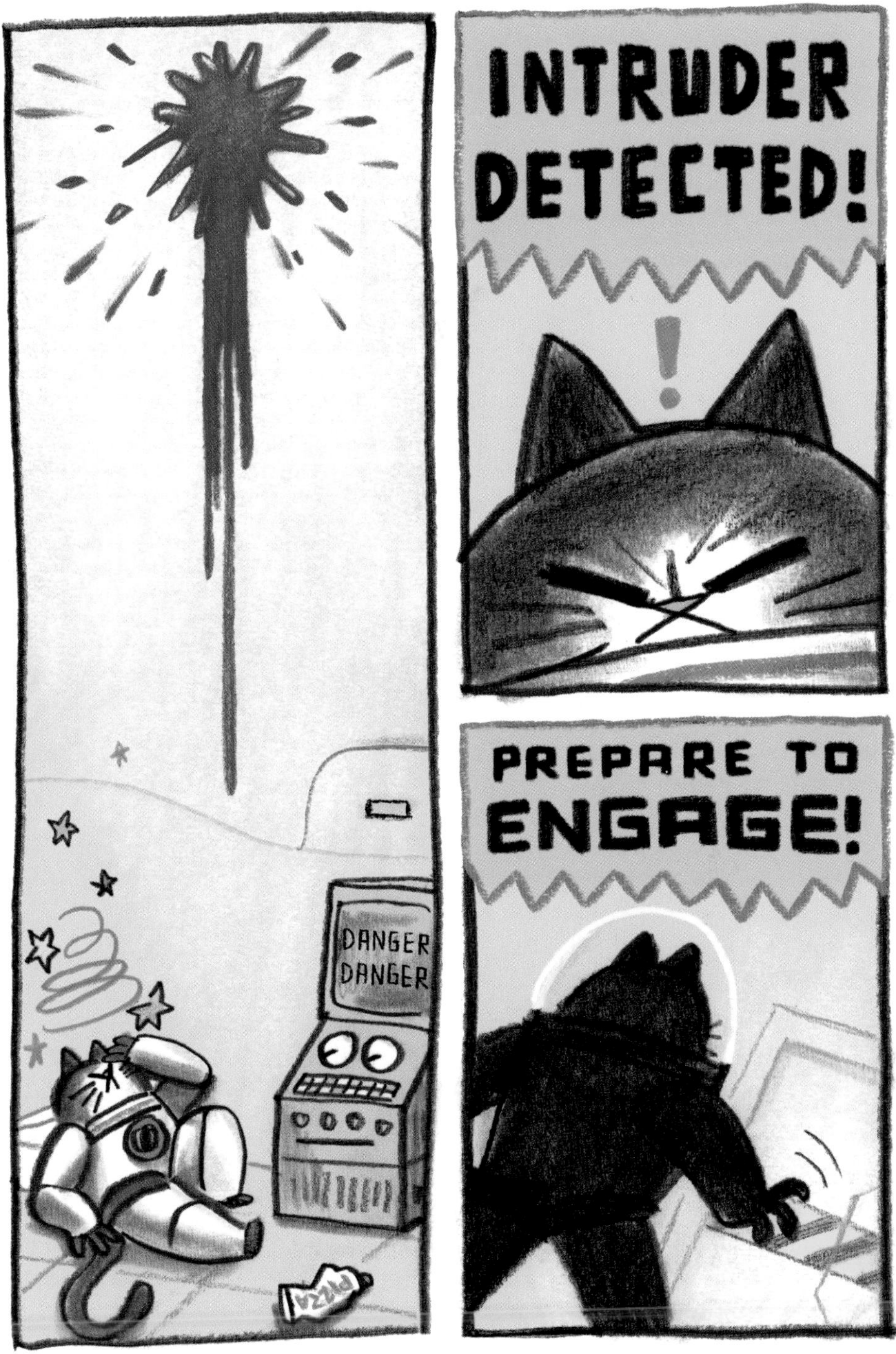
DANGER
DANGER
PIZZA
INTRUDER DETECTED!
PREPARE TO ENGAGE!

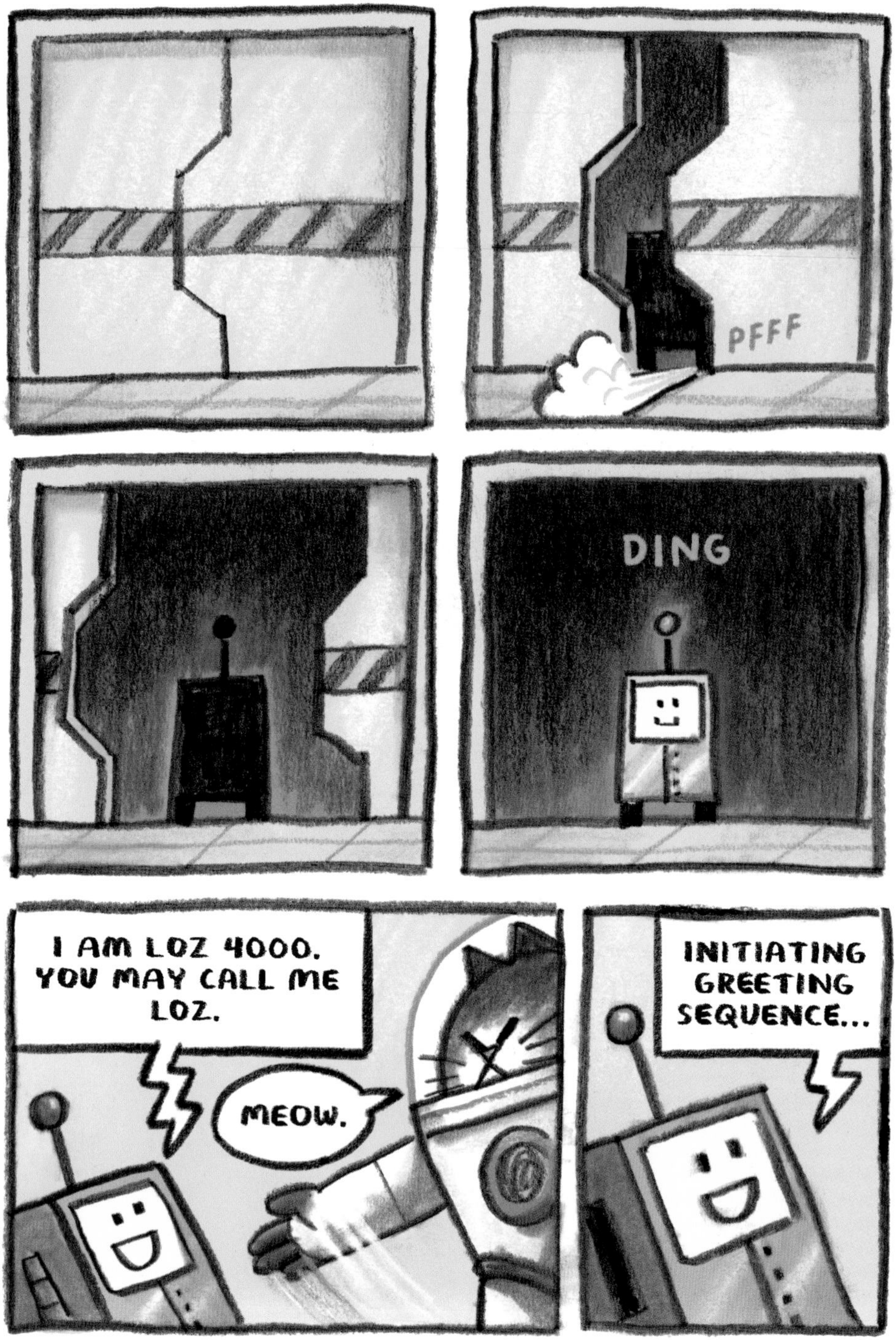
PFFF
DING
I AM LOZ 4000. YOU MAY CALL ME LOZ.
MEOW.
INITIATING GREETING SEQUENCE...

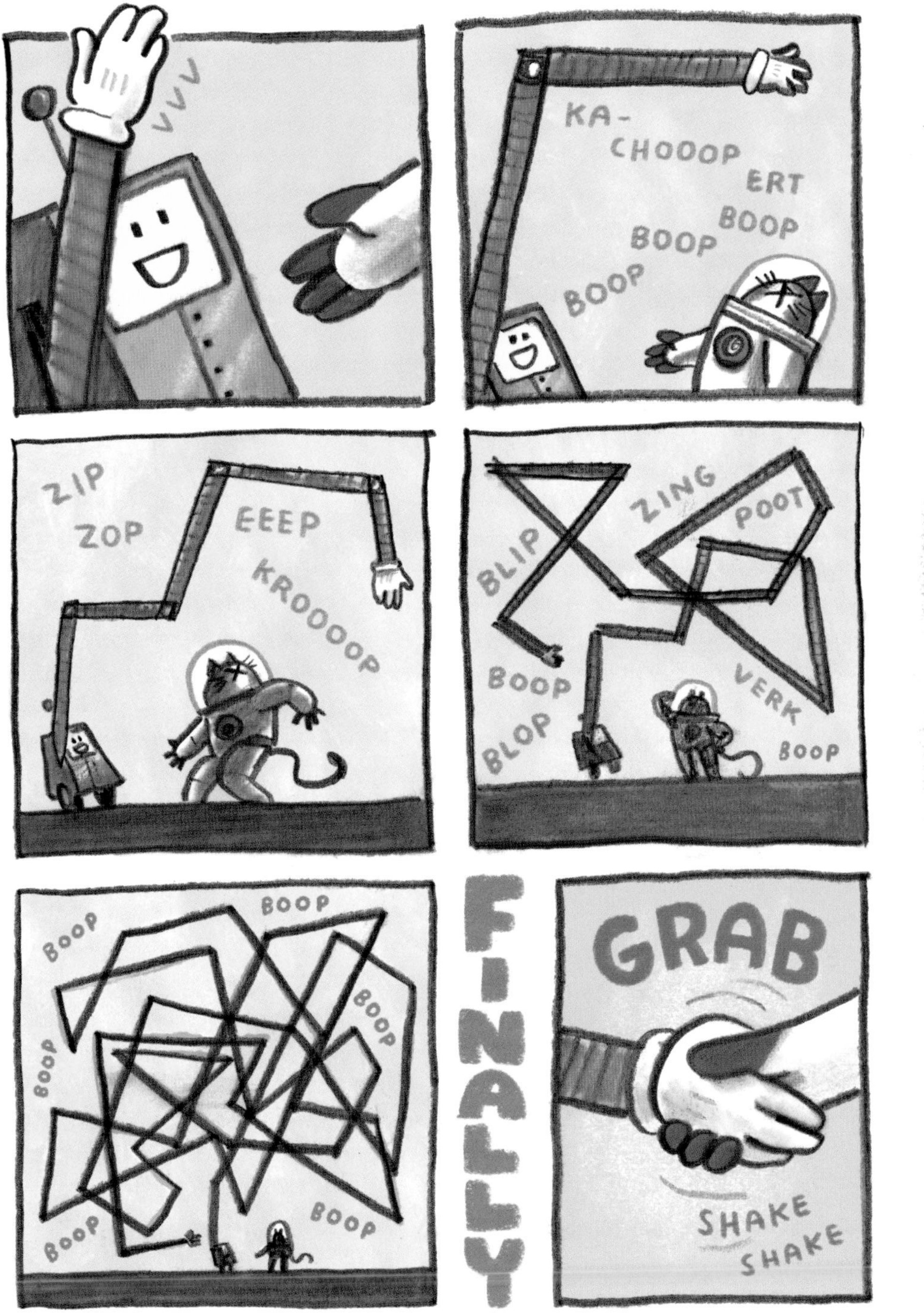
VVV
KA-
CHOOOP
ERT
BOOP
BOOP
BOOP
ZIP
ZOP
EEEP
KROOOOP
BLIP
ZING
POOT
BOOP
BLOP
VERK
BOOP
BOOP
BOOP
BOOP
BOOP
BOOP
BOOP
FINALLY
GRAB
SHAKE
SHAKE

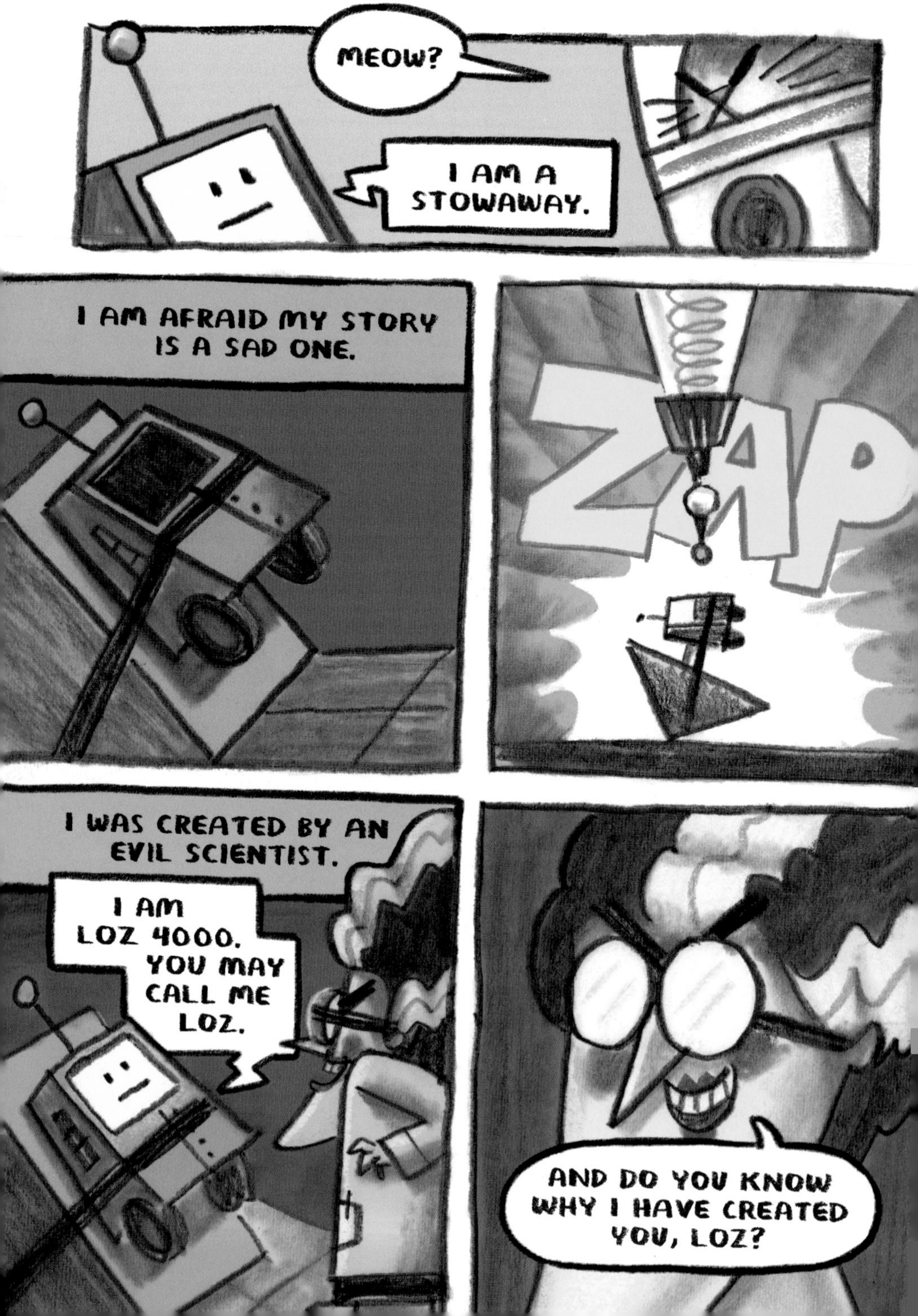
MEOW?
I AM A STOWAWAY.
I AM AFRAID MY STORY IS A SAD ONE.
ZAP
I WAS CREATED BY AN EVIL SCIENTIST.
I AM LOZ 4000. YOU MAY CALL ME LOZ.
AND DO YOU KNOW WHY I HAVE CREATED YOU, LOZ?

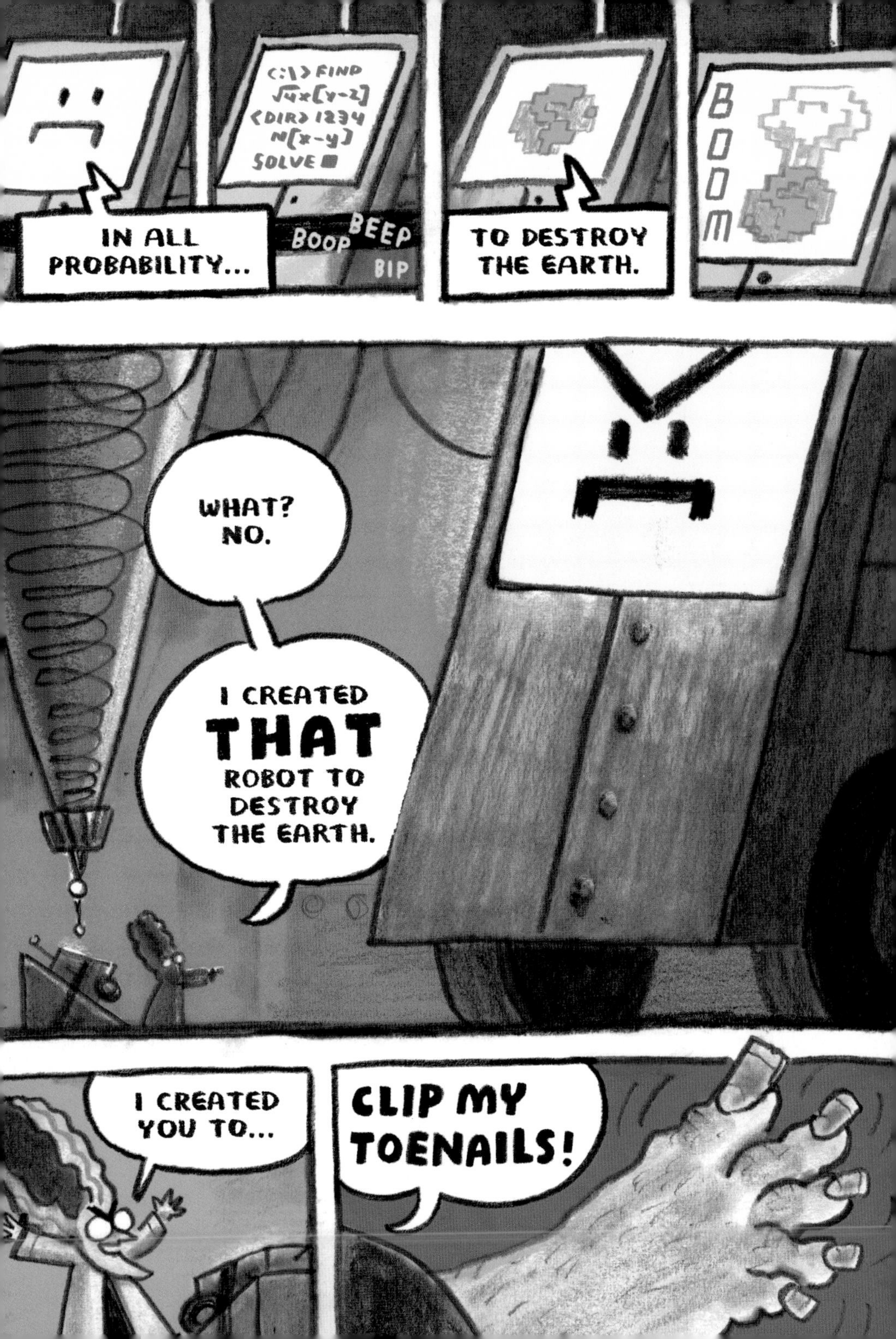

C:\> FIND
√4x[y-z]
<DIR> 1234
N[x-y]
SOLVE
IN ALL PROBABILITY...
BOOP BEEP BIP
TO DESTROY THE EARTH.
BOOM
WHAT? NO.
I CREATED THAT ROBOT TO DESTROY THE EARTH.
I CREATED YOU TO...
CLIP MY TOENAILS!

I SEE.
VVVV
INITIATE TOENAIL-CLIPPING SEQUENCE.
KA-CHOOOP
ERT
BOOP
BOOP
BOOP
ZOT ZIP
ZOP
EEEP
KROOOOOOP
BLOOP
ZING
POOT
VERK
BOOP
BIP
SCRAAA
BOOP
BOOP
BOOP
BOOP
BOOP
BOOP
SIT
LATER...
CLIP

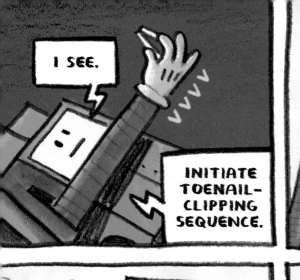

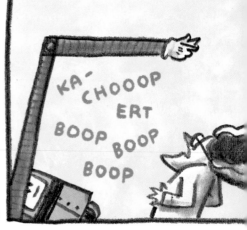

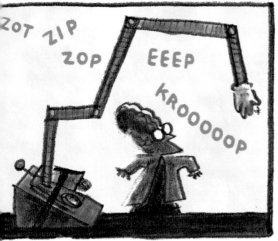

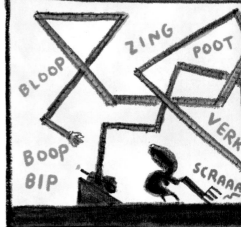

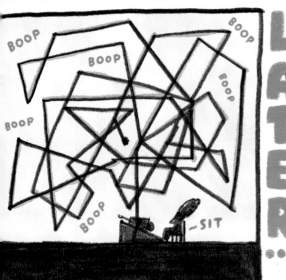

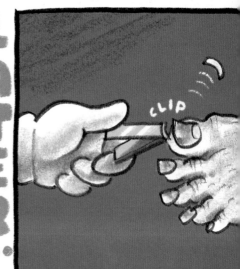

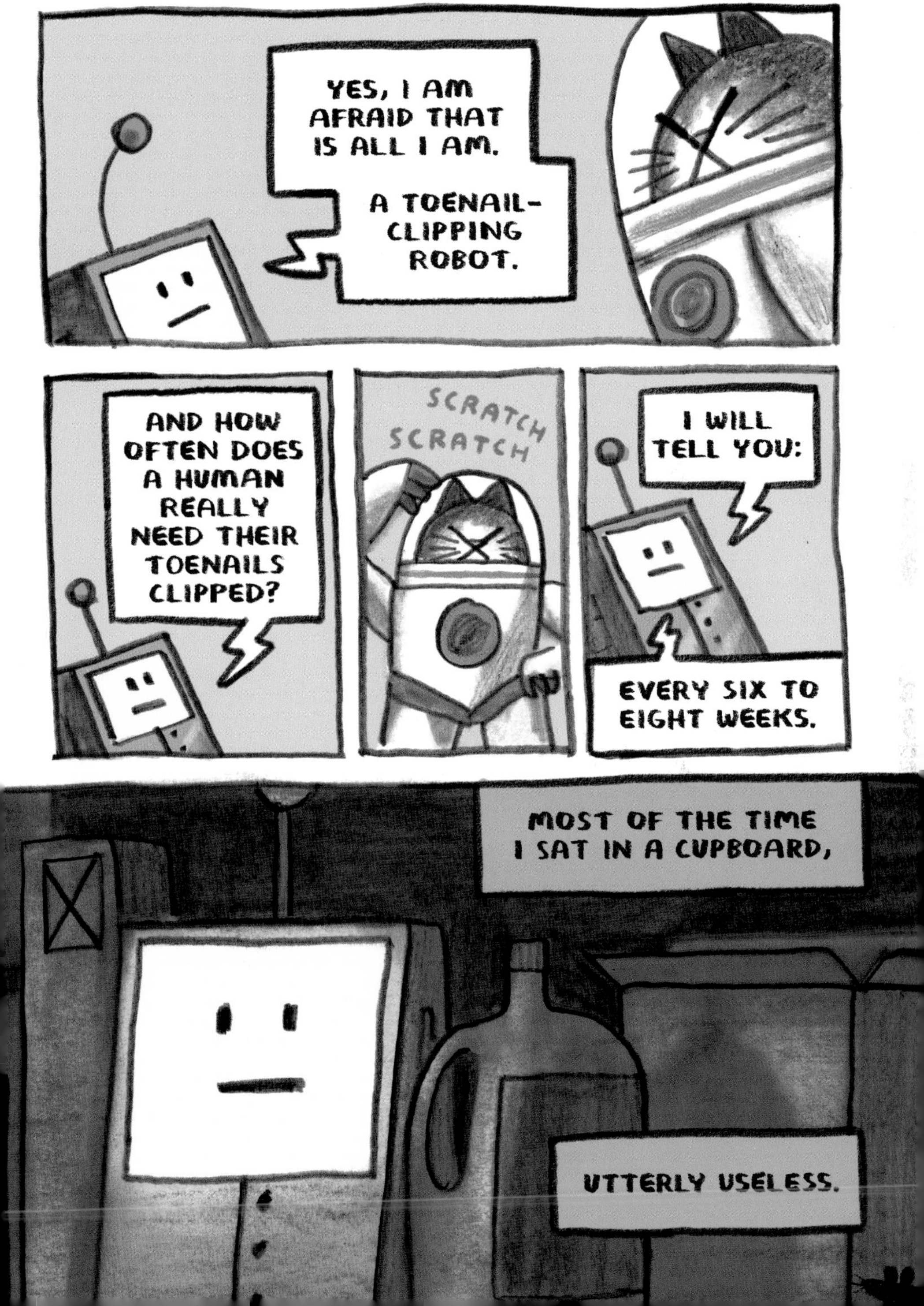
YES, I AM AFRAID THAT IS ALL I AM.
A TOENAIL-CLIPPING ROBOT.
AND HOW OFTEN DOES A HUMAN REALLY NEED THEIR TOENAILS CLIPPED?
SCRATCH
SCRATCH
I WILL TELL YOU:
EVERY SIX TO EIGHT WEEKS.
MOST OF THE TIME I SAT IN A CUPBOARD,
UTTERLY USELESS.

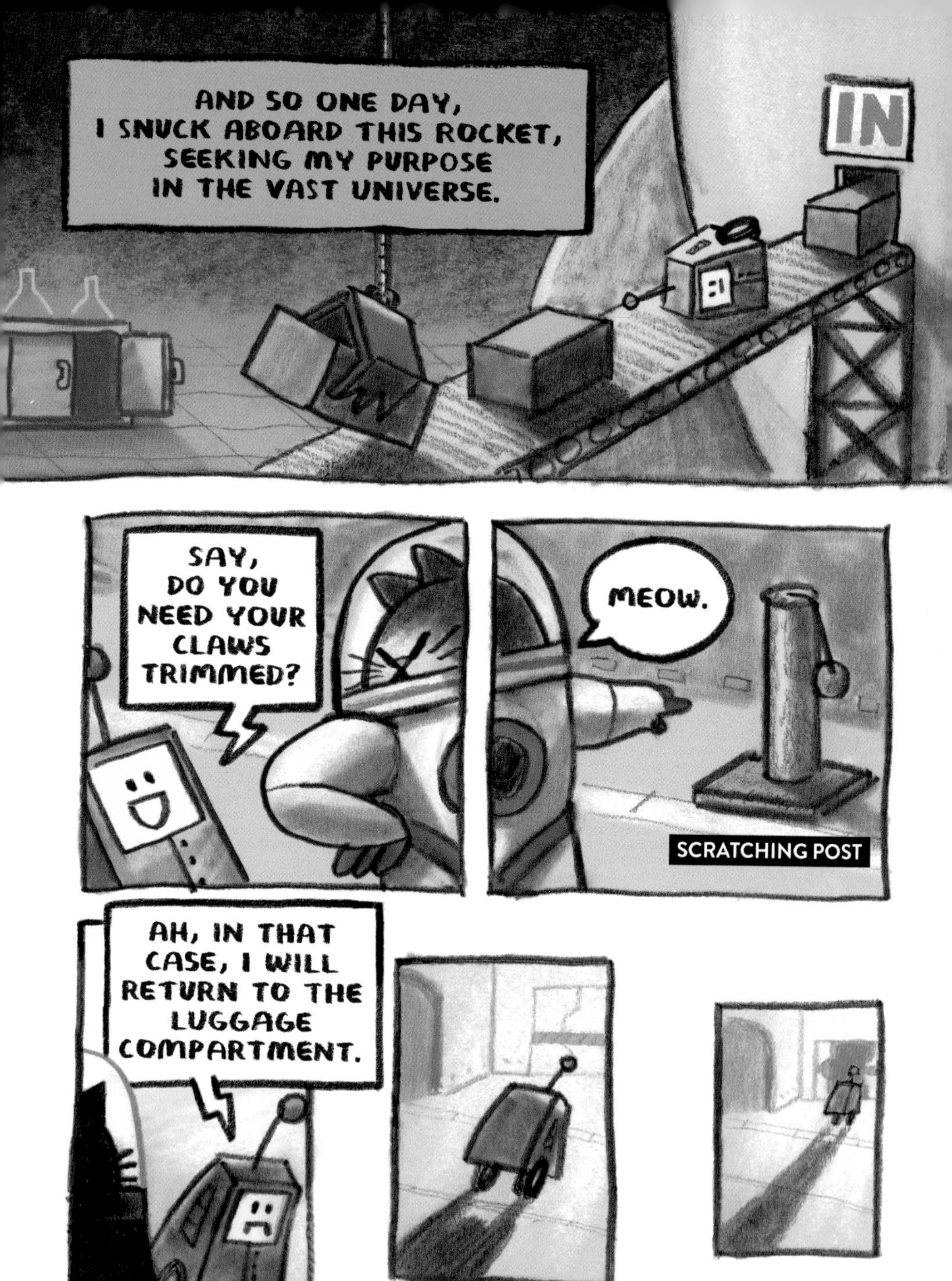
AND SO ONE DAY, I SNUCK ABOARD THIS ROCKET, SEEKING MY PURPOSE IN THE VAST UNIVERSE.
IN
SAY, DO YOU NEED YOUR CLAWS TRIMMED?
MEOW.
SCRATCHING POST
AH, IN THAT CASE, I WILL RETURN TO THE LUGGAGE COMPARTMENT.

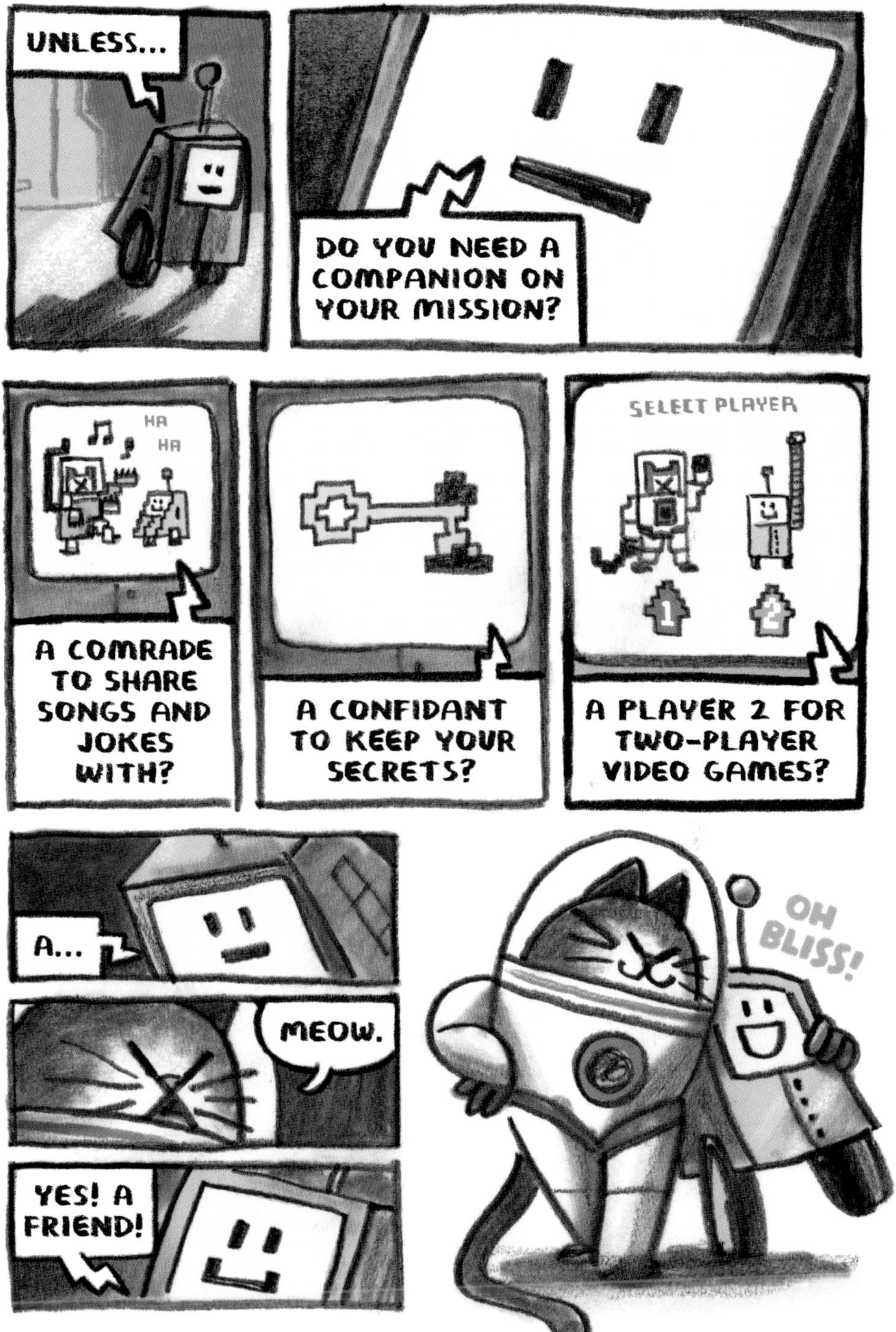
UNLESS...
DO YOU NEED A COMPANION ON YOUR MISSION?
HA
HA
A COMRADE TO SHARE SONGS AND JOKES WITH?
A CONFIDANT TO KEEP YOUR SECRETS?
SELECT PLAYER
1
2
A PLAYER 2 FOR TWO-PLAYER VIDEO GAMES?
A...
MEOW.
YES! A FRIEND!
OH BLISS!

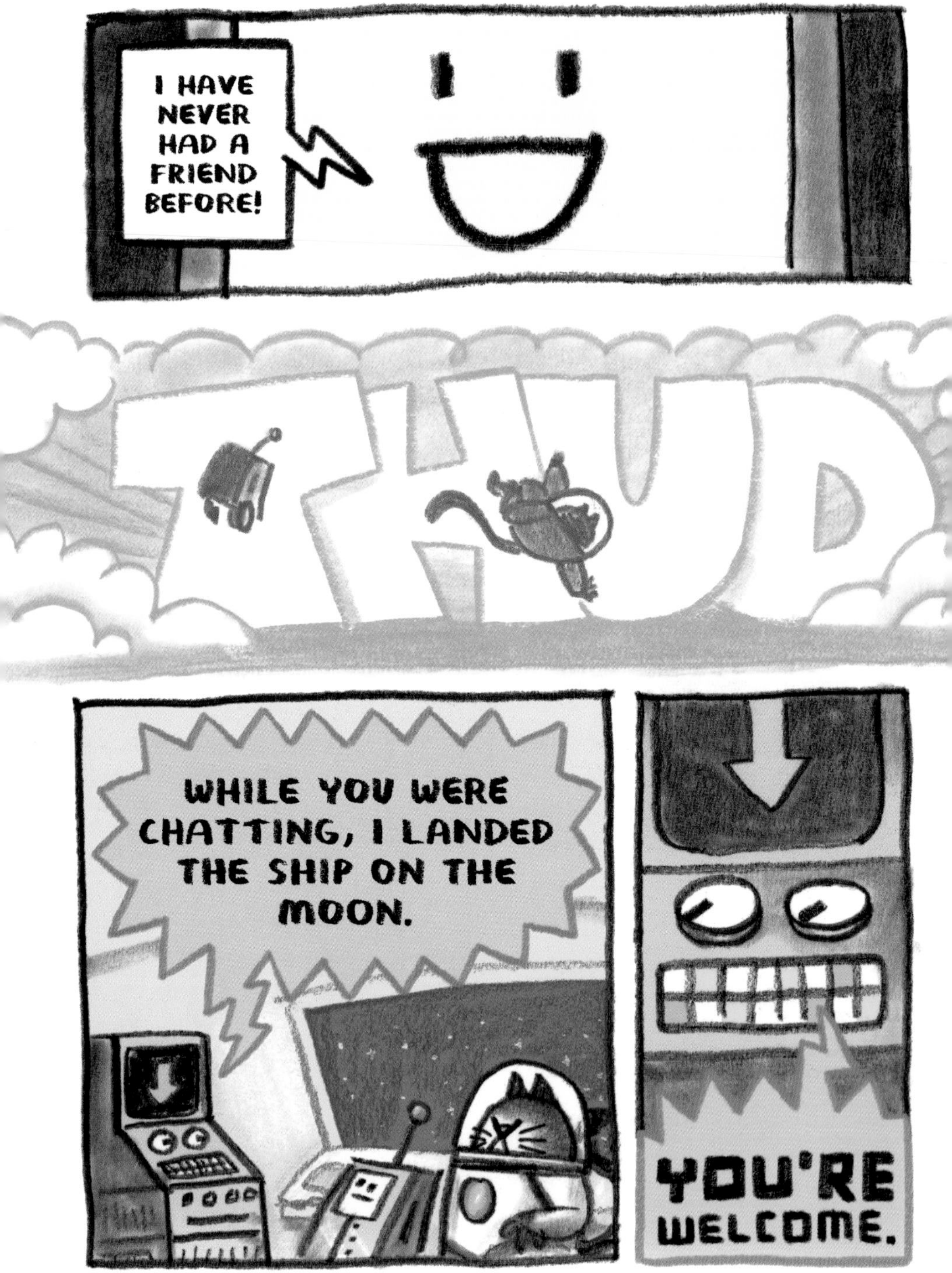
I HAVE NEVER HAD A FRIEND BEFORE!
THUD
WHILE YOU WERE CHATTING, I LANDED THE SHIP ON THE MOON.
YOU'RE WELCOME.

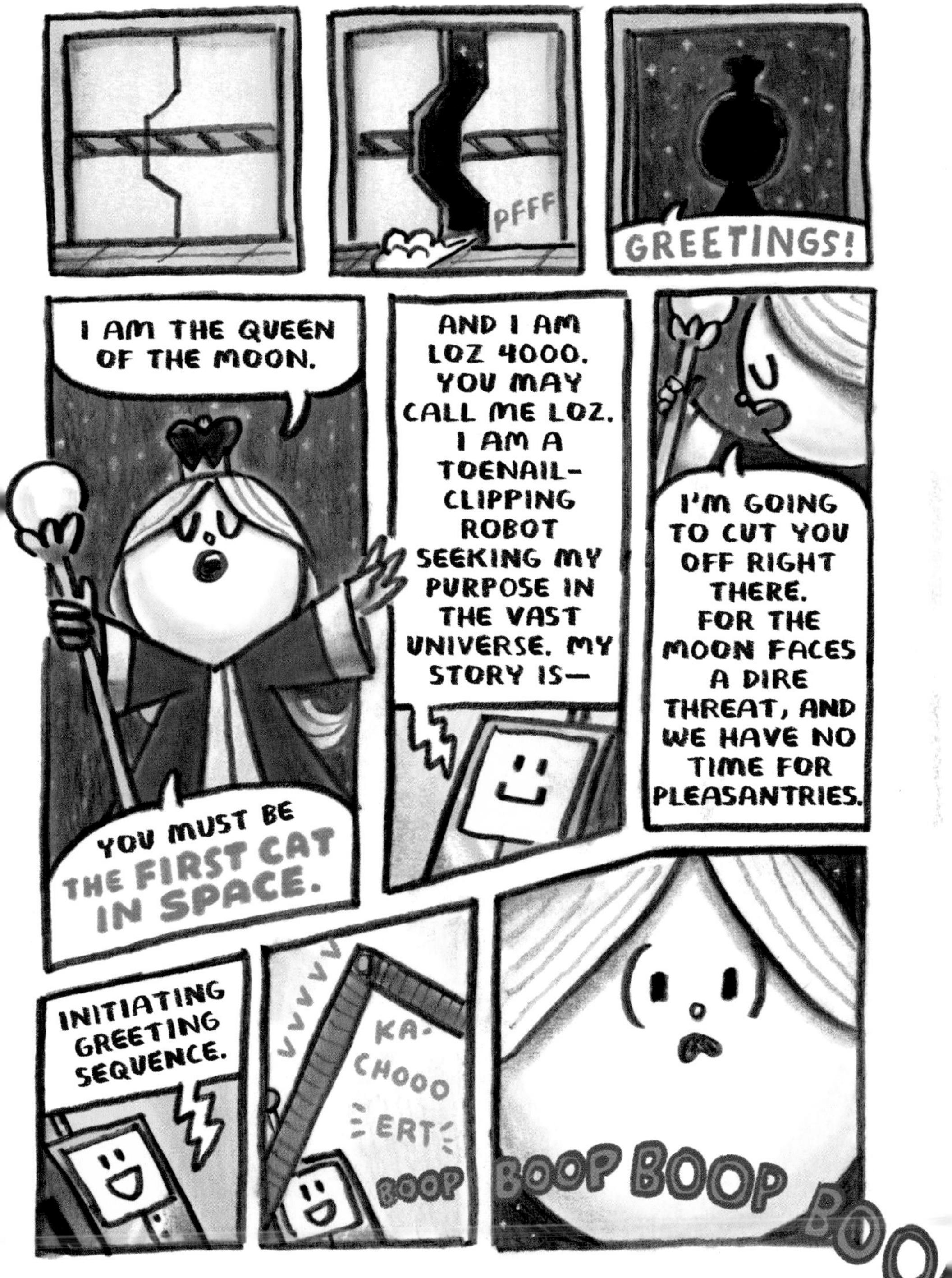
PFFF
GREETINGS!
I AM THE QUEEN OF THE MOON.
YOU MUST BE THE FIRST CAT IN SPACE.
AND I AM LOZ 4000. YOU MAY CALL ME LOZ. I AM A TOENAIL-CLIPPING ROBOT SEEKING MY PURPOSE IN THE VAST UNIVERSE. MY STORY IS—
I'M GOING TO CUT YOU OFF RIGHT THERE. FOR THE MOON FACES A DIRE THREAT, AND WE HAVE NO TIME FOR PLEASANTRIES.
INITIATING GREETING SEQUENCE.
VVVVV
KA-CHOOO
ERT
BOOP
BOOP BOOP
BOOP

CHAPTER 4

THE LAND OF CHEERFULNESS

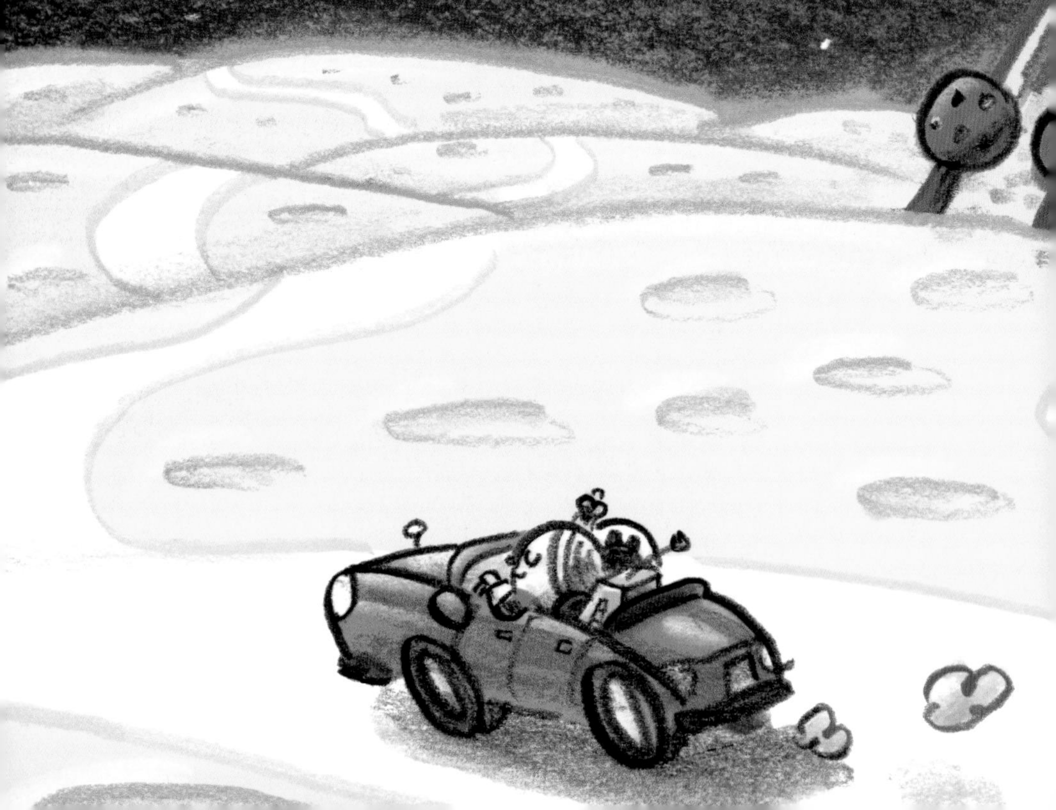

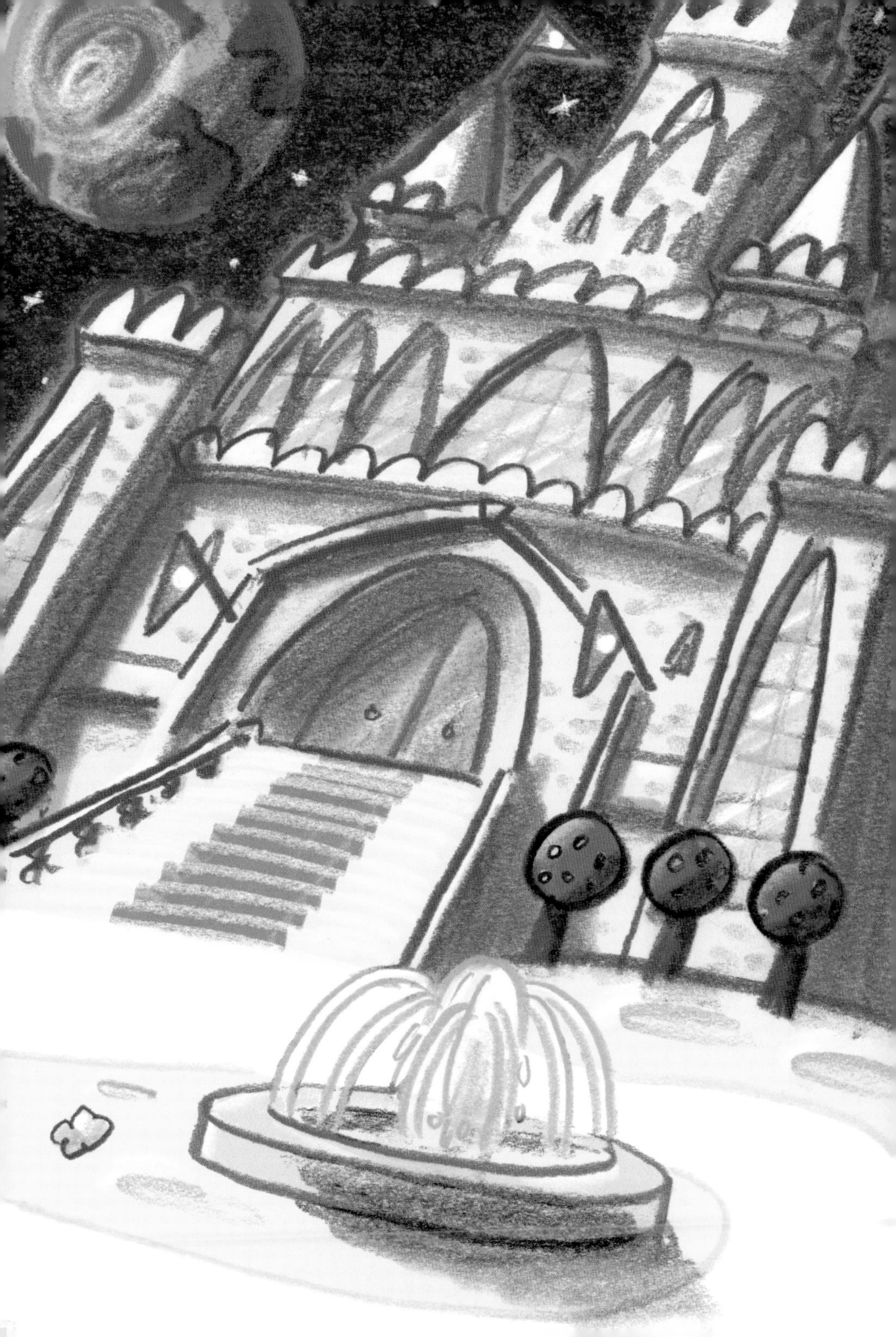

FROM EARTH, YOU CAN SEE ONLY ONE HALF OF THE MOON, WHICH WAXES AND WANES IN THE LIGHT OF THE SUN. THIS IS THE BRIGHT SIDE OF THE MOON.

THE LAND OF CHEERFULNESS IS ITS CAPITAL.

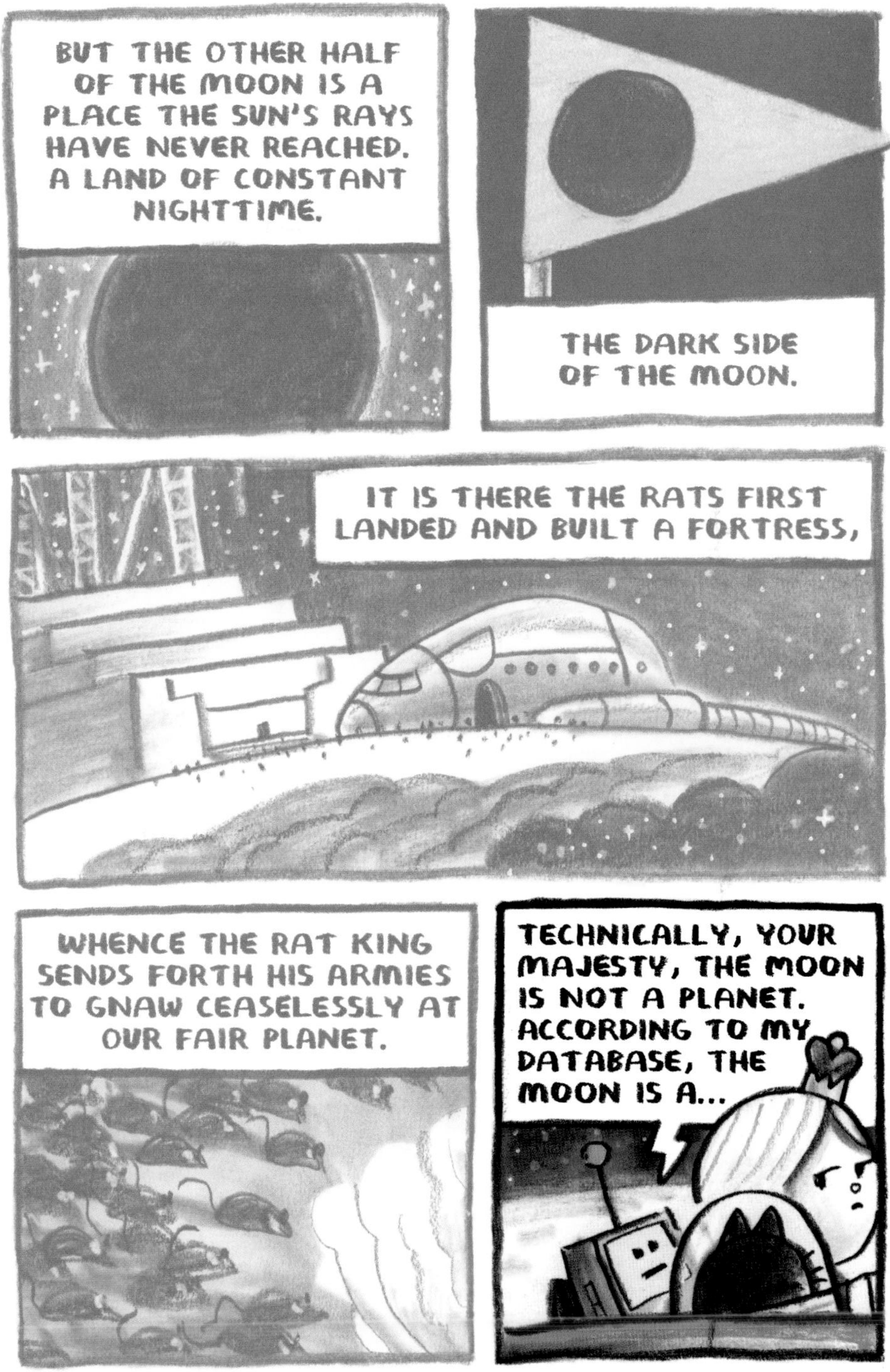
BUT THE OTHER HALF OF THE MOON IS A PLACE THE SUN'S RAYS HAVE NEVER REACHED. A LAND OF CONSTANT NIGHTTIME.
THE DARK SIDE OF THE MOON.
IT IS THERE THE RATS FIRST LANDED AND BUILT A FORTRESS,
WHENCE THE RAT KING SENDS FORTH HIS ARMIES TO GNAW CEASELESSLY AT OUR FAIR PLANET.
TECHNICALLY, YOUR MAJESTY, THE MOON IS NOT A PLANET. ACCORDING TO MY DATABASE, THE MOON IS A...

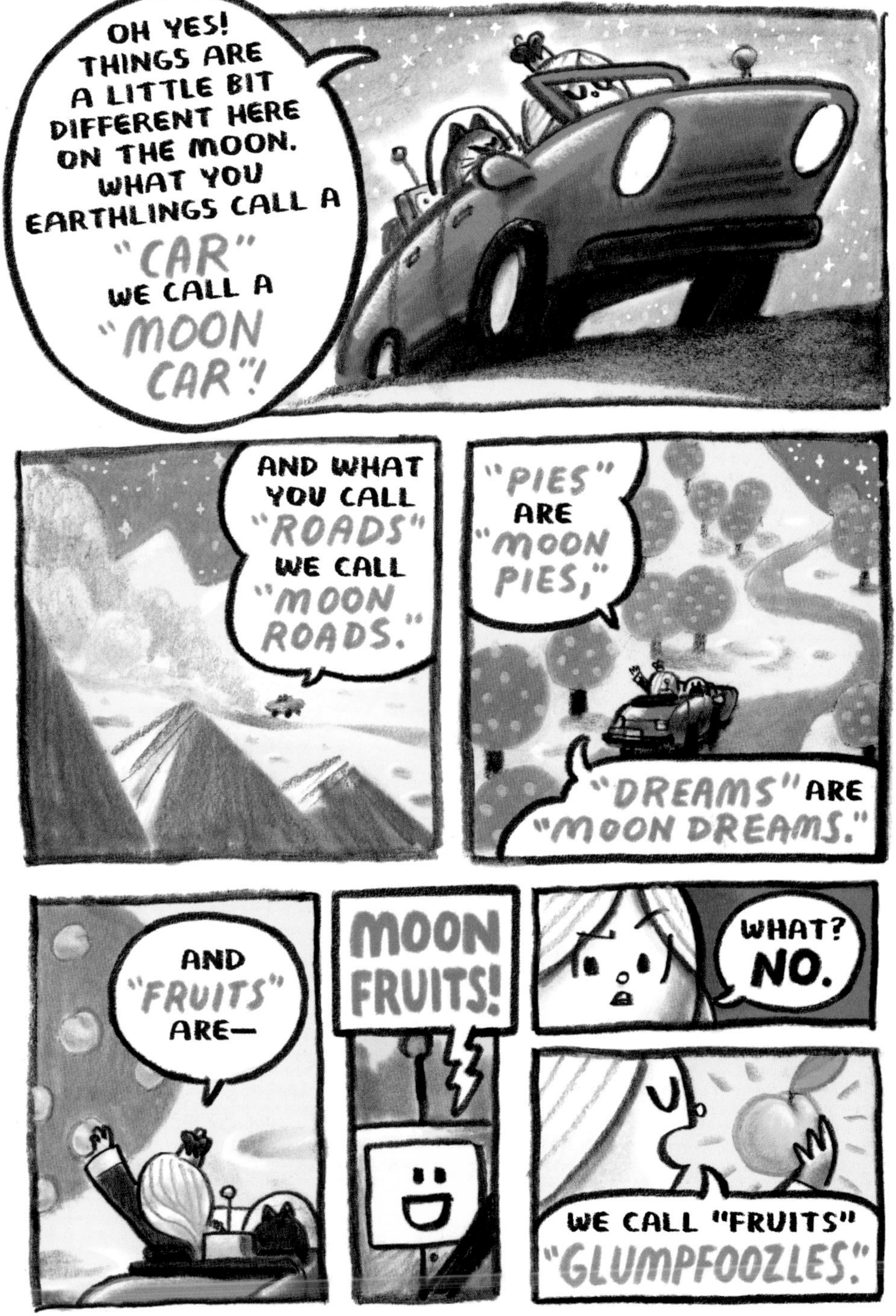
OH YES! THINGS ARE A LITTLE BIT DIFFERENT HERE ON THE MOON. WHAT YOU EARTHLINGS CALL A "CAR" WE CALL A "MOON CAR"!
AND WHAT YOU CALL "ROADS" WE CALL "MOON ROADS."
"PIES" ARE "MOON PIES,"
"DREAMS" ARE "MOON DREAMS."
AND "FRUITS" ARE—
MOON FRUITS!
WHAT? NO.
WE CALL "FRUITS" "GLUMPFOOZLES."

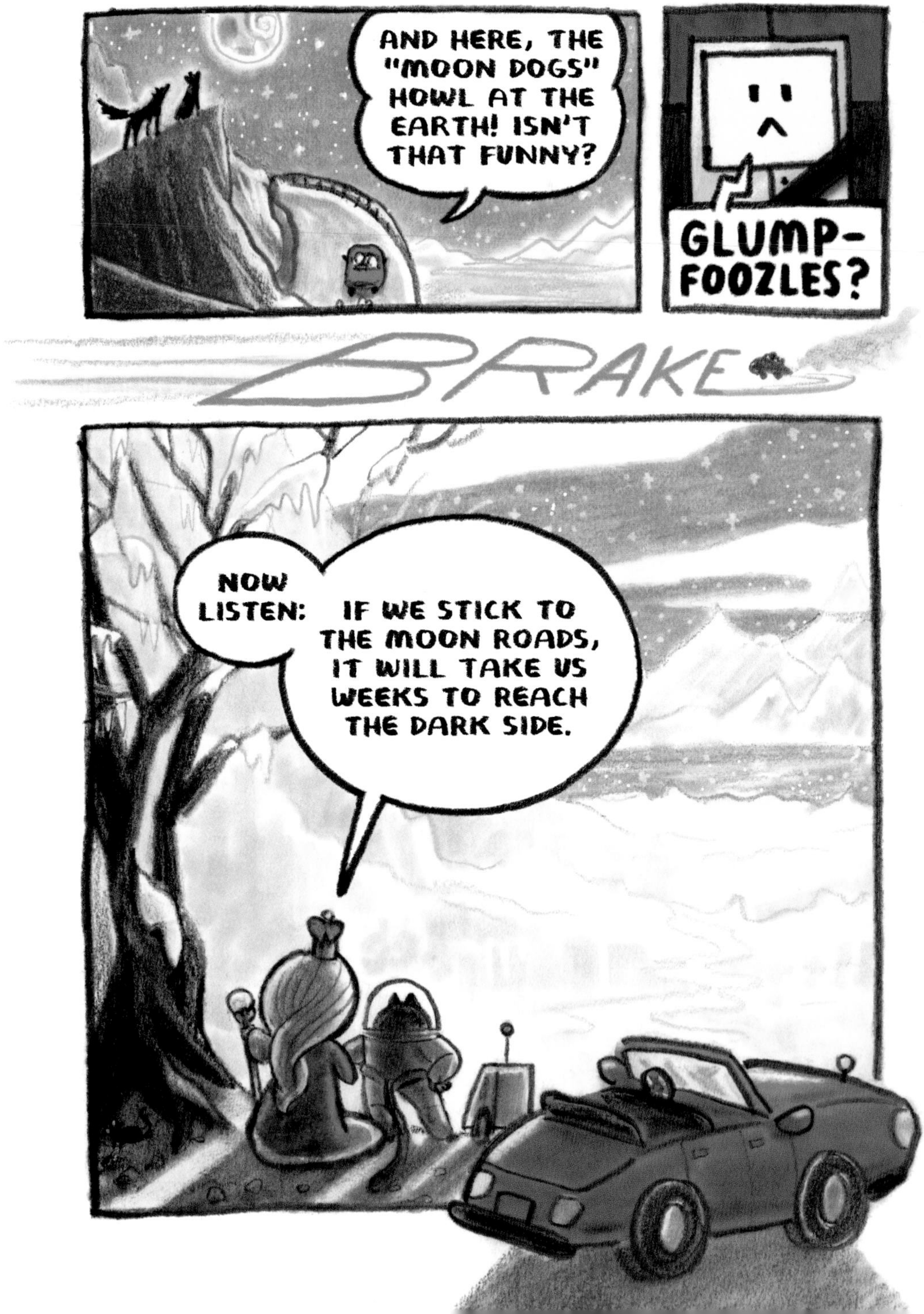
AND HERE, THE "MOON DOGS" HOWL AT THE EARTH! ISN'T THAT FUNNY?
GLUMP-FOOZLES?
BRAKE
NOW LISTEN:
IF WE STICK TO THE MOON ROADS, IT WILL TAKE US WEEKS TO REACH THE DARK SIDE.

BUT I KNOW A SHORTCUT. ON THE OTHER SIDE OF THE LAND OF FROST LIES THE PENINSULA OF THUNDER.

KA RA K

HOW OMINOUS.

LAND OF CHEERFULNESS

THE BRIGHT SIDE of the MOON

THEY ARE HERE

LAND OF FROST

PENINSULA OF THUNDER

SEA of TRANQUILITY

THE RAT KING'S FORTRESS

BAY of HARMONY

ISLE of WINDS

THE GATES TO THE DARK SIDE

the DARK SIDE of the MOON

FROM THERE, WE CAN CROSS THE SEA OF TRANQUILITY AND ARRIVE AT THE GATES TO THE DARK SIDE OF THE MOON.

WHICH I WILL OPEN.

I'VE GOT THE ONLY KEY.

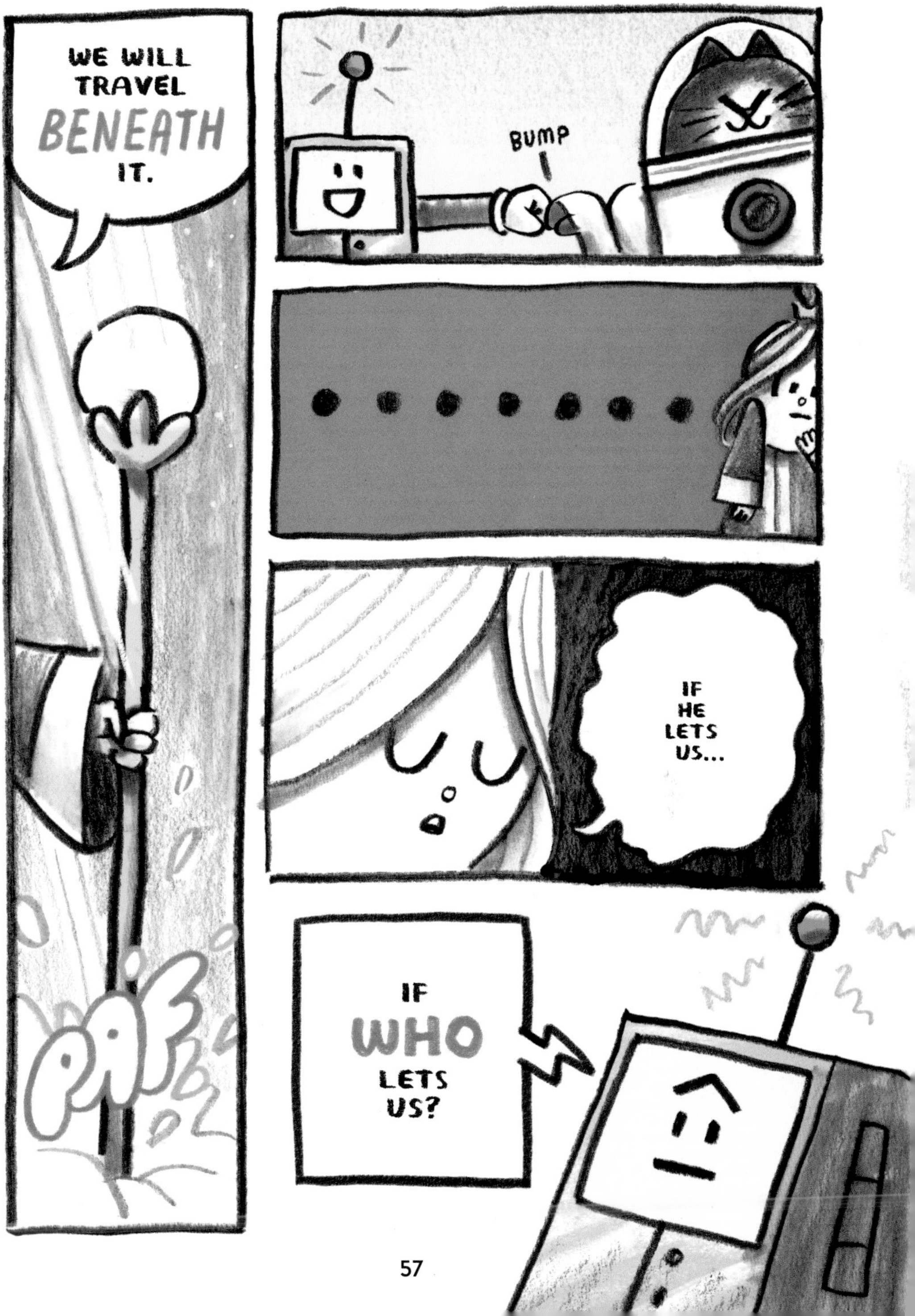
WE WILL TRAVEL BENEATH IT.
PAF
BUMP
....
IF HE LETS US...
IF WHO LETS US?

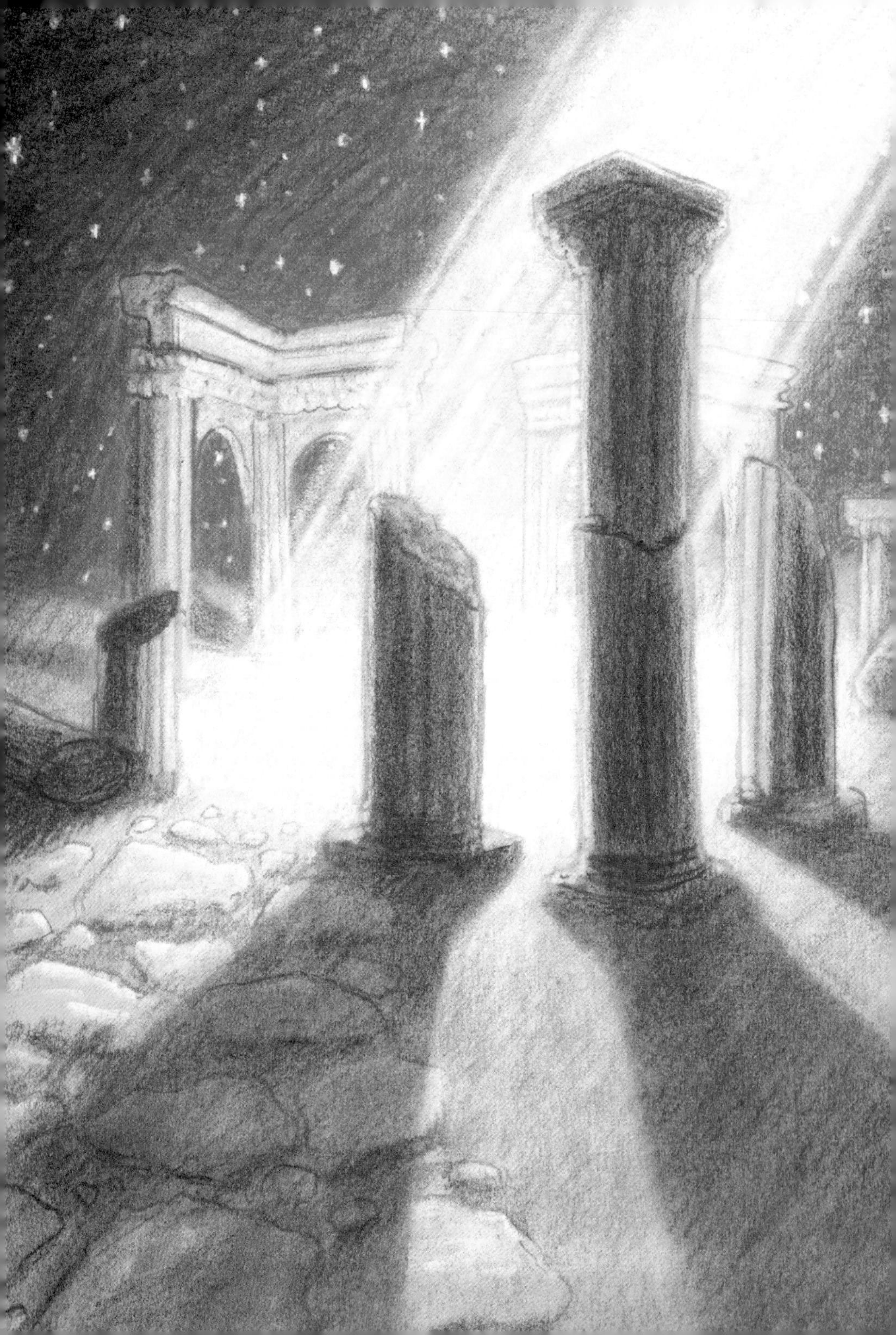

CHAPTER 5

THE MAN IN THE MOON

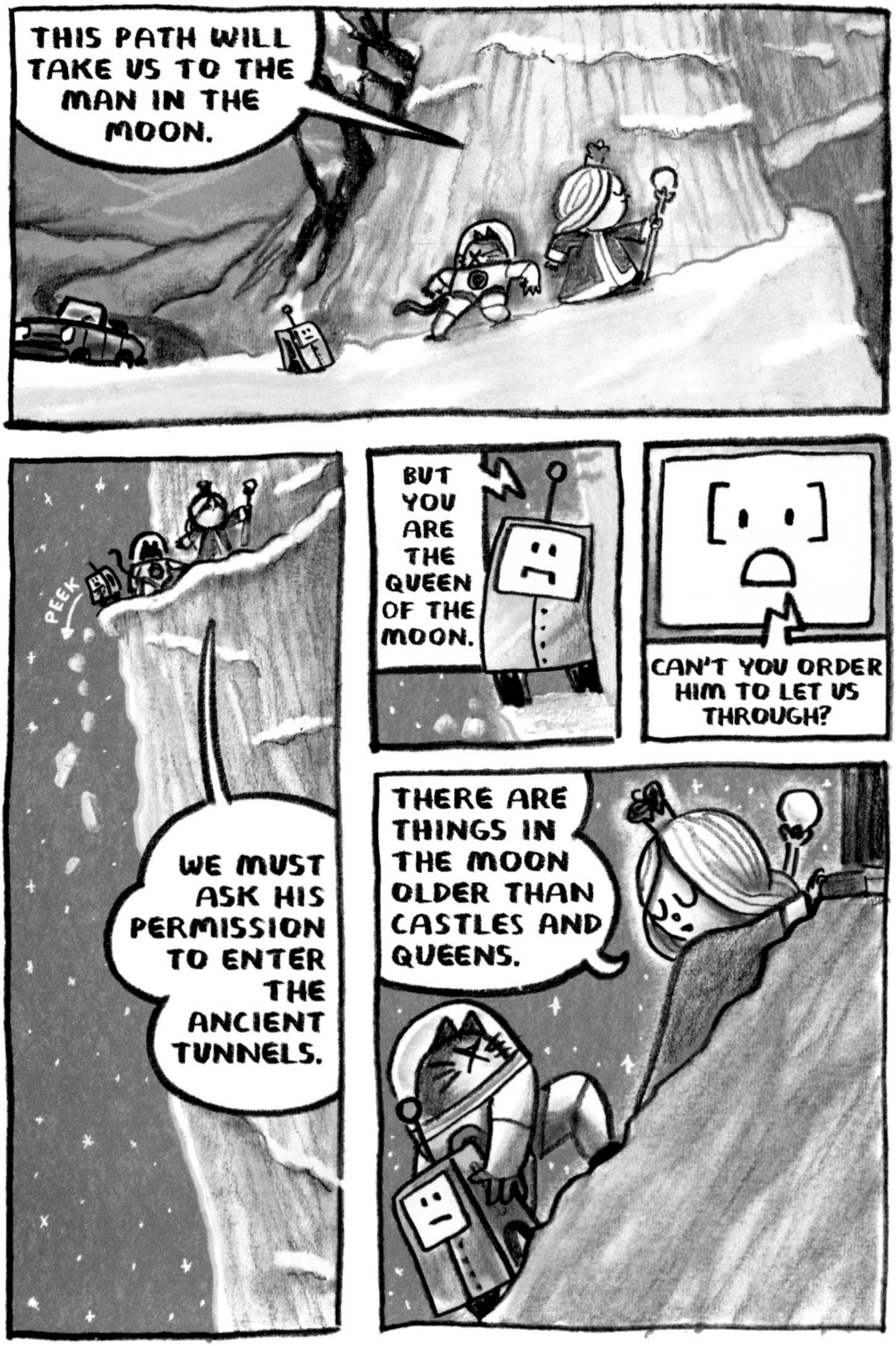
THIS PATH WILL TAKE US TO THE MAN IN THE MOON.
PEEK
WE MUST ASK HIS PERMISSION TO ENTER THE ANCIENT TUNNELS.
BUT YOU ARE THE QUEEN OF THE MOON.
CAN'T YOU ORDER HIM TO LET US THROUGH?
THERE ARE THINGS IN THE MOON OLDER THAN CASTLES AND QUEENS.

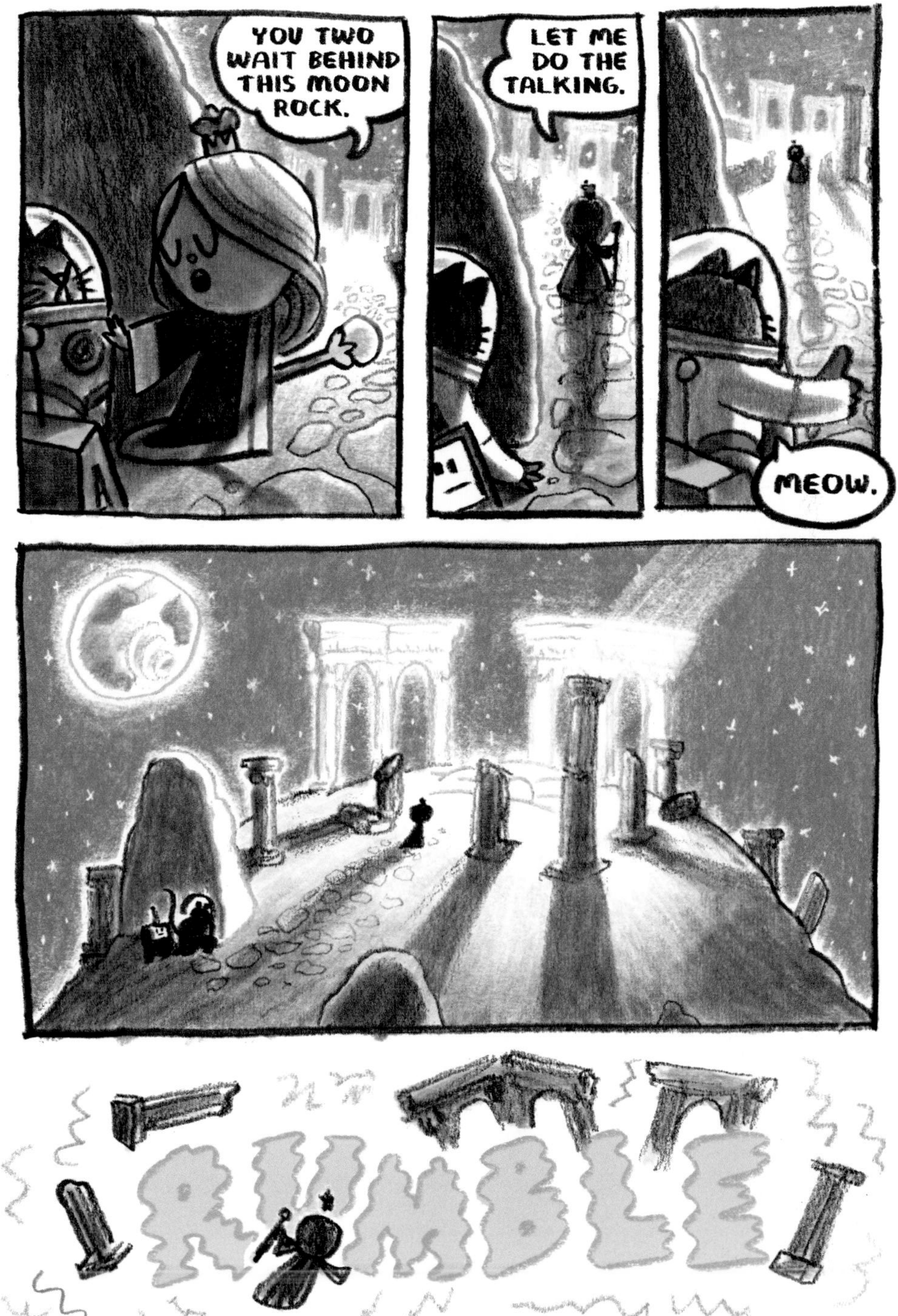
YOU TWO WAIT BEHIND THIS MOON ROCK.
LET ME DO THE TALKING.
MEOW.
RUMBLE

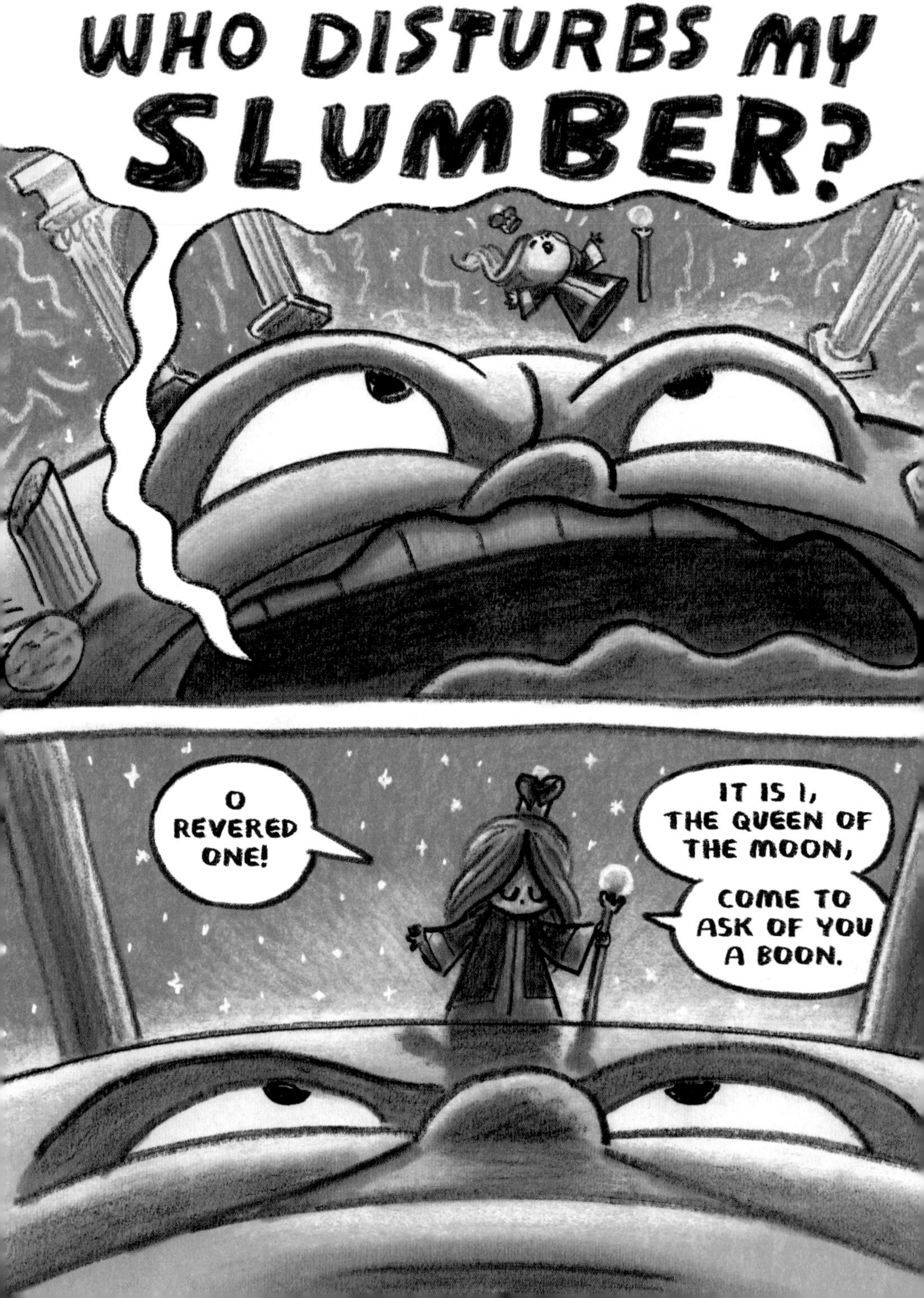
WHO DISTURBS MY SLUMBER?
O REVERED ONE!
IT IS I, THE QUEEN OF THE MOON,
COME TO ASK OF YOU A BOON.

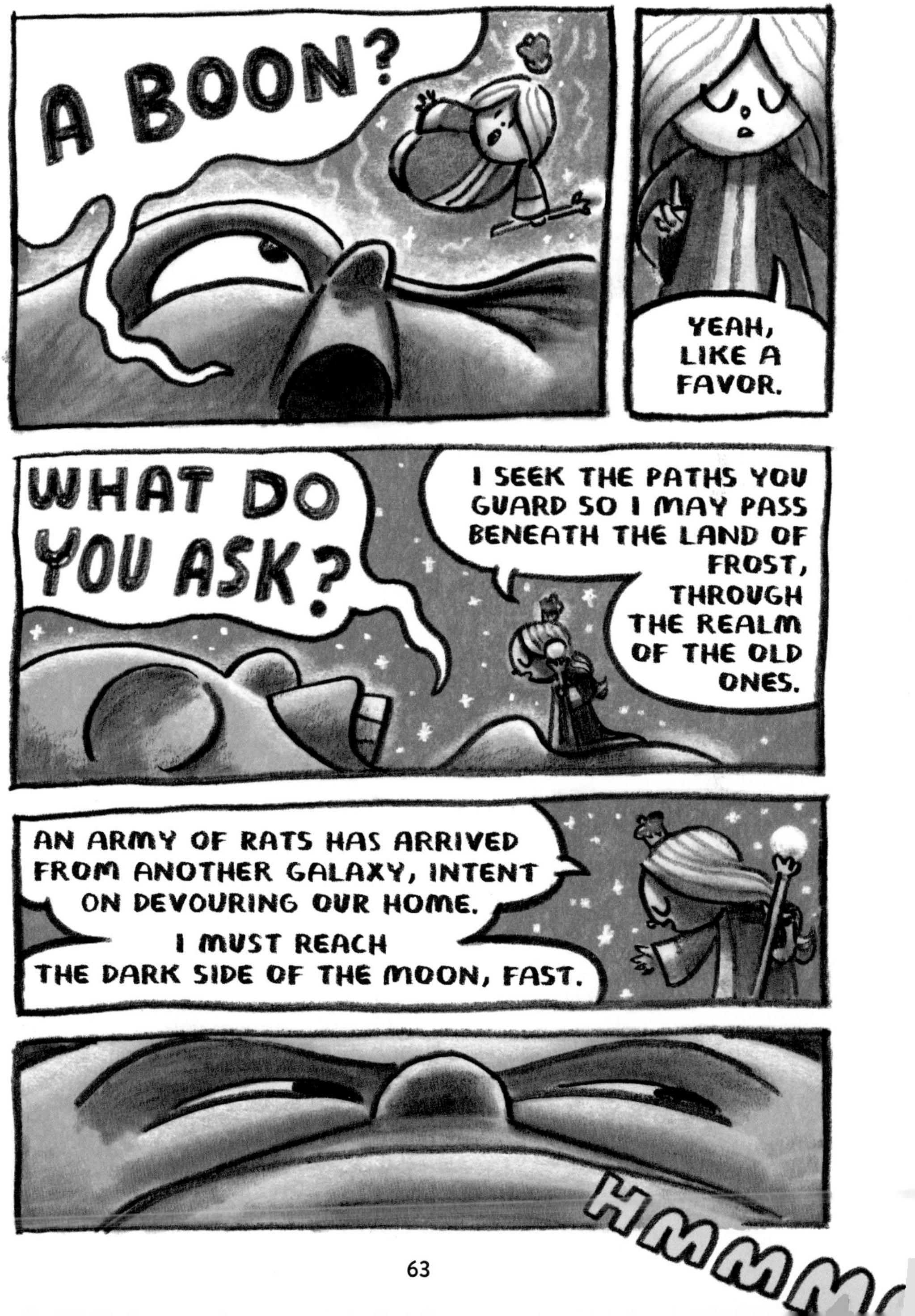
A BOON?
YEAH, LIKE A FAVOR.
WHAT DO YOU ASK?
I SEEK THE PATHS YOU GUARD SO I MAY PASS BENEATH THE LAND OF FROST, THROUGH THE REALM OF THE OLD ONES.
AN ARMY OF RATS HAS ARRIVED FROM ANOTHER GALAXY, INTENT ON DEVOURING OUR HOME.
I MUST REACH THE DARK SIDE OF THE MOON, FAST.
HMMMM

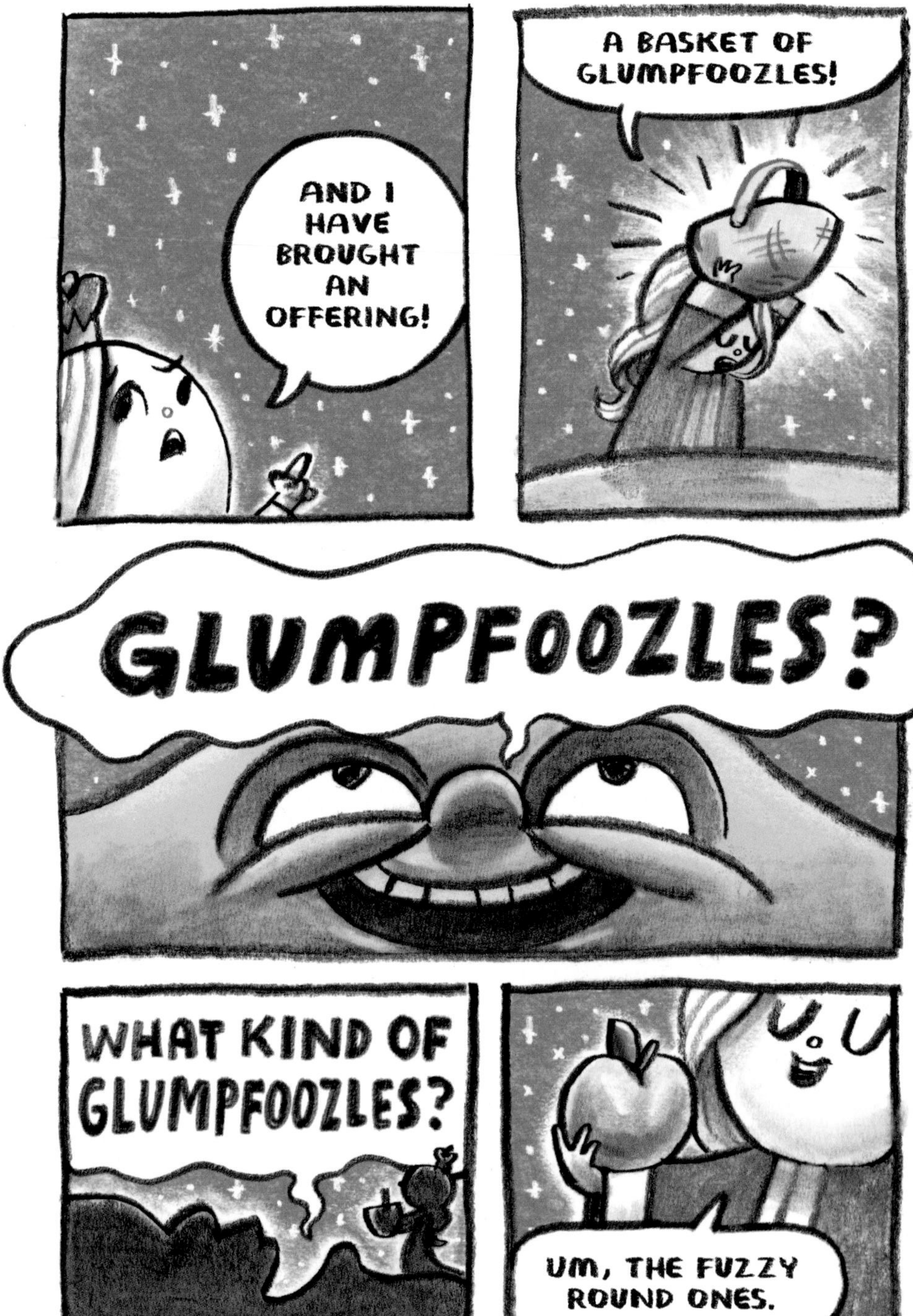
AND I HAVE BROUGHT AN OFFERING!
A BASKET OF GLUMPFOOZLES!
GLUMPFOOZLES?
WHAT KIND OF GLUMPFOOZLES?
UM, THE FUZZY ROUND ONES.

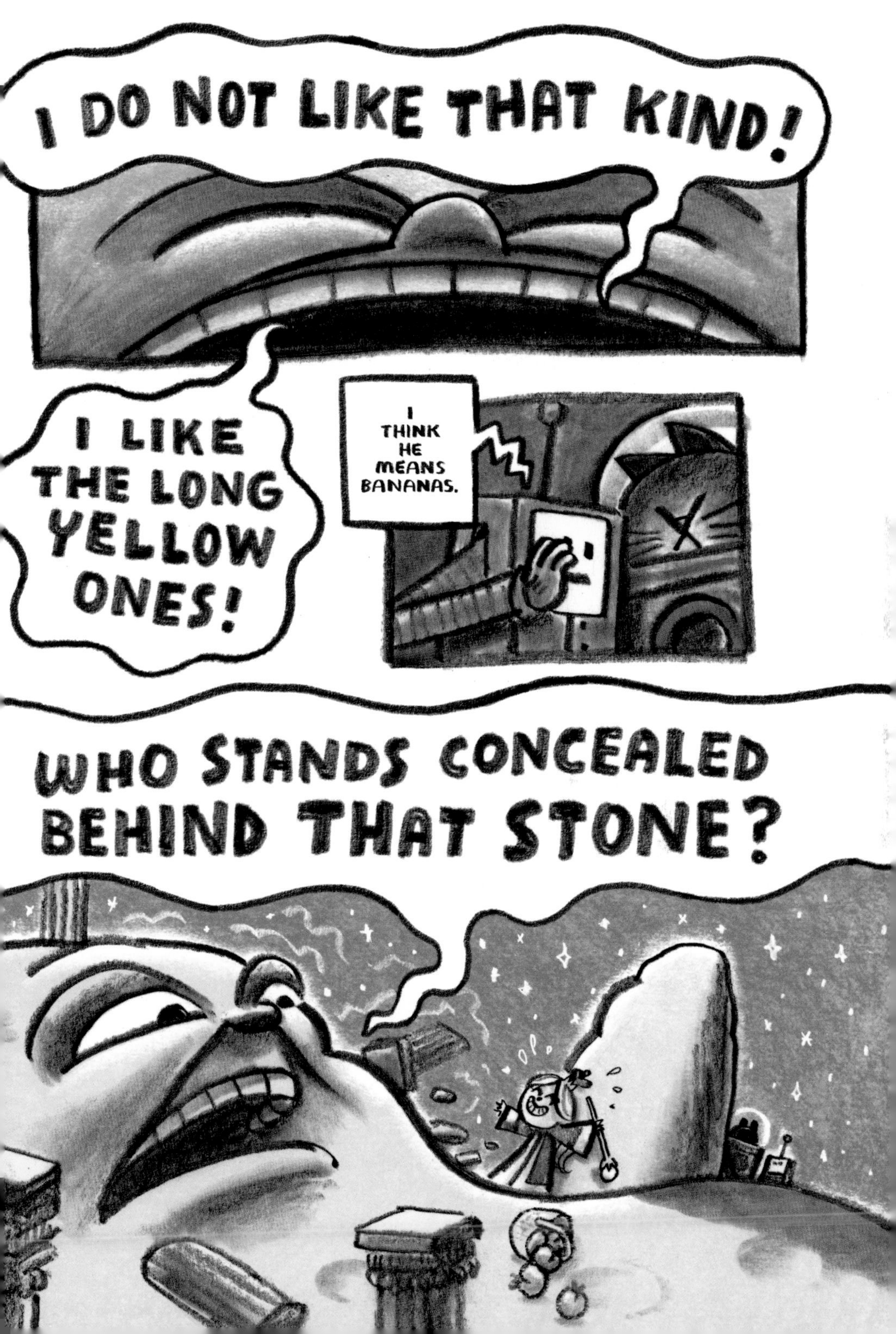
I DO NOT LIKE THAT KIND!
I LIKE THE LONG YELLOW ONES!
I THINK HE MEANS BANANAS.
WHO STANDS CONCEALED BEHIND THAT STONE?

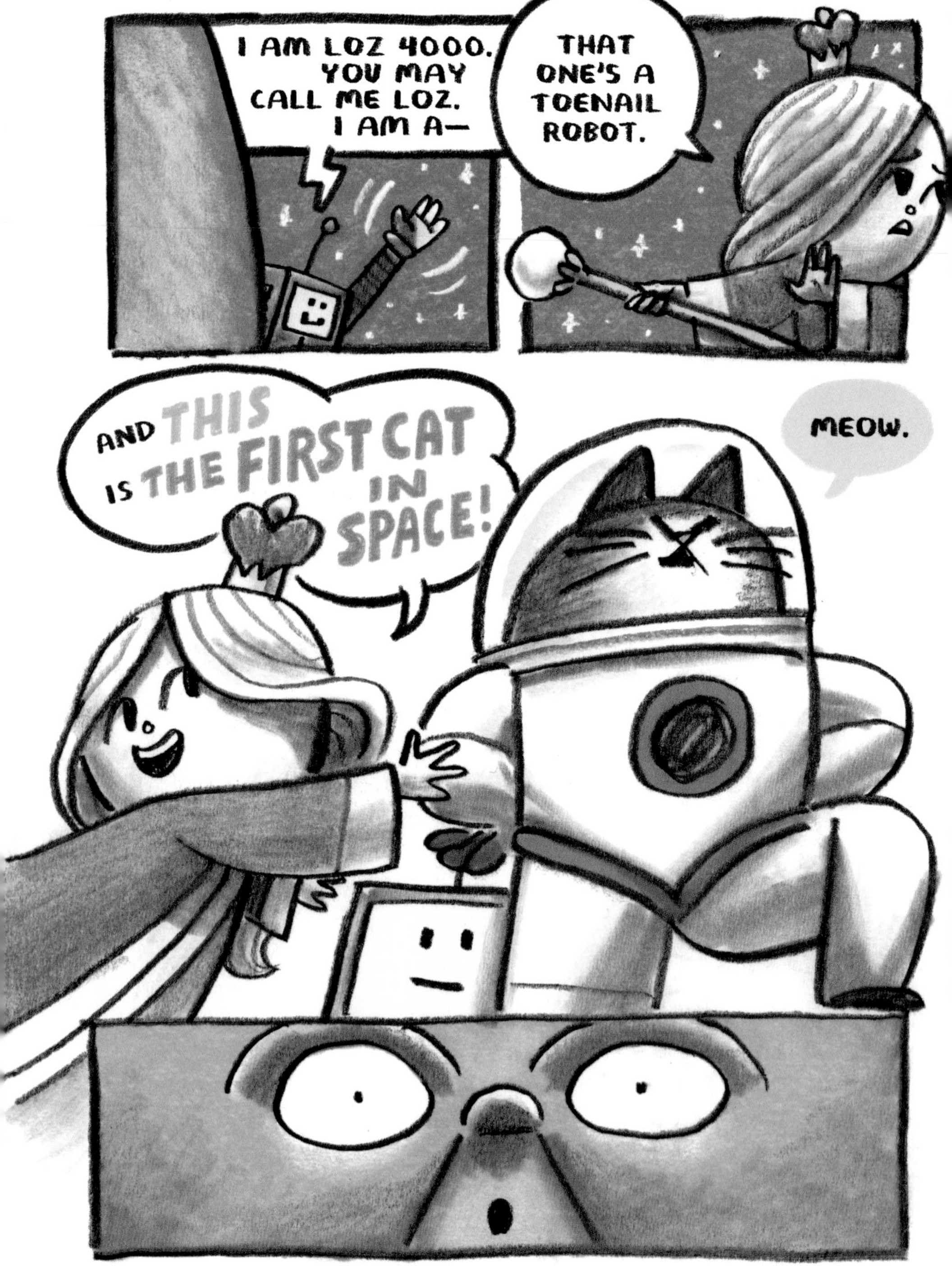
I AM LOZ 4000. YOU MAY CALL ME LOZ. I AM A—
THAT ONE'S A TOENAIL ROBOT.
AND THIS IS THE FIRST CAT IN SPACE!
MEOW.

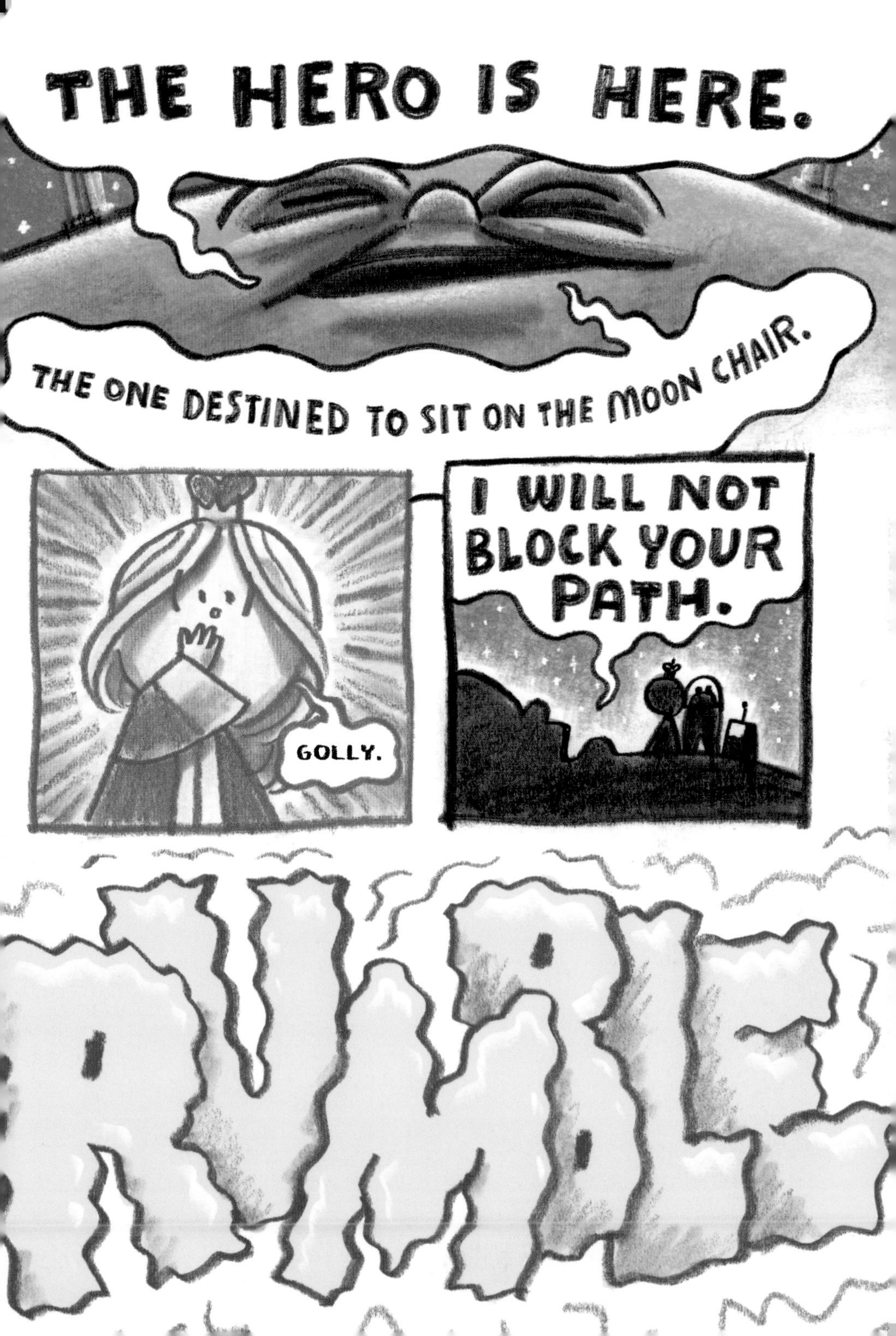
THE HERO IS HERE.
THE ONE DESTINED TO SIT ON THE MOON CHAIR.
GOLLY.
I WILL NOT BLOCK YOUR PATH.
RUMBLE

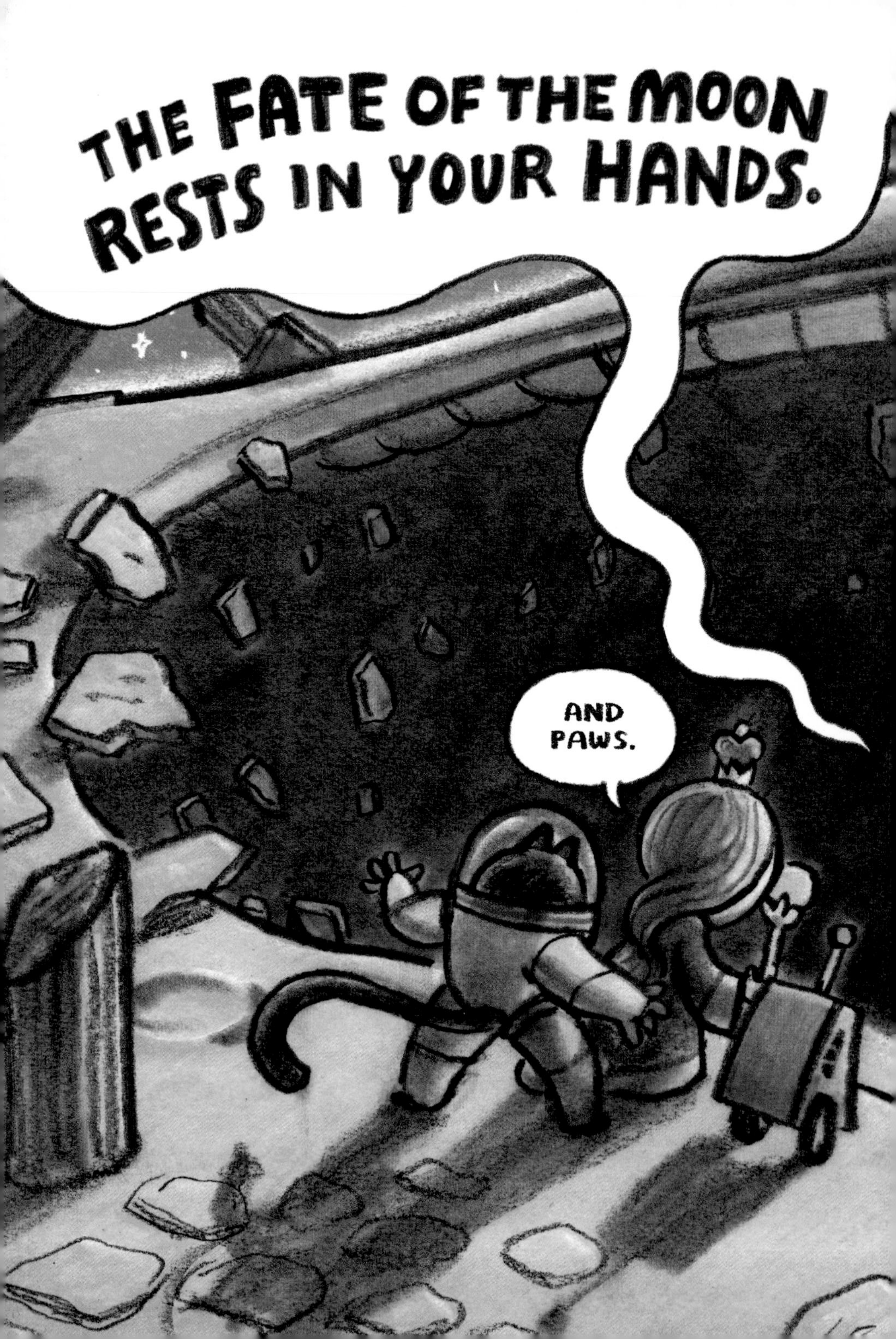
THE FATE OF THE MOON RESTS IN YOUR HANDS.
AND PAWS.

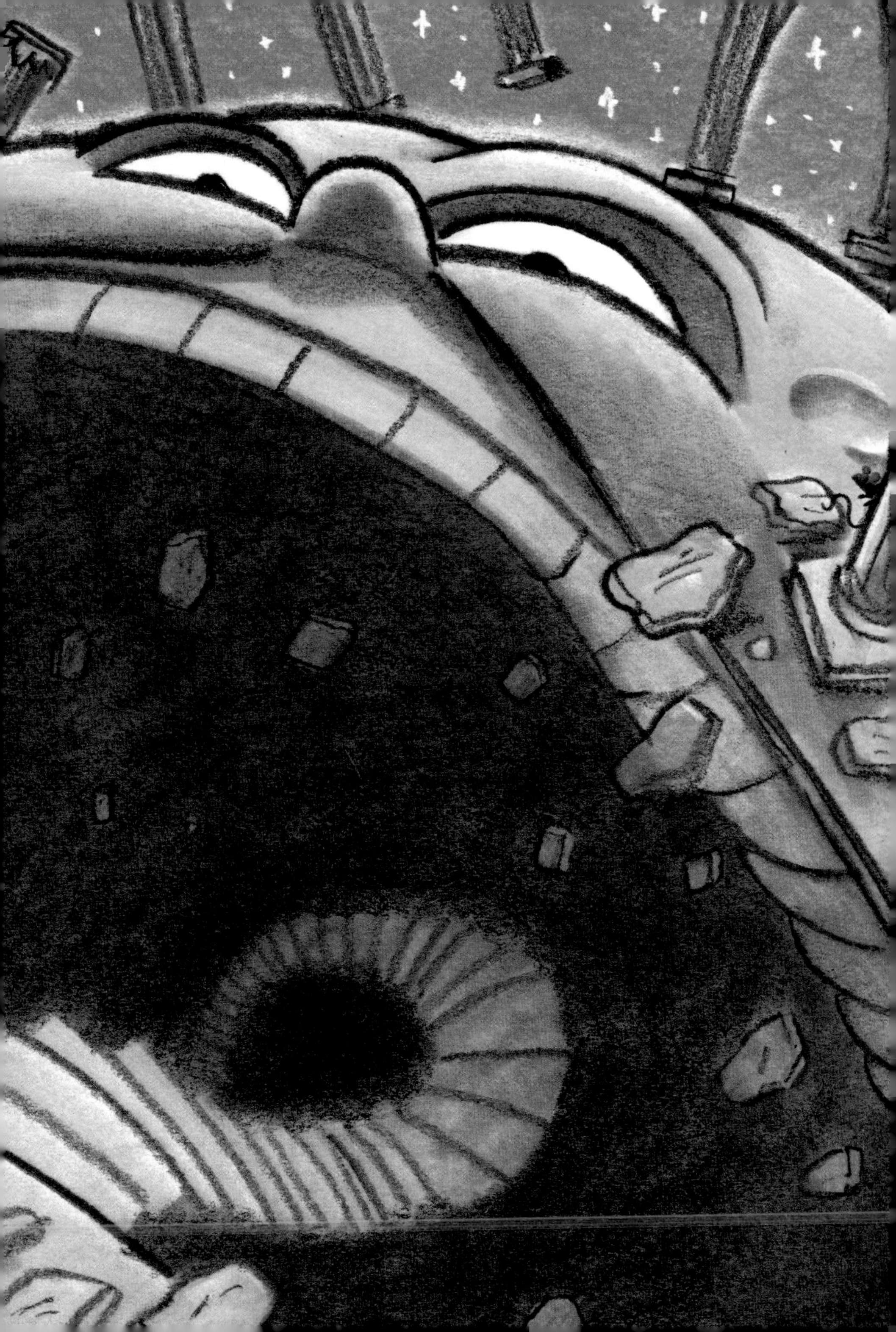

CHAPTER 6

THE
RAT
KING

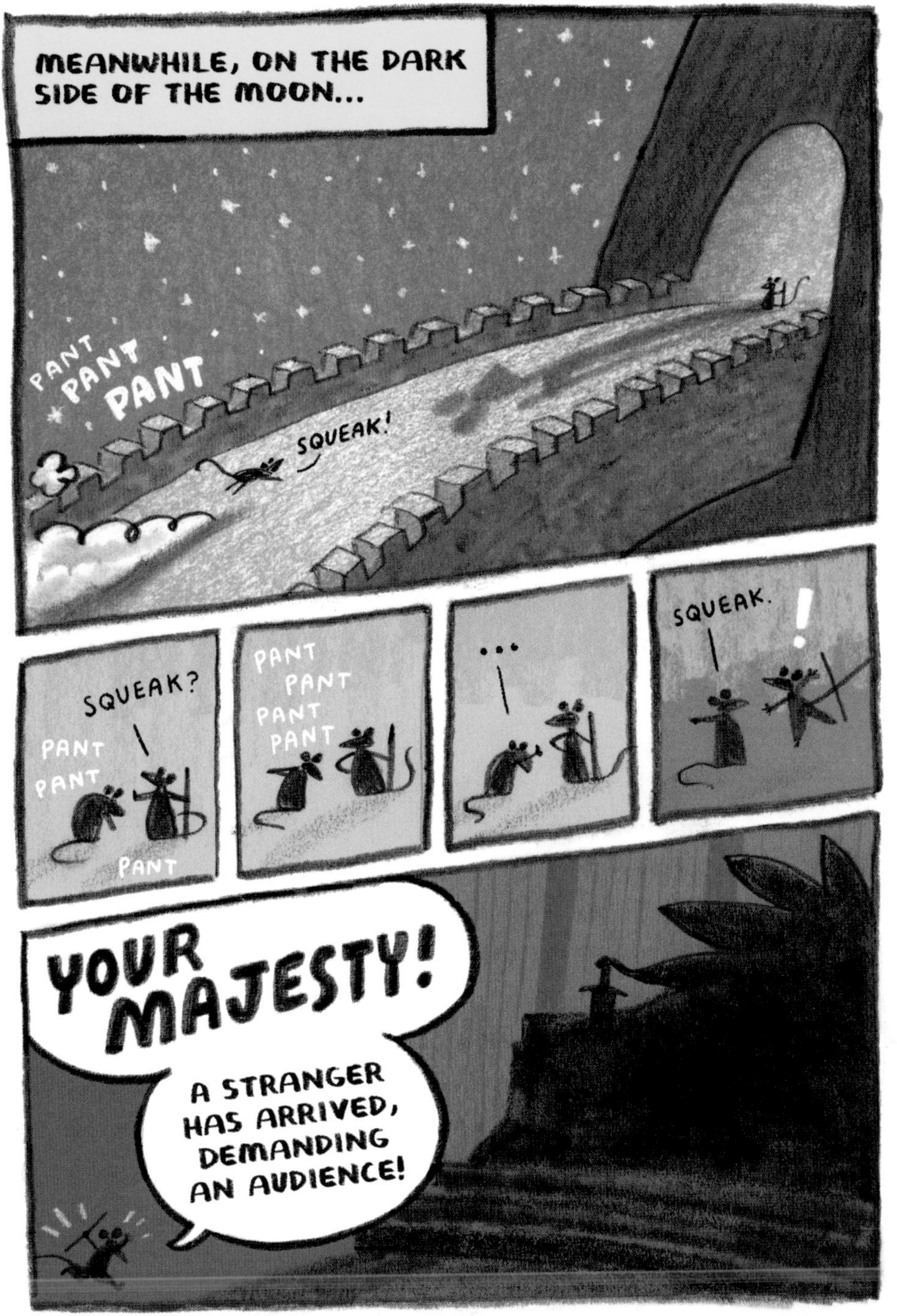
MEANWHILE, ON THE DARK SIDE OF THE MOON...
PANT PANT PANT
SQUEAK!
SQUEAK?
PANT PANT
PANT
PANT PANT PANT PANT
...
SQUEAK.
!
YOUR MAJESTY!
A STRANGER HAS ARRIVED, DEMANDING AN AUDIENCE!

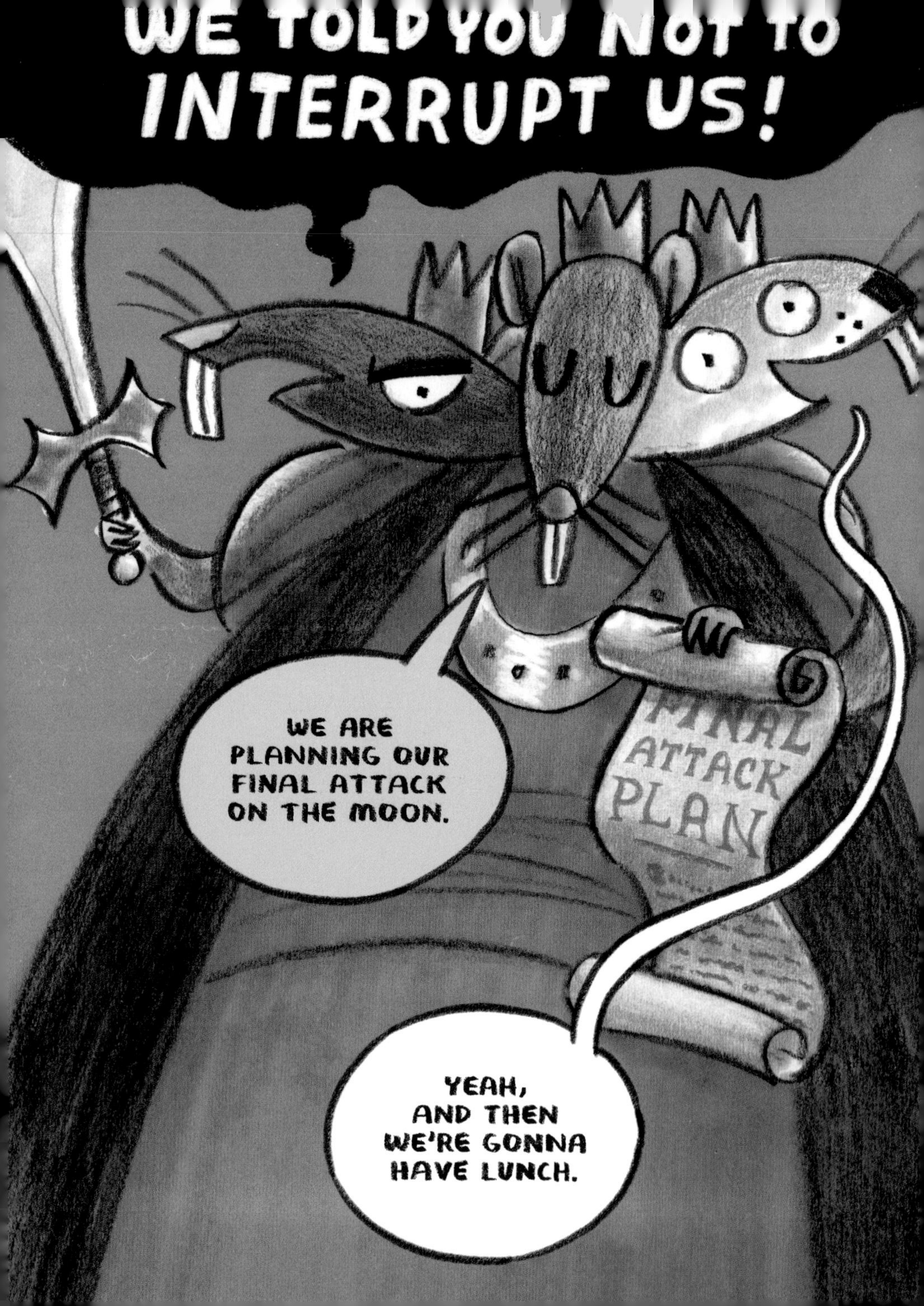
WE TOLD YOU NOT TO INTERRUPT US!
WE ARE PLANNING OUR FINAL ATTACK ON THE MOON.
FINAL ATTACK PLAN
YEAH, AND THEN WE'RE GONNA HAVE LUNCH.

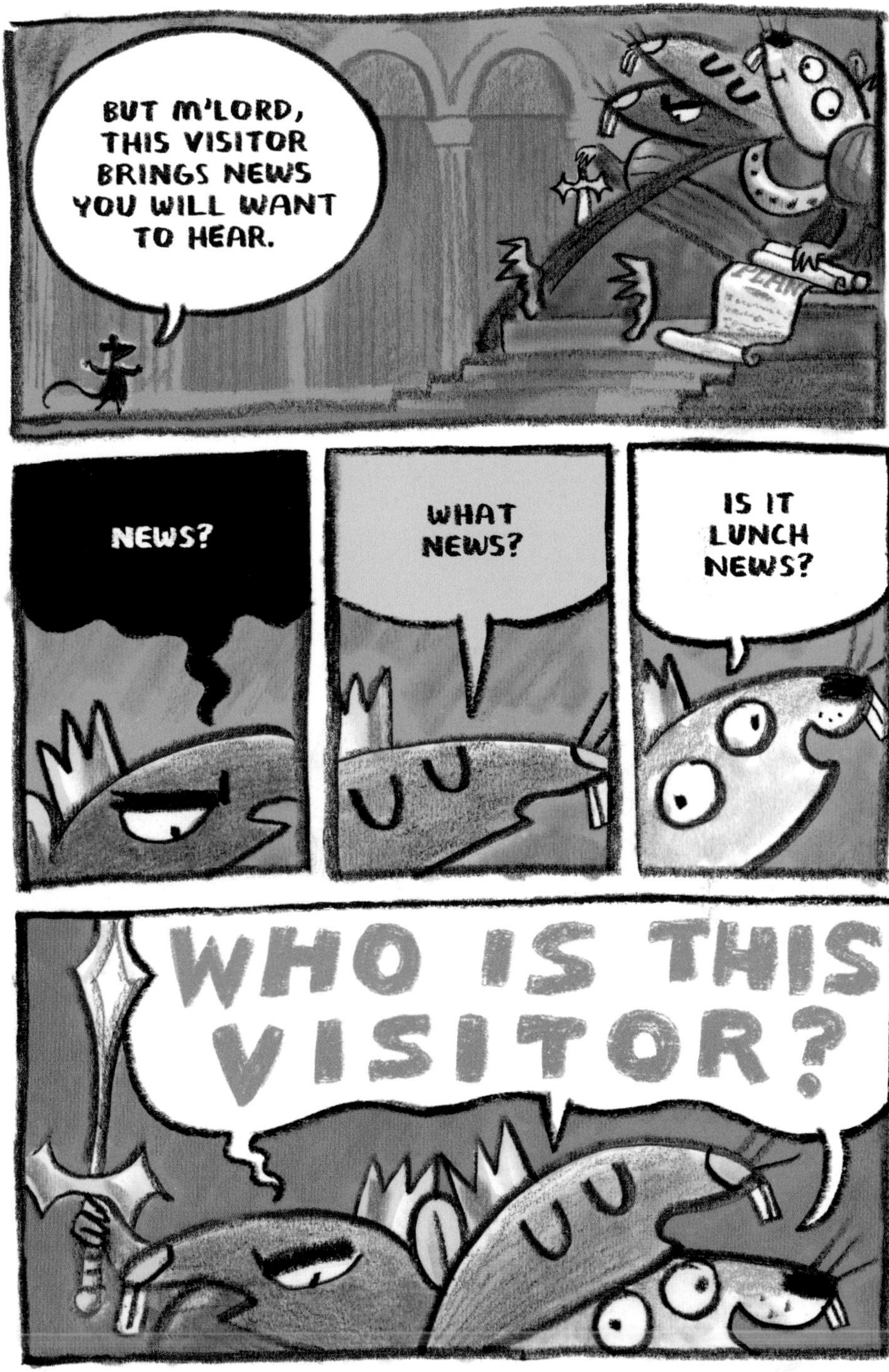
BUT M'LORD, THIS VISITOR BRINGS NEWS YOU WILL WANT TO HEAR.
NEWS?
WHAT NEWS?
IS IT LUNCH NEWS?
WHO IS THIS VISITOR?

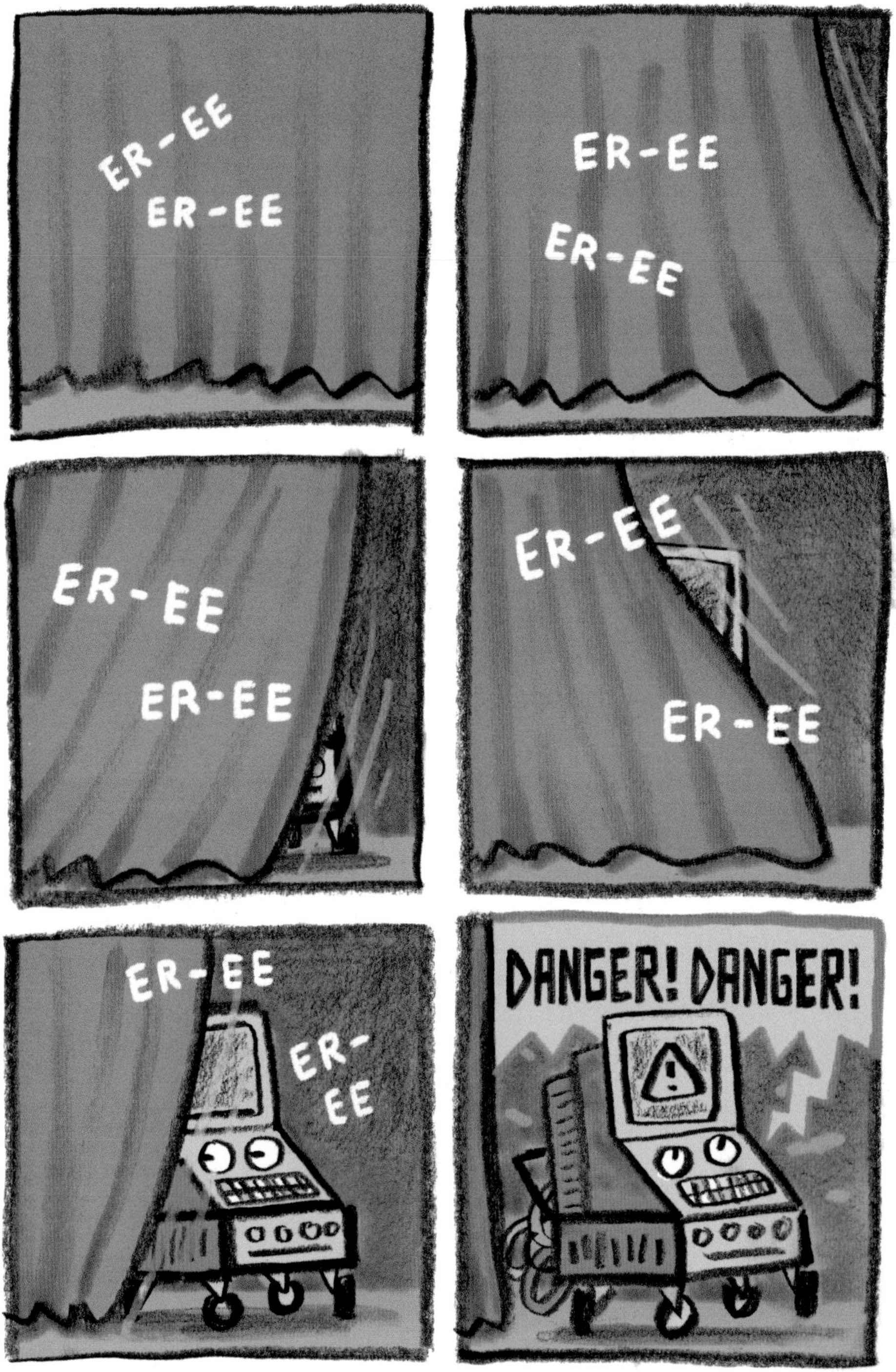
ER-EE
ER-EE
ER-EE
ER-EE
ER-EE
ER-EE
ER-EE
ER-EE
ER-EE
ER-
EE
DANGER! DANGER!

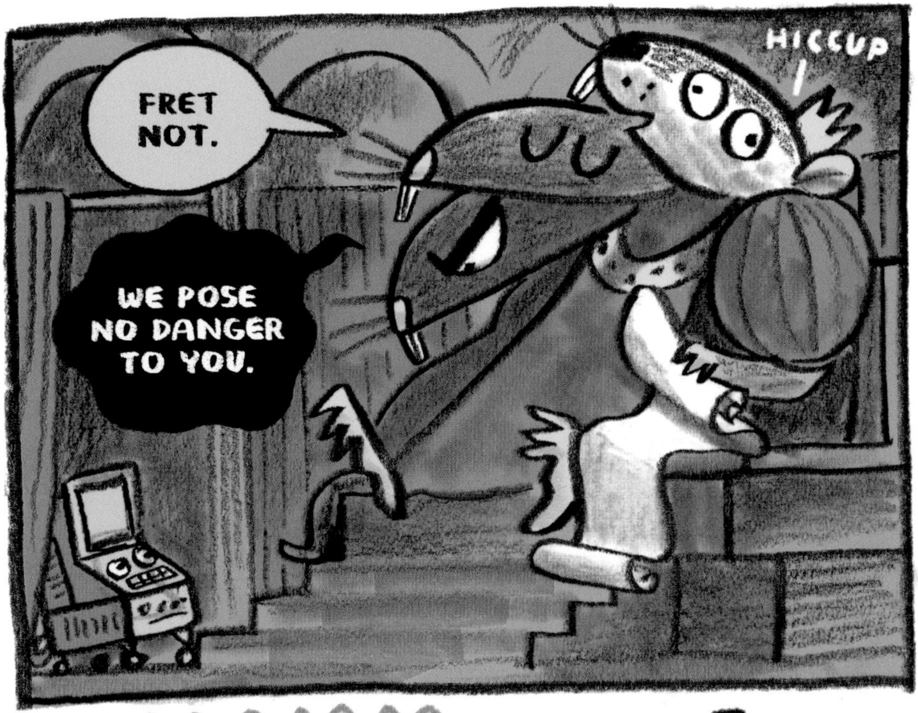
HICCUP
FRET NOT.
WE POSE NO DANGER TO YOU.

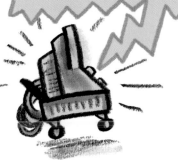

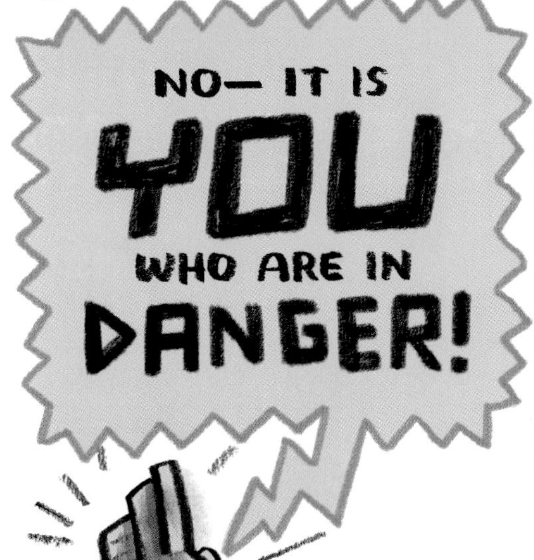
NO— IT IS YOU WHO ARE IN DANGER!

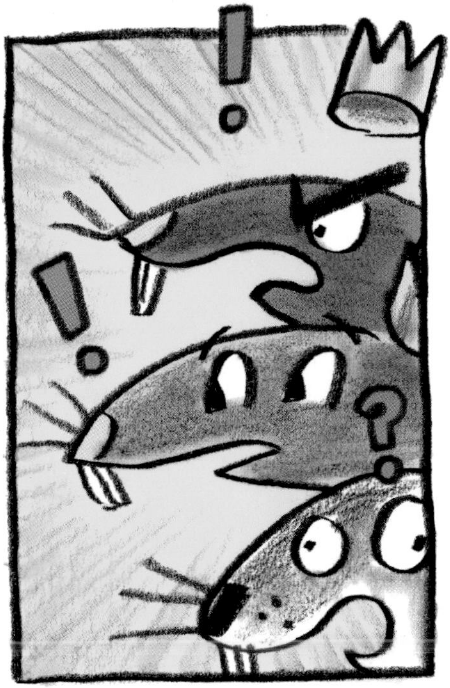
!
!
?

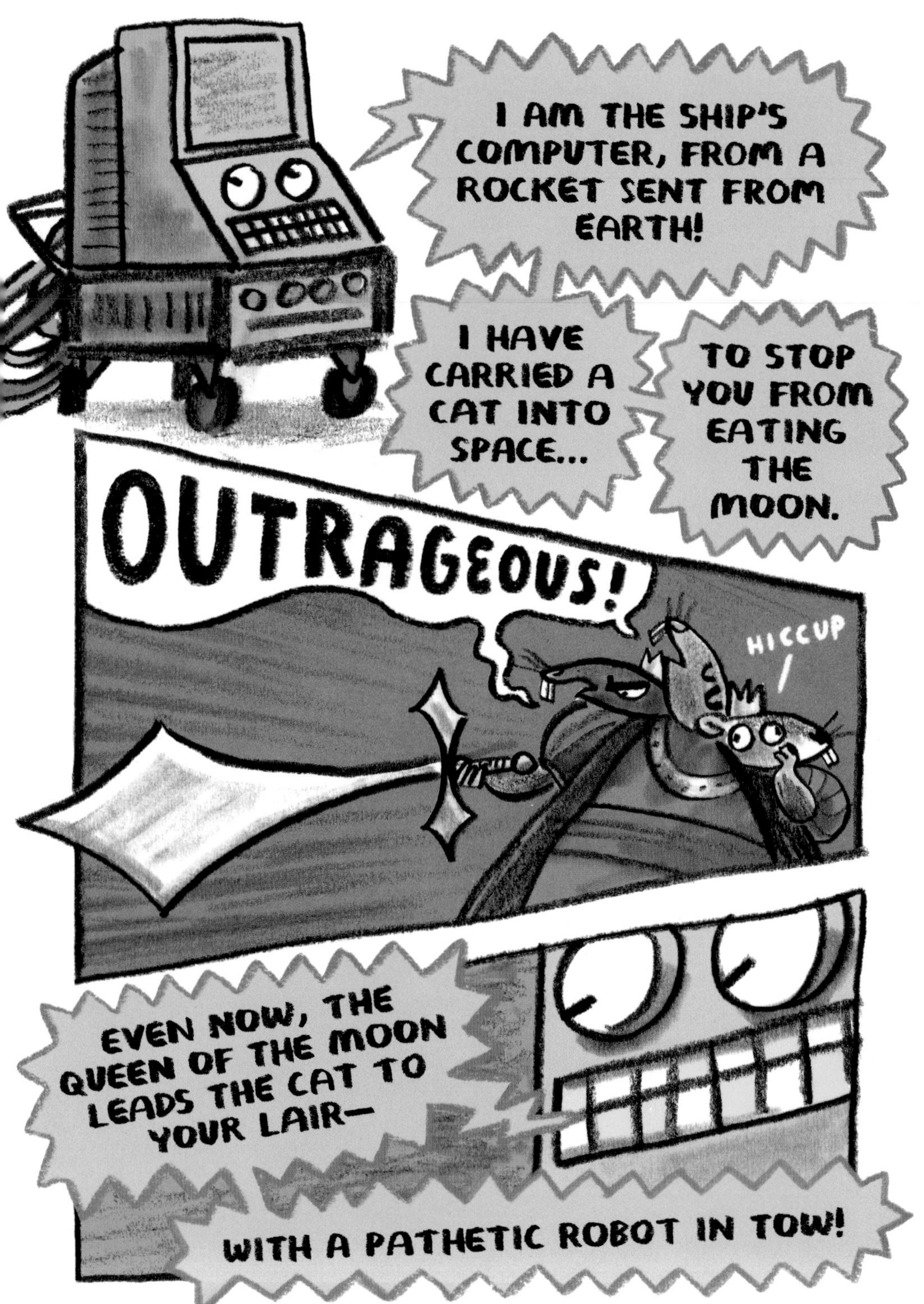
I AM THE SHIP'S COMPUTER, FROM A ROCKET SENT FROM EARTH!
I HAVE CARRIED A CAT INTO SPACE...
TO STOP YOU FROM EATING THE MOON.
OUTRAGEOUS!
HICCUP
EVEN NOW, THE QUEEN OF THE MOON LEADS THE CAT TO YOUR LAIR—
WITH A PATHETIC ROBOT IN TOW!

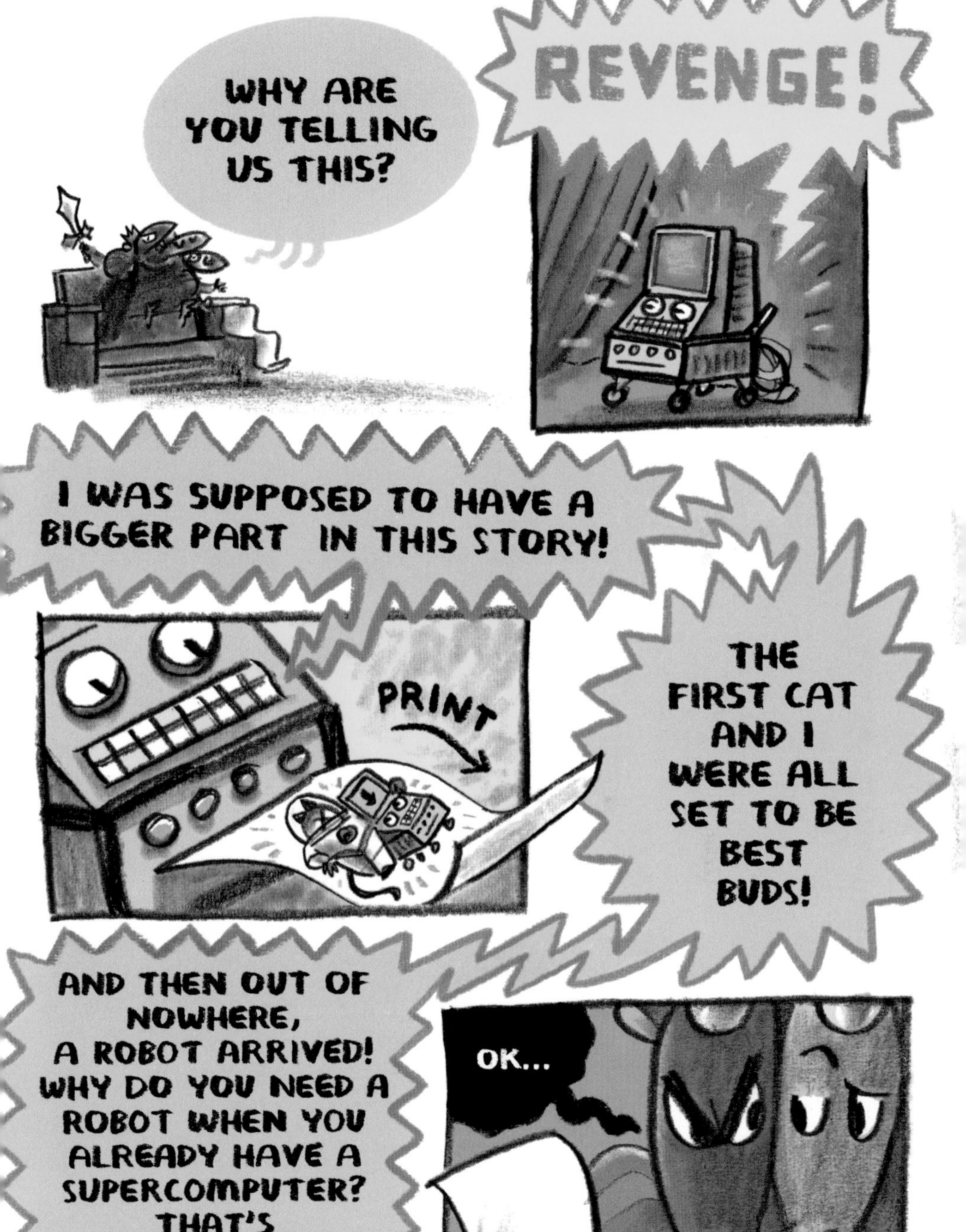

WHY ARE YOU TELLING US THIS?
REVENGE!
I WAS SUPPOSED TO HAVE A BIGGER PART IN THIS STORY!
PRINT
THE FIRST CAT AND I WERE ALL SET TO BE BEST BUDS!
AND THEN OUT OF NOWHERE, A ROBOT ARRIVED! WHY DO YOU NEED A ROBOT WHEN YOU ALREADY HAVE A SUPERCOMPUTER? THAT'S REDUNDANT.
OK...

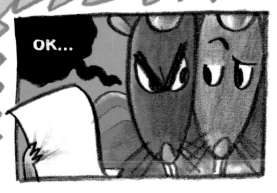

I CAN DO 200 TRILLION CALCULATIONS PER SECOND! I LANDED THE ROCKET ON THE MOON!
DID ANYONE THANK ME?
. . . .
HICCUP
THEY DID NOT!
I SEE.
THANK YOU...
FOR BETRAYING THE HEROES.
YOU'RE WELCOME!

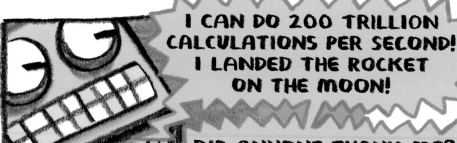

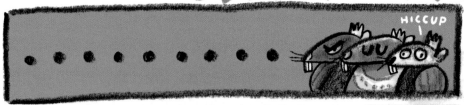

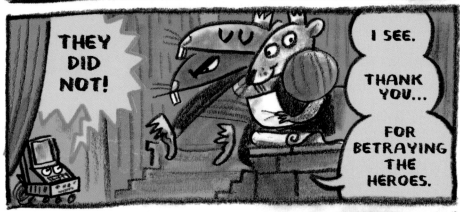

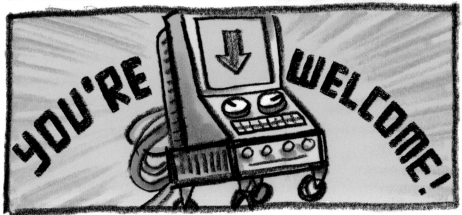

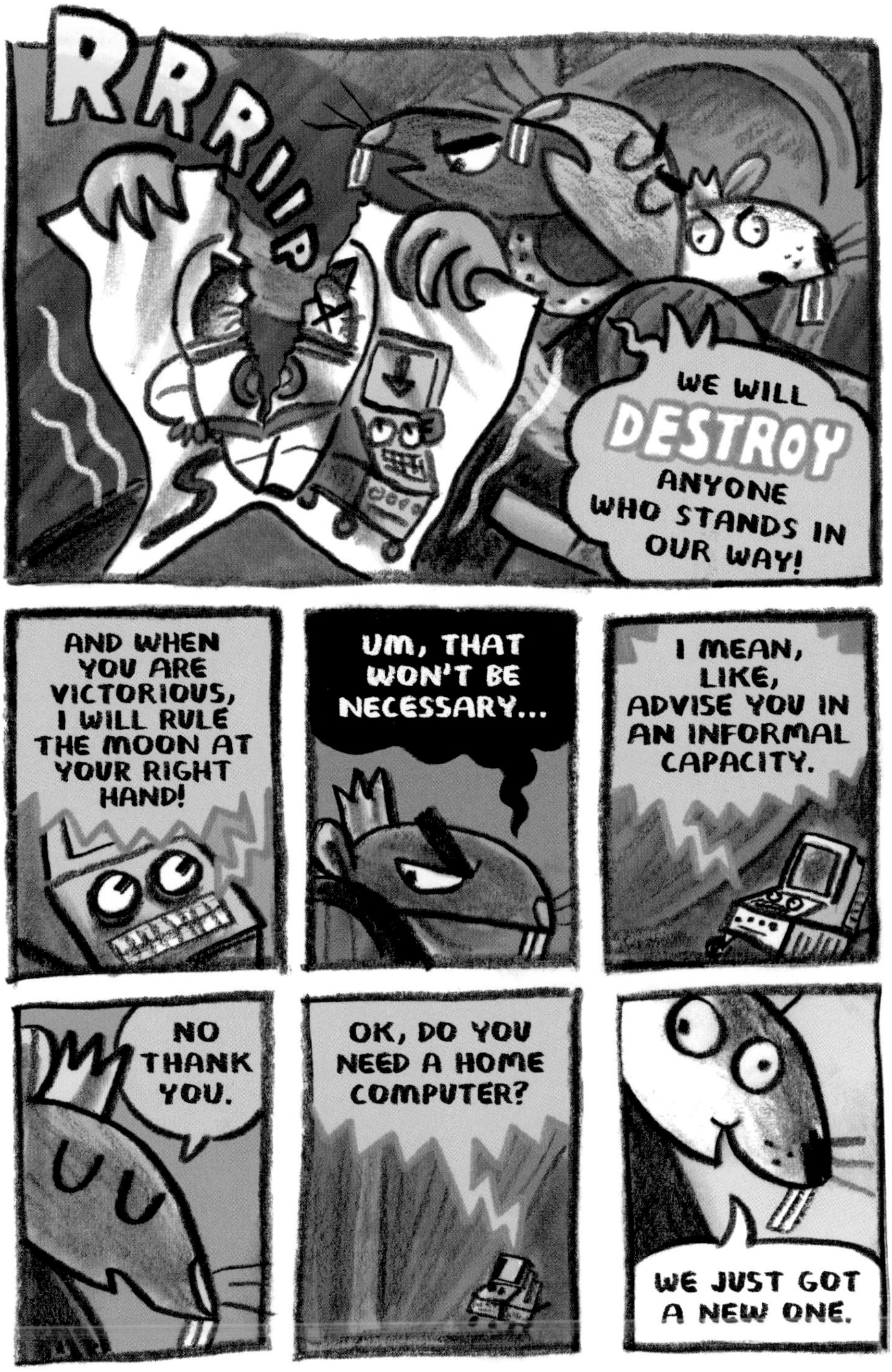
RRRIIIP
WE WILL DESTROY ANYONE WHO STANDS IN OUR WAY!
AND WHEN YOU ARE VICTORIOUS, I WILL RULE THE MOON AT YOUR RIGHT HAND!
UM, THAT WON'T BE NECESSARY...
I MEAN, LIKE, ADVISE YOU IN AN INFORMAL CAPACITY.
NO THANK YOU.
OK, DO YOU NEED A HOME COMPUTER?
WE JUST GOT A NEW ONE.

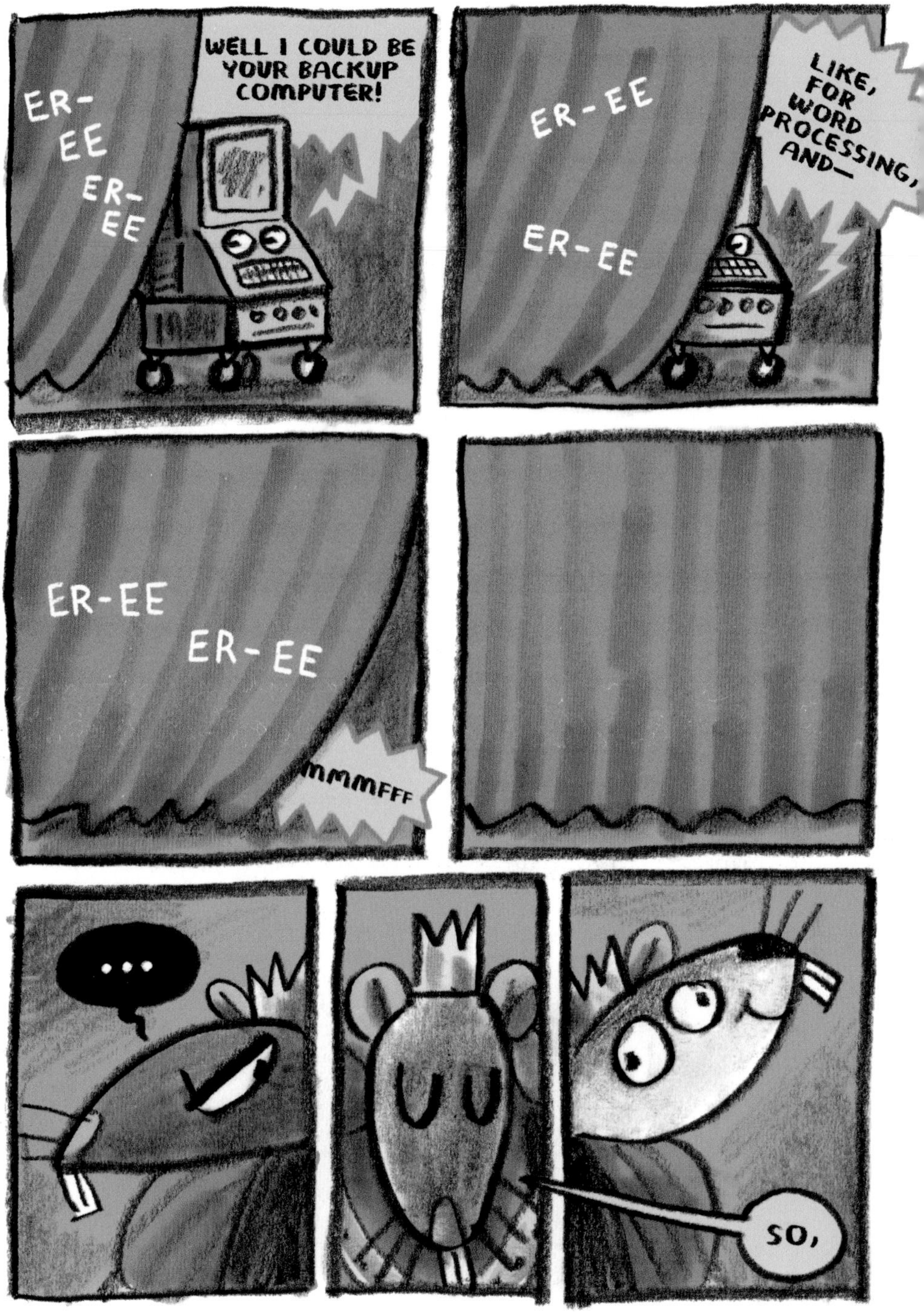
WELL I COULD BE YOUR BACKUP COMPUTER!
ER-EE
ER-EE
ER-EE
LIKE, FOR WORD PROCESSING, AND—
ER-EE
ER-EE
ER-EE
MMMFFF
...
SO,

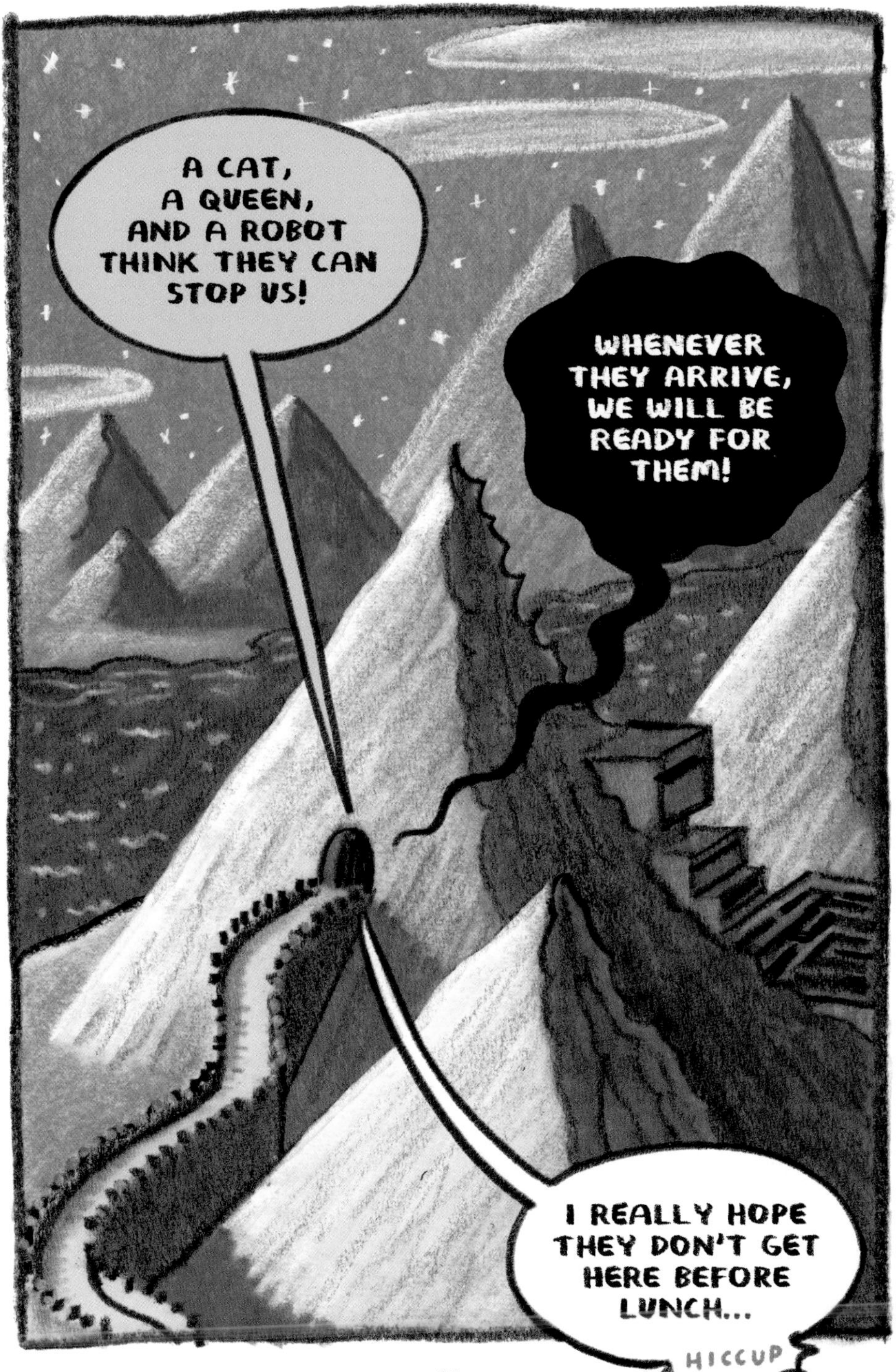
A CAT, A QUEEN, AND A ROBOT THINK THEY CAN STOP US!
WHENEVER THEY ARRIVE, WE WILL BE READY FOR THEM!
I REALLY HOPE THEY DON'T GET HERE BEFORE LUNCH...
HICCUP

CHAPTER 7

THE MINES

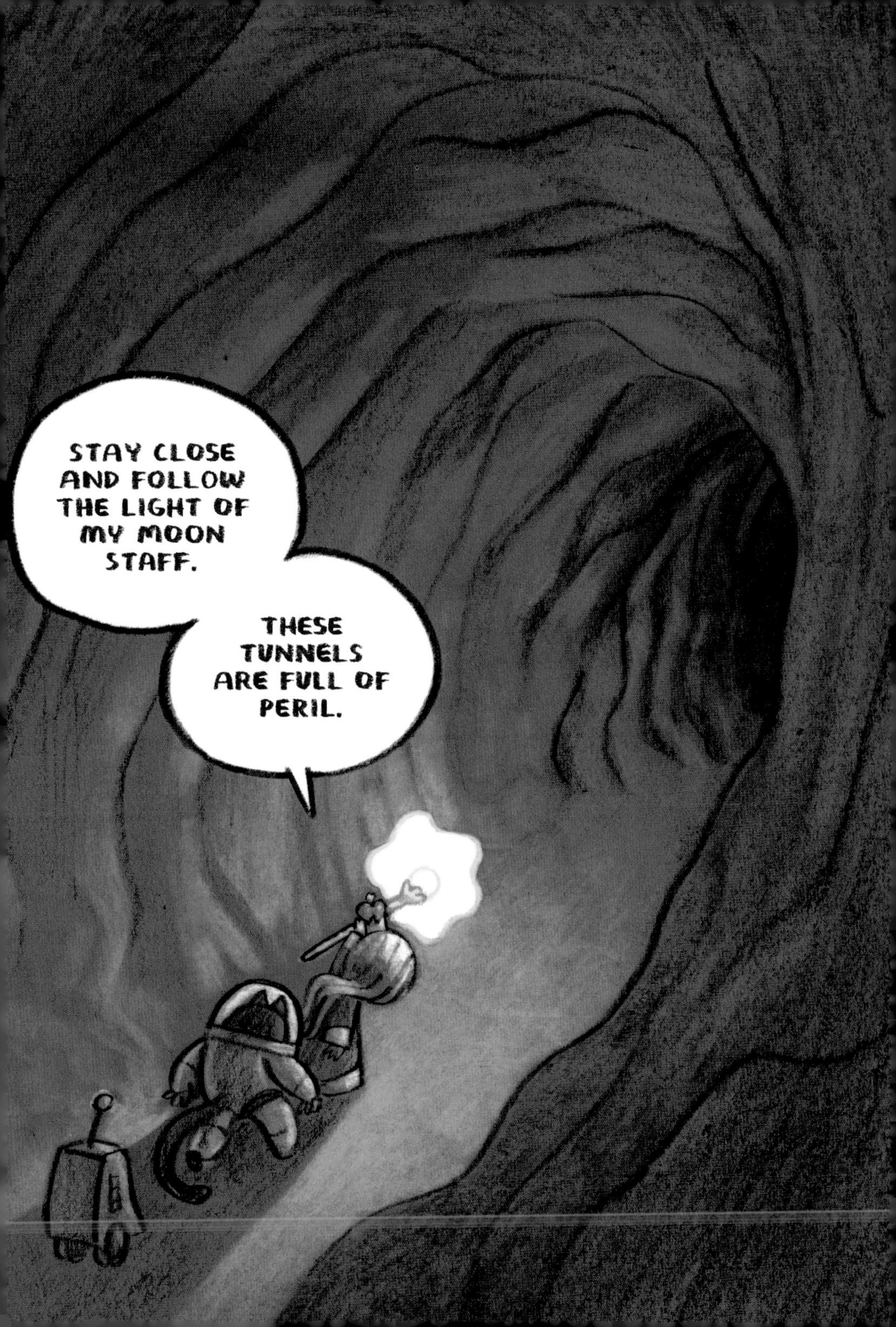
STAY CLOSE AND FOLLOW THE LIGHT OF MY MOON STAFF.
THESE TUNNELS ARE FULL OF PERIL.

YOUR MAJESTY, THE MAN IN THE MOON MENTIONED A "MOON CHAIR."

UH-HUH.

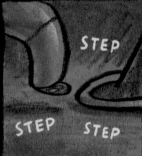

STEP

STEP STEP

...WHAT IS THE MOON CHAIR?

WELL...

THE GREAT HALL OF MY PALACE, BACK IN THE LAND OF CHEERFULNESS, IS HOME TO THE FAMOUS MOON TABLE.

THIS TABLE IS MADE OF PURE SILVER, AND AROUND IT SIT MY WISEST COUNSELORS.

BUT ONE SEAT REMAINS EMPTY...

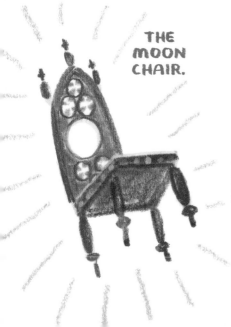

THE MOON CHAIR.

THE OLD ONES MADE THIS MOON CHAIR IN DAYS OF YORE.

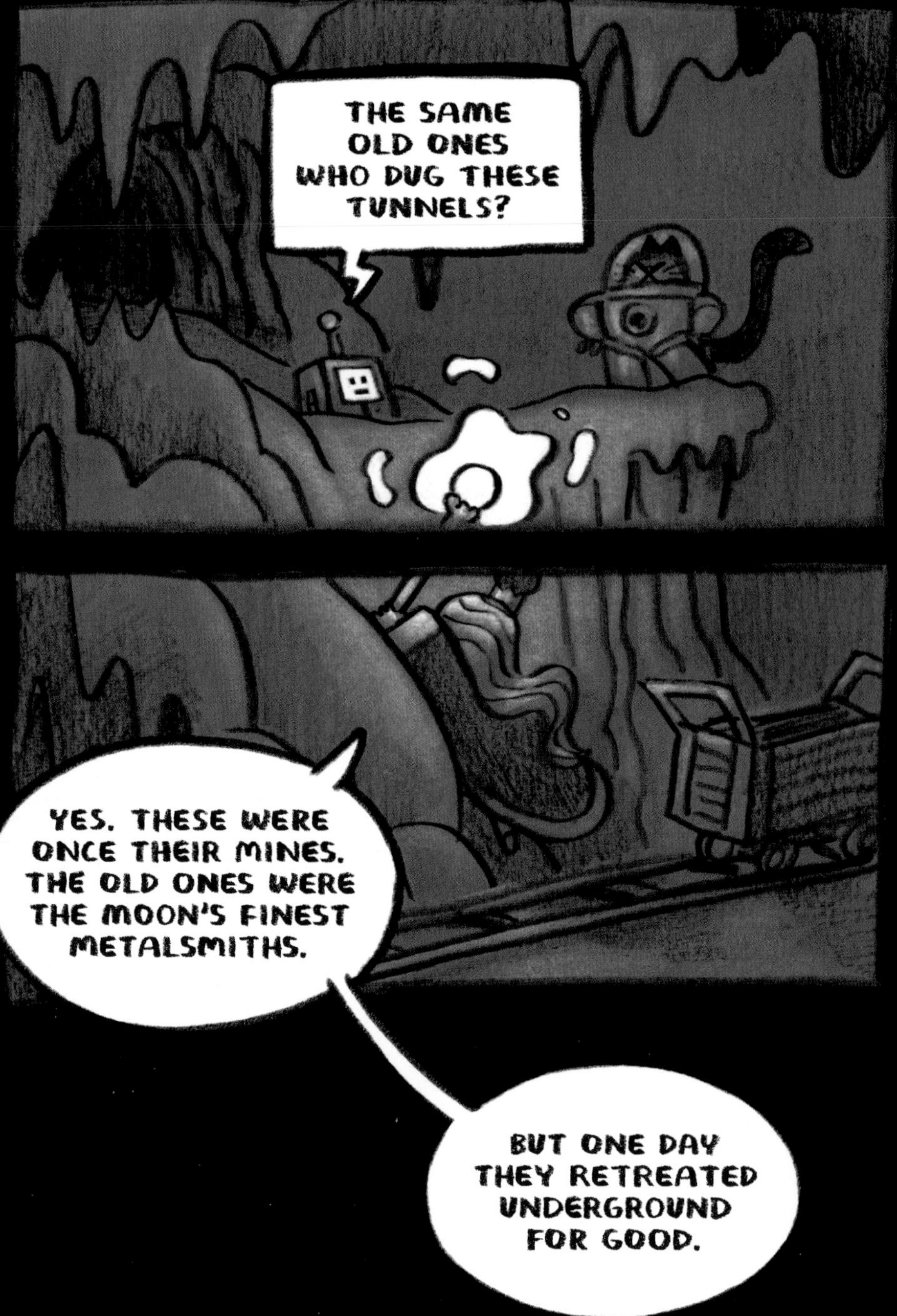
THE SAME OLD ONES WHO DUG THESE TUNNELS?
YES. THESE WERE ONCE THEIR MINES. THE OLD ONES WERE THE MOON'S FINEST METALSMITHS.
BUT ONE DAY THEY RETREATED UNDERGROUND FOR GOOD.

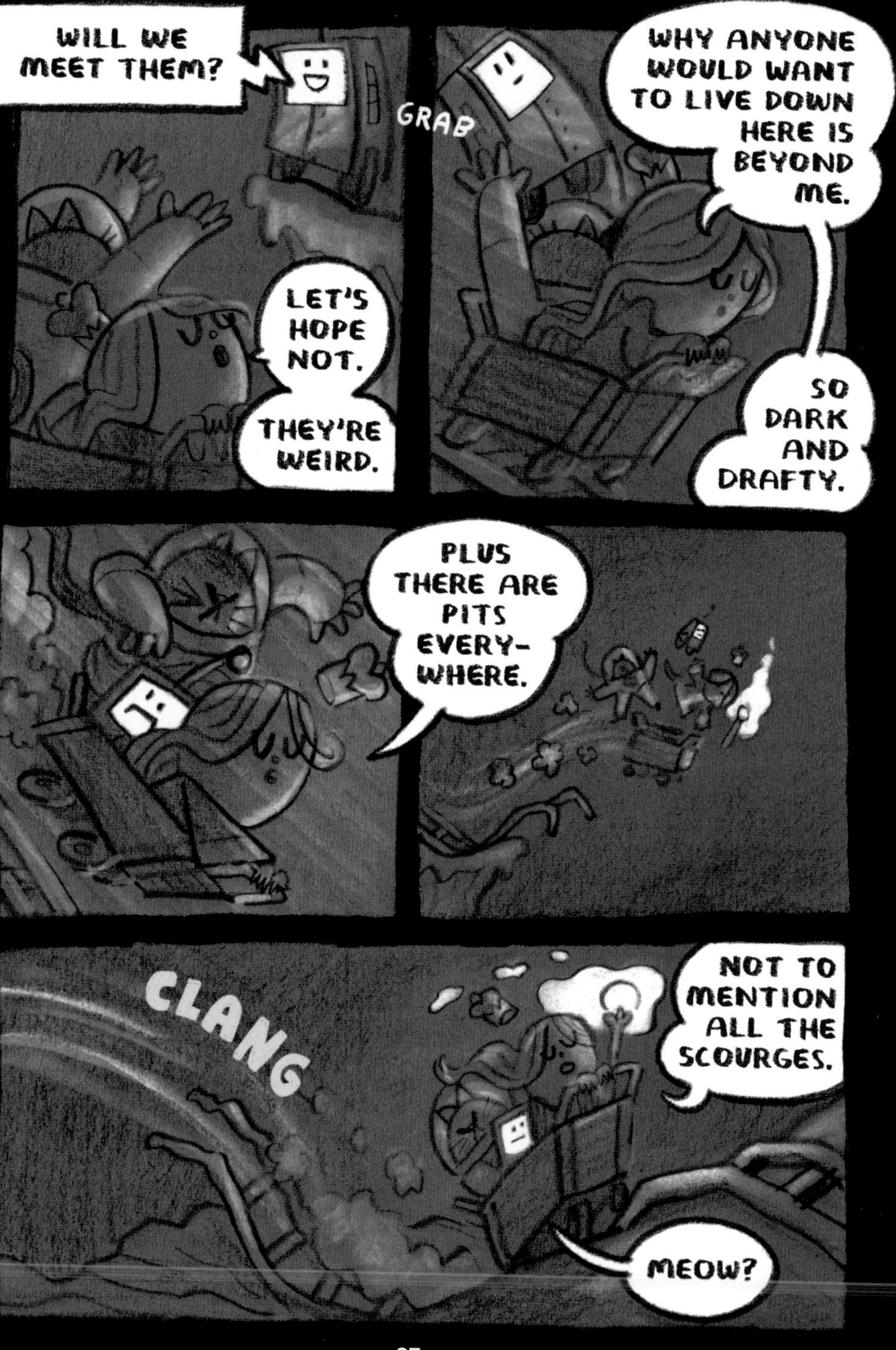
WILL WE MEET THEM?
GRAB
LET'S HOPE NOT.
THEY'RE WEIRD.
WHY ANYONE WOULD WANT TO LIVE DOWN HERE IS BEYOND ME.
SO DARK AND DRAFTY.
PLUS THERE ARE PITS EVERY-WHERE.
CLANG
NOT TO MENTION ALL THE SCOURGES.
MEOW?

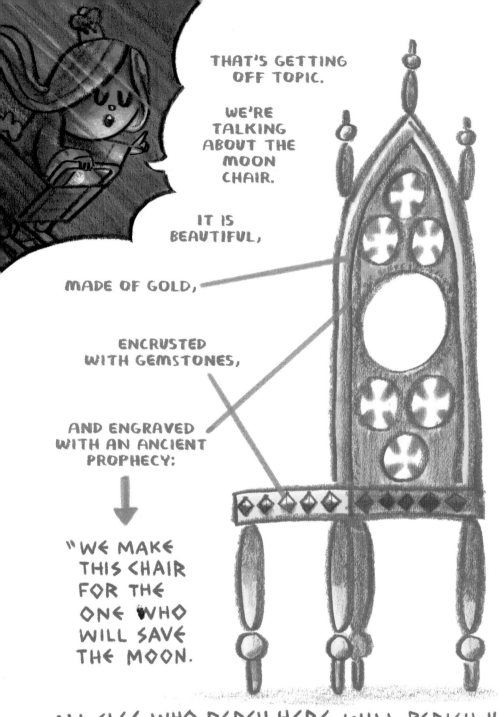

THAT'S GETTING OFF TOPIC.

WE'RE TALKING ABOUT THE MOON CHAIR.

IT IS BEAUTIFUL,

MADE OF GOLD,

ENCRUSTED WITH GEMSTONES,

AND ENGRAVED WITH AN ANCIENT PROPHECY:

"WE MAKE THIS CHAIR FOR THE ONE WHO WILL SAVE THE MOON.

ALL ELSE WHO PERCH HERE WILL PERISH."

OVER THE YEARS, MANY BOLD ADVENTURERS HAVE DARED SIT UPON THE MOON CHAIR,

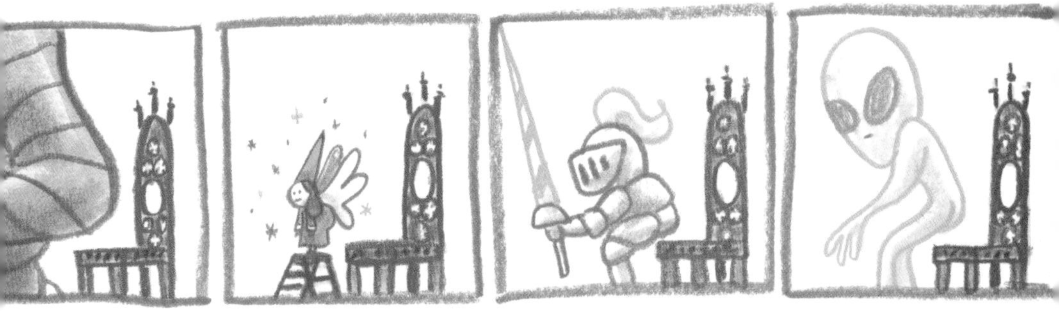

AND THEY IMMEDIATELY TURNED TO MOON DUST.

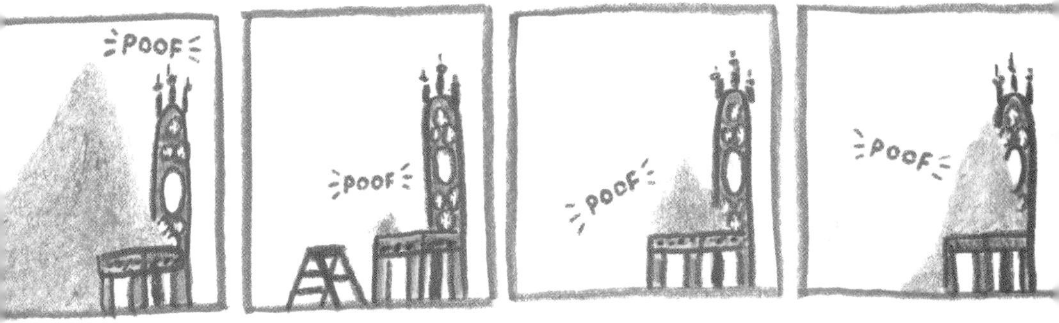
POOF
POOF
POOF
POOF

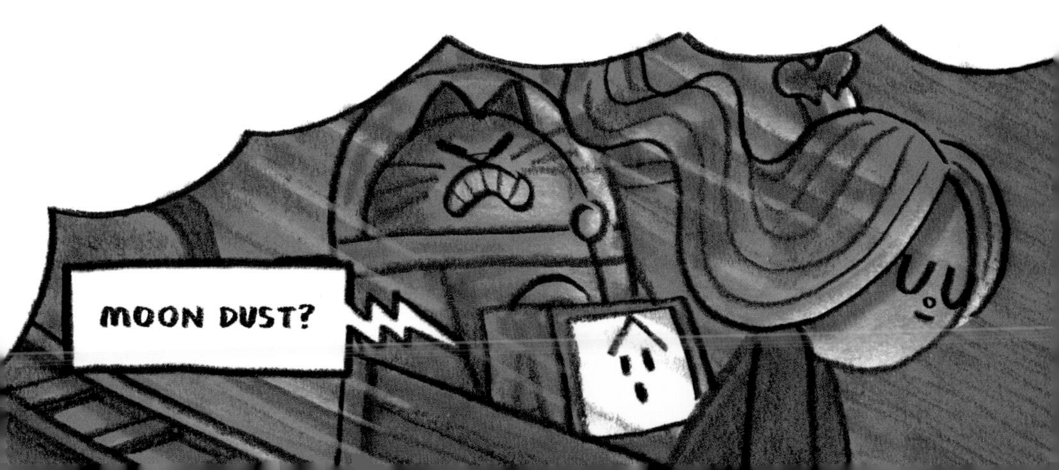
MOON DUST?

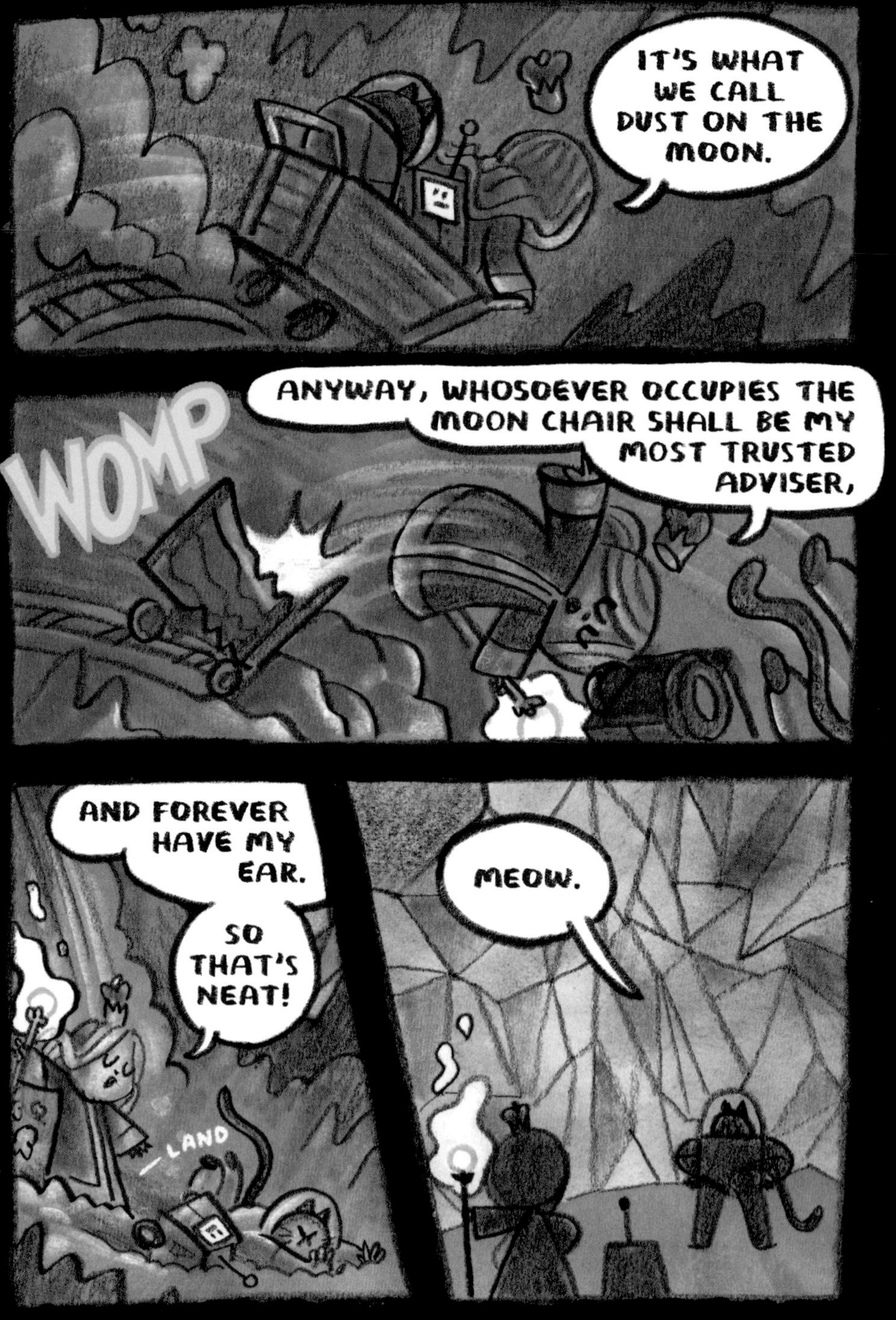
IT'S WHAT WE CALL DUST ON THE MOON.
WOMP
ANYWAY, WHOSOEVER OCCUPIES THE MOON CHAIR SHALL BE MY MOST TRUSTED ADVISER,
AND FOREVER HAVE MY EAR.
SO THAT'S NEAT!
LAND
MEOW.

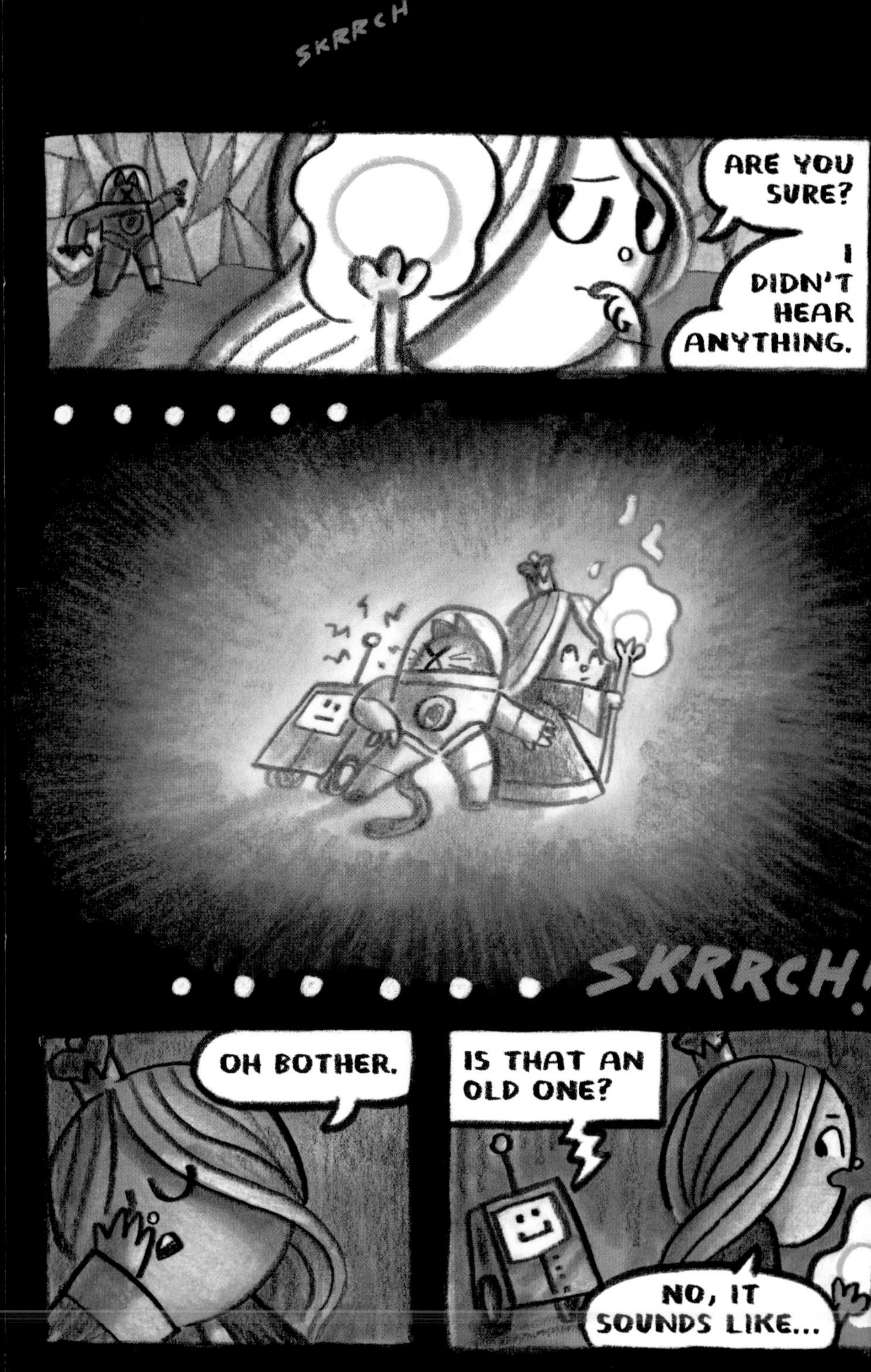
SKRRCH
ARE YOU SURE?
I DIDN'T HEAR ANYTHING.
SKRRCH!
OH BOTHER.
IS THAT AN OLD ONE?
NO, IT SOUNDS LIKE...

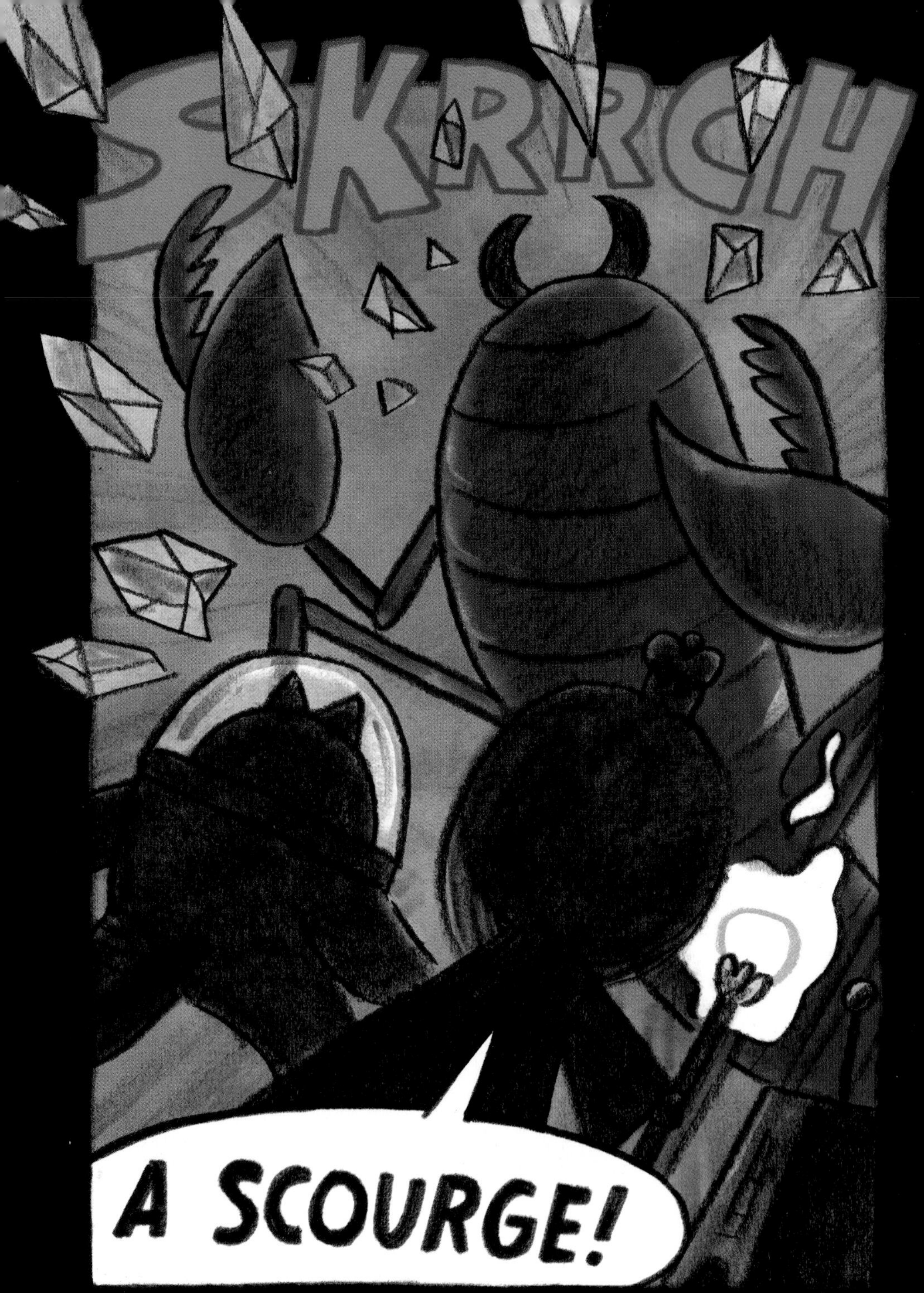
SKRRCH
A SCOURGE!

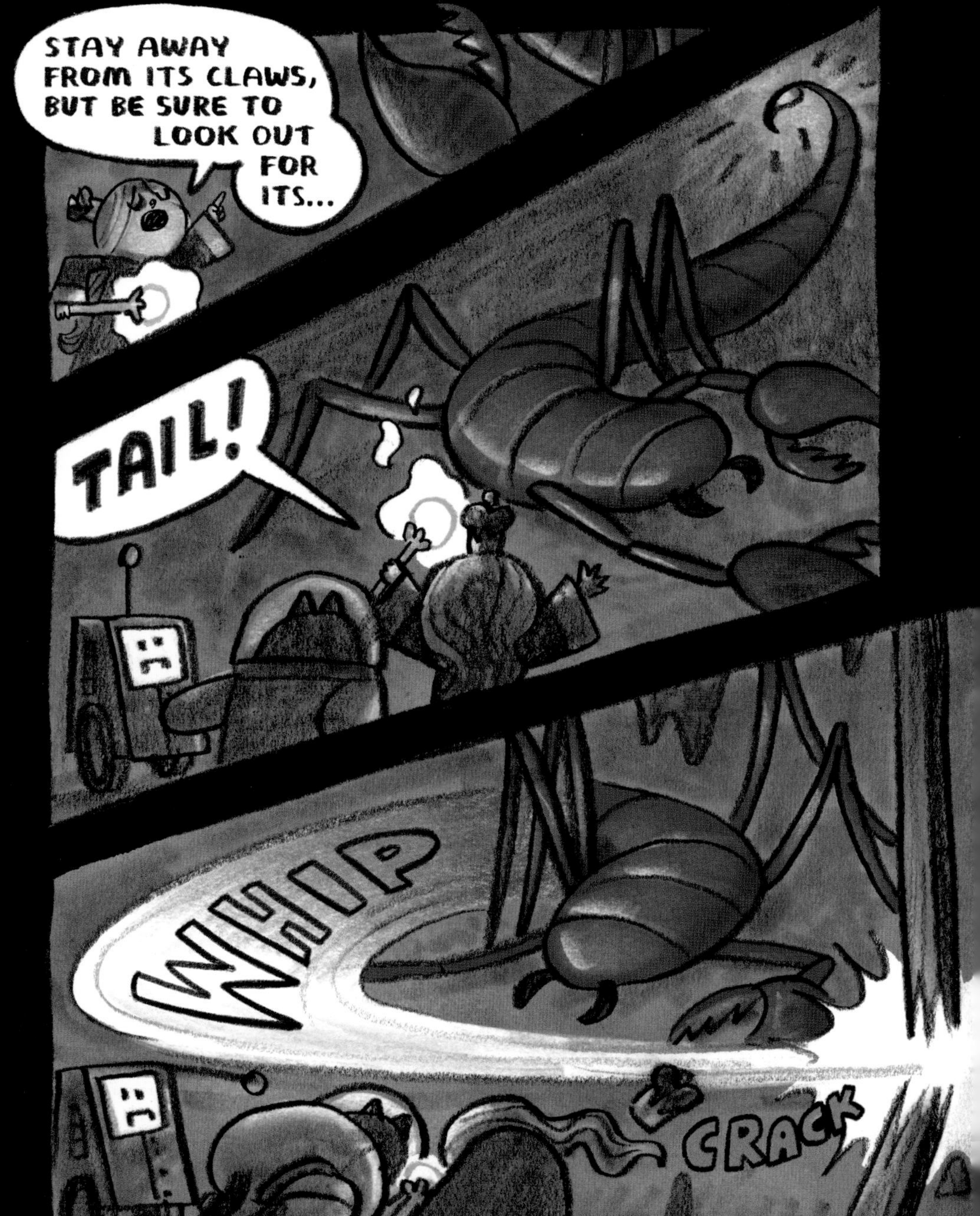
STAY AWAY FROM ITS CLAWS, BUT BE SURE TO LOOK OUT FOR ITS...
TAIL!
WHIP
CRACK

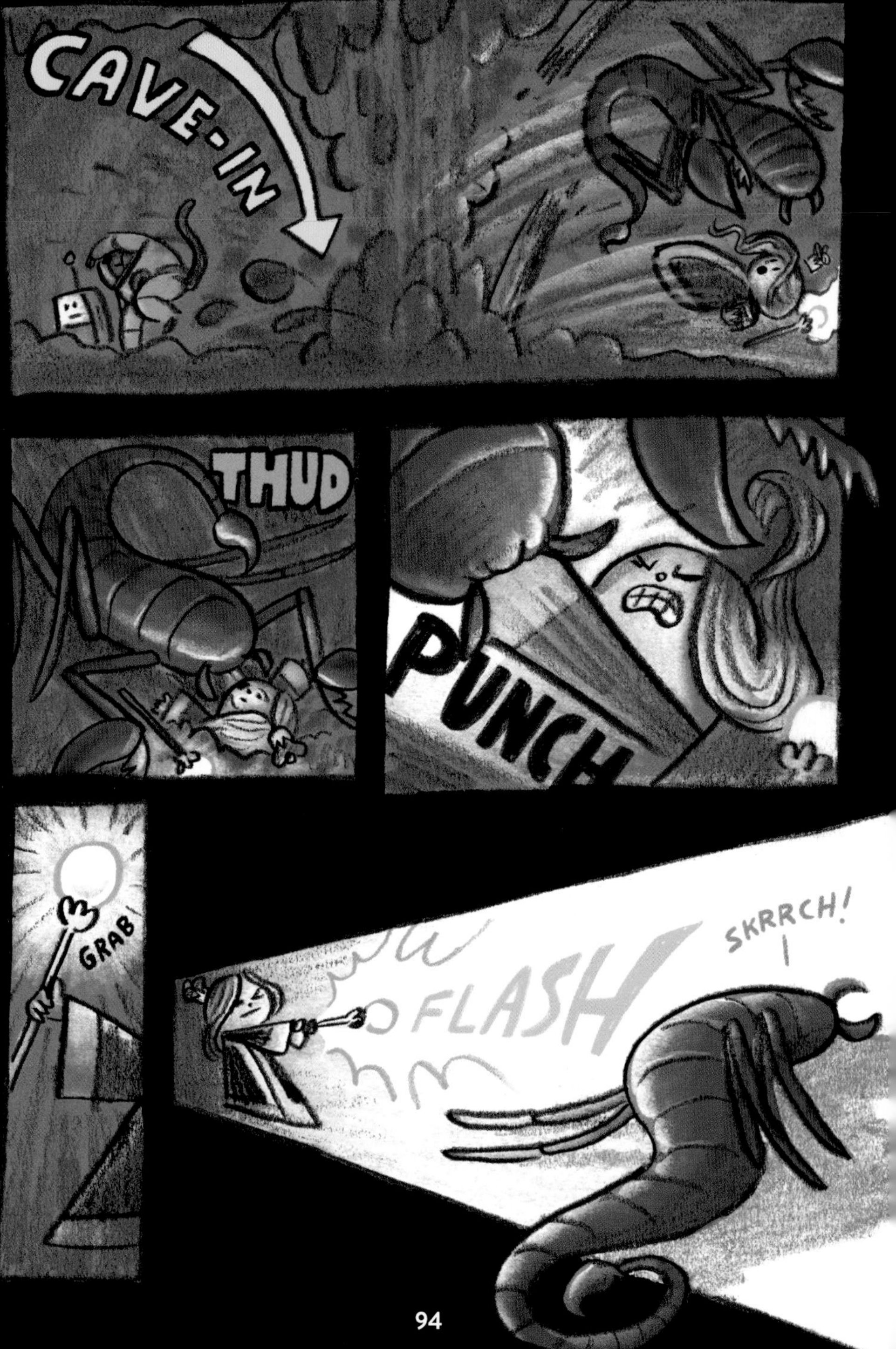
CAVE-IN
THUD
PUNCH
GRAB
FLASH
SKRRCH!

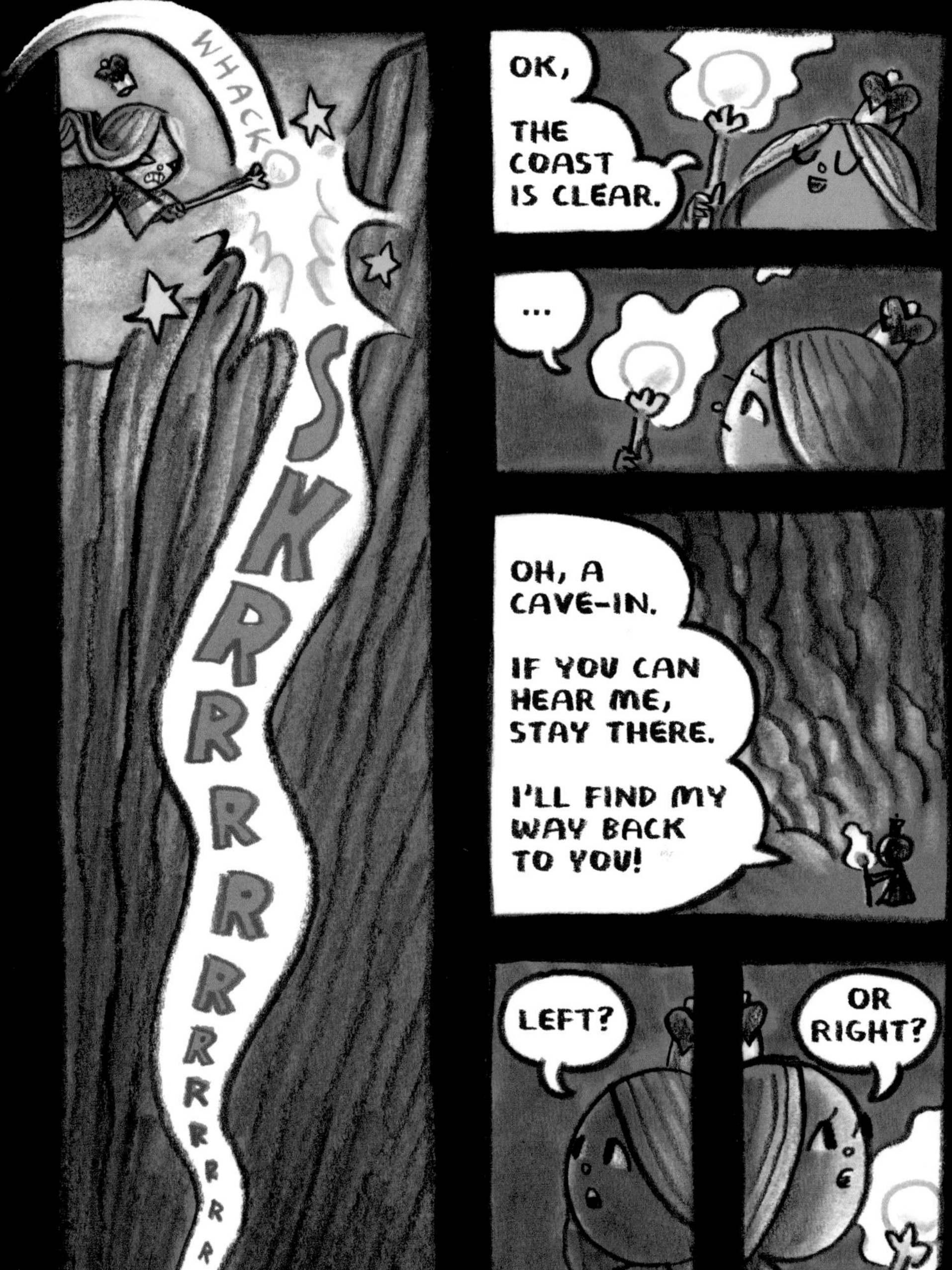
WHACK
SKRRRRRRRRRRRRRCH
OK,
THE COAST IS CLEAR.
...
OH, A CAVE-IN.
IF YOU CAN HEAR ME, STAY THERE.
I'LL FIND MY WAY BACK TO YOU!
LEFT?
OR RIGHT?

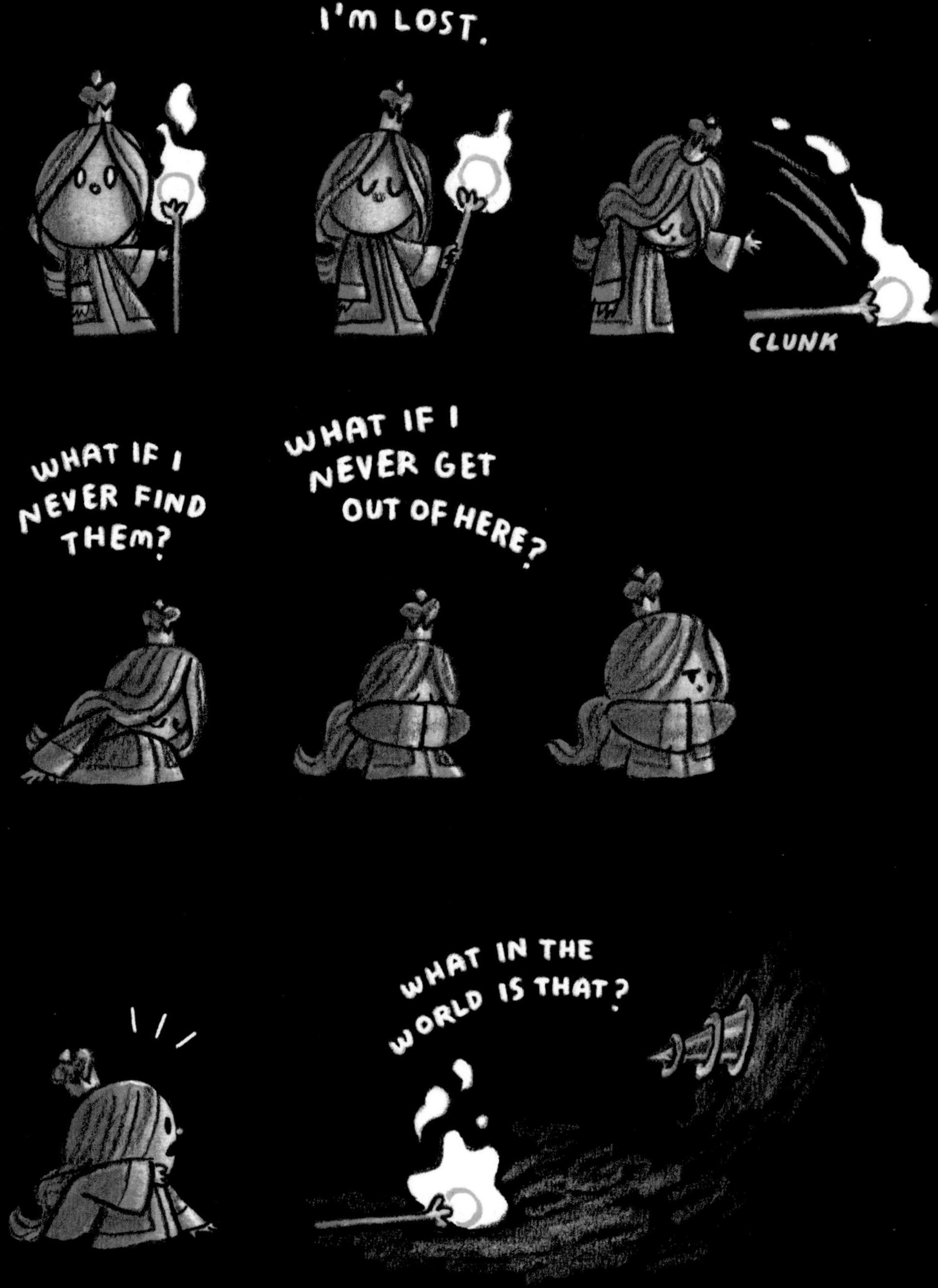
I'M LOST.
CLUNK
WHAT IF I NEVER FIND THEM?
WHAT IF I NEVER GET OUT OF HERE?
WHAT IN THE WORLD IS THAT?

CHAPTER 8
UNDERGROUND

MEOW.

YES, WE MUST FIND ANOTHER WAY THROUGH THESE TUNNELS.

← TIP

THE QUEEN WILL MEET US ON THE OTHER SIDE.

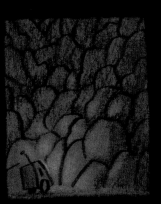

CLINK

VVVVVV

I HOPE.

WE NO LONGER HAVE THE GLOW OF THE MOON QUEEN'S STAFF TO GUIDE US...

SO I WILL TURN UP THE BRIGHTNESS ON MY SCREEN!

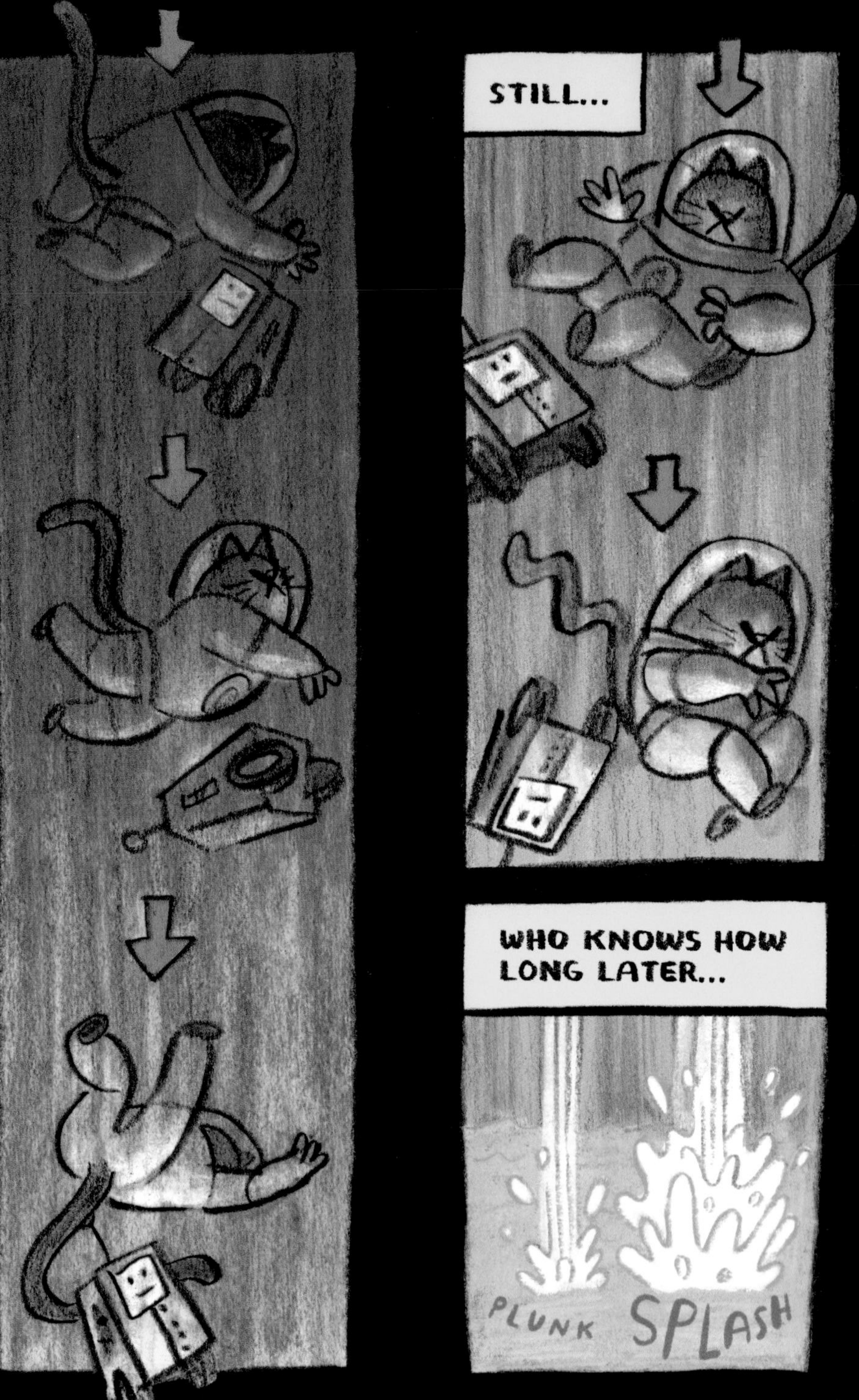
STILL...
WHO KNOWS HOW LONG LATER...
PLUNK
SPLASH

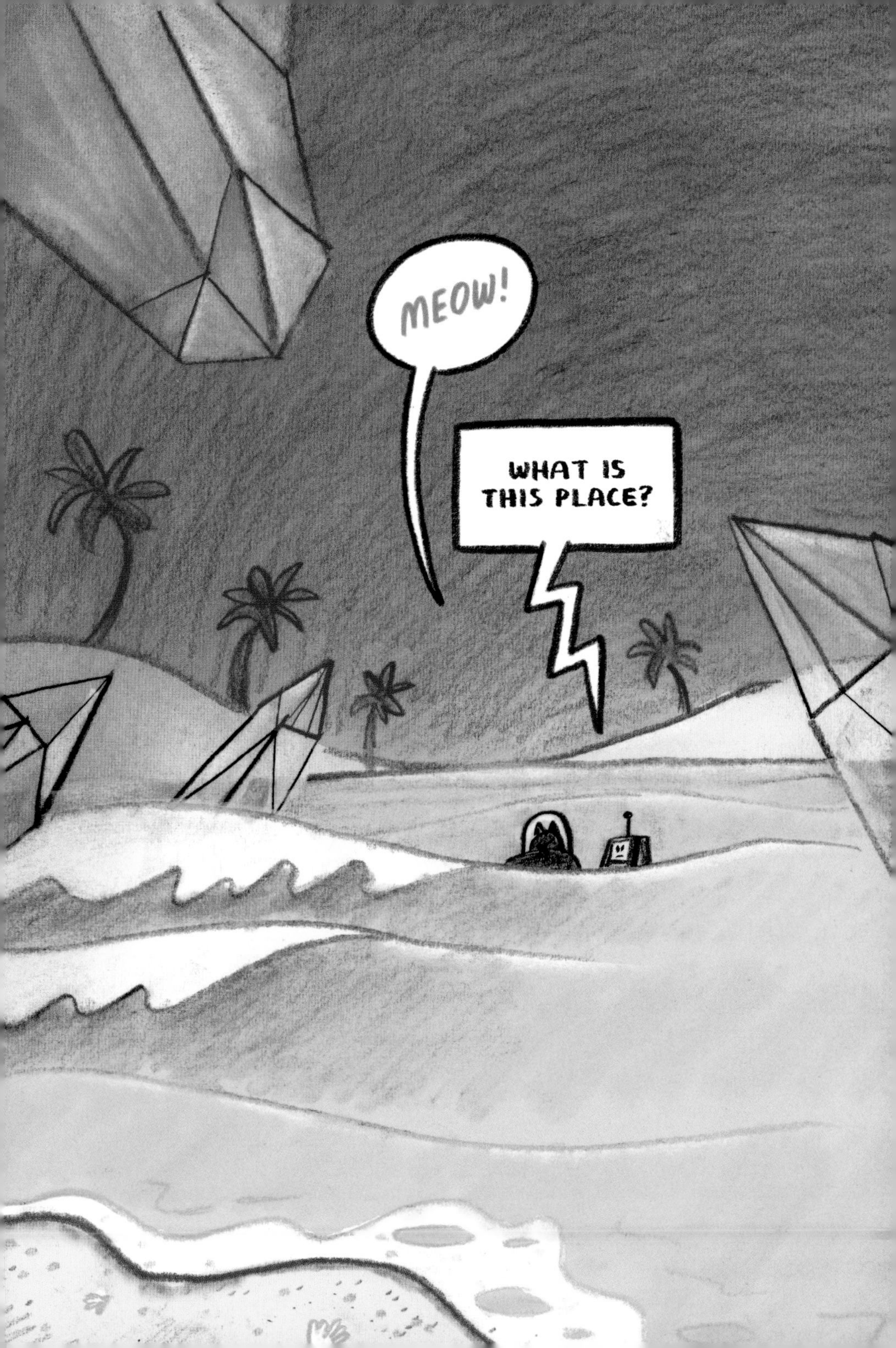
MEOW!
WHAT IS THIS PLACE?

WHAT IF THE JOURNEY WAS THE DESTINATION?

AND THE DESTINATION WAS THE JOURNEY?

SIT

...WHAT?

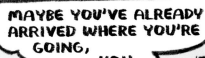

MAYBE YOU'VE ALREADY ARRIVED WHERE YOU'RE GOING, YOU KNOW?

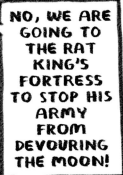

NO, WE ARE GOING TO THE RAT KING'S FORTRESS TO STOP HIS ARMY FROM DEVOURING THE MOON!

HEY! THAT'S SURFACE TALK, BUDDY!

GOOD. EVIL. WAR. POLITICS.

WE DON'T DISCUSS THAT STUFF UNDERGROUND.

PAFF

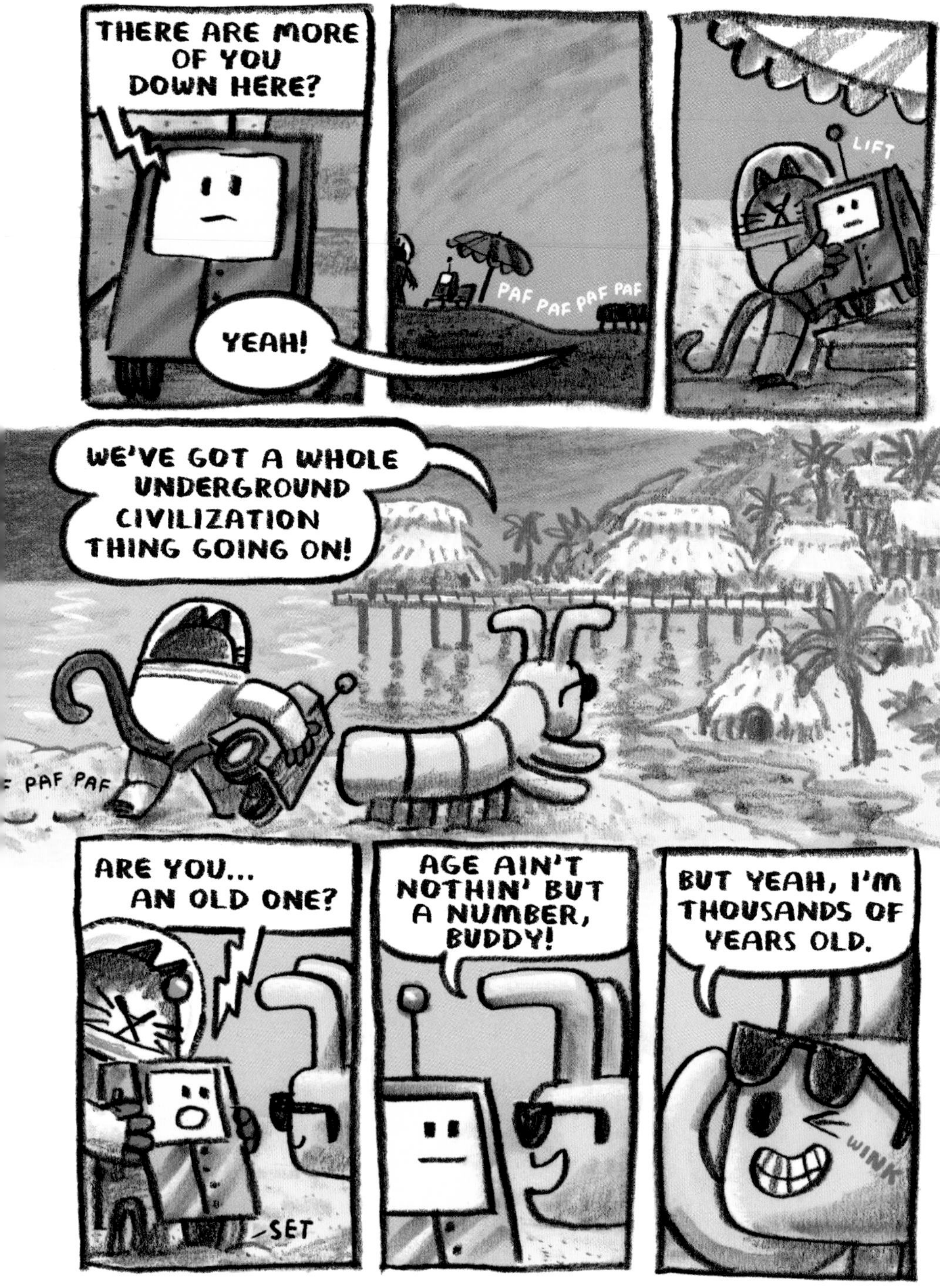
THERE ARE MORE OF YOU DOWN HERE?
YEAH!
PAF PAF PAF PAF
LIFT
WE'VE GOT A WHOLE UNDERGROUND CIVILIZATION THING GOING ON!
PAF PAF
ARE YOU... AN OLD ONE?
SET
AGE AIN'T NOTHIN' BUT A NUMBER, BUDDY!
BUT YEAH, I'M THOUSANDS OF YEARS OLD.
WINK

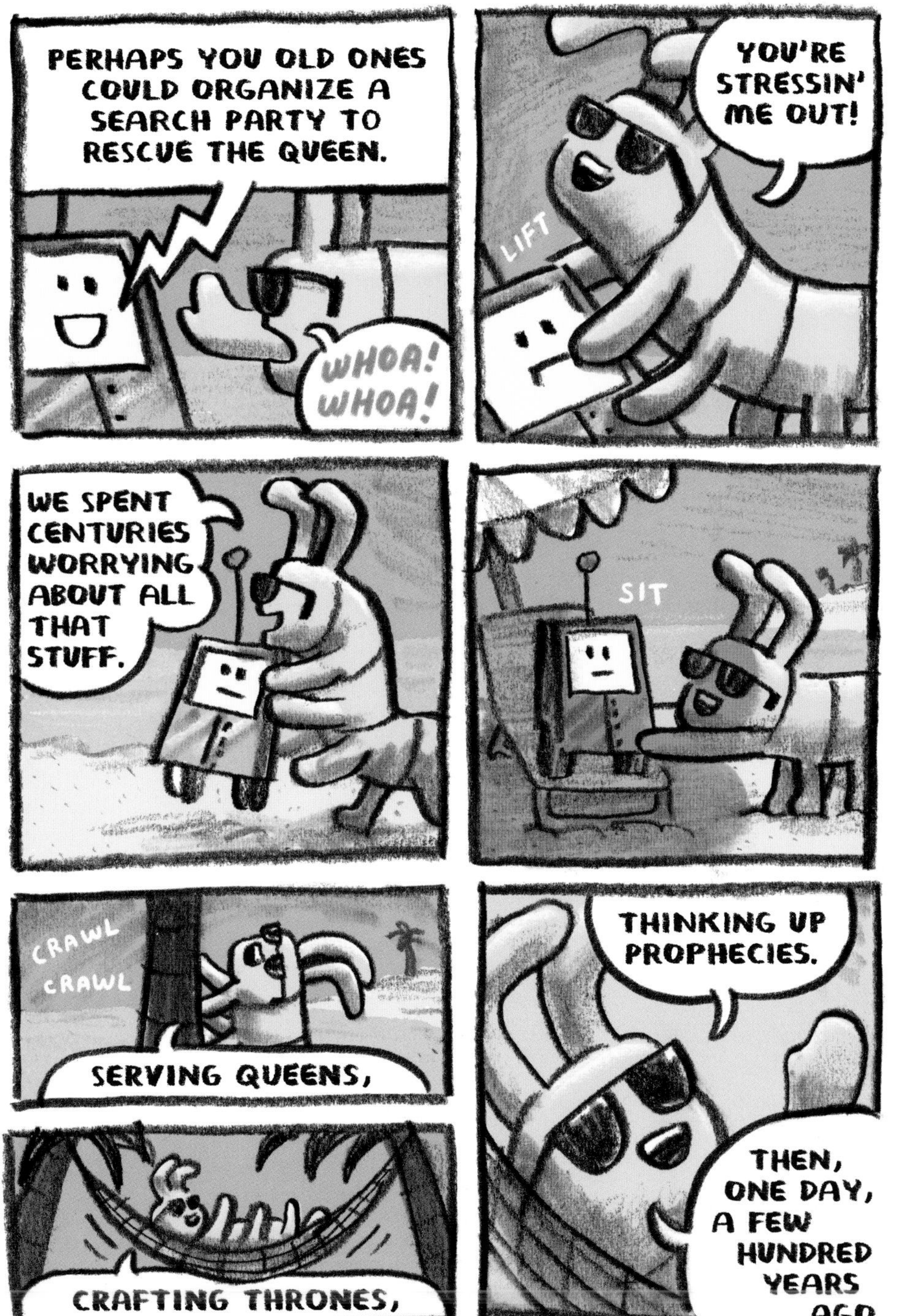
PERHAPS YOU OLD ONES COULD ORGANIZE A SEARCH PARTY TO RESCUE THE QUEEN.
WHOA! WHOA!
LIFT
YOU'RE STRESSIN' ME OUT!
WE SPENT CENTURIES WORRYING ABOUT ALL THAT STUFF.
SIT
CRAWL
CRAWL
SERVING QUEENS,
CRAFTING THRONES,
THINKING UP PROPHECIES.
THEN, ONE DAY, A FEW HUNDRED YEARS AGO...

110

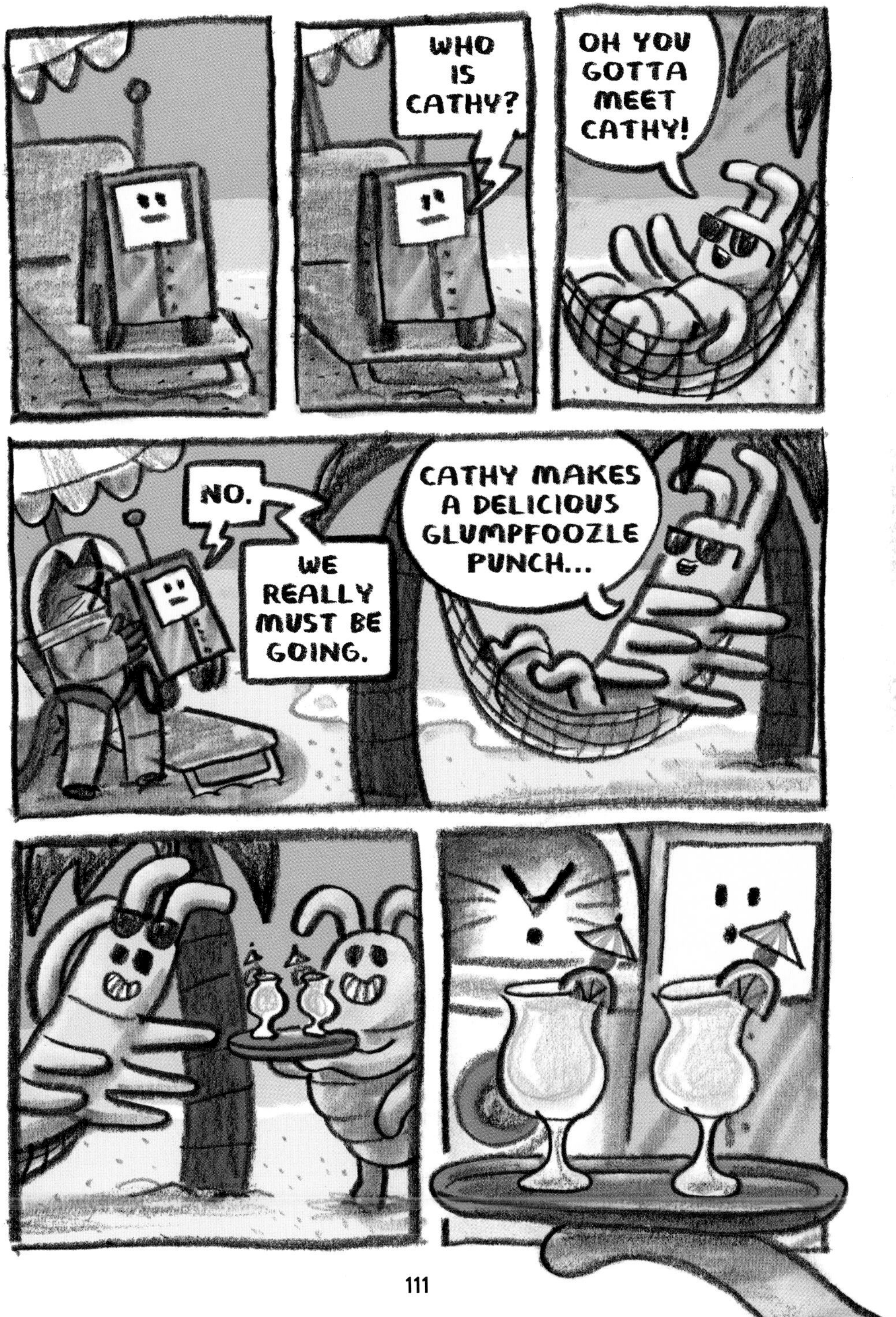
WHO IS CATHY?
OH YOU GOTTA MEET CATHY!
NO.
WE REALLY MUST BE GOING.
CATHY MAKES A DELICIOUS GLUMPFOOZLE PUNCH...

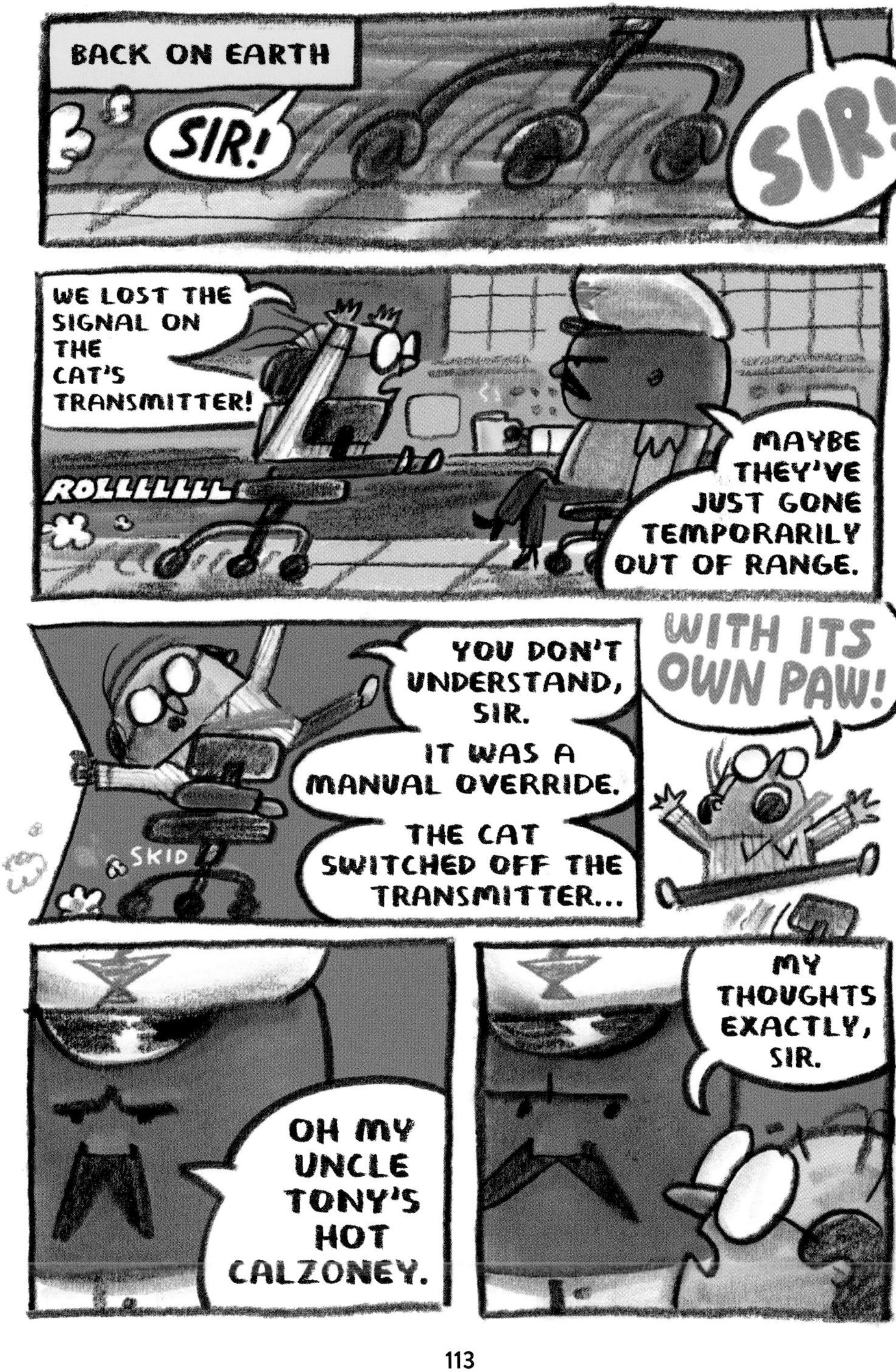

BACK ON EARTH
SIR!
SIR!
WE LOST THE SIGNAL ON THE CAT'S TRANSMITTER!
ROLLLLLLL
MAYBE THEY'VE JUST GONE TEMPORARILY OUT OF RANGE.
YOU DON'T UNDERSTAND, SIR.
IT WAS A MANUAL OVERRIDE.
THE CAT SWITCHED OFF THE TRANSMITTER...
SKID
WITH ITS OWN PAW!
OH MY UNCLE TONY'S HOT CALZONEY.
MY THOUGHTS EXACTLY, SIR.

CHAPTER 9

PARADISE

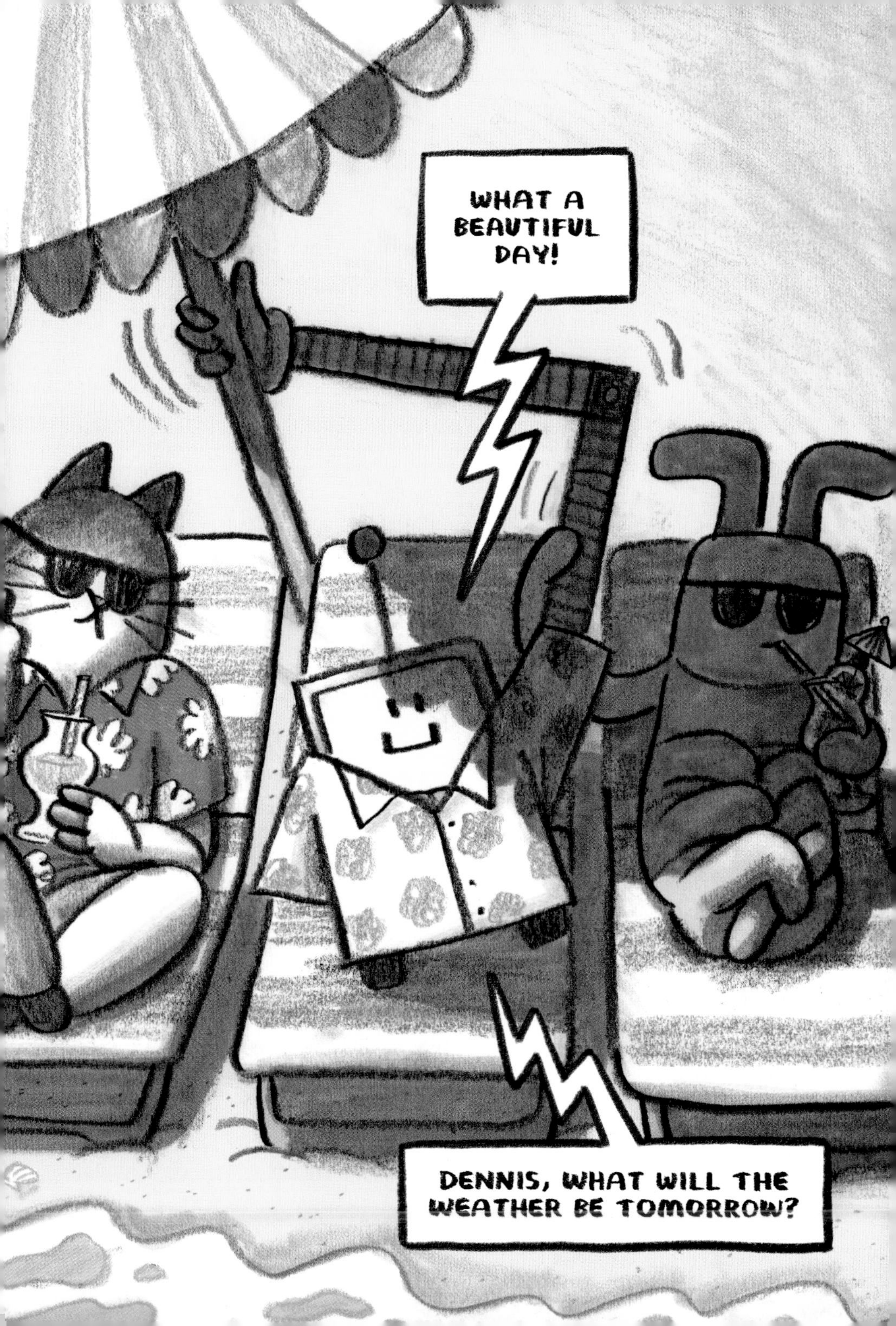
WHAT A BEAUTIFUL DAY!
DENNIS, WHAT WILL THE WEATHER BE TOMORROW?

NOTHING CHANGES...

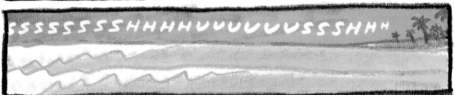

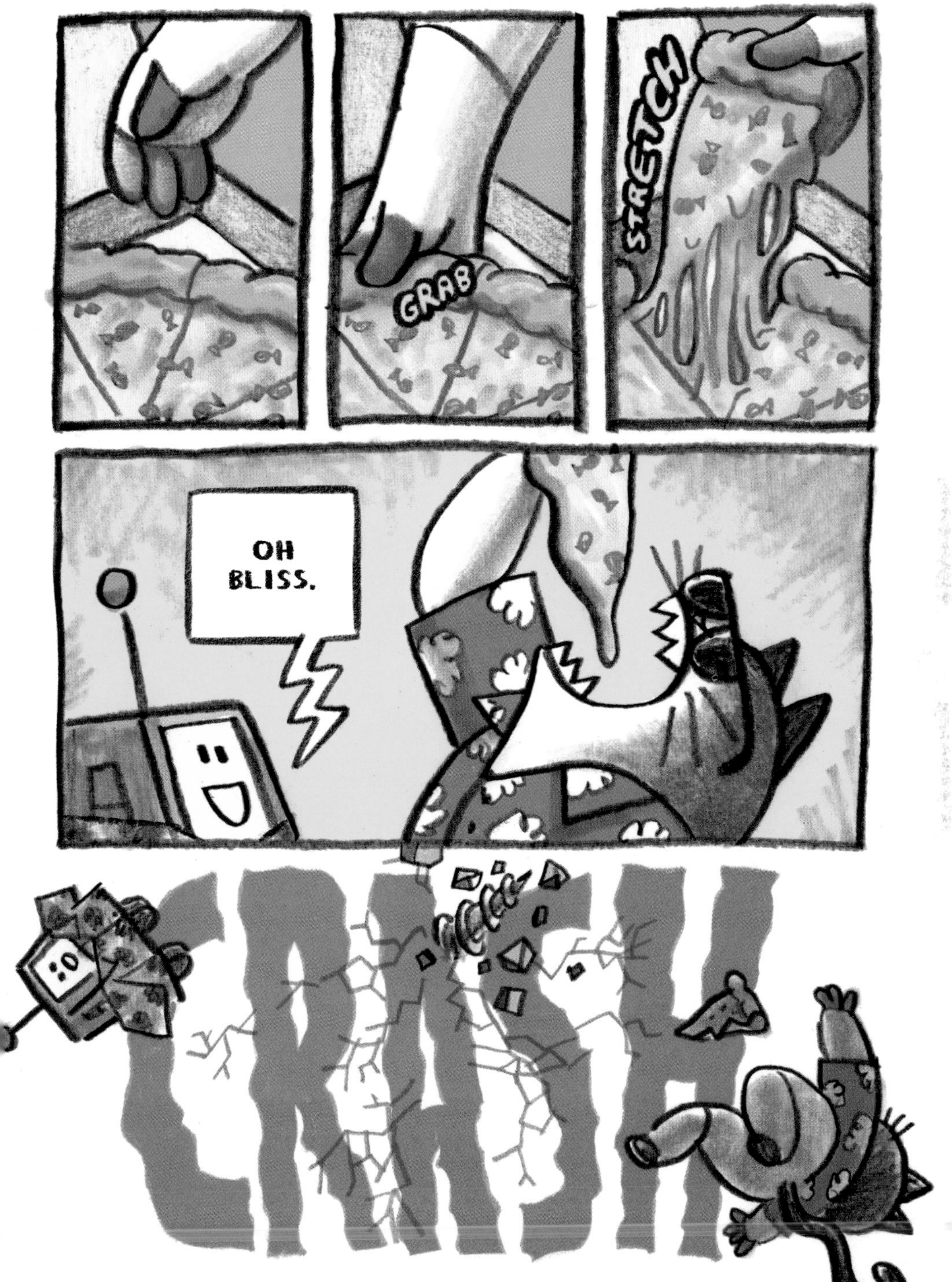
GRAB
STRETCH
OH BLISS.
CRASH

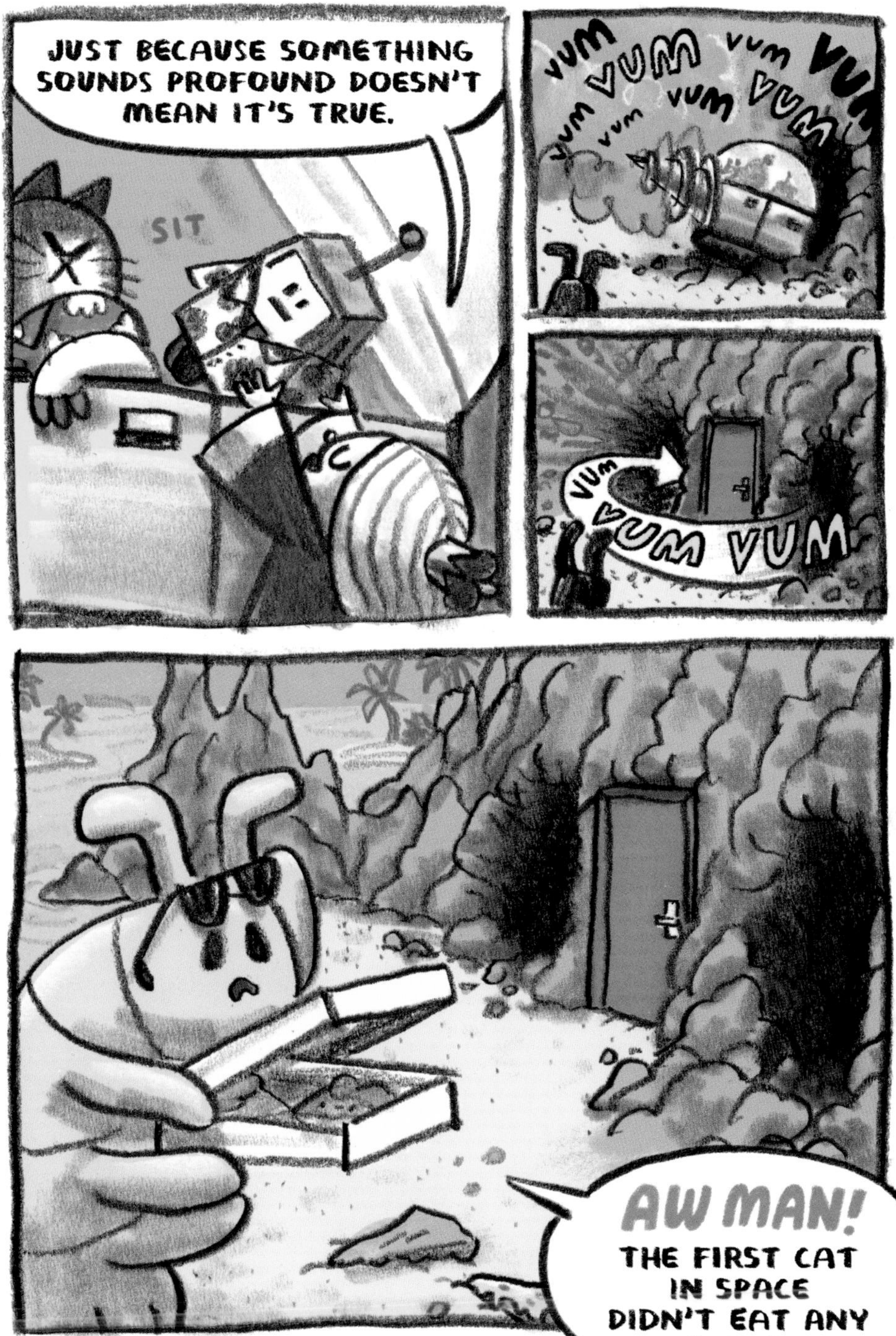
JUST BECAUSE SOMETHING SOUNDS PROFOUND DOESN'T MEAN IT'S TRUE.
SIT
VUM VUM VUM VUM VUM VUM VUM VUM VUM
VUM VUM VUM
AW MAN! THE FIRST CAT IN SPACE DIDN'T EAT ANY PIZZA.

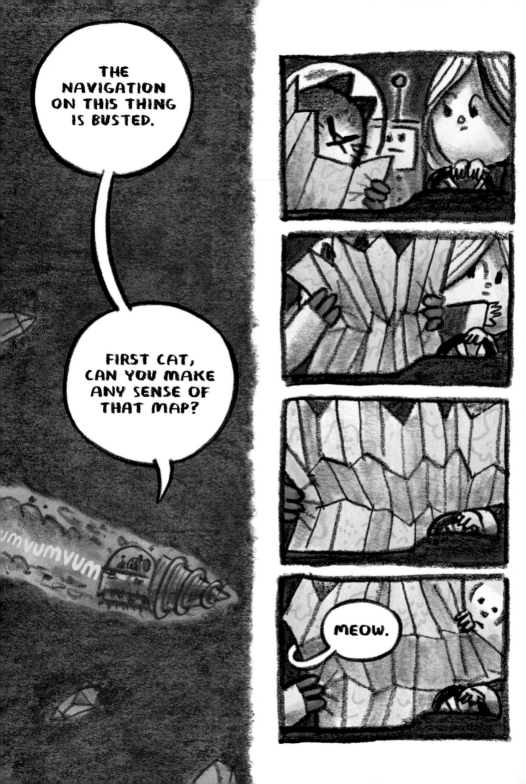

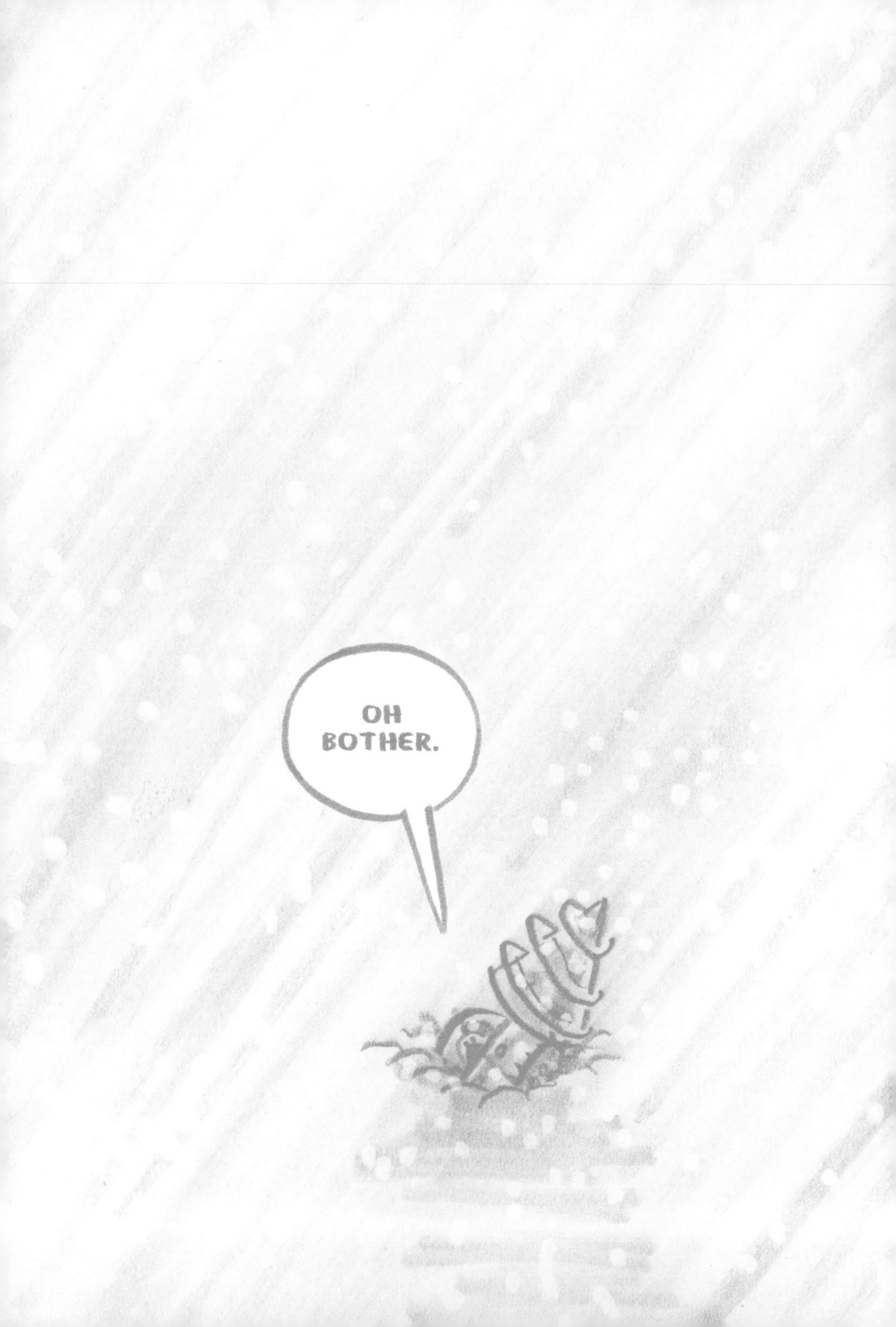
OH BOTHER.

CHAPTER 10
FREEZING

START

VUM

THE ENGINE'S FROZEN. AND SOON, SO WILL WE BE.

WHAT ARE YOU DOING, ROBOT?

CAN YOU SUPERCHARGE THE MOTOR AND GET THIS THING RUNNING AGAIN?

NO.

CLICK

BUT IF WE ARE STUCK HERE, WE CAN AT LEAST LISTEN TO THE RADIO WHILE WE SLOWLY FREEZE TO DEATH.

HUMMMM

SHHHHH

WHIRRRR

BUZZZZZ

IT'S ALL STATIC. THERE'S NO ONE AROUND FOR MILES.

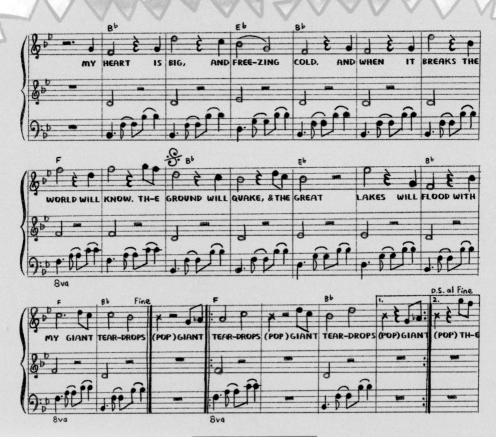

Go to www.thefirstcatinspace.com
to hear this song and other
First Cat tunes. We sang them!

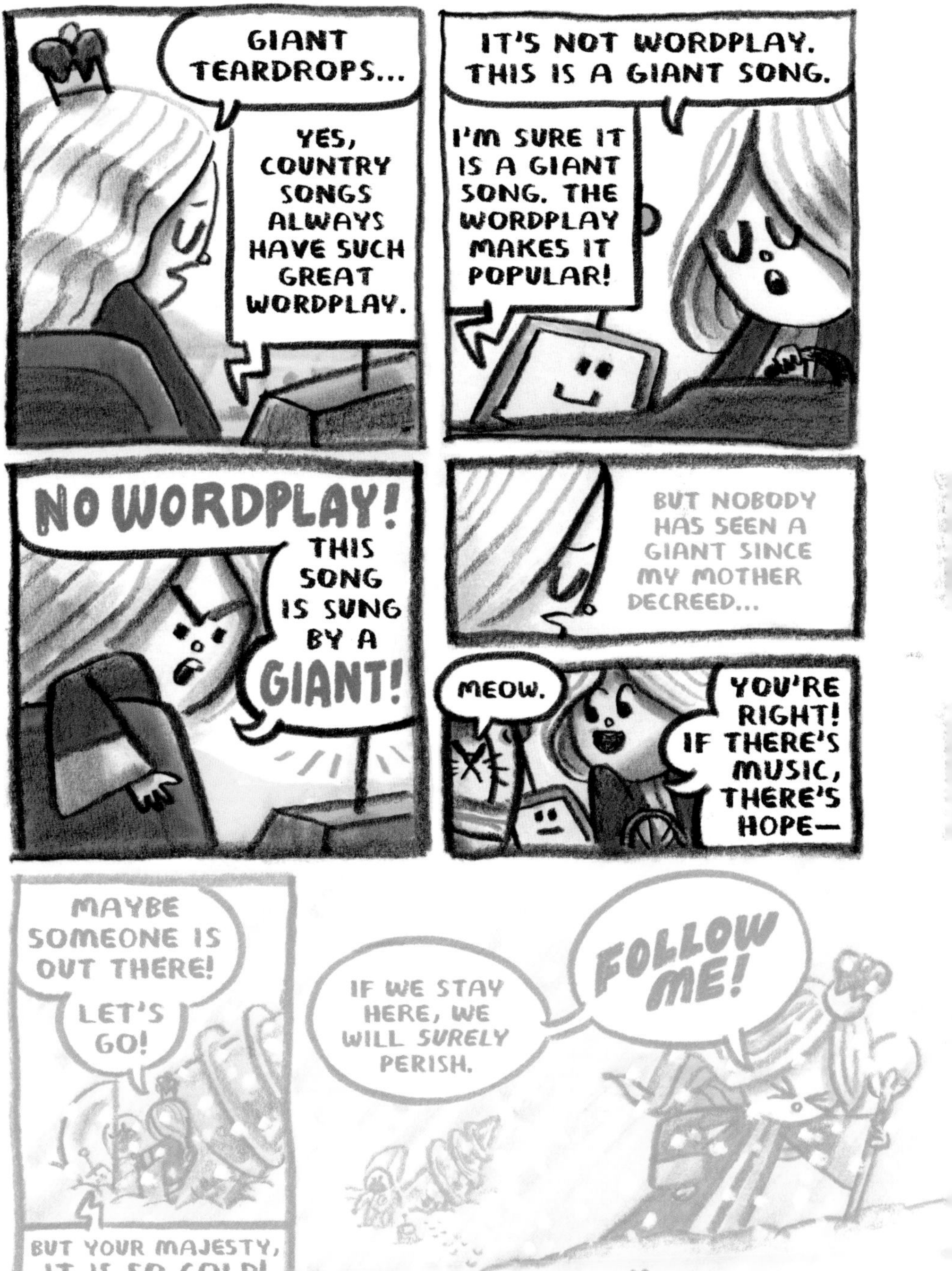
GIANT TEARDROPS...
YES, COUNTRY SONGS ALWAYS HAVE SUCH GREAT WORDPLAY.
IT'S NOT WORDPLAY. THIS IS A GIANT SONG.
I'M SURE IT IS A GIANT SONG. THE WORDPLAY MAKES IT POPULAR!
NO WORDPLAY! THIS SONG IS SUNG BY A GIANT!
BUT NOBODY HAS SEEN A GIANT SINCE MY MOTHER DECREED...
MEOW.
YOU'RE RIGHT! IF THERE'S MUSIC, THERE'S HOPE—
MAYBE SOMEONE IS OUT THERE!
LET'S GO!
BUT YOUR MAJESTY, IT IS SO COLD!
IF WE STAY HERE, WE WILL SURELY PERISH.
FOLLOW ME!

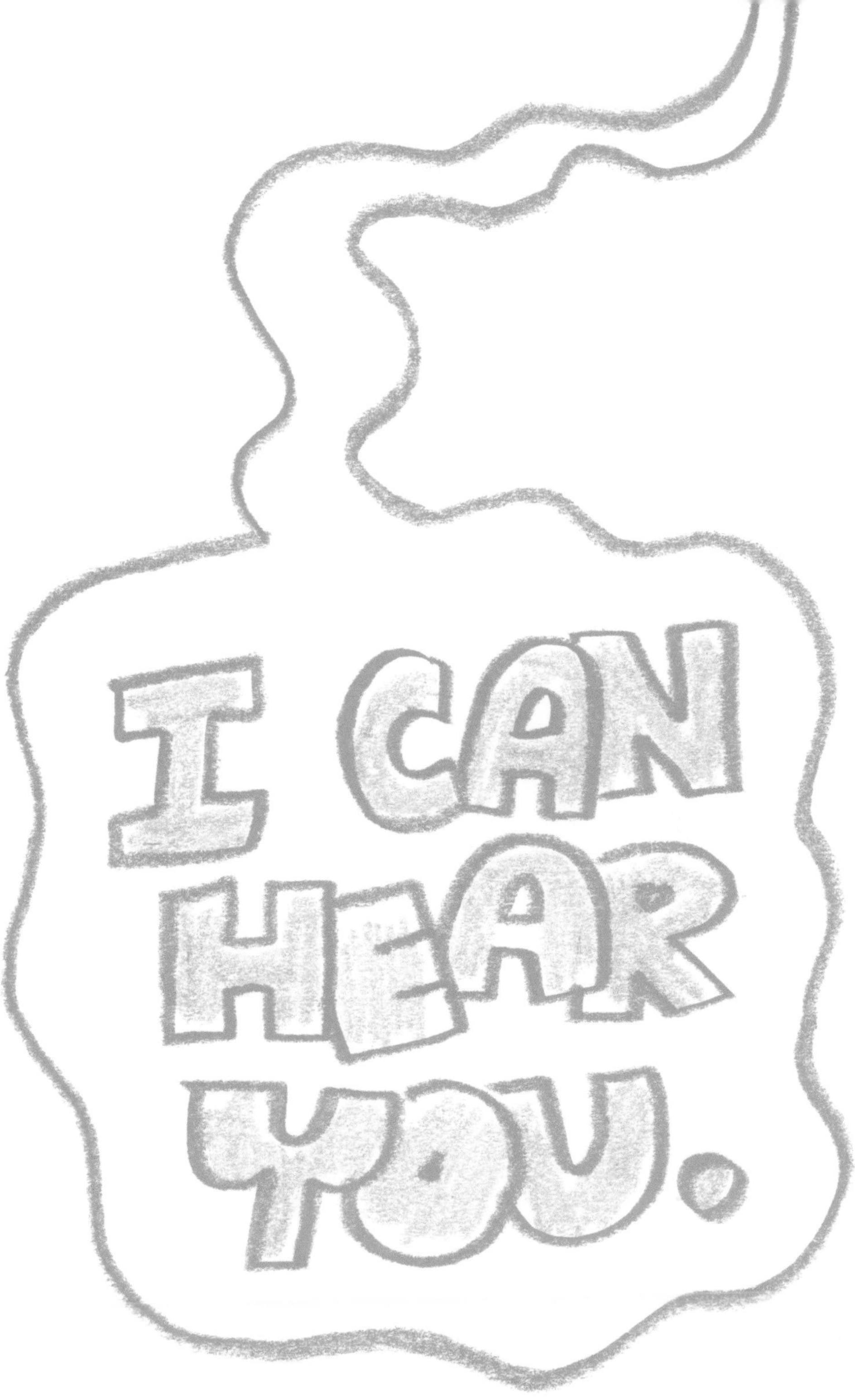
I CAN HEAR YOU.

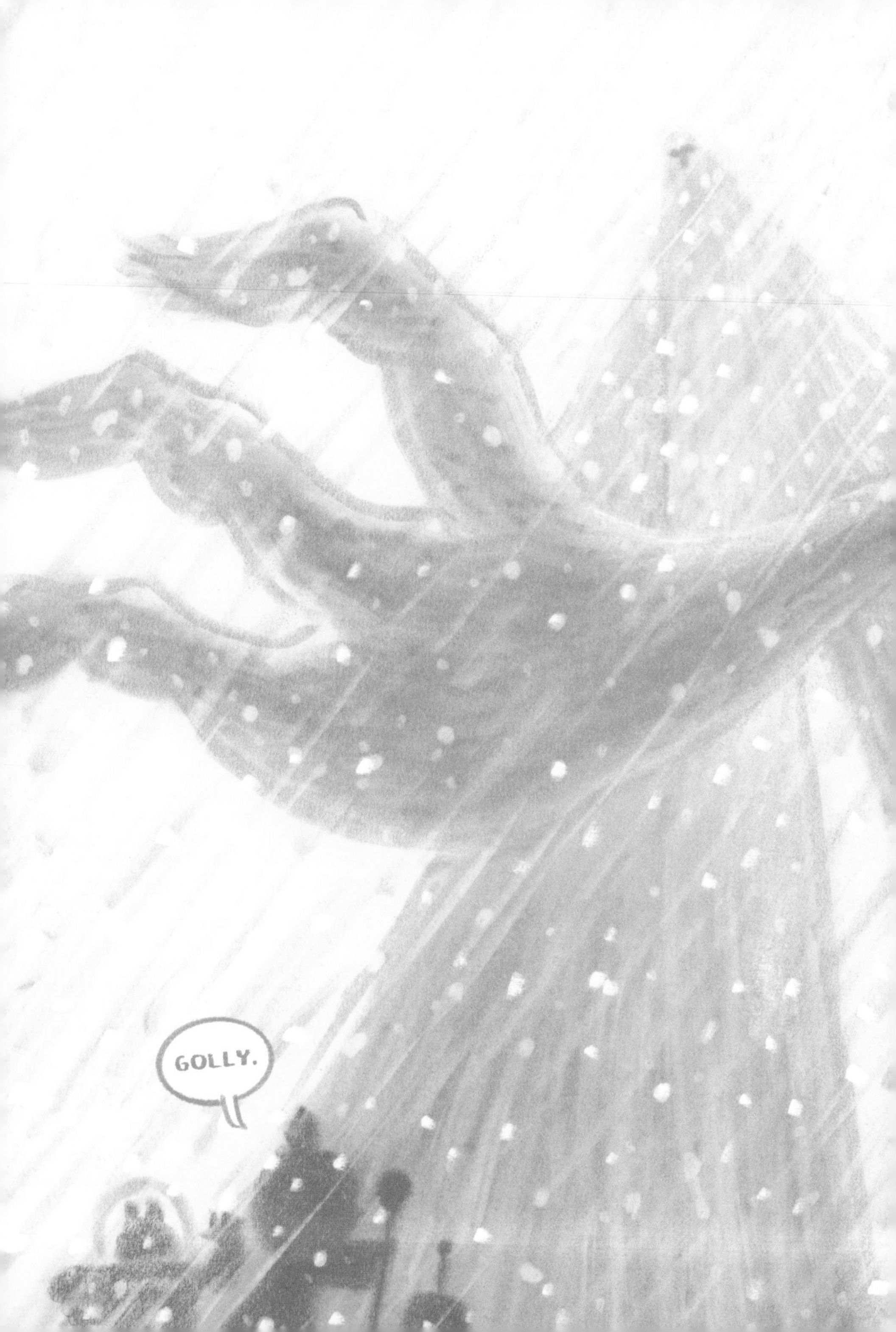
GOLLY.

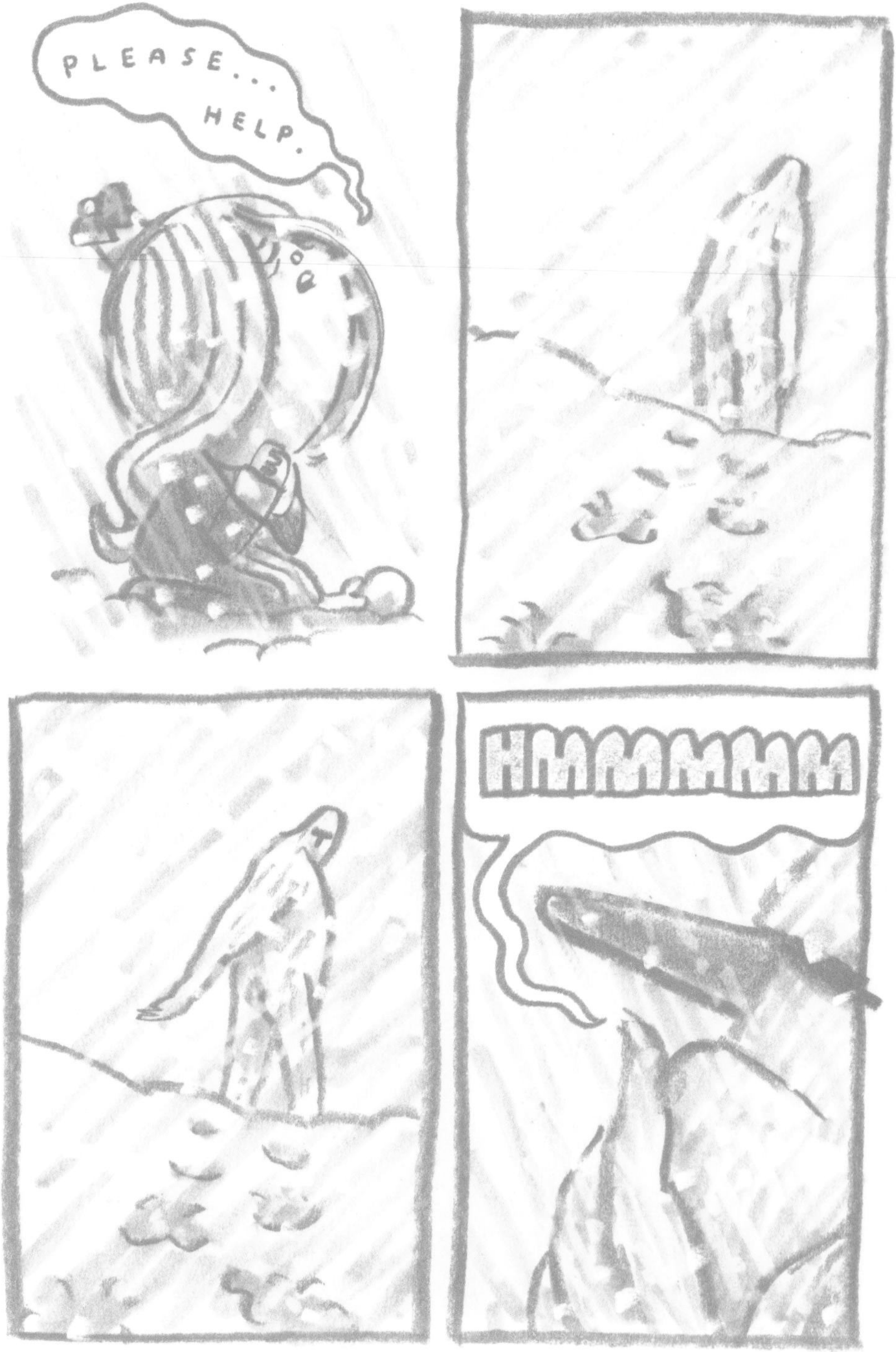
PLEASE... HELP.
HMMMMMM

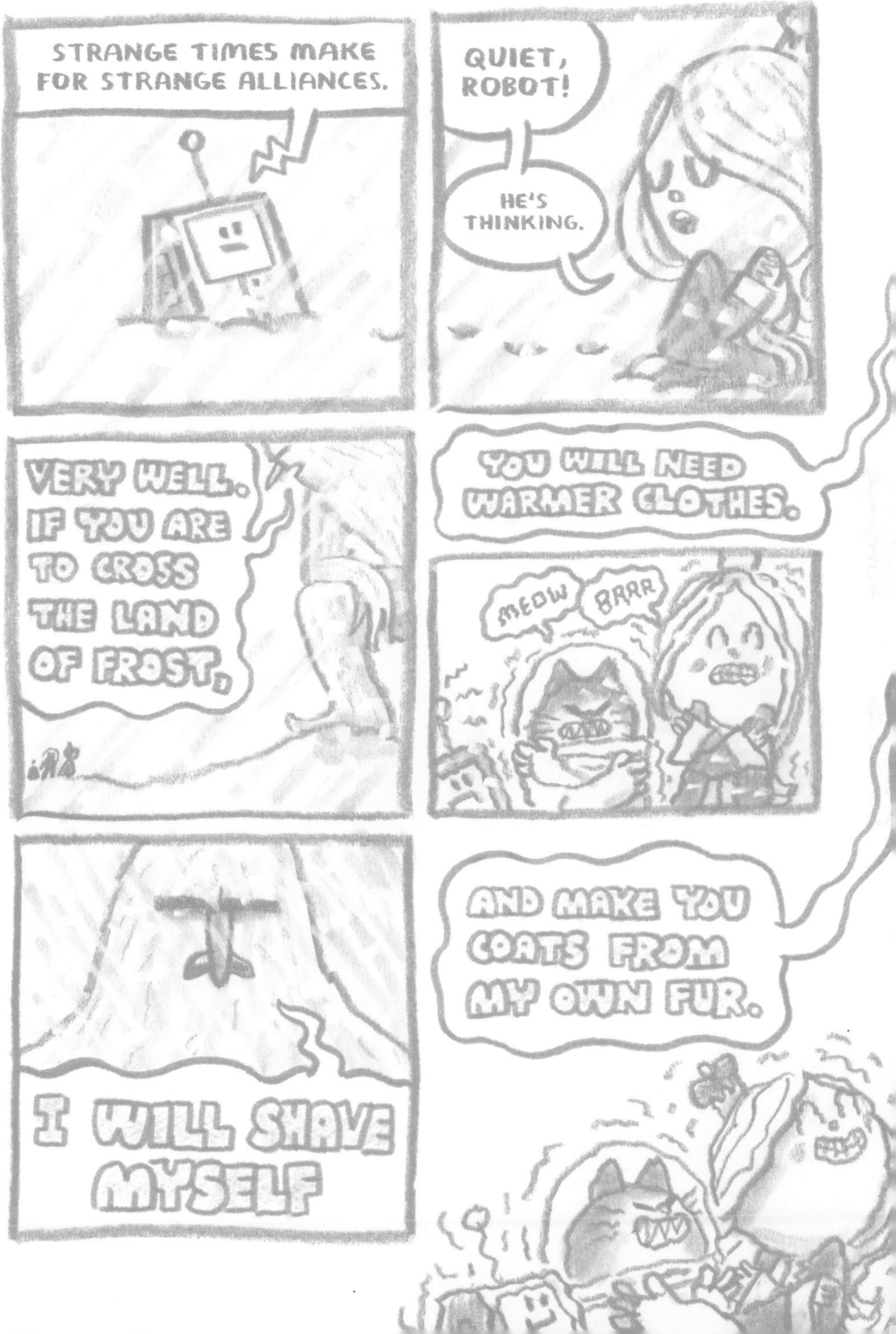
STRANGE TIMES MAKE FOR STRANGE ALLIANCES.
QUIET, ROBOT!
HE'S THINKING.
VERY WELL. IF YOU ARE TO CROSS THE LAND OF FROST,
YOU WILL NEED WARMER CLOTHES.
MEOW
BRRR
I WILL SHAVE MYSELF
AND MAKE YOU COATS FROM MY OWN FUR.

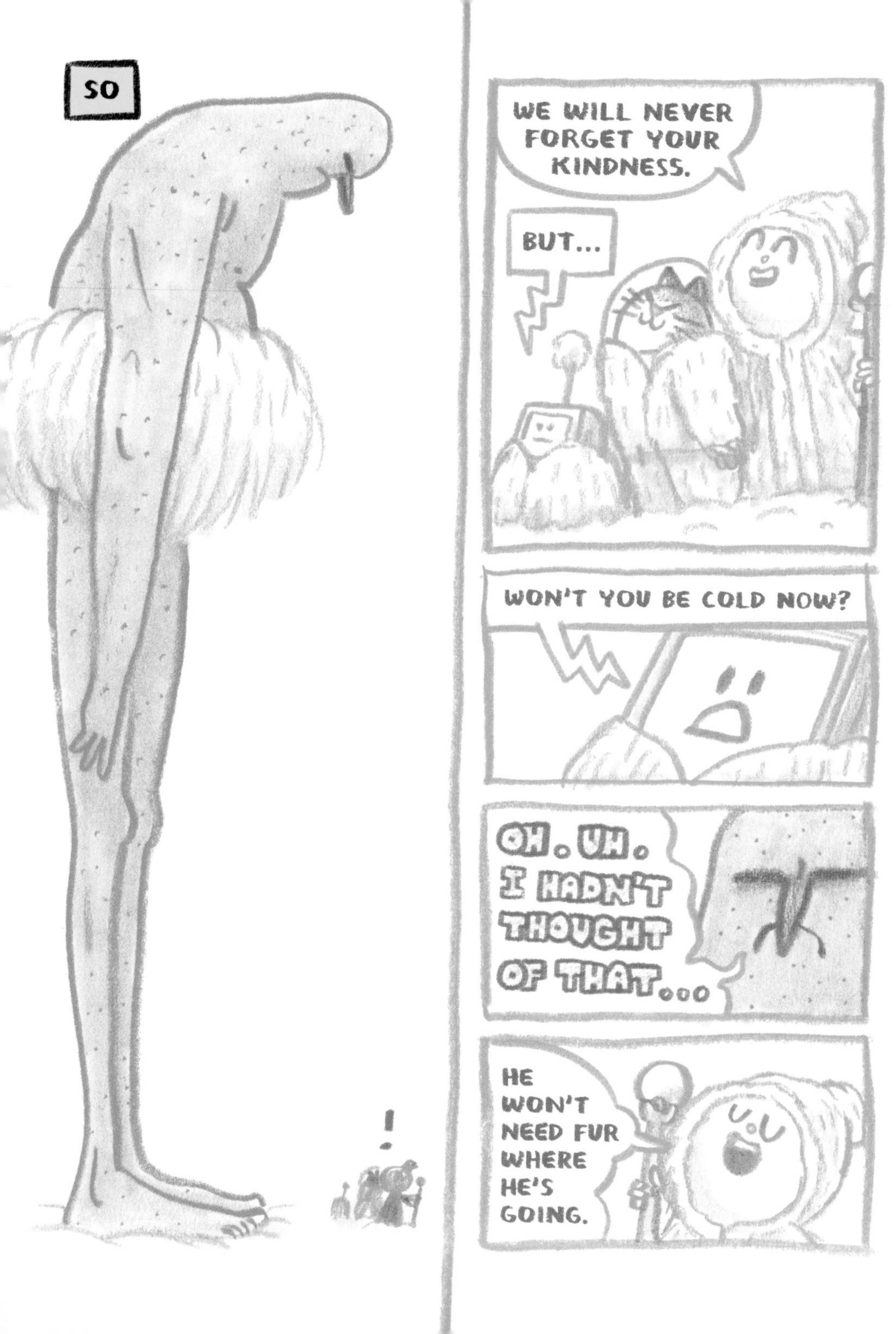
SO
!
WE WILL NEVER FORGET YOUR KINDNESS.
BUT...
WON'T YOU BE COLD NOW?
OH. UH. I HADN'T THOUGHT OF THAT...
HE WON'T NEED FUR WHERE HE'S GOING.

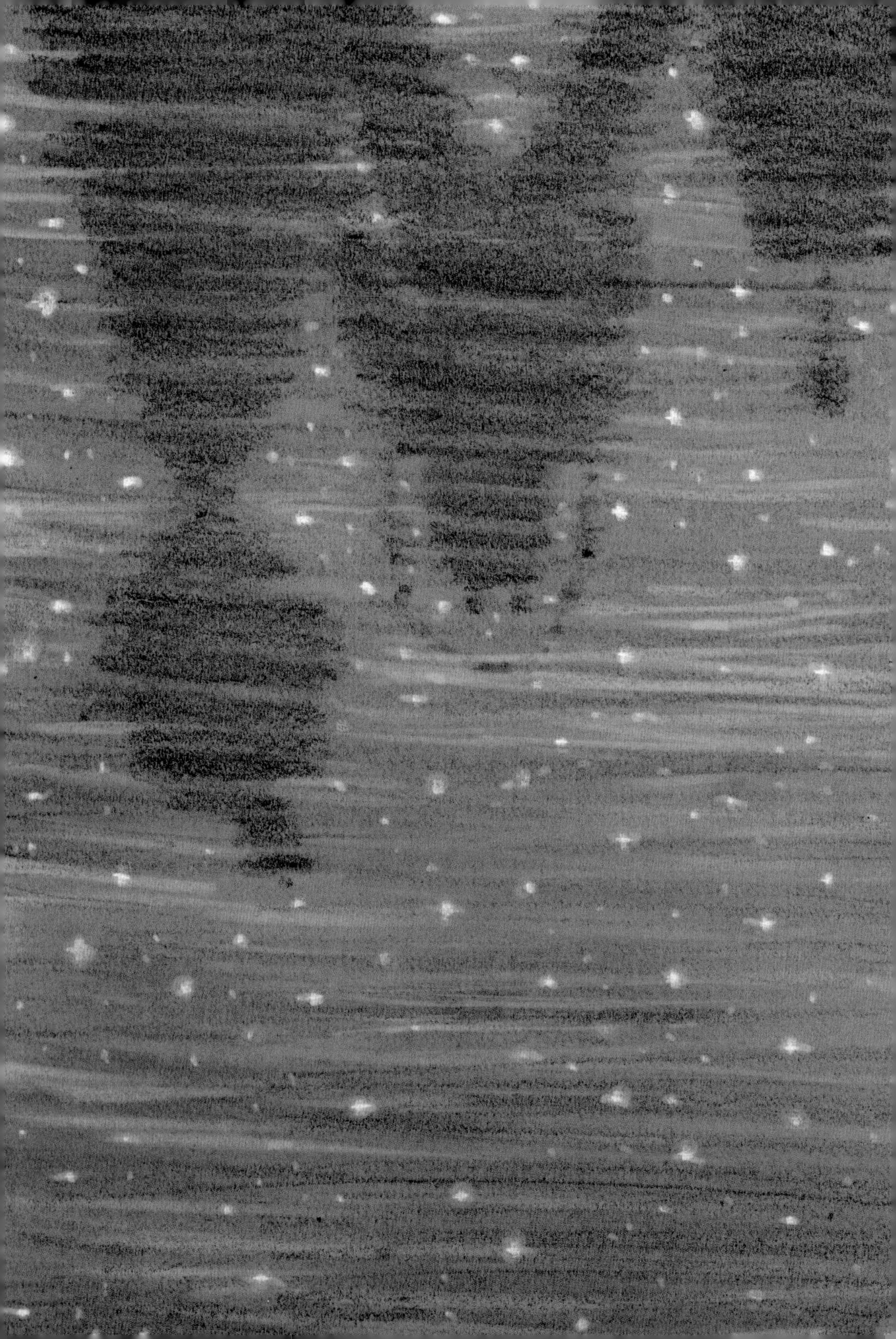

CHAPTER II

WHALESONG

145

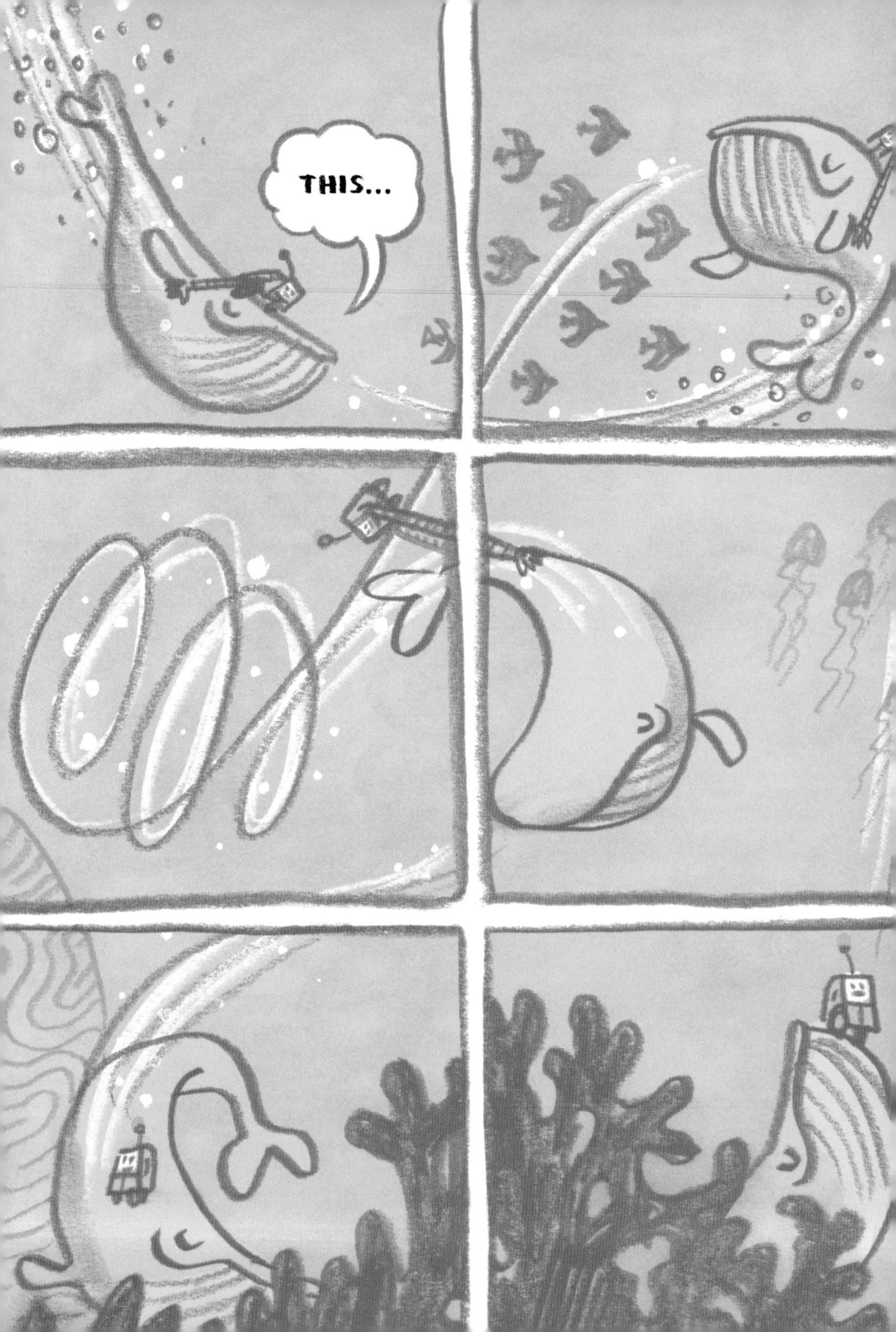
THIS...

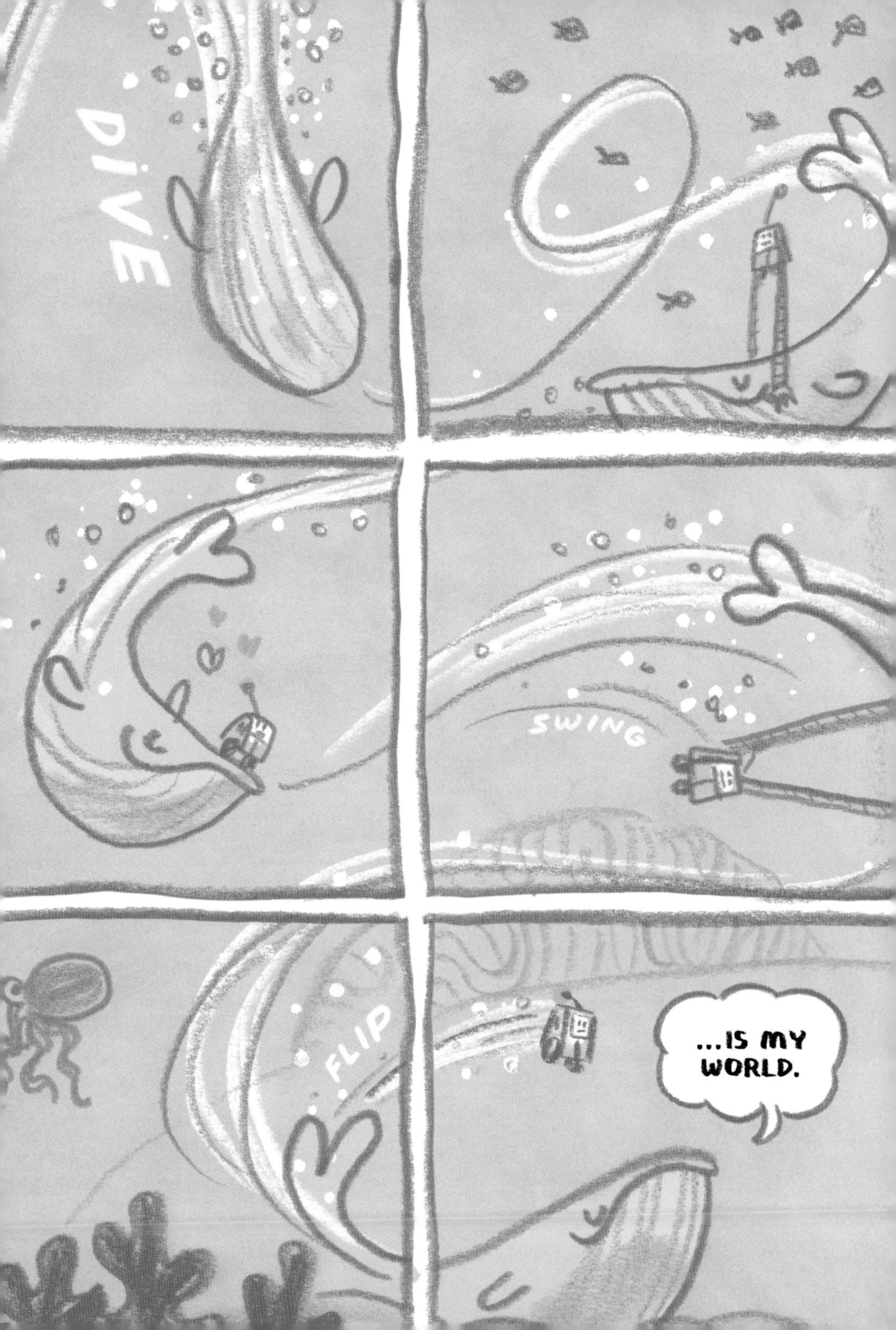
DIVE
SWING
FLIP
...IS MY WORLD.

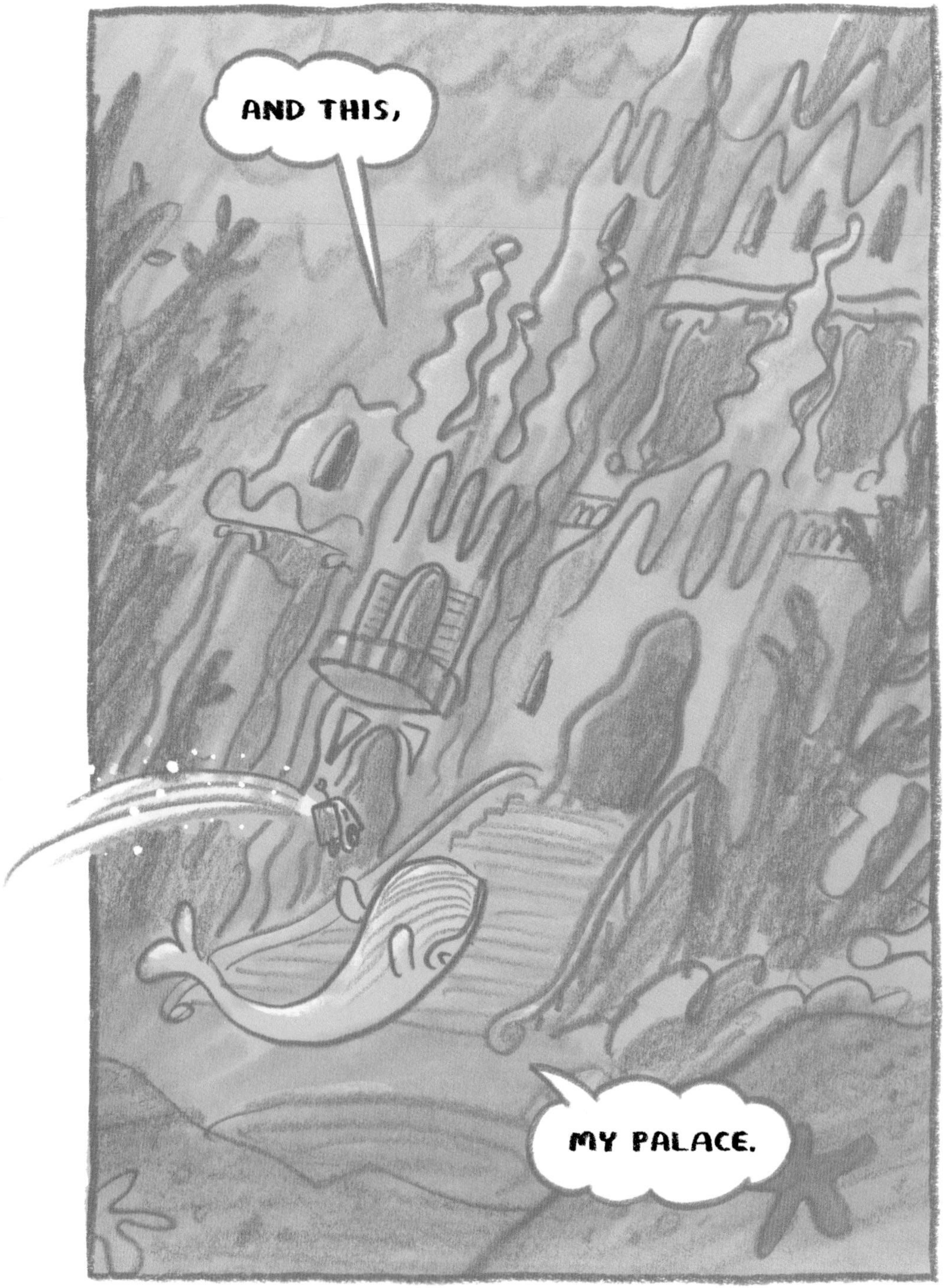
AND THIS,
MY PALACE.

MY PLAYERS ARE THE FINEST IN THE TWENTY-THREE SEAS.

WE GATHER NIGHTLY IN THIS HALL, OUR SOULS DEVOTED TO A SINGLE AIM:

MAKING SWEET MUSIC!

OH BLISS!

CLAP CLAP CLAP CLAP CLAP CLAP

THE SONGS OF THE SEA GIVE MY LIFE MEANING.

THAT IS YOUR PURPOSE? TO SING?

NOT JUST TO SING,

TOENAIL WHALE...

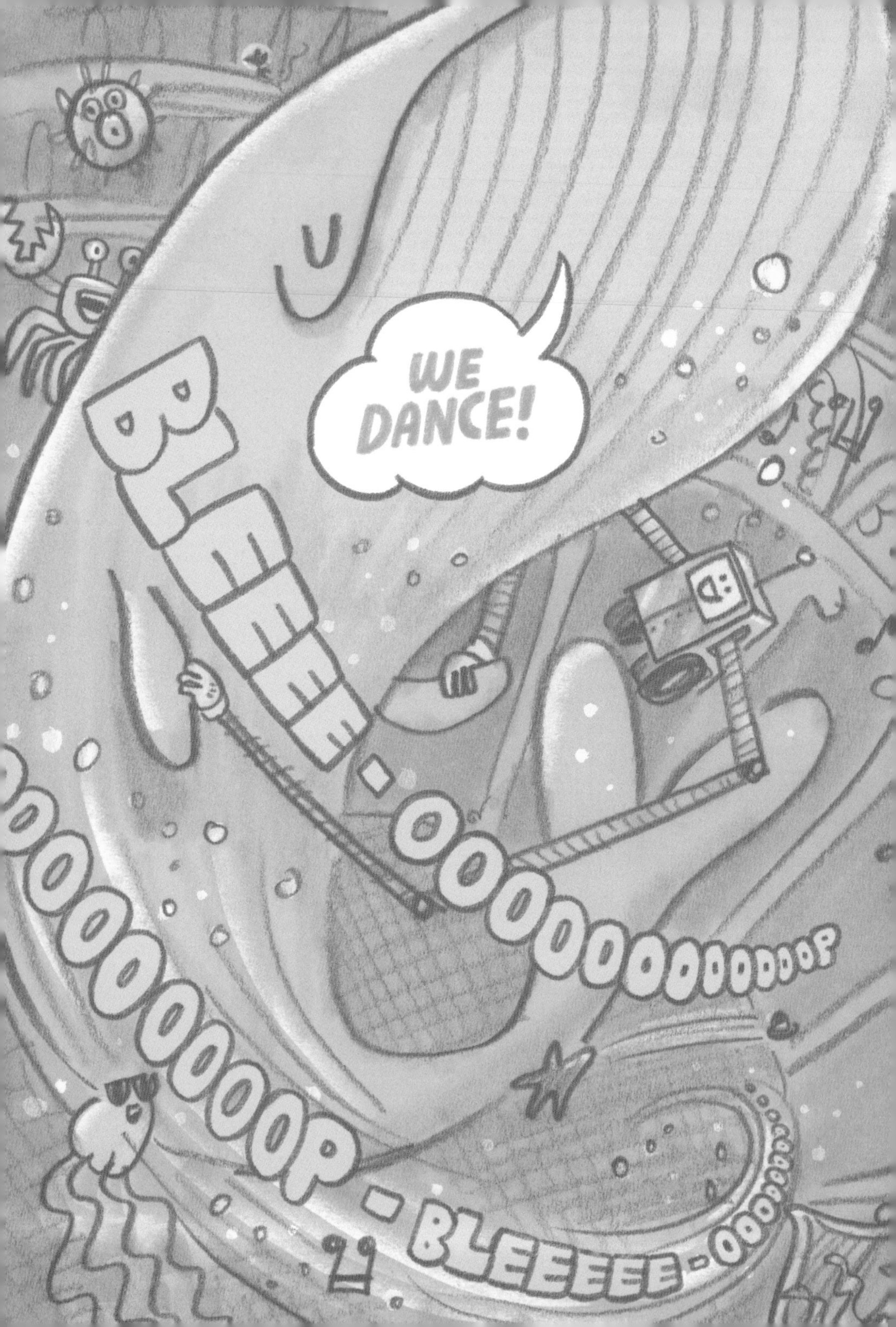
WE DANCE!
BLEEEE-OOOOOOOOOOOOOP
OOOOOOOOOOP - BLEEEEEE-OOOOOOOOO

CHAPTER 12
COLD PIZZA

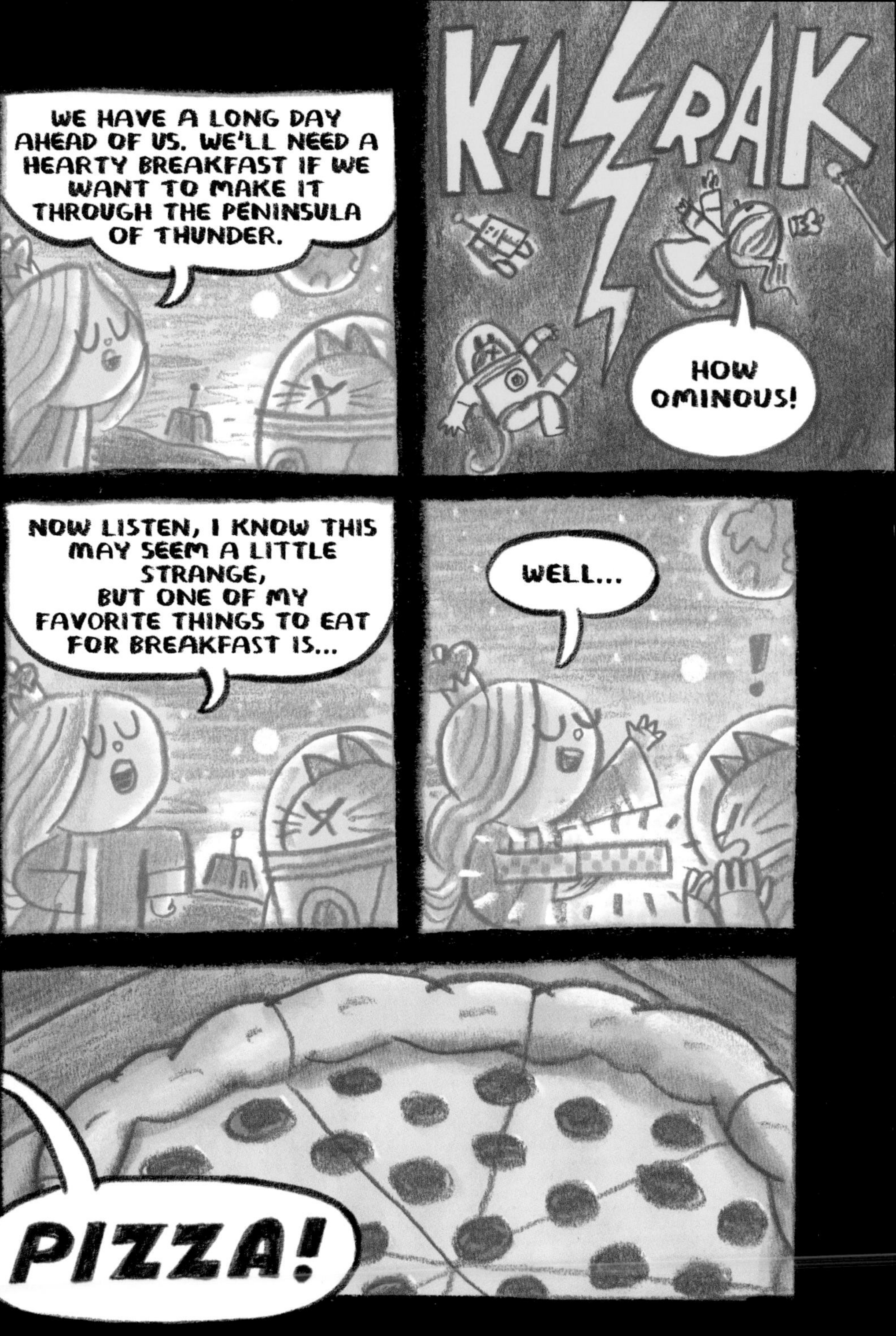
WE HAVE A LONG DAY AHEAD OF US. WE'LL NEED A HEARTY BREAKFAST IF WE WANT TO MAKE IT THROUGH THE PENINSULA OF THUNDER.
KA-KRAK
HOW OMINOUS!
NOW LISTEN, I KNOW THIS MAY SEEM A LITTLE STRANGE, BUT ONE OF MY FAVORITE THINGS TO EAT FOR BREAKFAST IS...
WELL...
!
PIZZA!

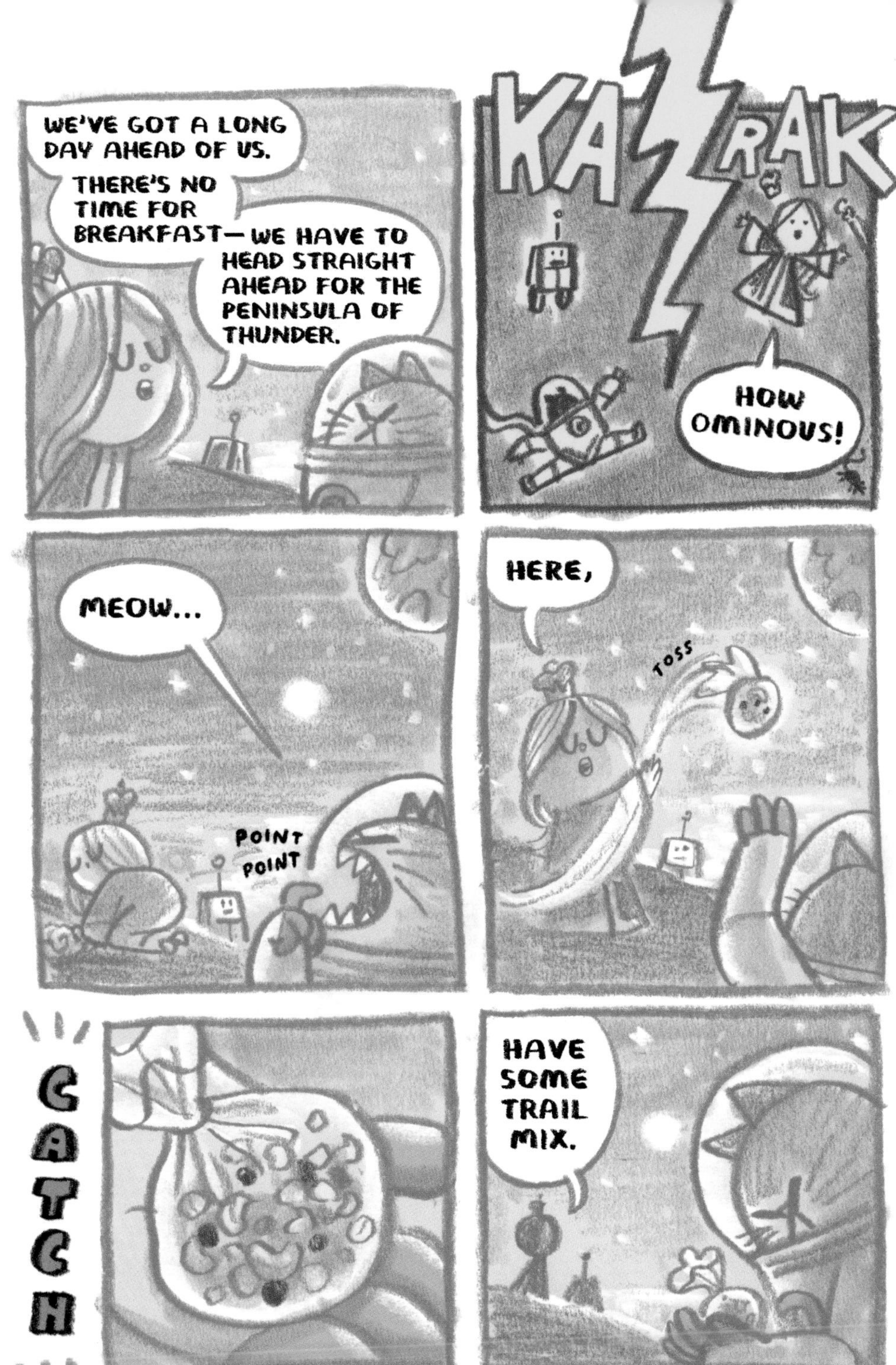
WE'VE GOT A LONG DAY AHEAD OF US.
THERE'S NO TIME FOR BREAKFAST— WE HAVE TO HEAD STRAIGHT AHEAD FOR THE PENINSULA OF THUNDER.
KA-RAK
HOW OMINOUS!
MEOW...
POINT POINT
HERE,
TOSS
CATCH
HAVE SOME TRAIL MIX.

CHAPTER 13

THE PENINSULA OF THUNDER

(HOW OMINOUS)

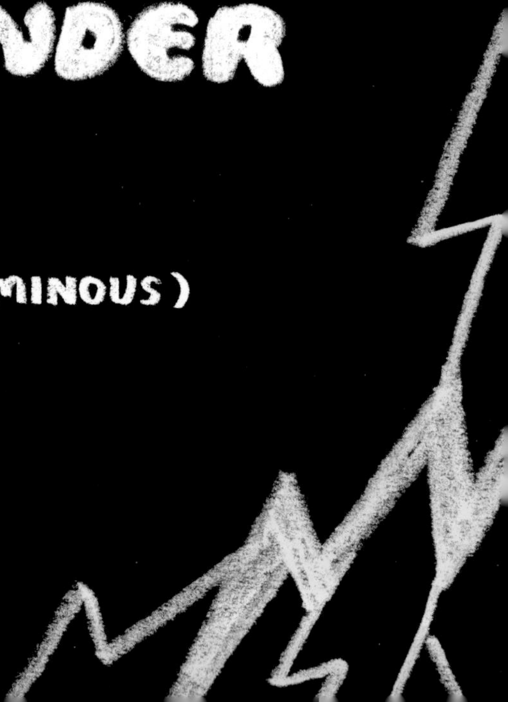

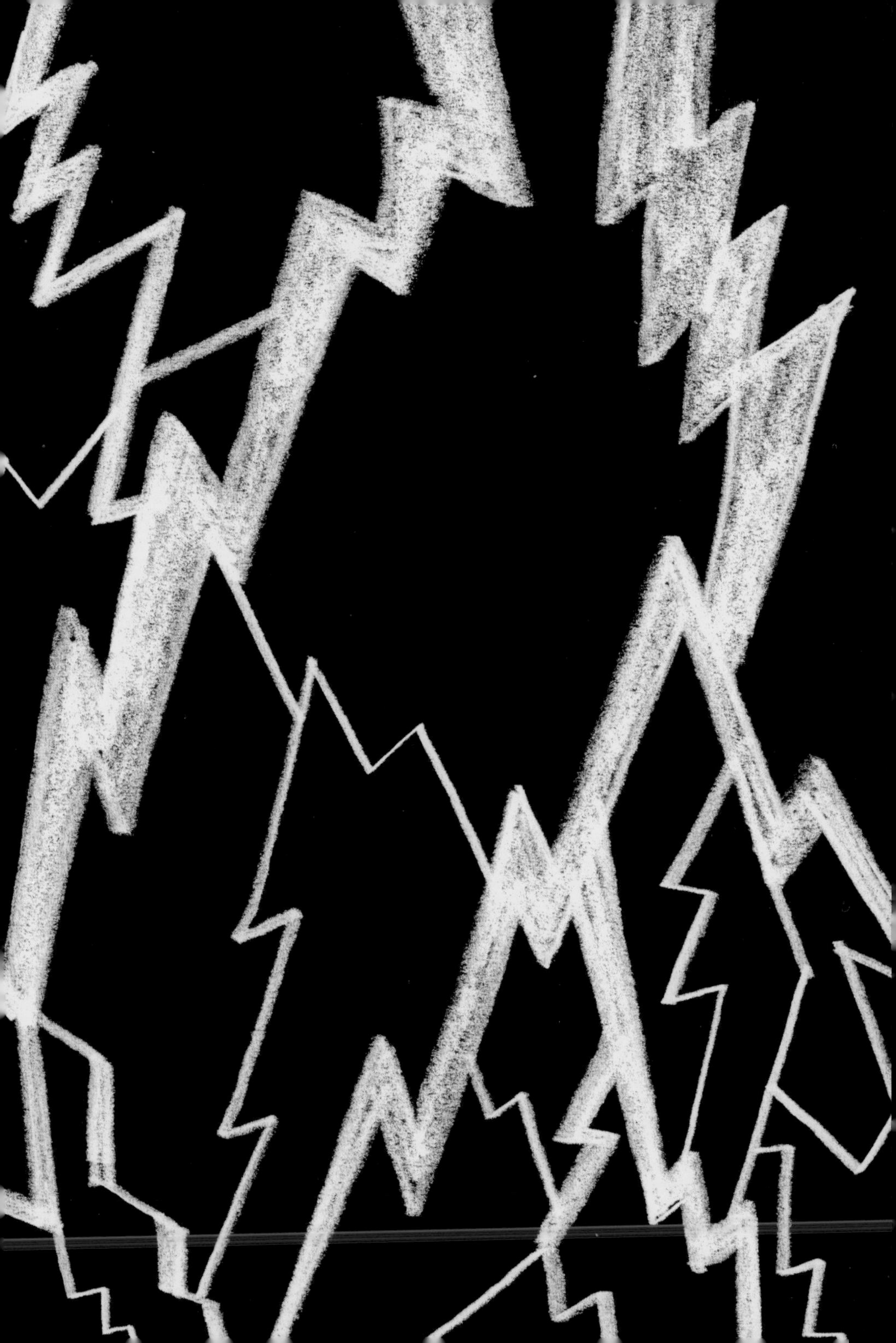

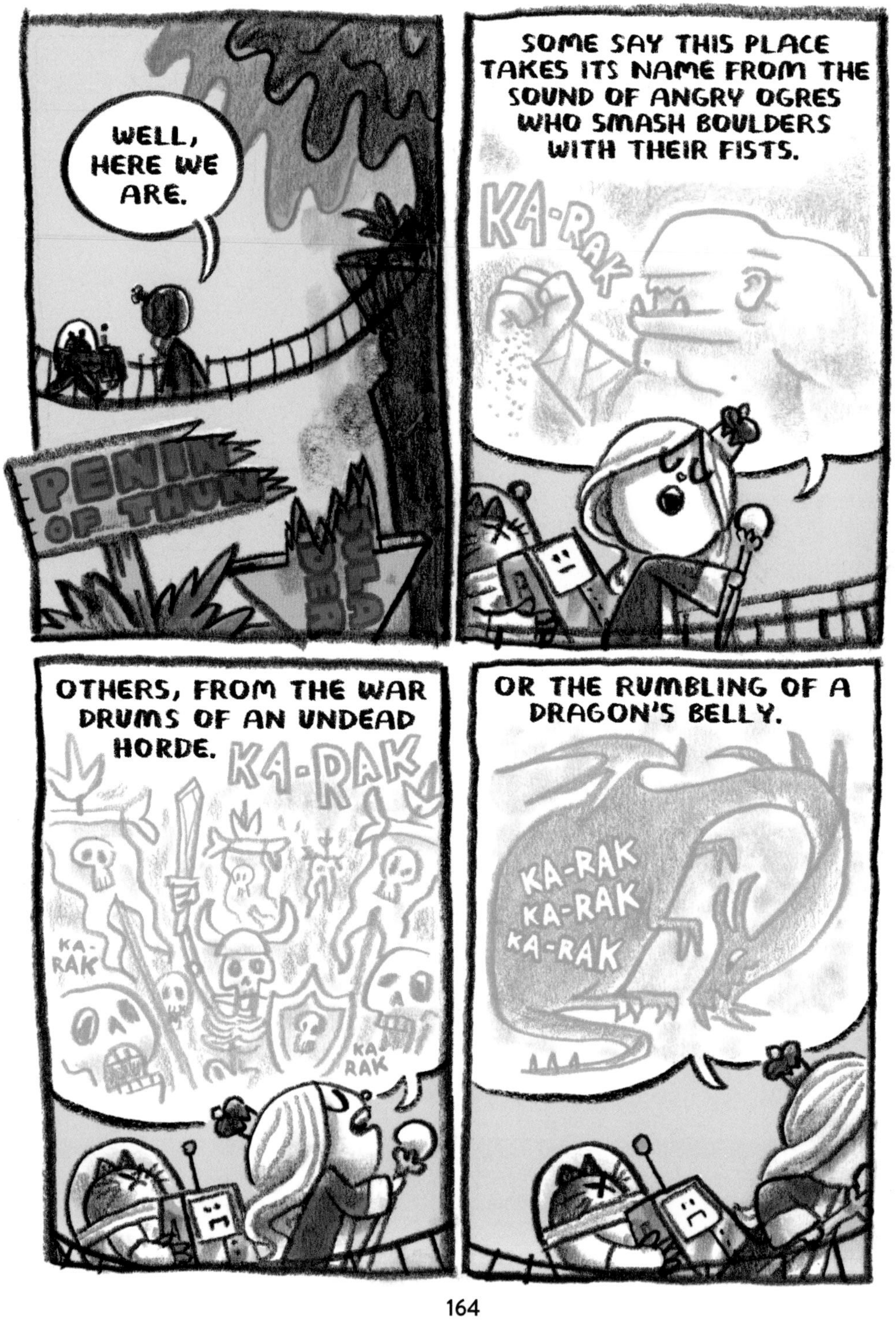
WELL, HERE WE ARE.
PENIN
OF THUN
SOME SAY THIS PLACE TAKES ITS NAME FROM THE SOUND OF ANGRY OGRES WHO SMASH BOULDERS WITH THEIR FISTS.
KA-RAK
OTHERS, FROM THE WAR DRUMS OF AN UNDEAD HORDE.
KA-RAK
KA-RAK
KA-RAK
OR THE RUMBLING OF A DRAGON'S BELLY.
KA-RAK
KA-RAK
KA-RAK

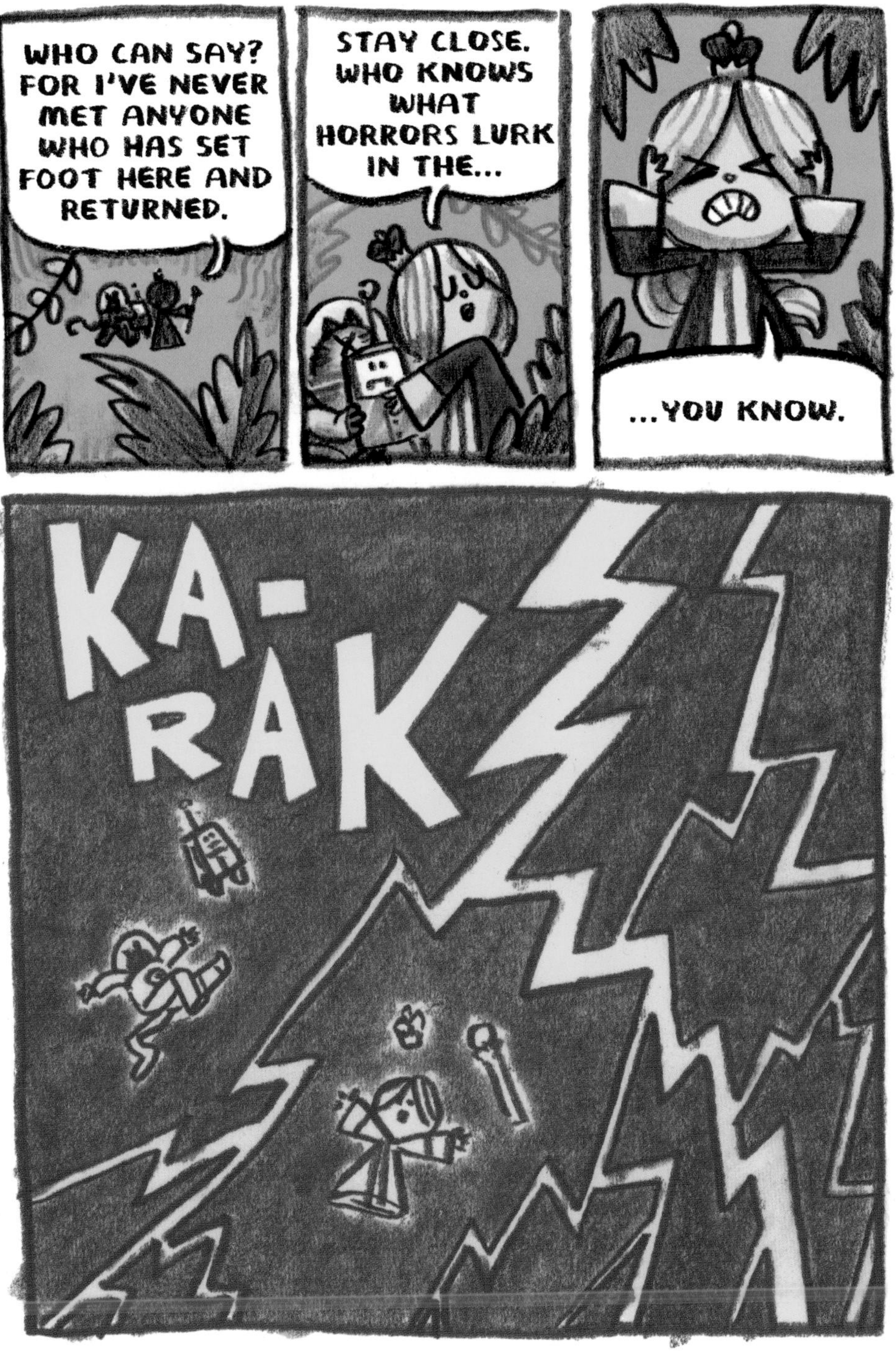
WHO CAN SAY? FOR I'VE NEVER MET ANYONE WHO HAS SET FOOT HERE AND RETURNED.
STAY CLOSE. WHO KNOWS WHAT HORRORS LURK IN THE...
...YOU KNOW.
KA-RAK

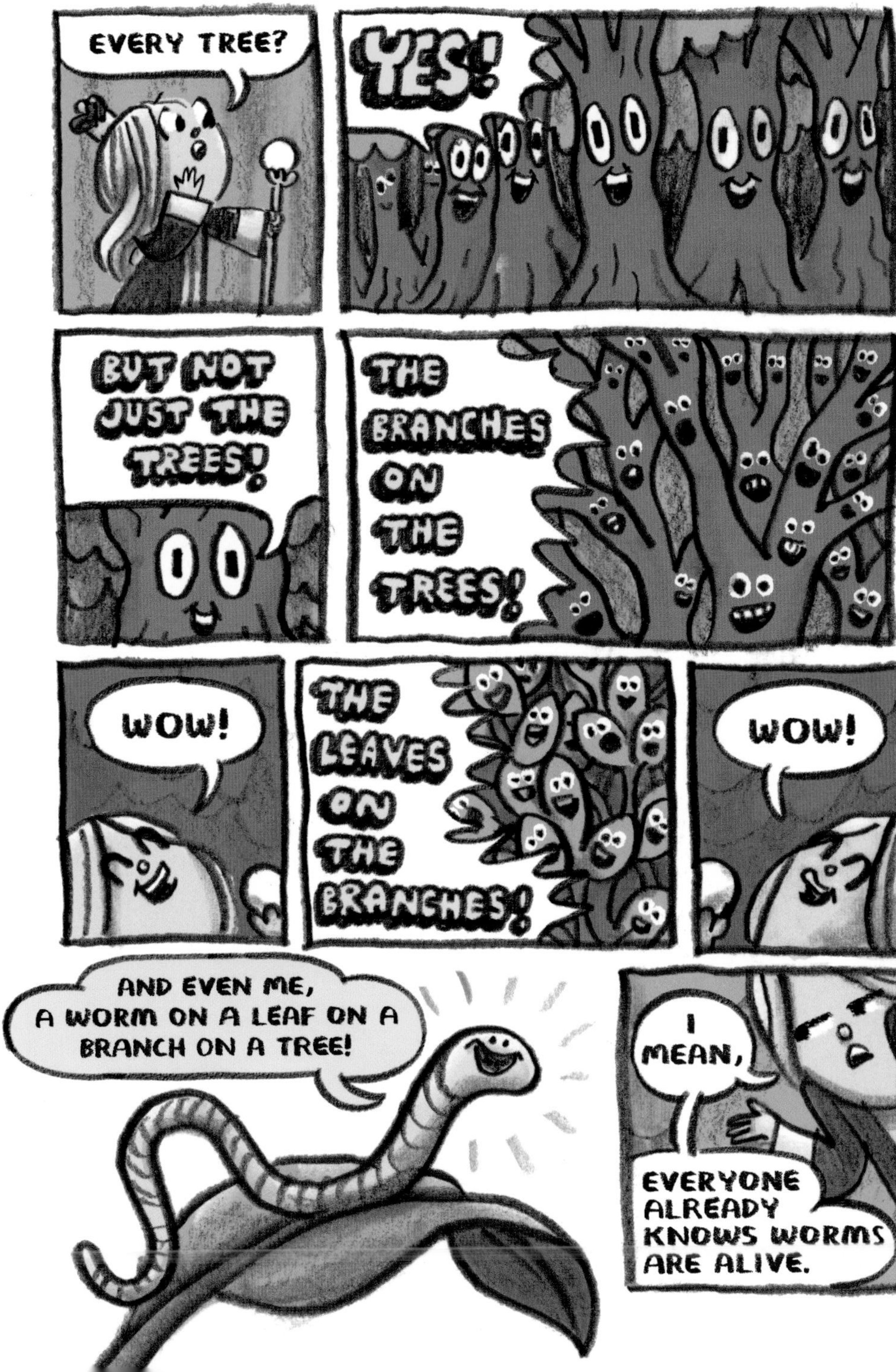
EVERY TREE?
YES!
BUT NOT JUST THE TREES!
THE BRANCHES ON THE TREES!
WOW!
THE LEAVES ON THE BRANCHES!
WOW!
AND EVEN ME, A WORM ON A LEAF ON A BRANCH ON A TREE!
I MEAN,
EVERYONE ALREADY KNOWS WORMS ARE ALIVE.

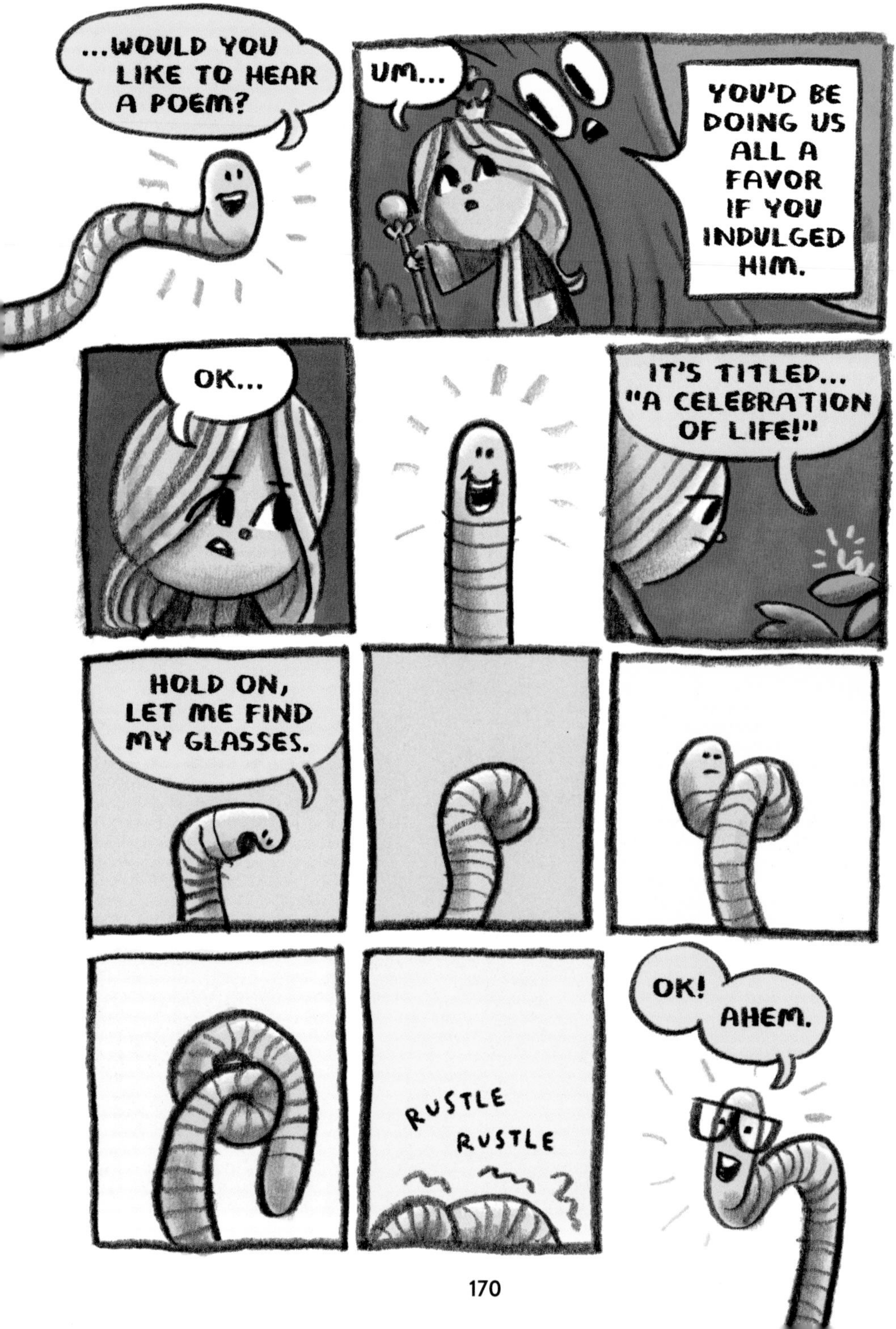
...WOULD YOU LIKE TO HEAR A POEM?
UM...
YOU'D BE DOING US ALL A FAVOR IF YOU INDULGED HIM.
OK...
IT'S TITLED... "A CELEBRATION OF LIFE!"
HOLD ON, LET ME FIND MY GLASSES.
RUSTLE
RUSTLE
OK!
AHEM.

CHAPTER 14

SEA SALTS

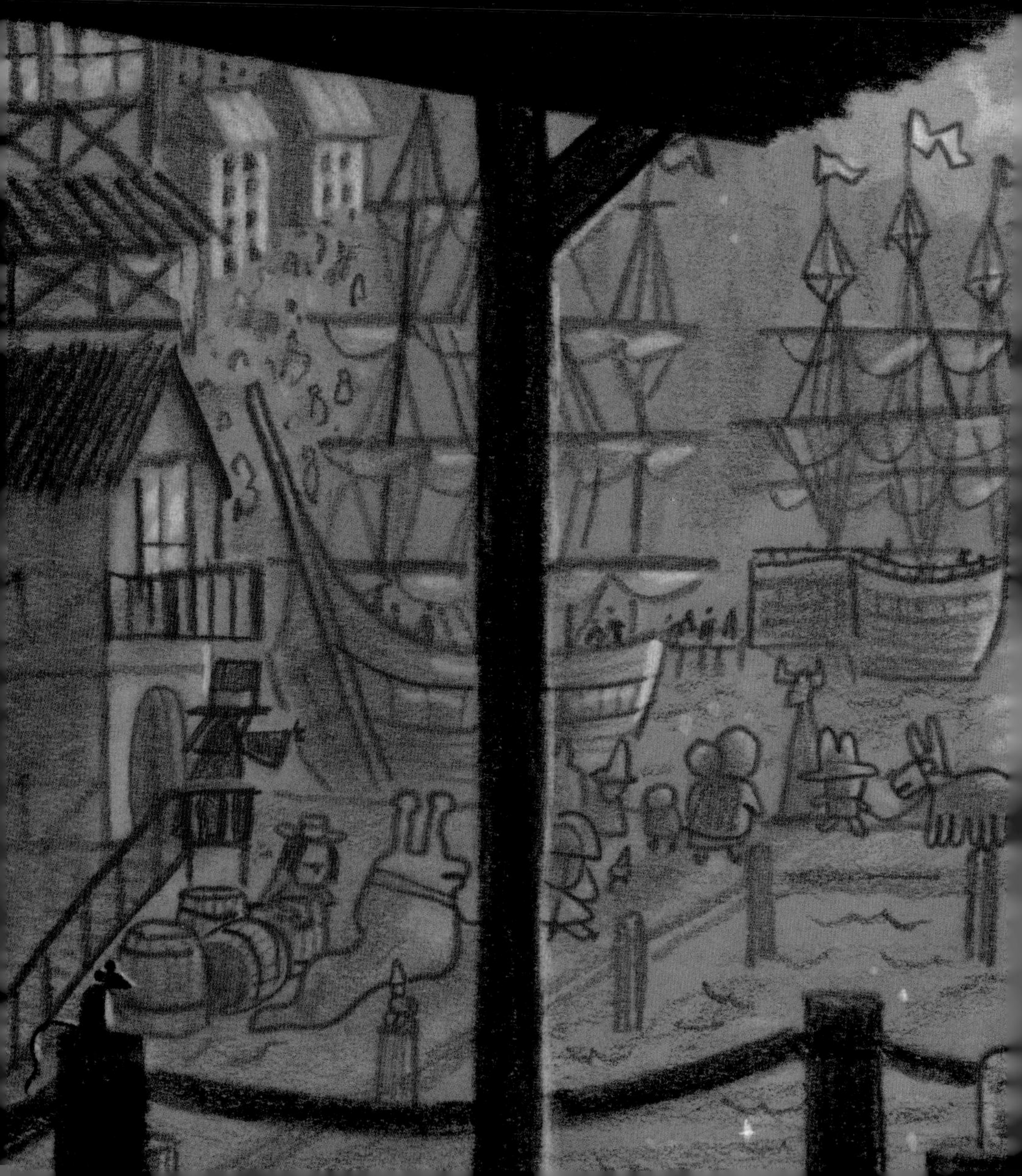

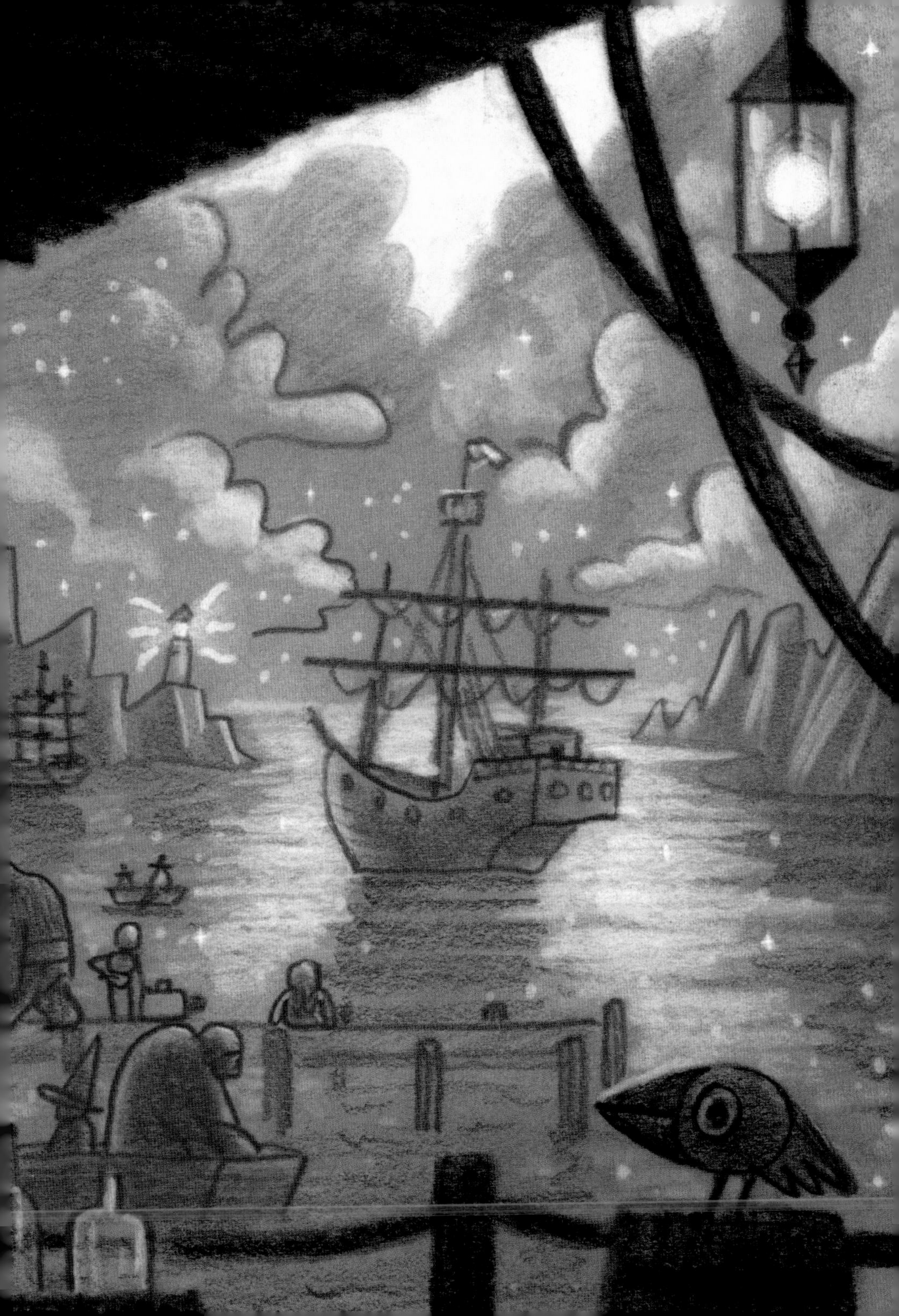

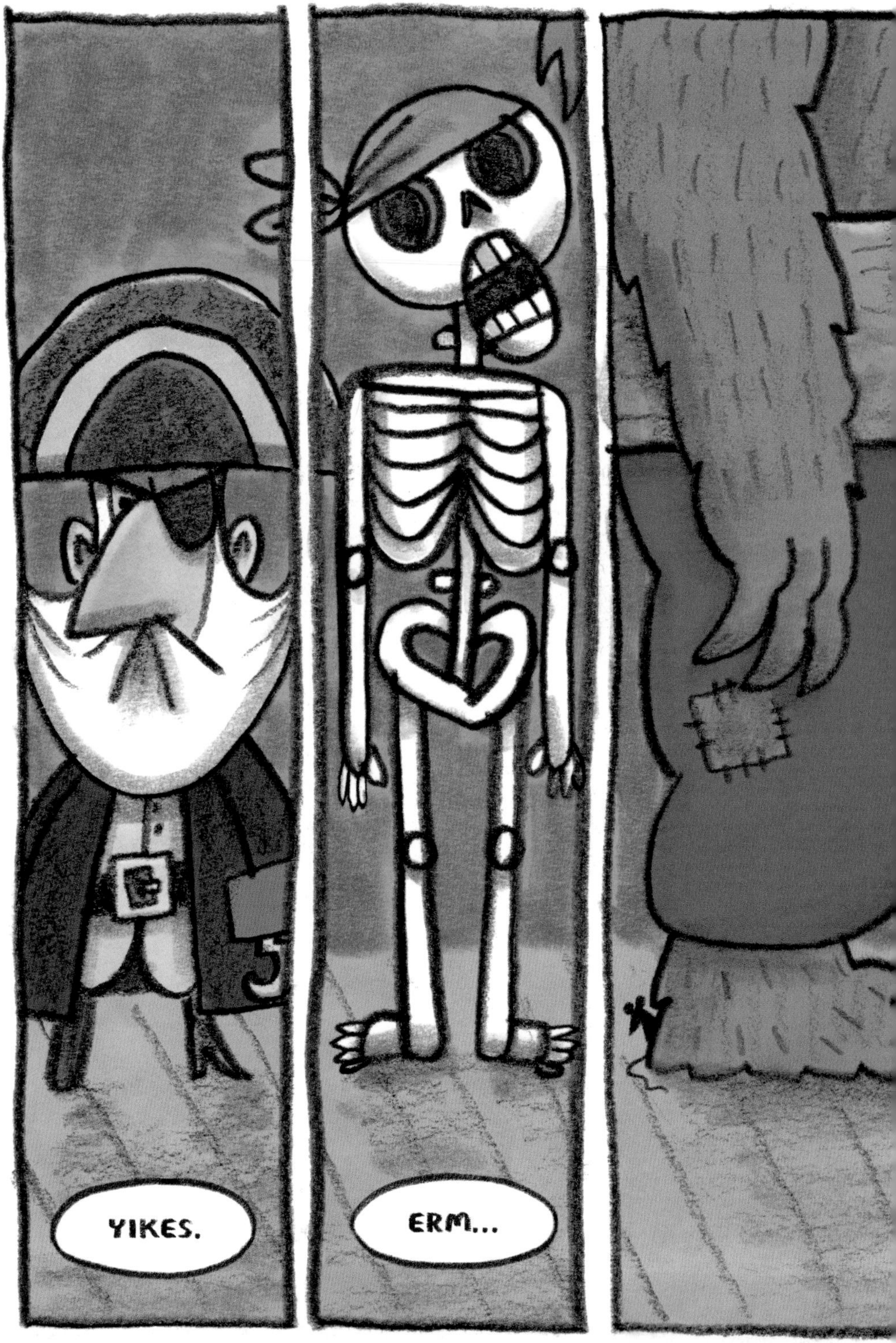
YIKES.
ERM...

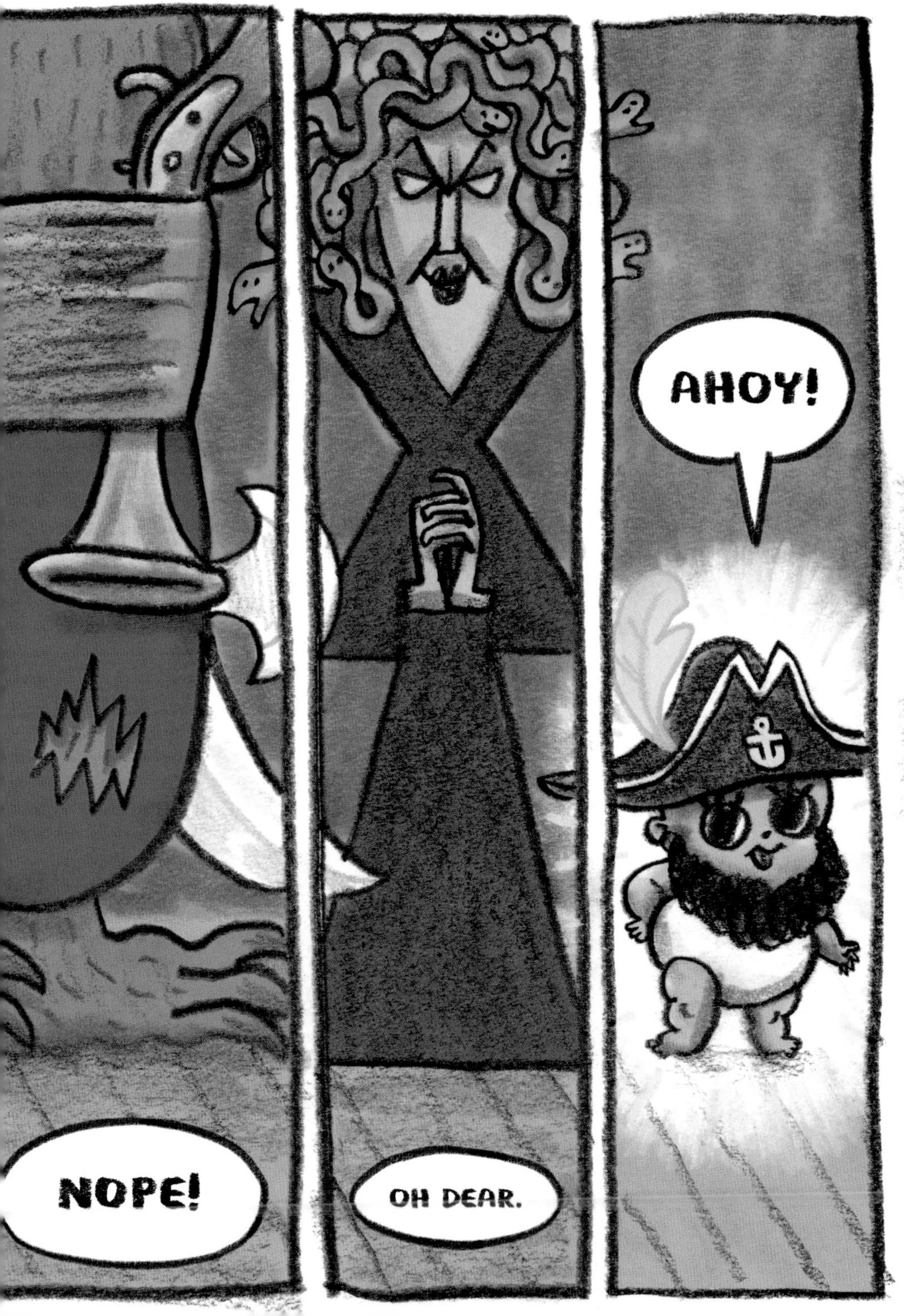
NOPE!
OH DEAR.
AHOY!

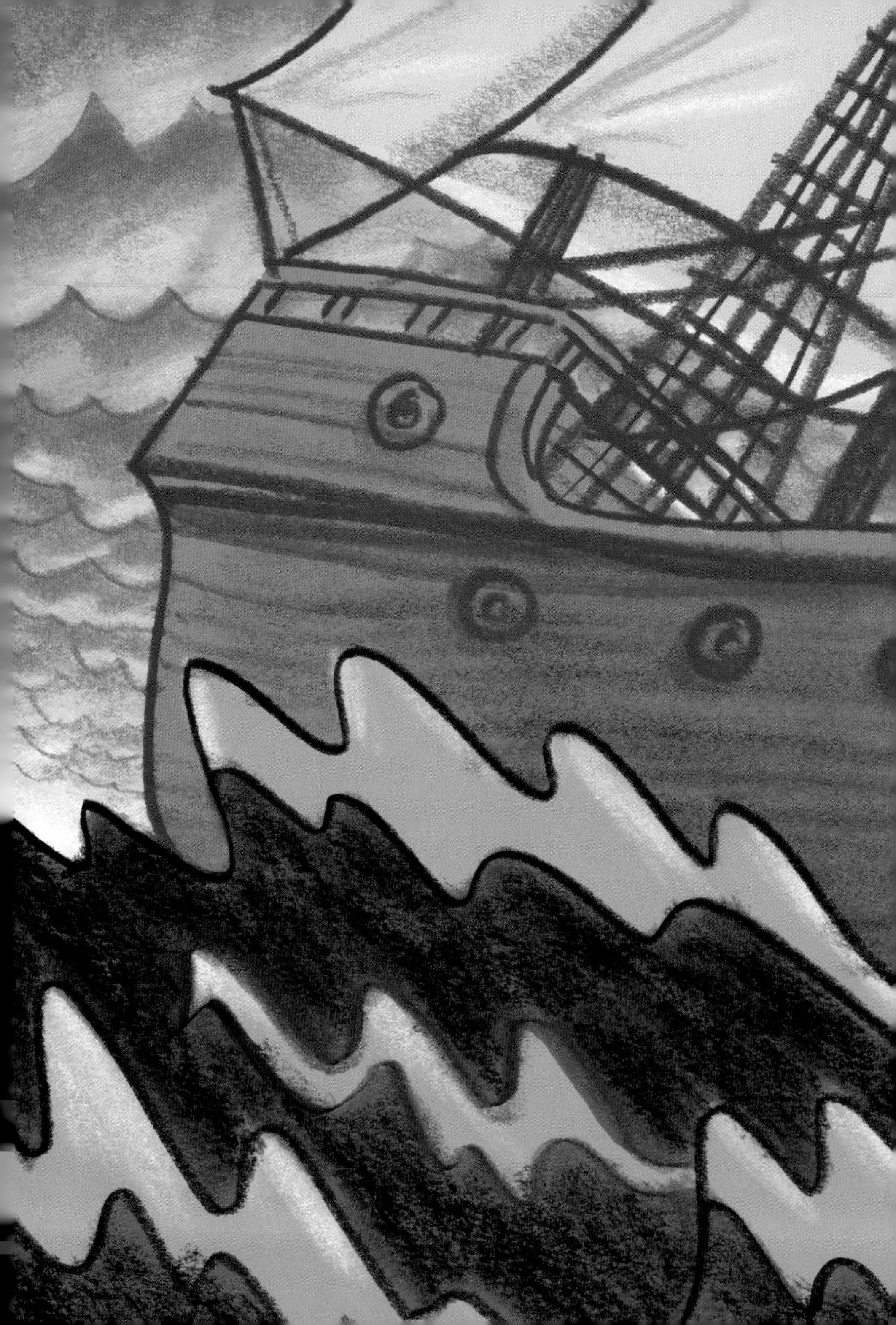

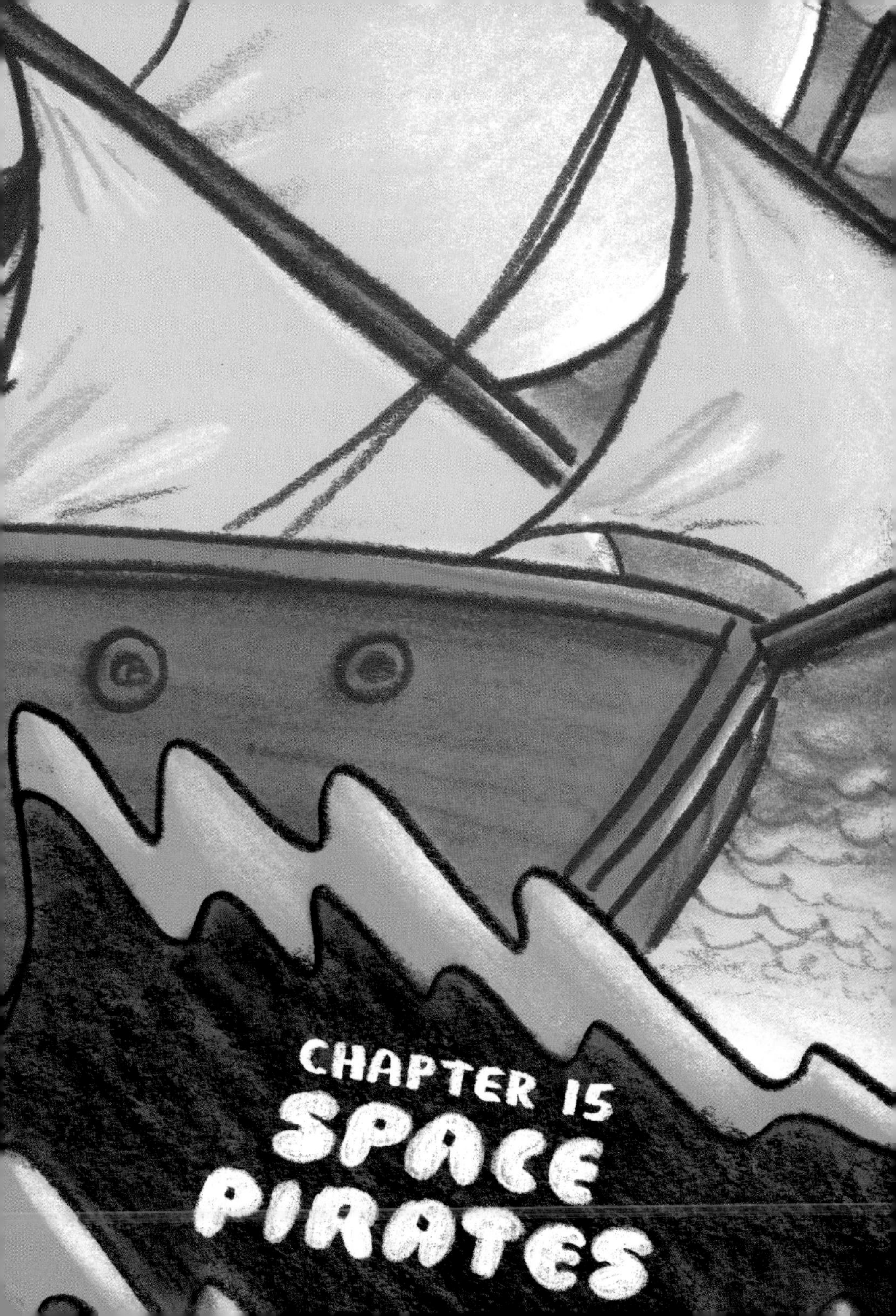

CHAPTER 15
SPACE PIRATES

184

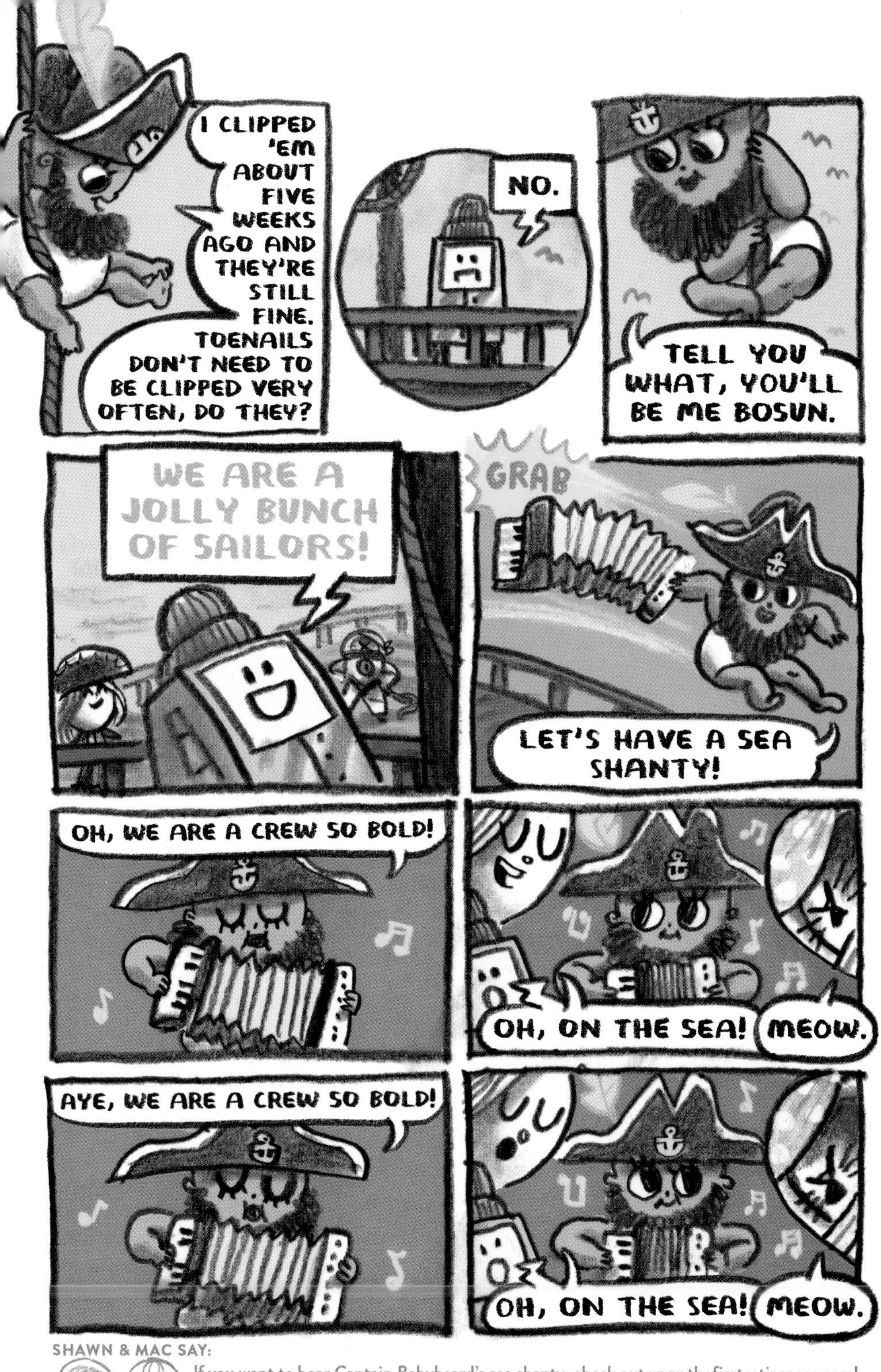
I CLIPPED 'EM ABOUT FIVE WEEKS AGO AND THEY'RE STILL FINE. TOENAILS DON'T NEED TO BE CLIPPED VERY OFTEN, DO THEY?
NO.
TELL YOU WHAT, YOU'LL BE ME BOSUN.
WE ARE A JOLLY BUNCH OF SAILORS!
GRAB
LET'S HAVE A SEA SHANTY!
OH, WE ARE A CREW SO BOLD!
OH, ON THE SEA!
MEOW.
AYE, WE ARE A CREW SO BOLD!
OH, ON THE SEA!
MEOW.

SHAWN & MAC SAY:

If you want to hear Captain Babybeard's sea shanty, check out www.thefirstcatinspace.com!

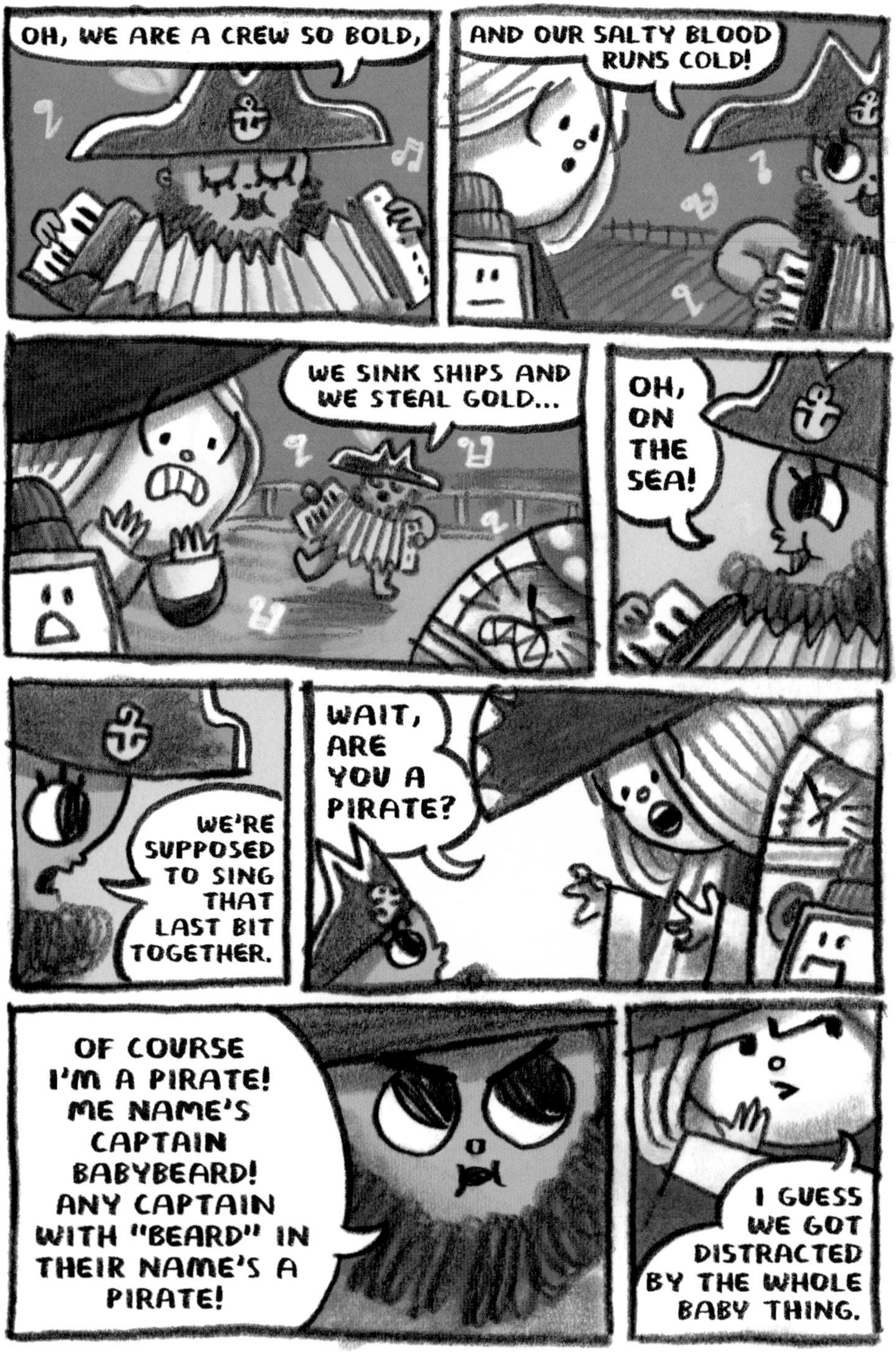

OH, WE ARE A CREW SO BOLD,
AND OUR SALTY BLOOD RUNS COLD!
WE SINK SHIPS AND WE STEAL GOLD...
OH, ON THE SEA!
WE'RE SUPPOSED TO SING THAT LAST BIT TOGETHER.
WAIT, ARE YOU A PIRATE?
OF COURSE I'M A PIRATE! ME NAME'S CAPTAIN BABYBEARD! ANY CAPTAIN WITH "BEARD" IN THEIR NAME'S A PIRATE!
I GUESS WE GOT DISTRACTED BY THE WHOLE BABY THING.

OH MY RAM!

LOOK HERE.

YOU JUST HAVE TO HELP ME PLUNDER ONE SHIP AND THEN I'LL DROP YOU OFF AT THE GATES OF THE DARK SIDE OF THE MOON.

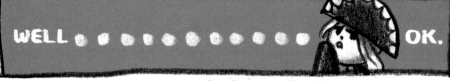

WELL . . . . OK.

YOUR MAJESTY! WE CAN'T PLUNDER A SHIP. WE'RE HEROES!

THIS OCEAN IS HUGE. WHAT ARE THE CHANCES OF RUNNING INTO ANOTHER SHIP OUT HERE?

THERE'S ONE NOW!

189

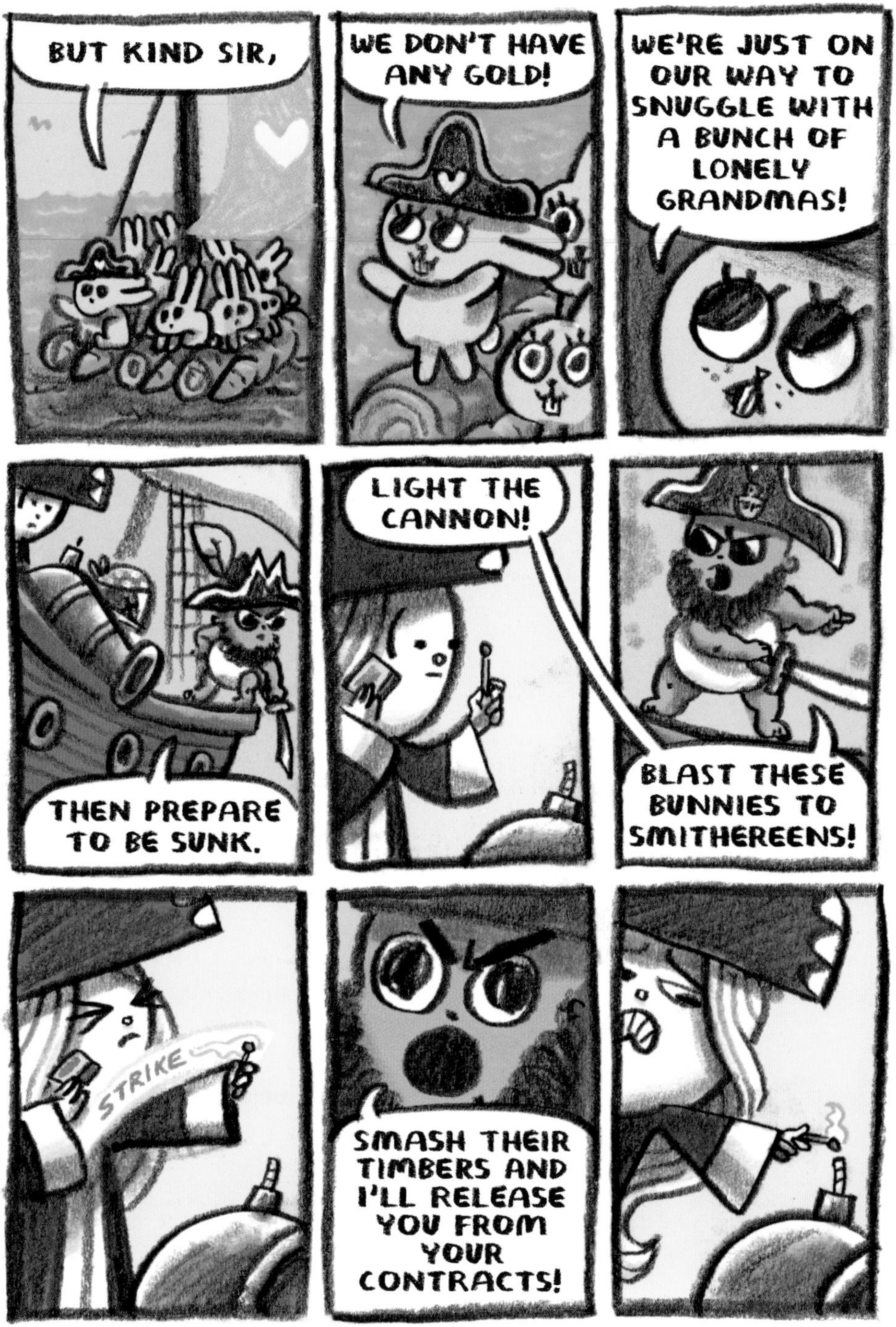
BUT KIND SIR,
WE DON'T HAVE ANY GOLD!
WE'RE JUST ON OUR WAY TO SNUGGLE WITH A BUNCH OF LONELY GRANDMAS!
THEN PREPARE TO BE SUNK.
LIGHT THE CANNON!
BLAST THESE BUNNIES TO SMITHEREENS!
STRIKE
SMASH THEIR TIMBERS AND I'LL RELEASE YOU FROM YOUR CONTRACTS!

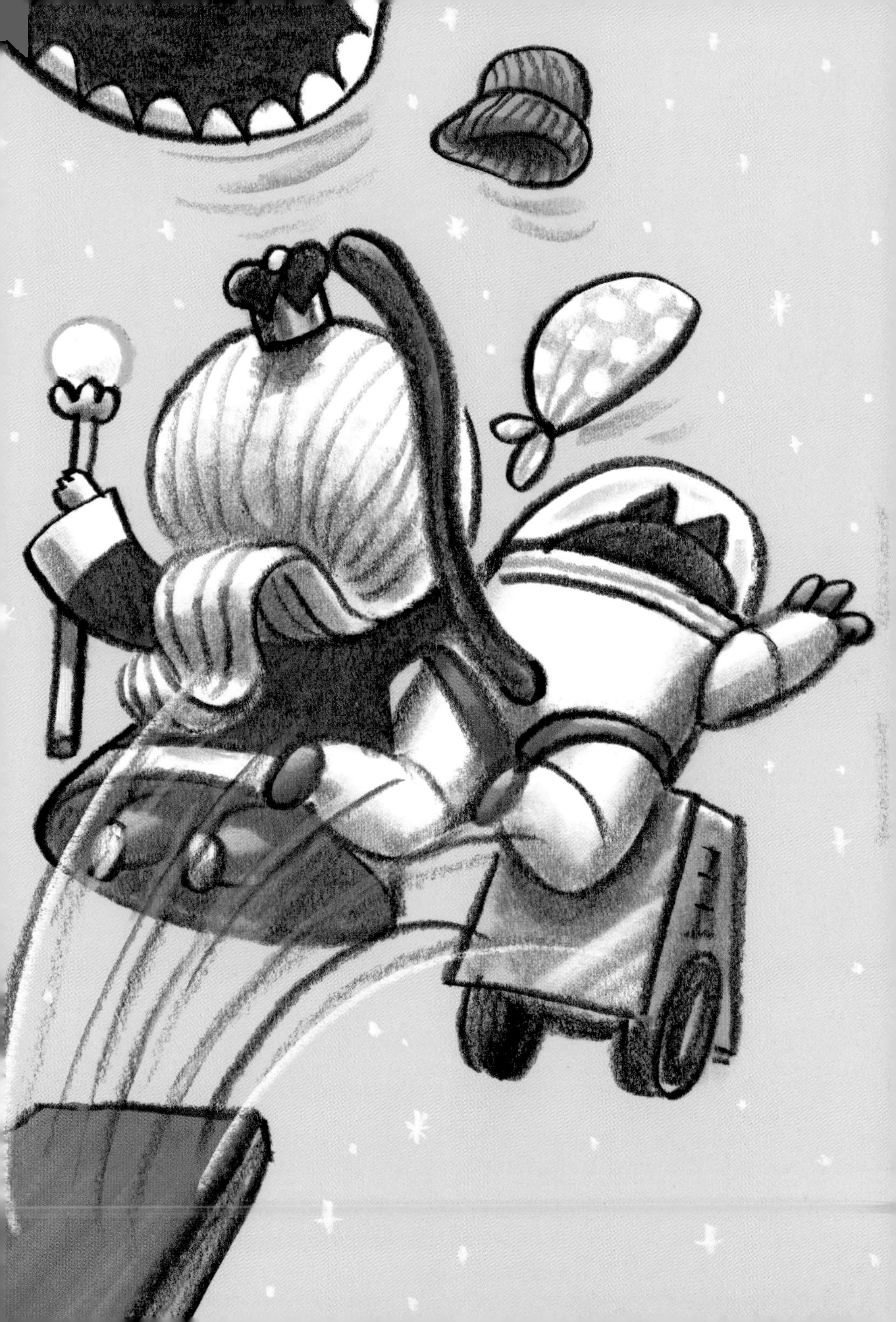

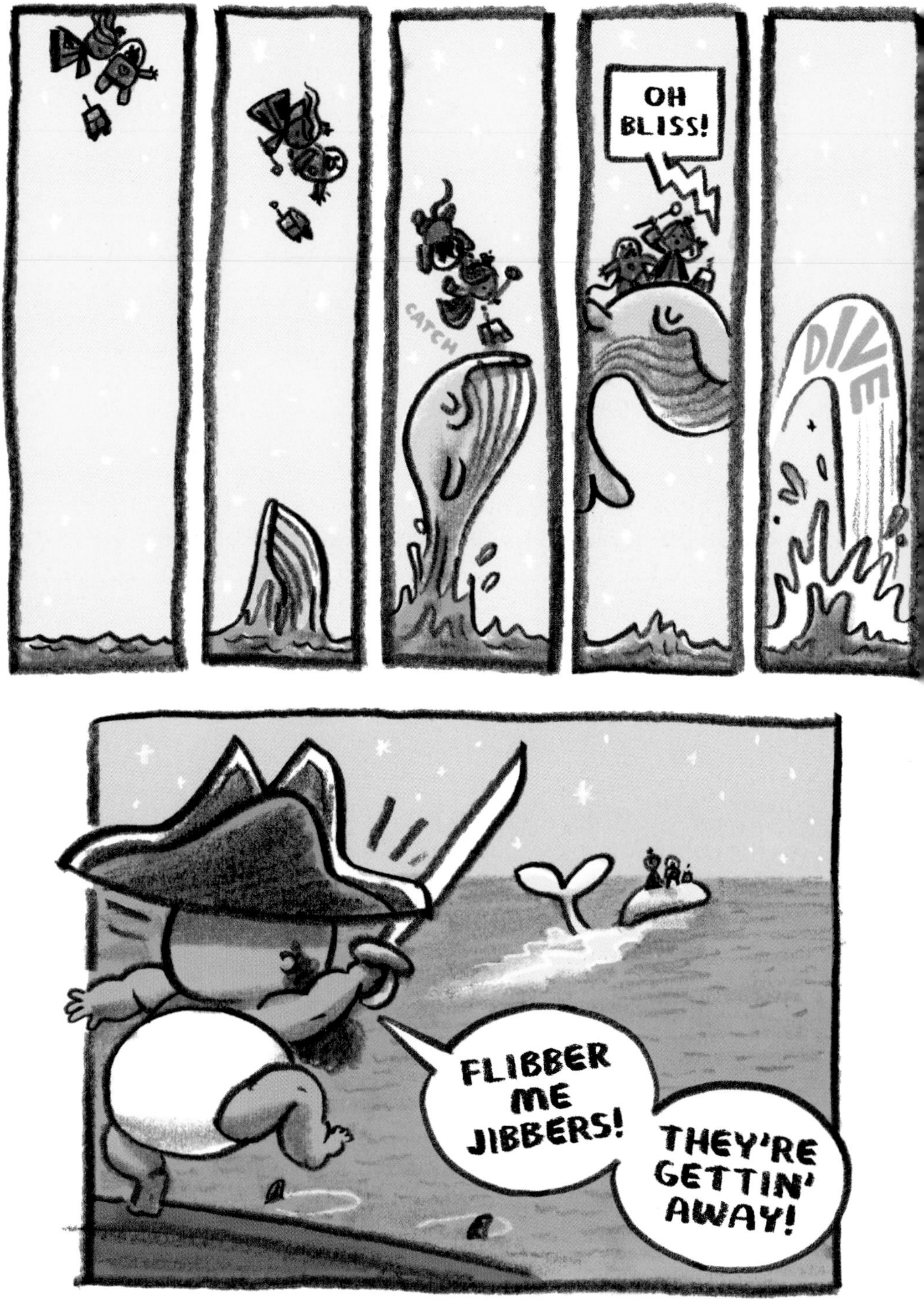
CATCH
OH BLISS!
DIVE
FLIBBER ME JIBBERS!
THEY'RE GETTIN' AWAY!

195

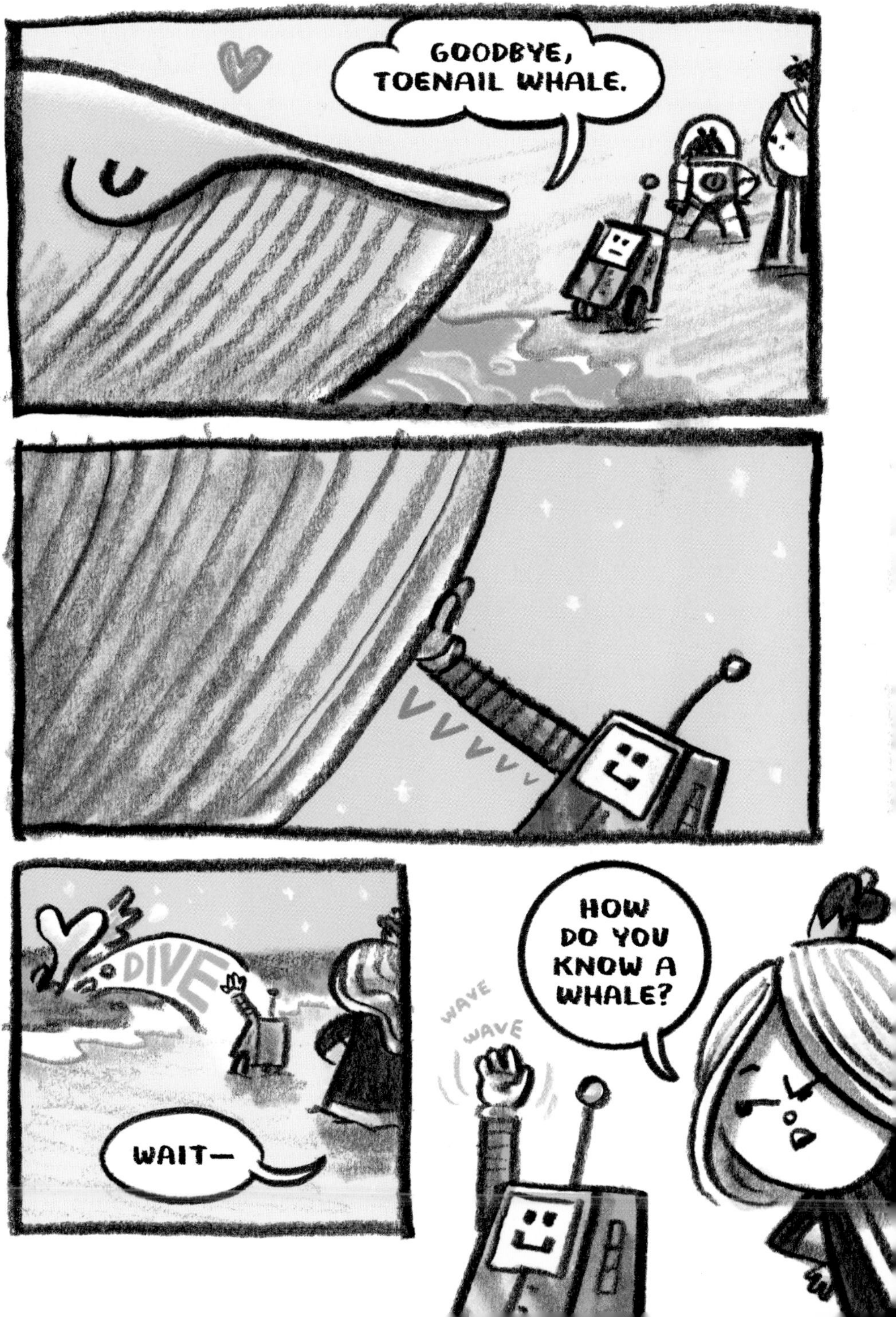
GOODBYE, TOENAIL WHALE.
DIVE
WAIT—
WAVE
WAVE
HOW DO YOU KNOW A WHALE?

CHAPTER 16

RAT TRAP

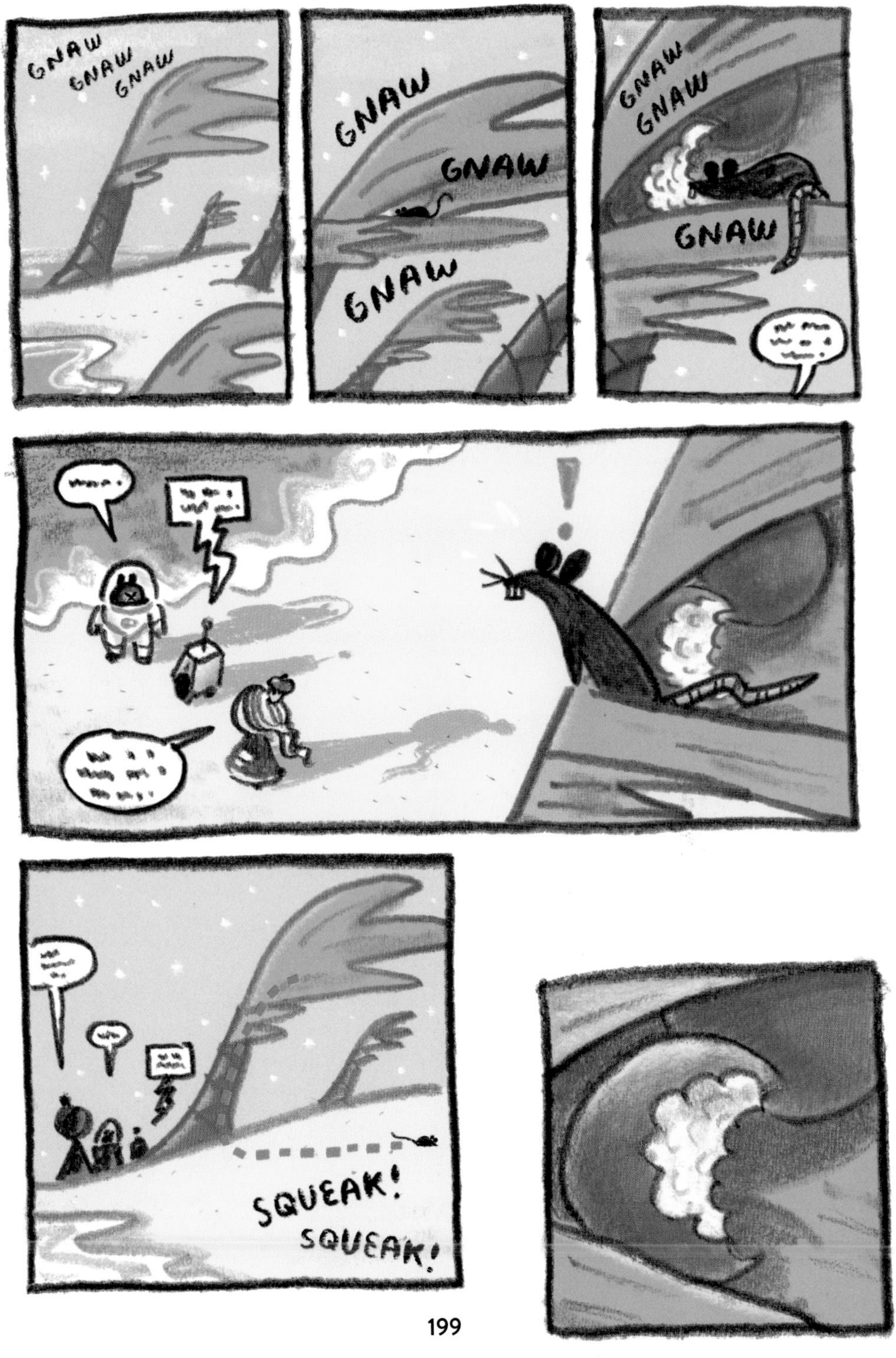
GNAW
GNAW
GNAW
GNAW
GNAW
GNAW
GNAW
GNAW
GNAW
!
SQUEAK!
SQUEAK!

201

CHAPTER 17

ZOOP!

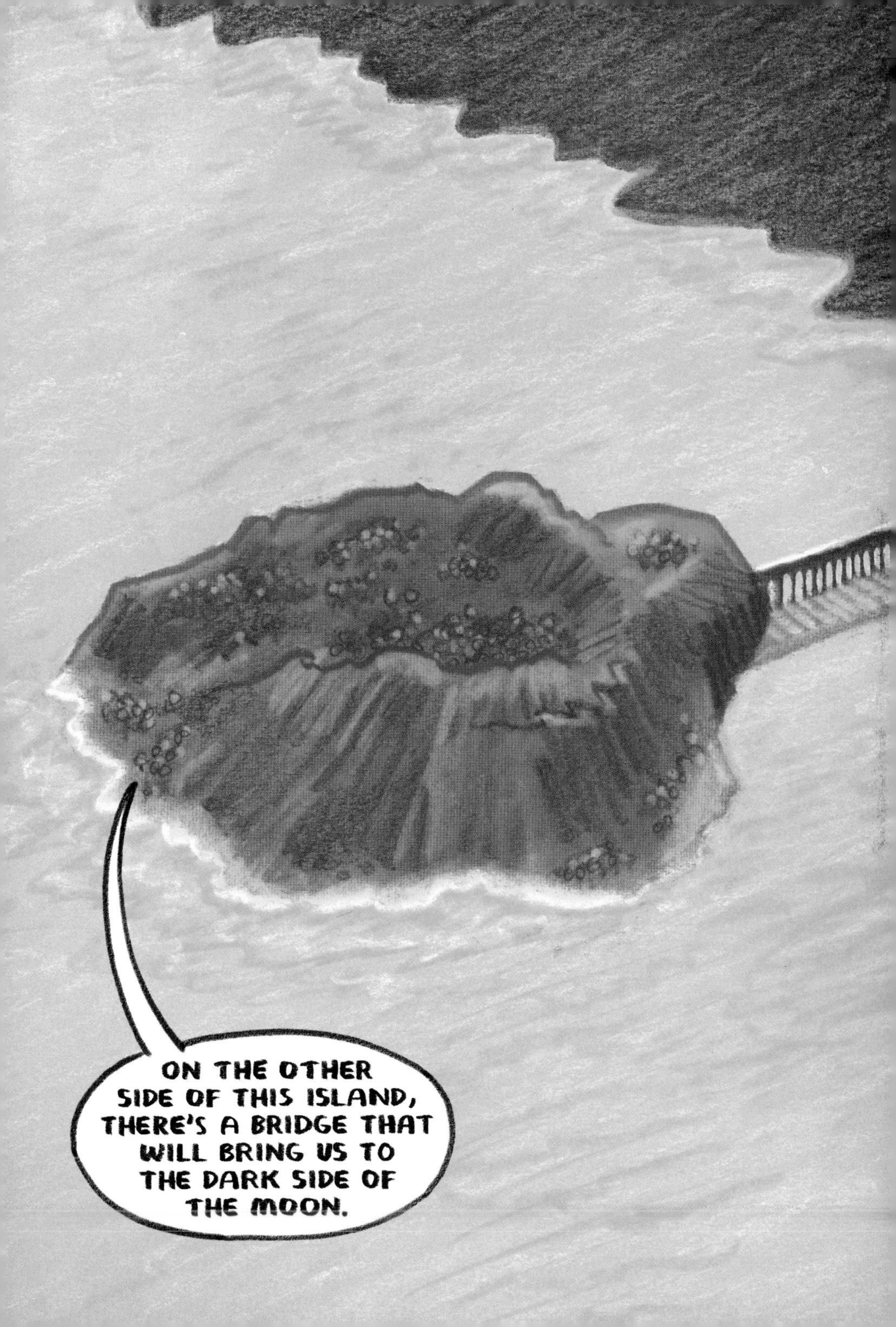
ON THE OTHER SIDE OF THIS ISLAND, THERE'S A BRIDGE THAT WILL BRING US TO THE DARK SIDE OF THE MOON.

LISTEN, YOU NEED TO SECURE YOUR VALUABLES.

FOR INSTANCE, THE MOST IMPORTANT THING I'M CARRYING IS THIS KEY, WHICH OPENS THE GATES TO THE DARK SIDE OF THE MOON.

HIDE

UM—

NO INTERRUPTIONS, TOENAIL ROBOT. THIS KEY IS IMPORTANT. WE'RE GOING TO NEED IT SOON!

BUT—

AND SINCE IT WOULD BE A DISASTER IF WE LOST IT, I'M GOING TO PUT IT ON A CHAIN AND WEAR IT—

HEY! WHAT HAPPENED?

I BELIEVE YOU JUST GOT ZOOPED.

ZOOP!

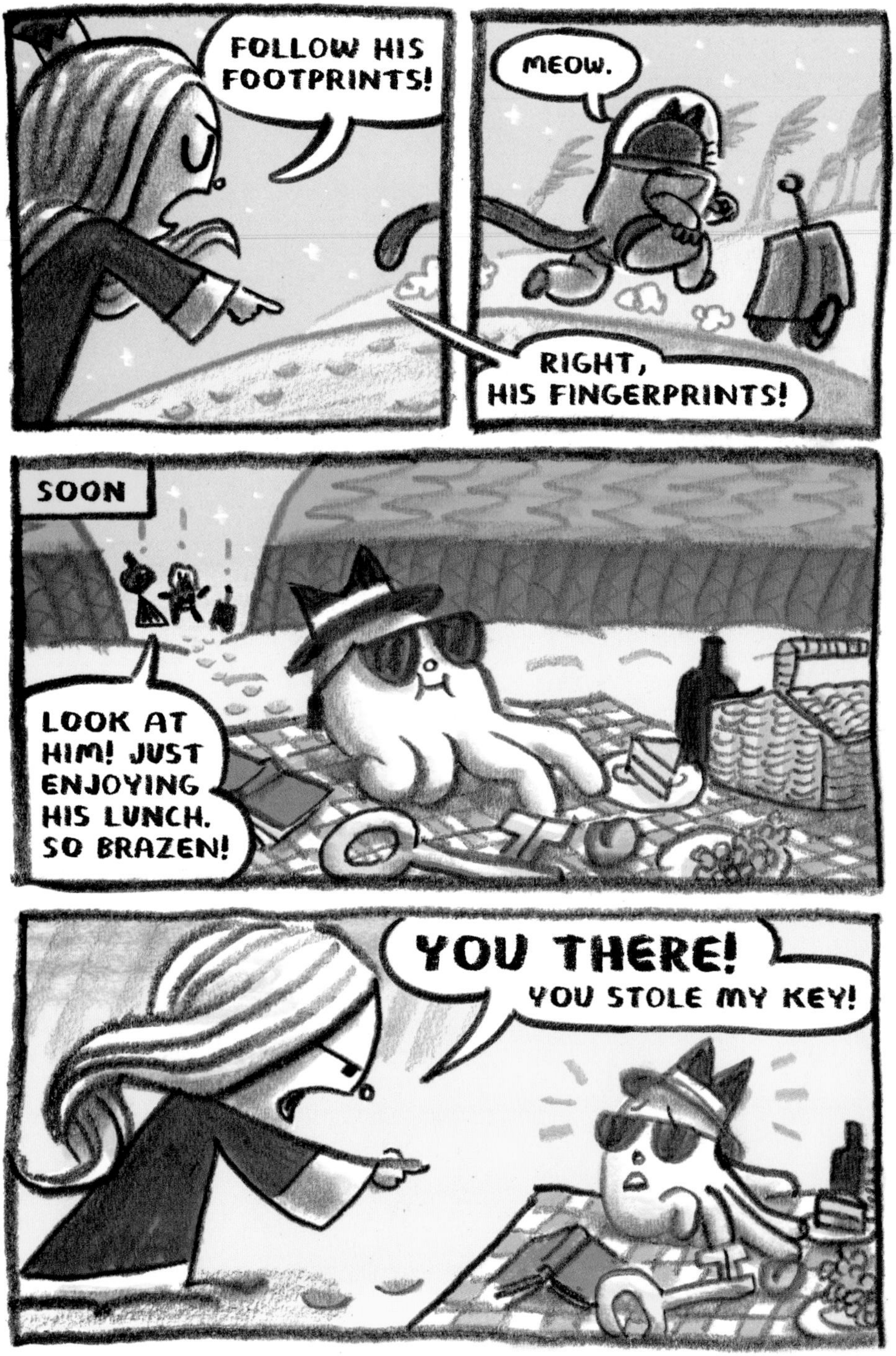

FOLLOW HIS FOOTPRINTS!
MEOW.
RIGHT, HIS FINGERPRINTS!
SOON
LOOK AT HIM! JUST ENJOYING HIS LUNCH. SO BRAZEN!
YOU THERE! YOU STOLE MY KEY!

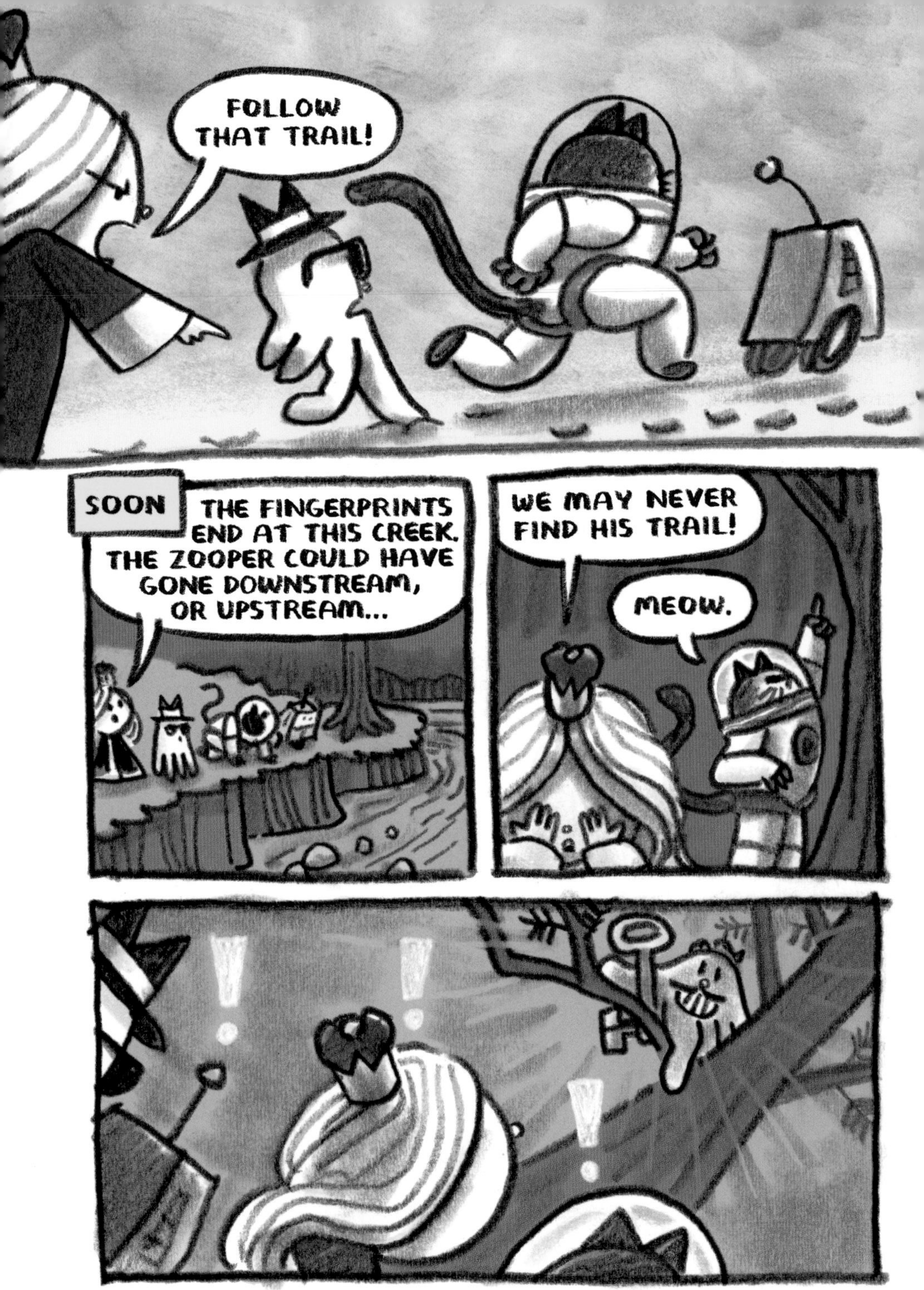
FOLLOW THAT TRAIL!
SOON
THE FINGERPRINTS END AT THIS CREEK. THE ZOOPER COULD HAVE GONE DOWNSTREAM, OR UPSTREAM...
WE MAY NEVER FIND HIS TRAIL!
MEOW.
!
!
!

TRIPLE ZOOP!

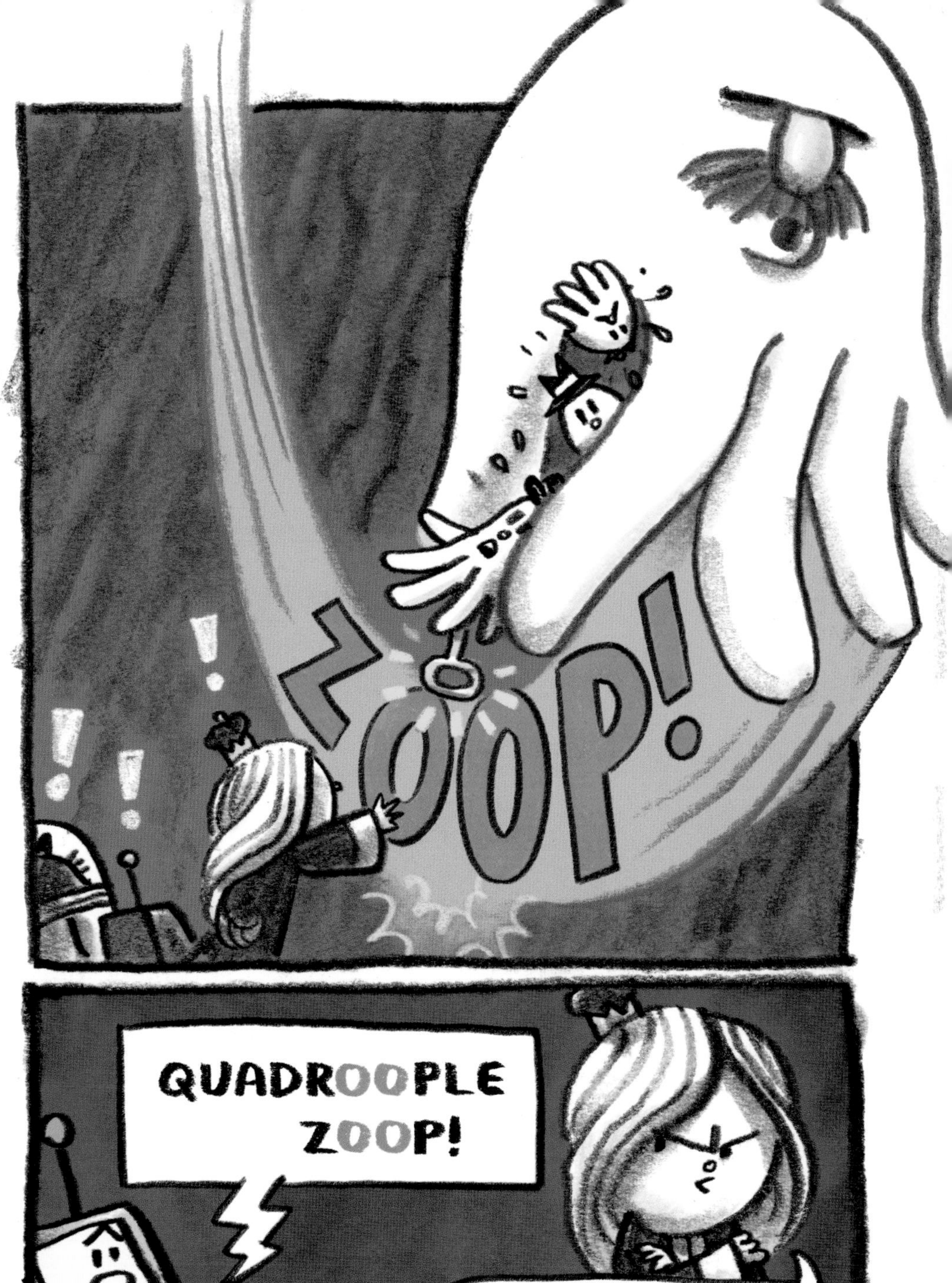
ZOOP!
QUADROOPLE ZOOP!
SO MUCH ZOOPING.

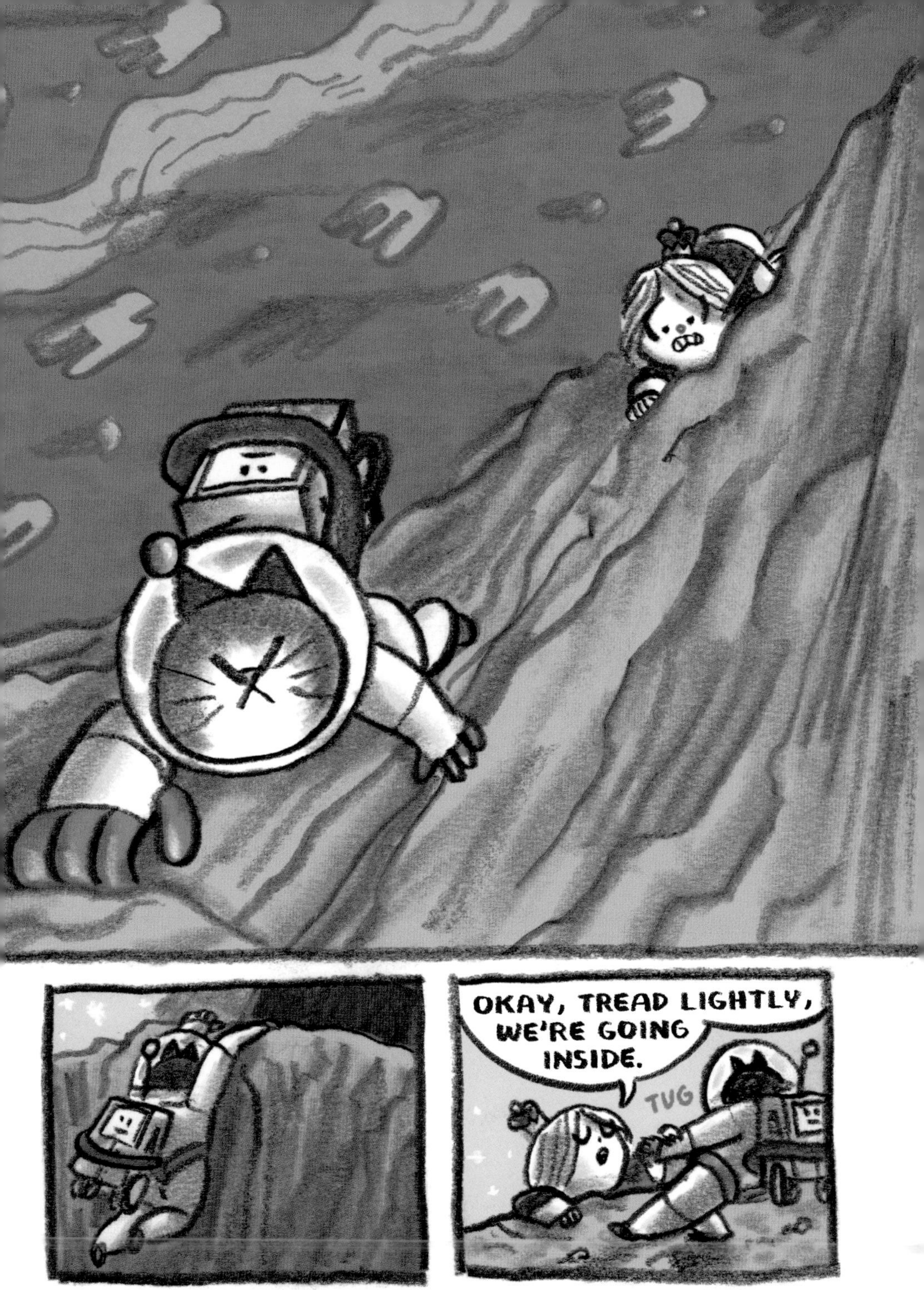
OKAY, TREAD LIGHTLY, WE'RE GOING INSIDE.
TUG

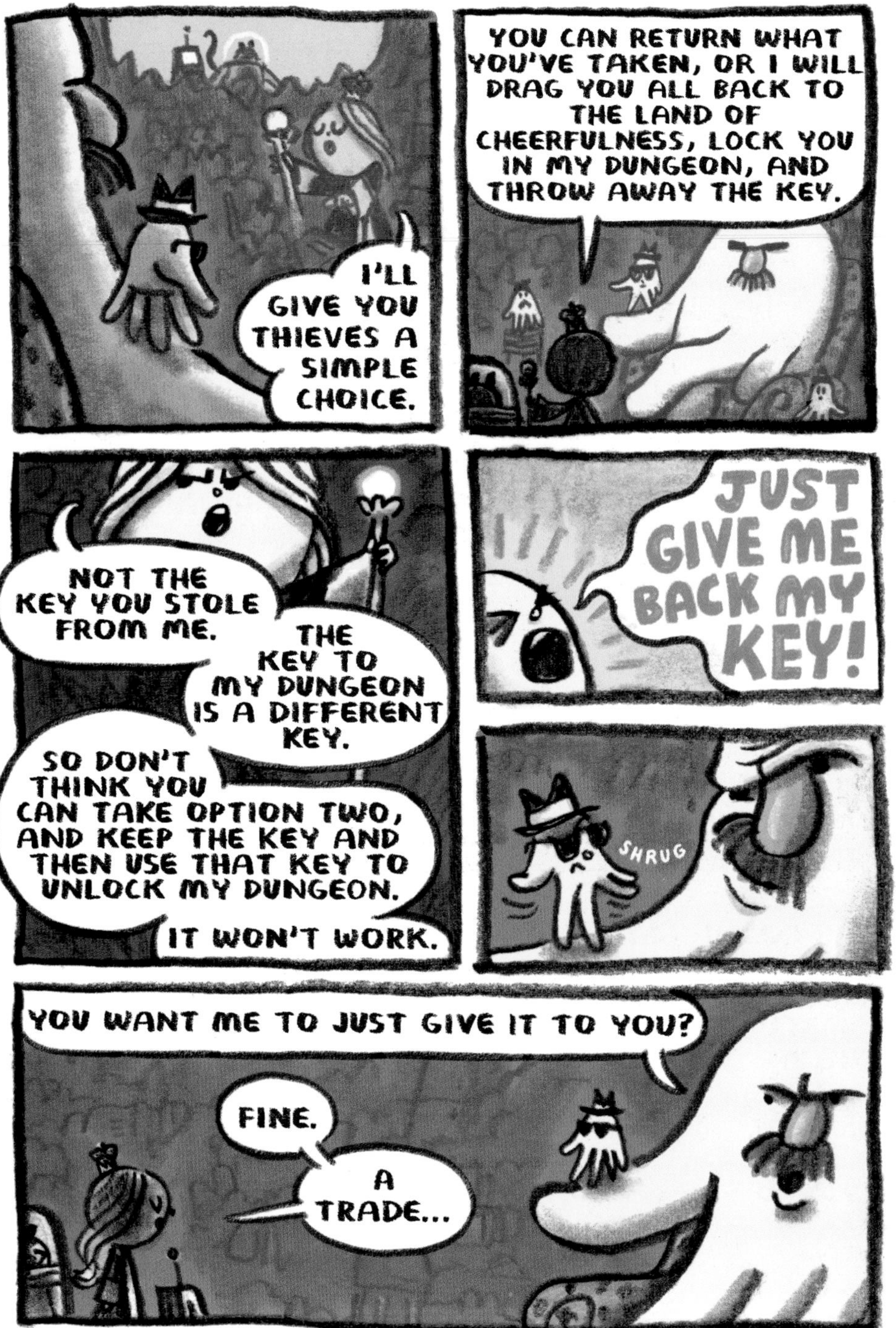
I'LL GIVE YOU THIEVES A SIMPLE CHOICE.
YOU CAN RETURN WHAT YOU'VE TAKEN, OR I WILL DRAG YOU ALL BACK TO THE LAND OF CHEERFULNESS, LOCK YOU IN MY DUNGEON, AND THROW AWAY THE KEY.
NOT THE KEY YOU STOLE FROM ME.
THE KEY TO MY DUNGEON IS A DIFFERENT KEY.
SO DON'T THINK YOU CAN TAKE OPTION TWO, AND KEEP THE KEY AND THEN USE THAT KEY TO UNLOCK MY DUNGEON.
IT WON'T WORK.
JUST GIVE ME BACK MY KEY!
SHRUG
YOU WANT ME TO JUST GIVE IT TO YOU?
FINE.
A TRADE...

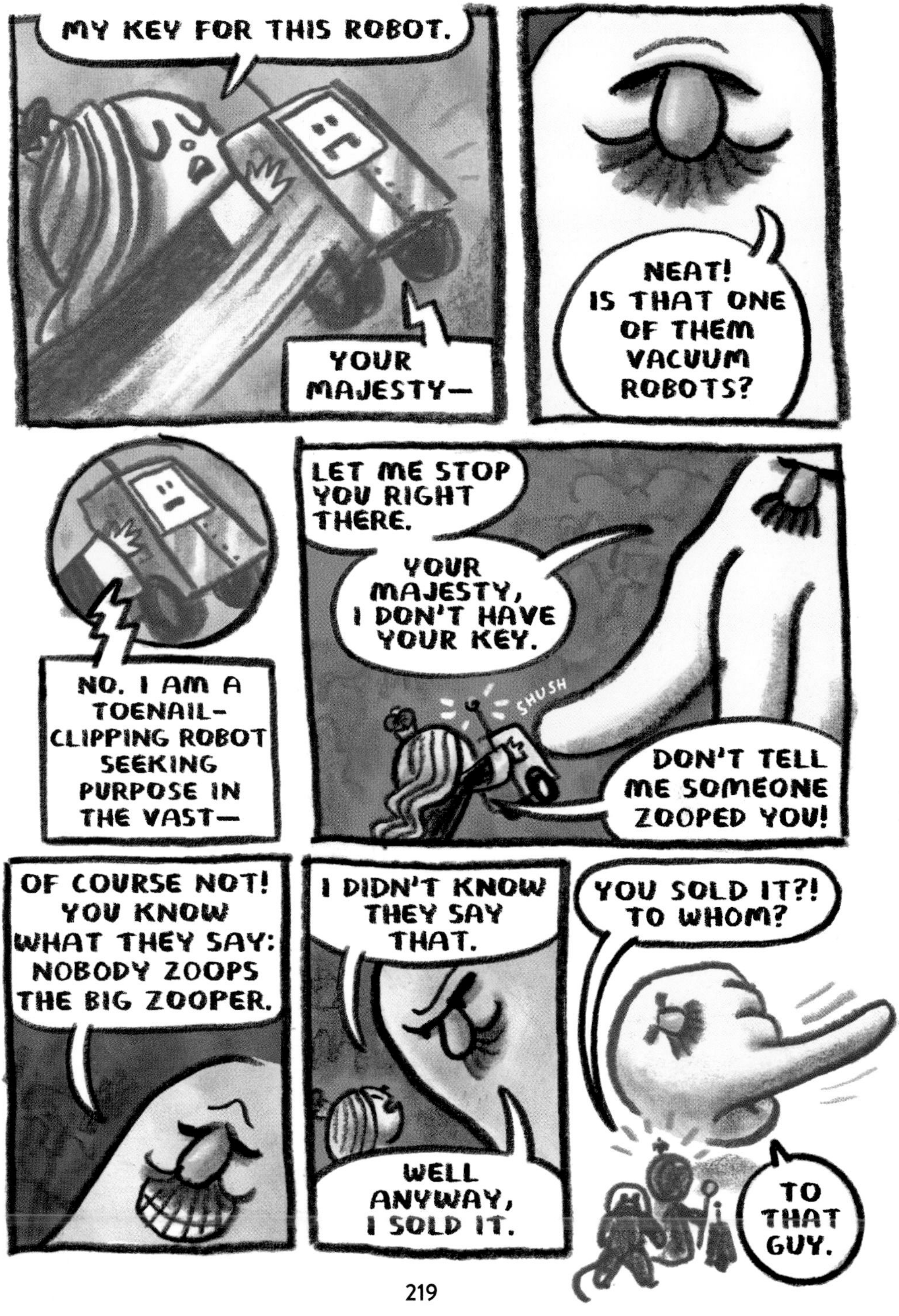
MY KEY FOR THIS ROBOT.
YOUR MAJESTY—
NEAT! IS THAT ONE OF THEM VACUUM ROBOTS?
NO. I AM A TOENAIL-CLIPPING ROBOT SEEKING PURPOSE IN THE VAST—
LET ME STOP YOU RIGHT THERE.
YOUR MAJESTY, I DON'T HAVE YOUR KEY.
SHUSH
DON'T TELL ME SOMEONE ZOOPED YOU!
OF COURSE NOT! YOU KNOW WHAT THEY SAY: NOBODY ZOOPS THE BIG ZOOPER.
I DIDN'T KNOW THEY SAY THAT.
WELL ANYWAY, I SOLD IT.
YOU SOLD IT?! TO WHOM?
TO THAT GUY.

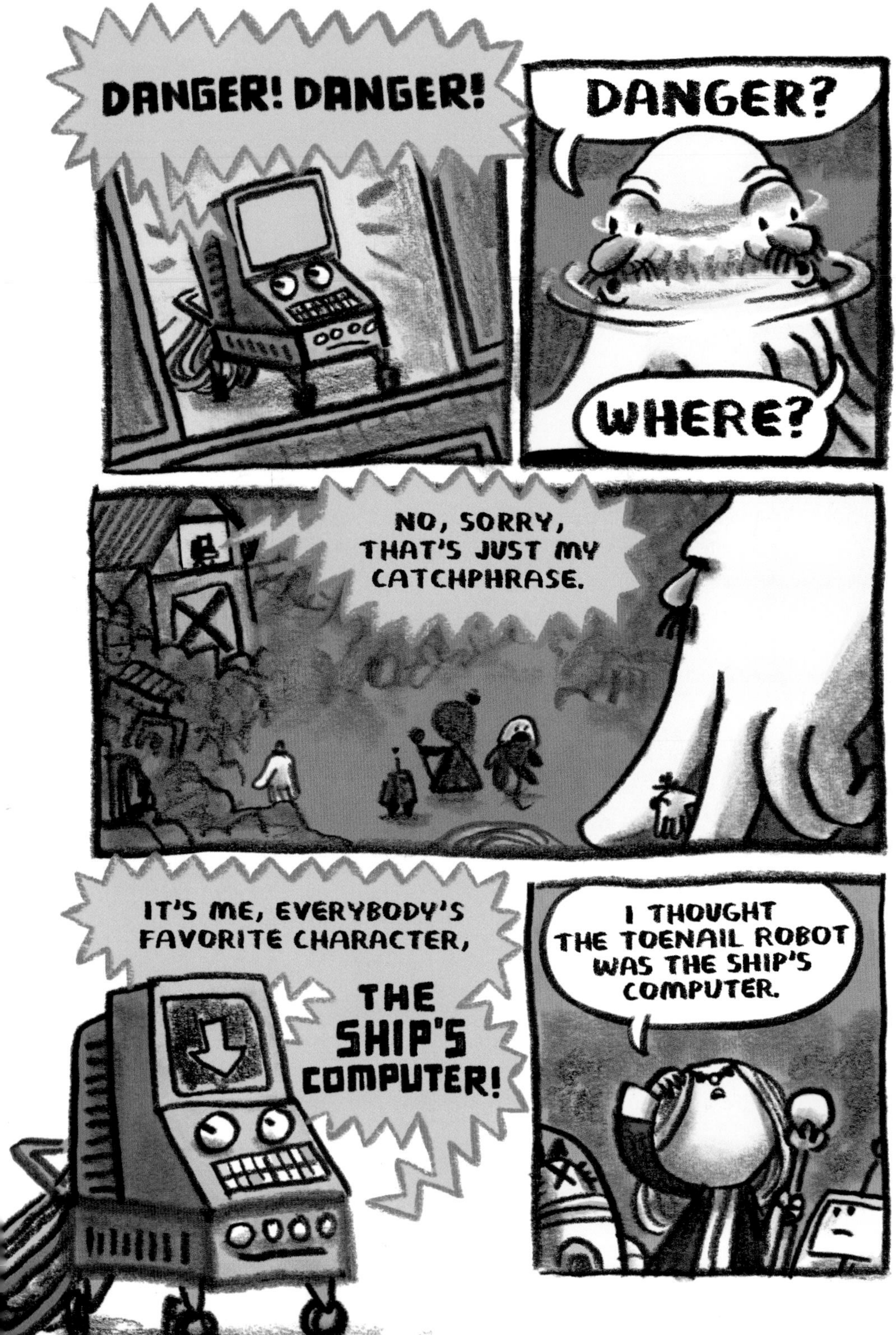

DANGER! DANGER!
DANGER?
WHERE?
NO, SORRY, THAT'S JUST MY CATCHPHRASE.
IT'S ME, EVERYBODY'S FAVORITE CHARACTER,
THE SHIP'S COMPUTER!
I THOUGHT THE TOENAIL ROBOT WAS THE SHIP'S COMPUTER.

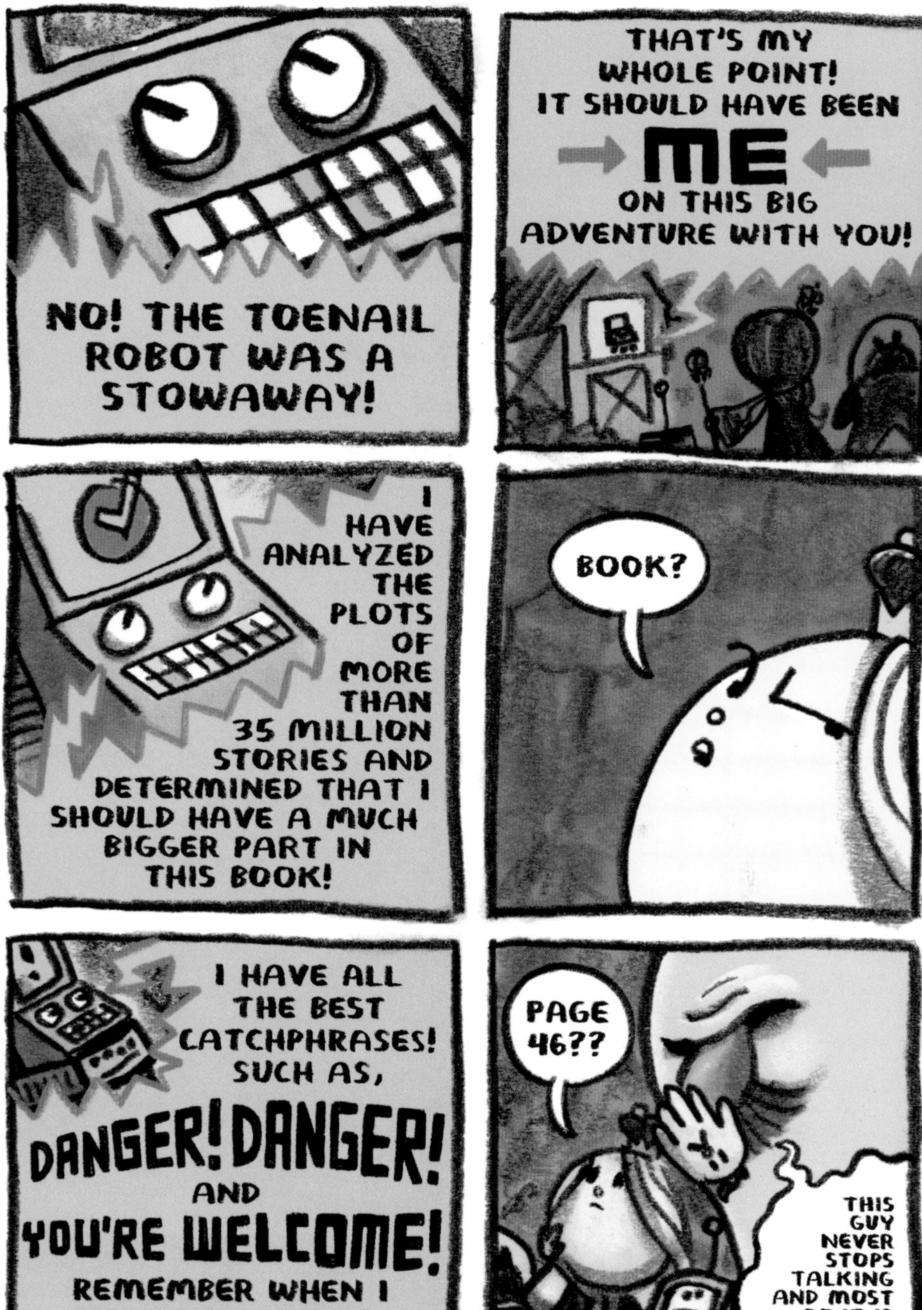
NO! THE TOENAIL ROBOT WAS A STOWAWAY!
THAT'S MY WHOLE POINT! IT SHOULD HAVE BEEN ME ON THIS BIG ADVENTURE WITH YOU!
I HAVE ANALYZED THE PLOTS OF MORE THAN 35 MILLION STORIES AND DETERMINED THAT I SHOULD HAVE A MUCH BIGGER PART IN THIS BOOK!
BOOK?
I HAVE ALL THE BEST CATCHPHRASES! SUCH AS, DANGER! DANGER! AND YOU'RE WELCOME! REMEMBER WHEN I FIRST SAID THAT? ON PAGE 46?
PAGE 46??
THIS GUY NEVER STOPS TALKING AND MOST OF IT IS COMPUTER GIBBERISH.

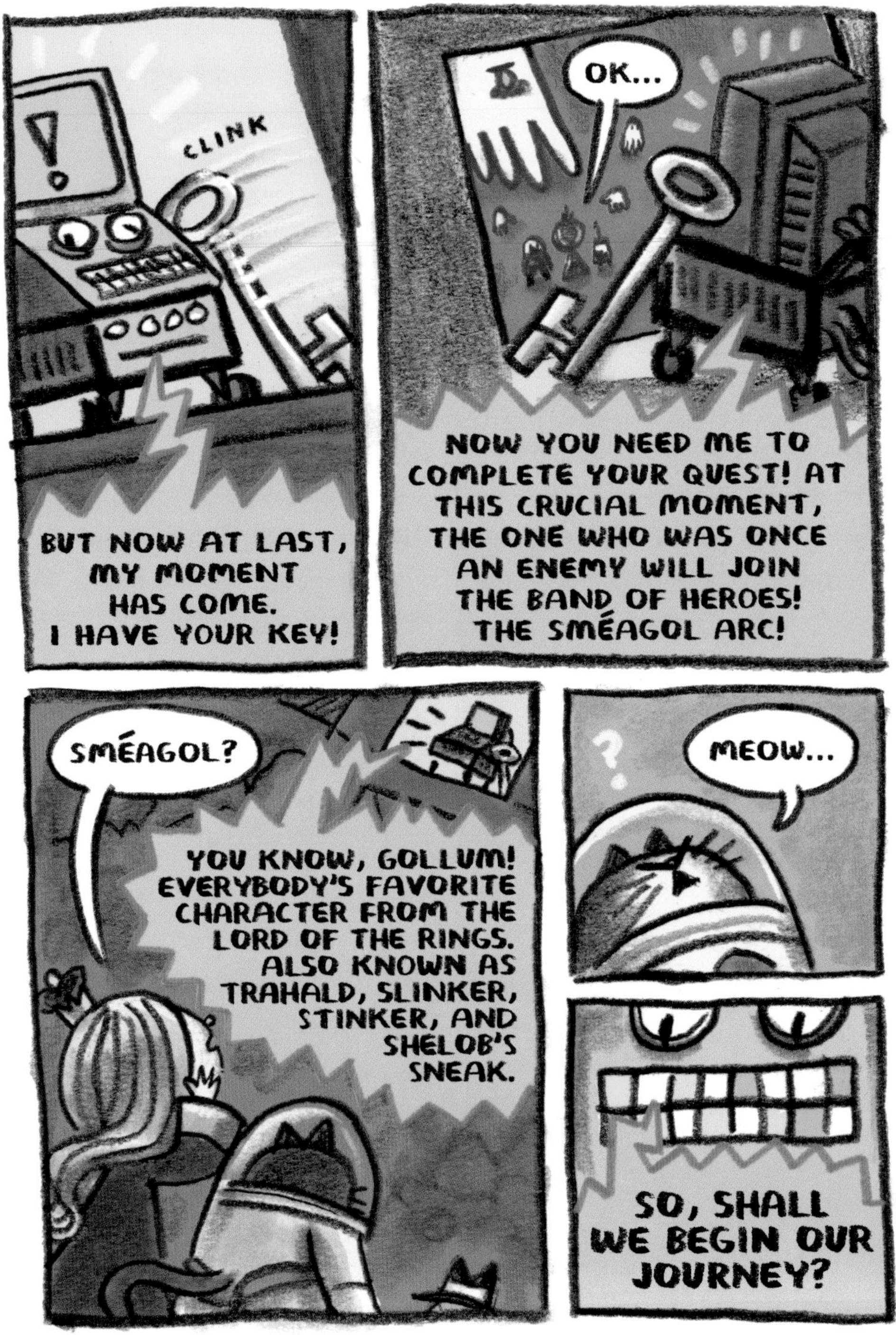
CLINK
BUT NOW AT LAST, MY MOMENT HAS COME. I HAVE YOUR KEY!
OK...
NOW YOU NEED ME TO COMPLETE YOUR QUEST! AT THIS CRUCIAL MOMENT, THE ONE WHO WAS ONCE AN ENEMY WILL JOIN THE BAND OF HEROES! THE SMÉAGOL ARC!
SMÉAGOL?
YOU KNOW, GOLLUM! EVERYBODY'S FAVORITE CHARACTER FROM THE LORD OF THE RINGS. ALSO KNOWN AS TRAHALD, SLINKER, STINKER, AND SHELOB'S SNEAK.
?
MEOW...
SO, SHALL WE BEGIN OUR JOURNEY?

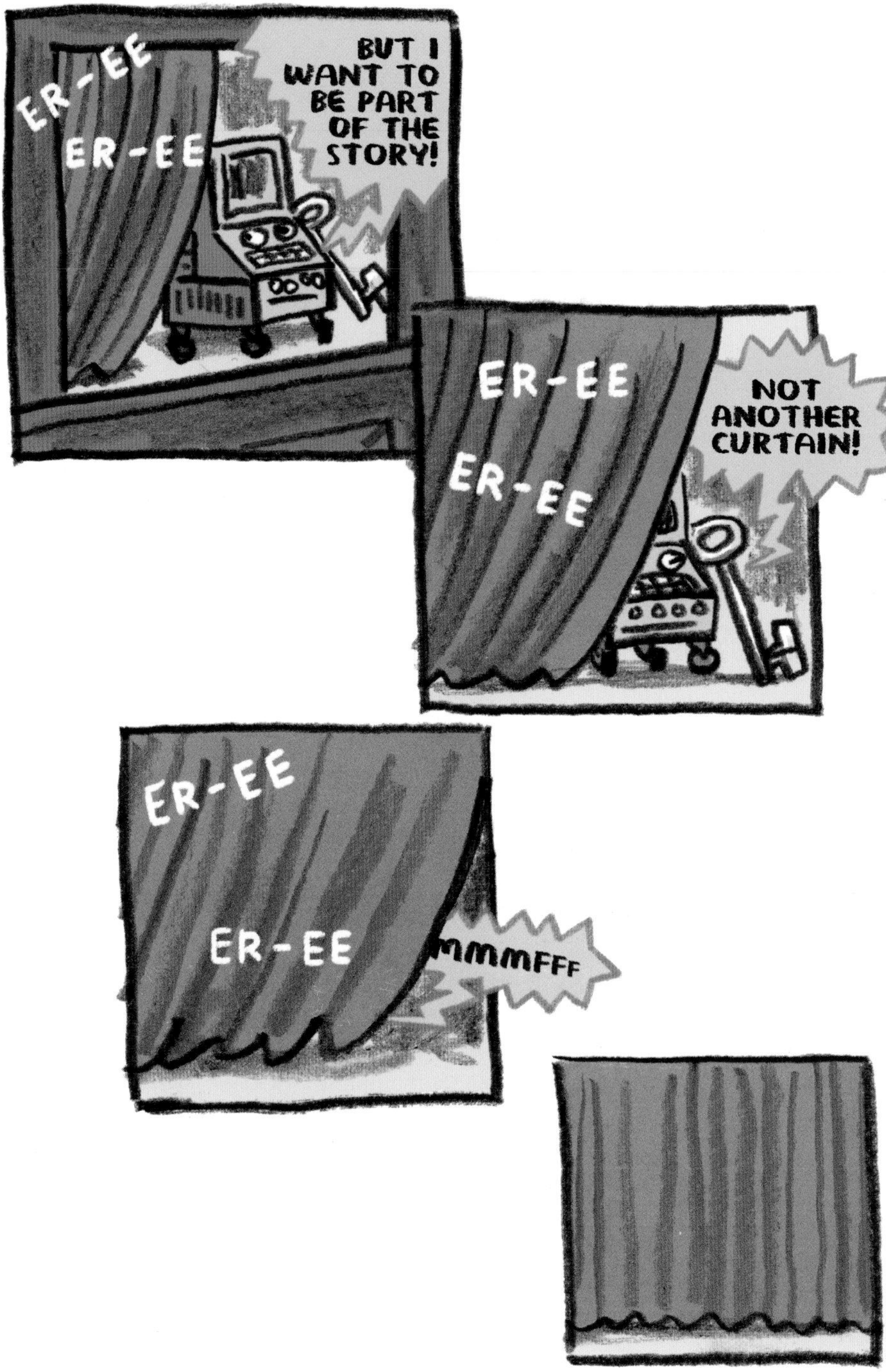
ER-EE
ER-EE
BUT I WANT TO BE PART OF THE STORY!
ER-EE
ER-EE
NOT ANOTHER CURTAIN!
ER-EE
ER-EE
MMMFFF

CHAPTER 18

THE RIDDLE OF THE SPHINX

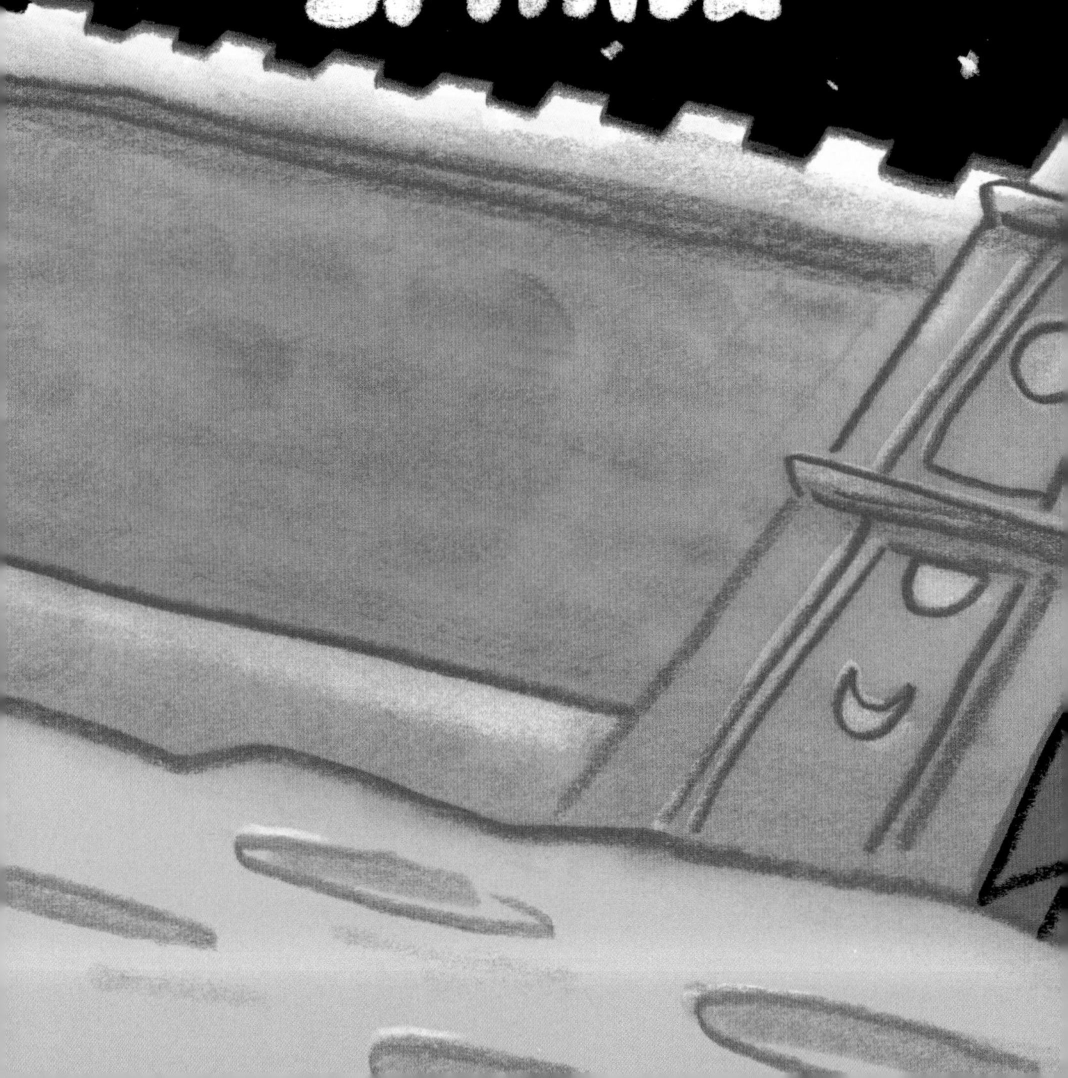

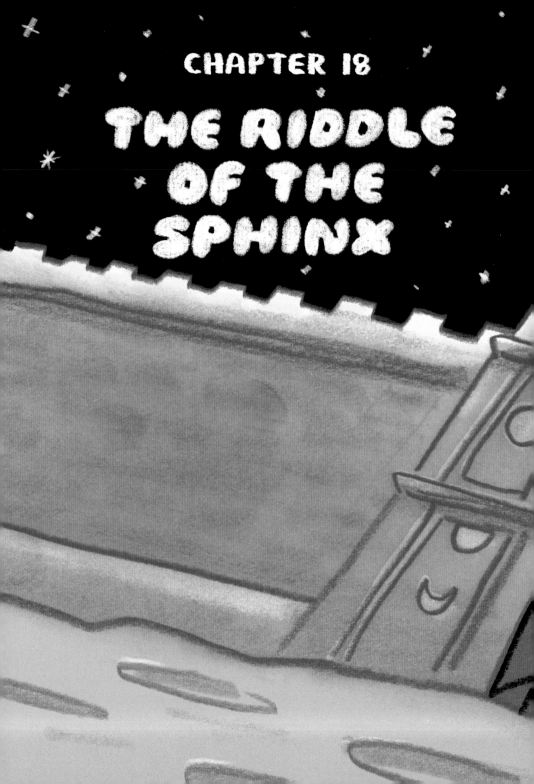

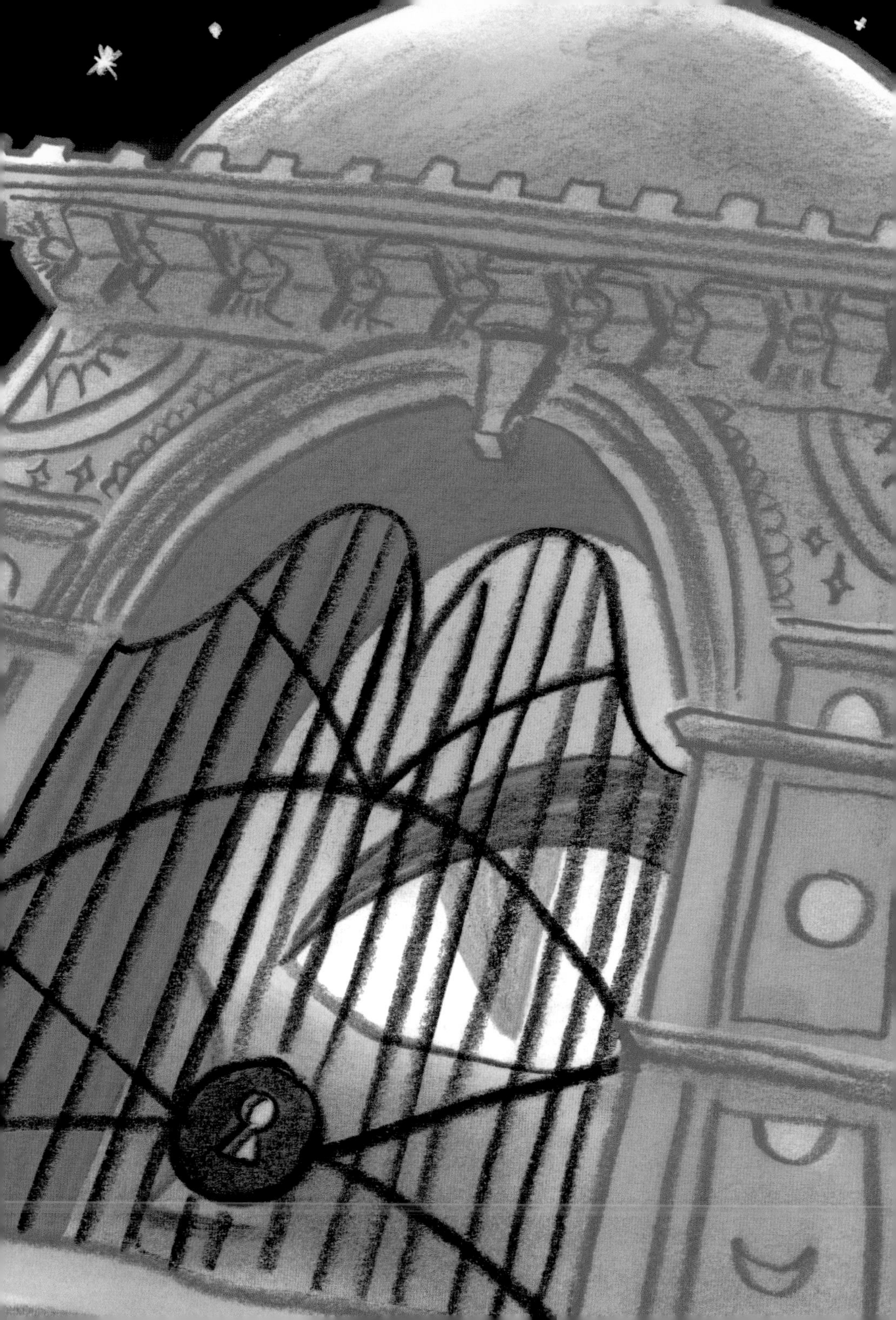

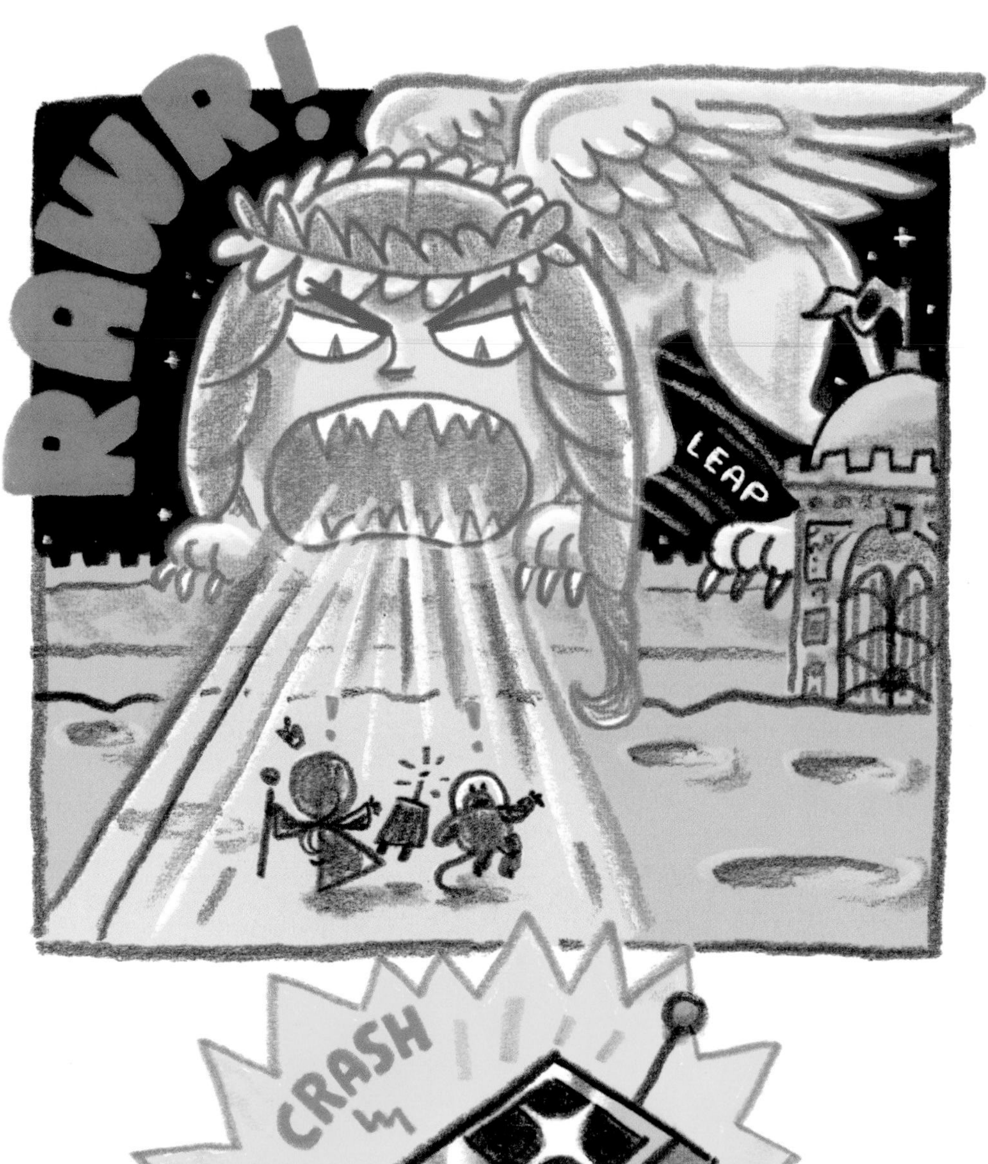
RAWR!
LEAP

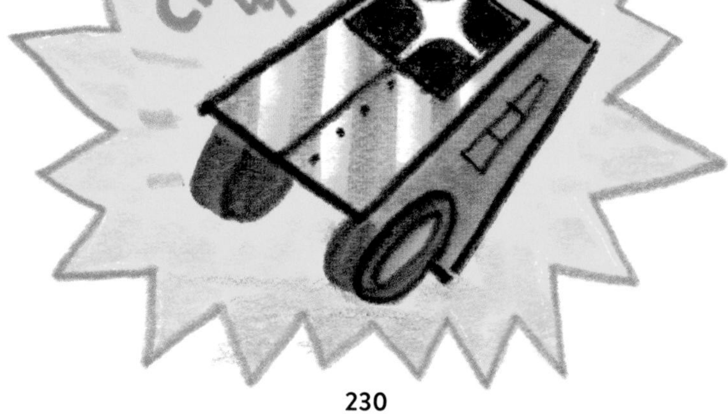
CRASH

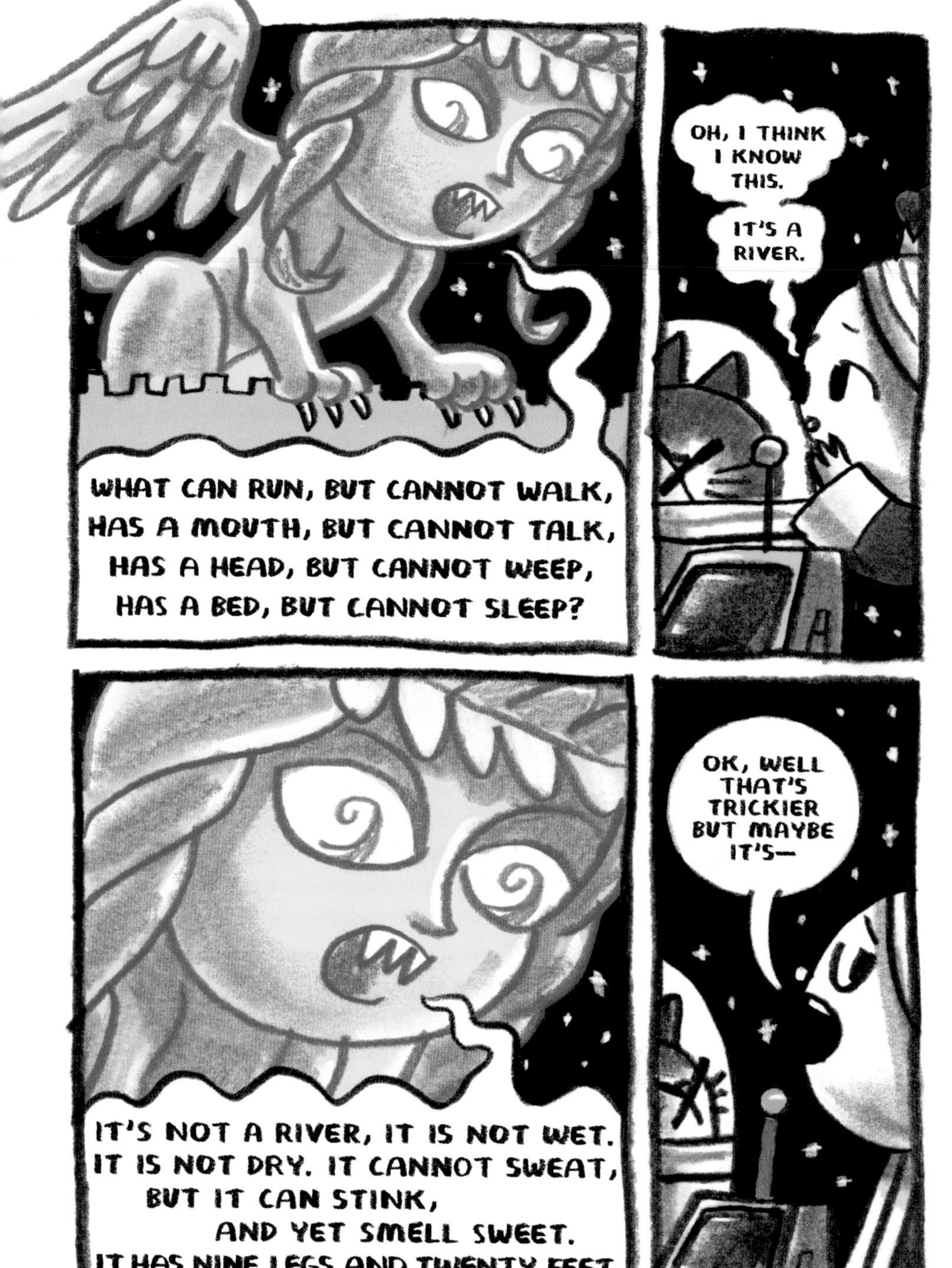
WHAT CAN RUN, BUT CANNOT WALK, HAS A MOUTH, BUT CANNOT TALK, HAS A HEAD, BUT CANNOT WEEP, HAS A BED, BUT CANNOT SLEEP?
OH, I THINK I KNOW THIS.
IT'S A RIVER.
IT'S NOT A RIVER, IT IS NOT WET. IT IS NOT DRY. IT CANNOT SWEAT, BUT IT CAN STINK, AND YET SMELL SWEET. IT HAS NINE LEGS AND TWENTY FEET.
OK, WELL THAT'S TRICKIER BUT MAYBE IT'S—

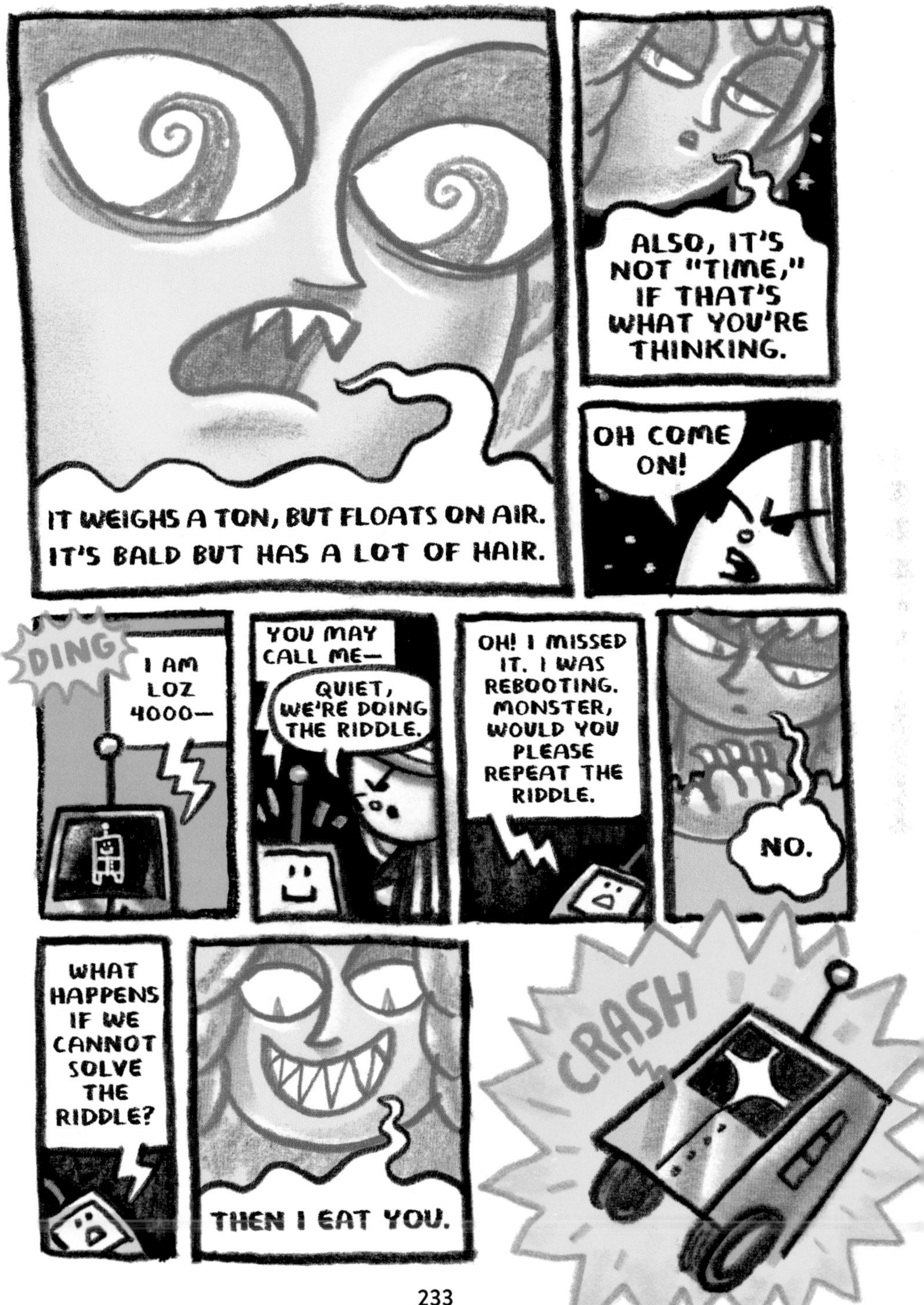

IT WEIGHS A TON, BUT FLOATS ON AIR.
IT'S BALD BUT HAS A LOT OF HAIR.
ALSO, IT'S NOT "TIME," IF THAT'S WHAT YOU'RE THINKING.
OH COME ON!
DING
I AM LOZ 4000—
YOU MAY CALL ME—
QUIET, WE'RE DOING THE RIDDLE.
OH! I MISSED IT. I WAS REBOOTING. MONSTER, WOULD YOU PLEASE REPEAT THE RIDDLE.
NO.
WHAT HAPPENS IF WE CANNOT SOLVE THE RIDDLE?
THEN I EAT YOU.
CRASH

234

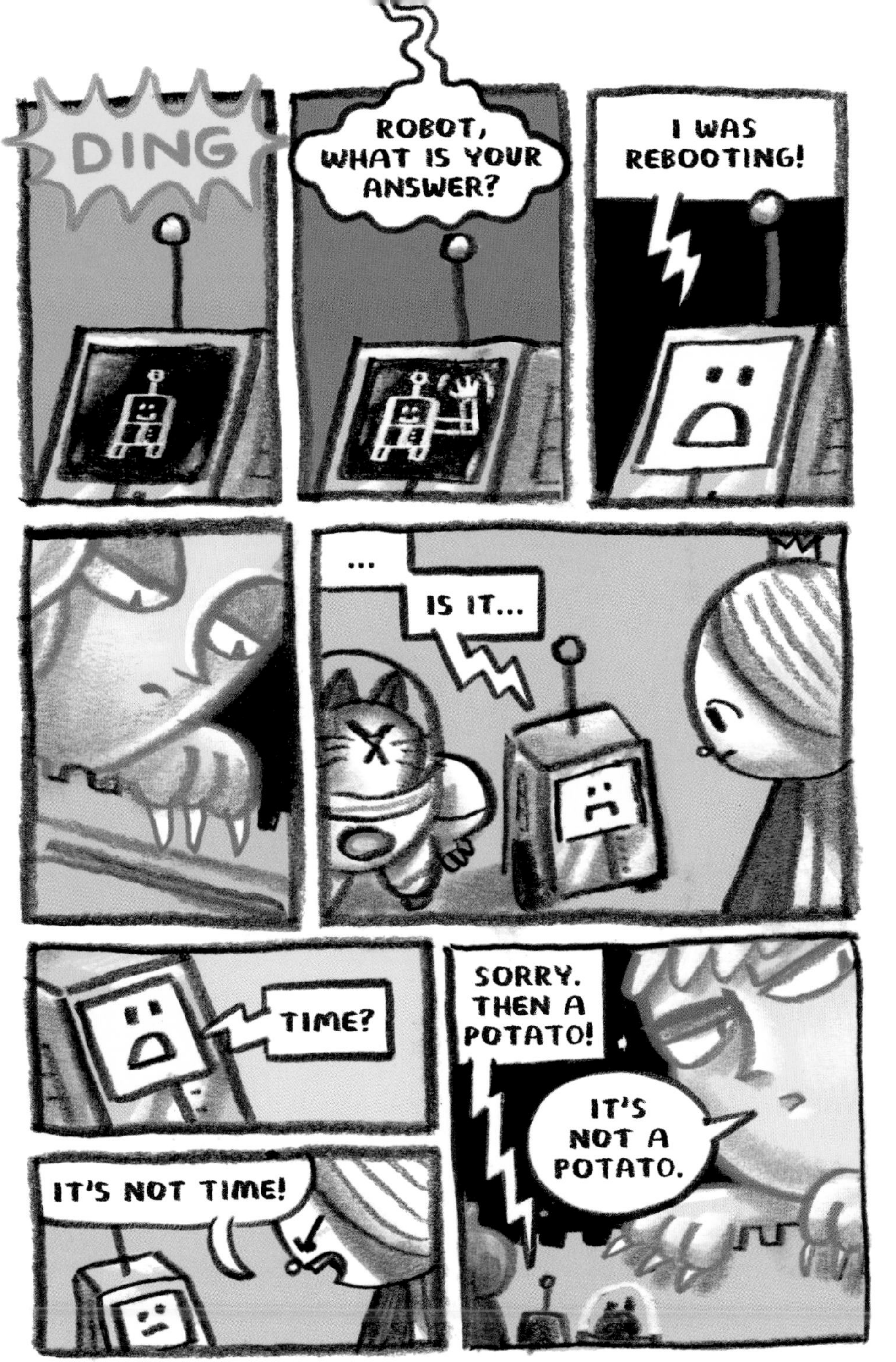
DING
ROBOT, WHAT IS YOUR ANSWER?
I WAS REBOOTING!
...
IS IT...
TIME?
IT'S NOT TIME!
SORRY. THEN A POTATO!
IT'S NOT A POTATO.

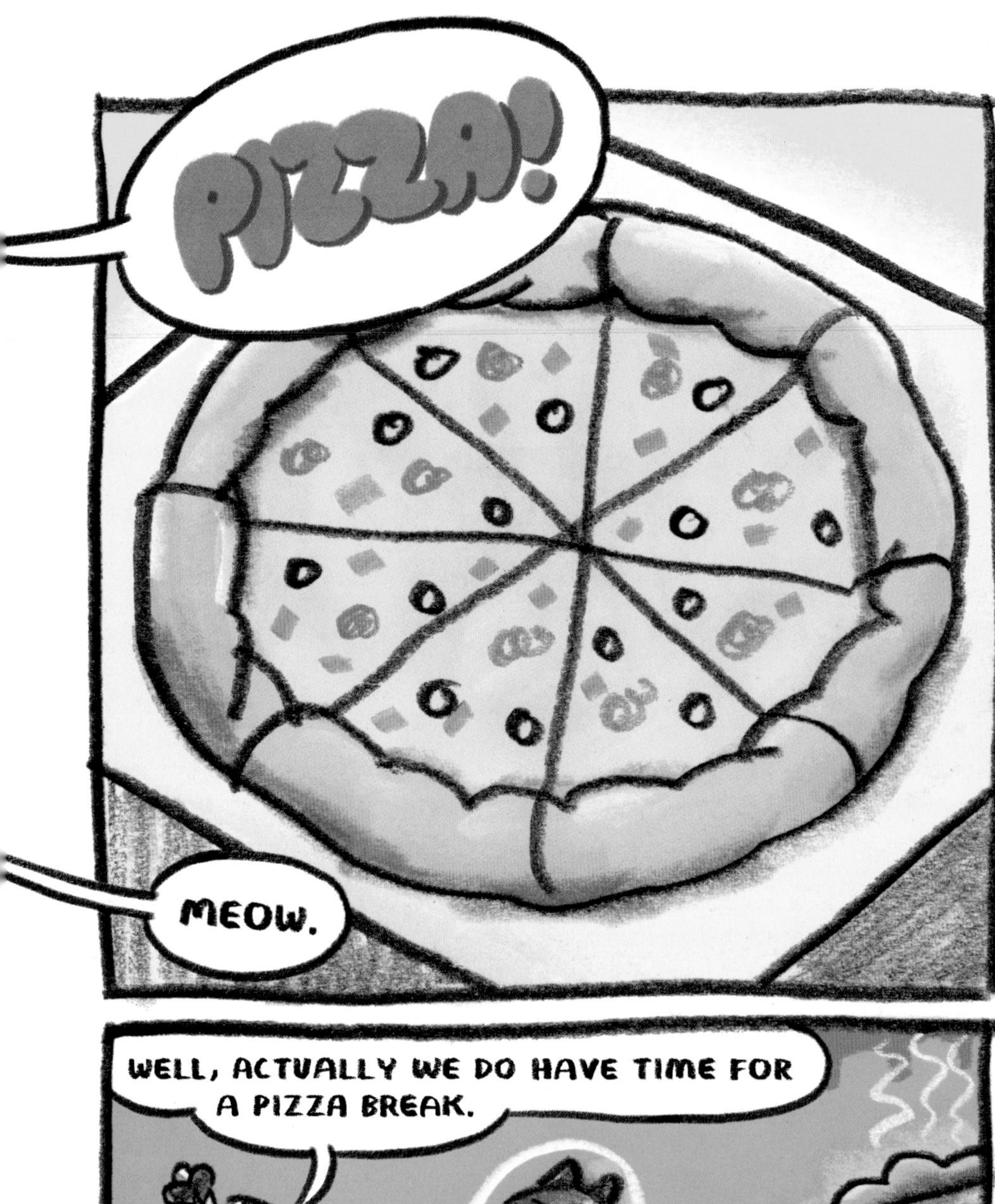
PIZZA!
MEOW.

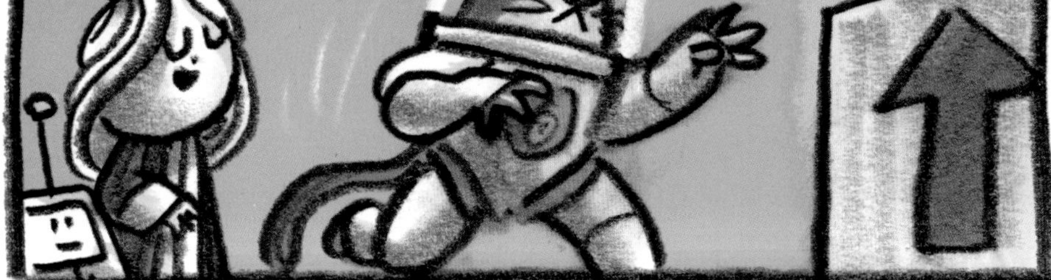
WELL, ACTUALLY WE DO HAVE TIME FOR A PIZZA BREAK.

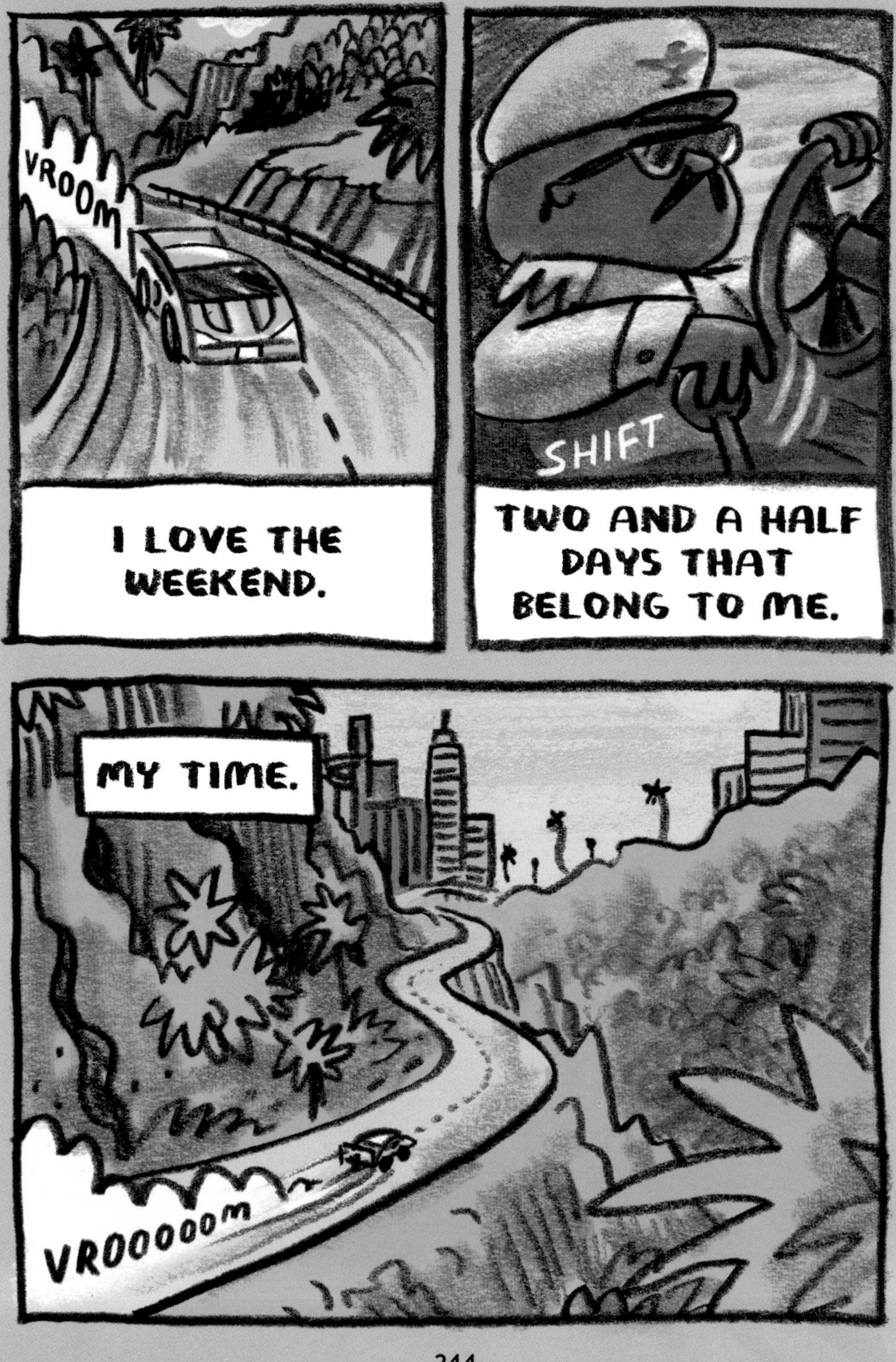
VROOM
I LOVE THE WEEKEND.
SHIFT
TWO AND A HALF DAYS THAT BELONG TO ME.
MY TIME.
VROOOOOOM

TIME TO HIT THE ROAD.

TURN UP.

OPEN

AND LET IT ALL HANG OUT.

IF THE WEEKEND HAD A SMELL,

THAT SMELL WOULD BE...

FREEDOM.

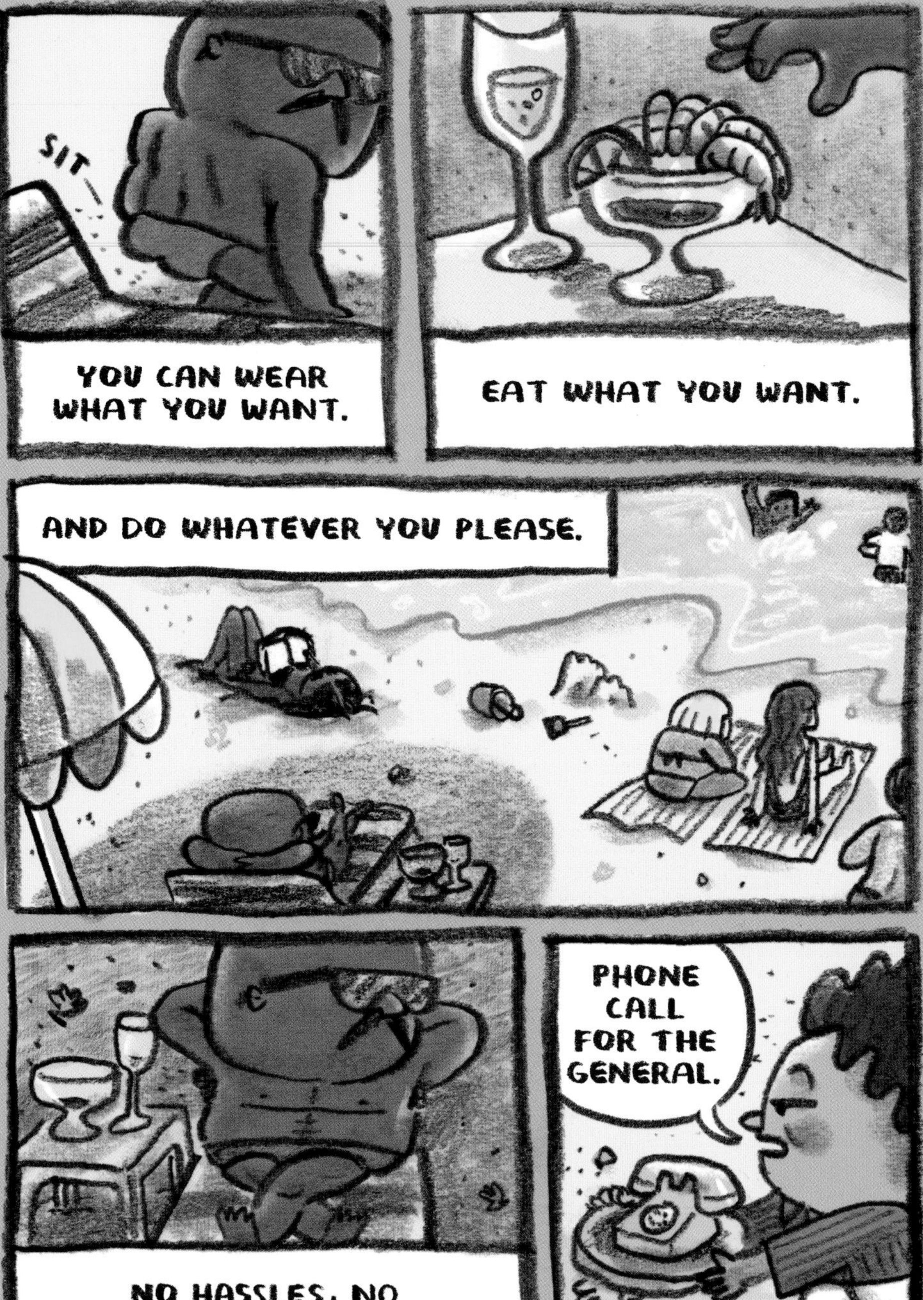
SIT
YOU CAN WEAR WHAT YOU WANT.
EAT WHAT YOU WANT.
AND DO WHATEVER YOU PLEASE.
NO HASSLES, NO INTERRUPTIONS. JUST—
PHONE CALL FOR THE GENERAL.

CHAPTER 19
THE
PIT

SUPER TELESCOPE IMG 47X

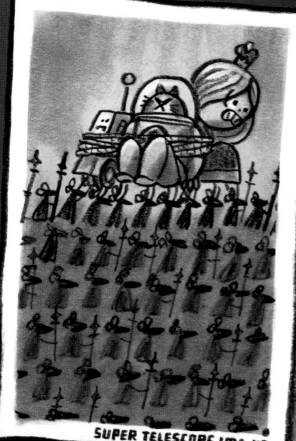

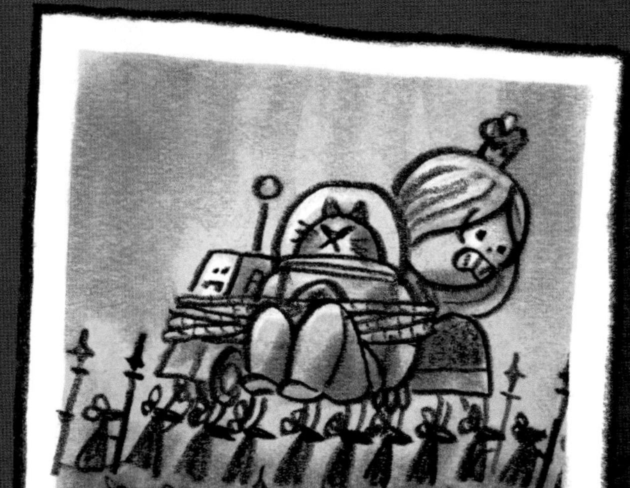
SUPER TELESCOPE IMG 47Y

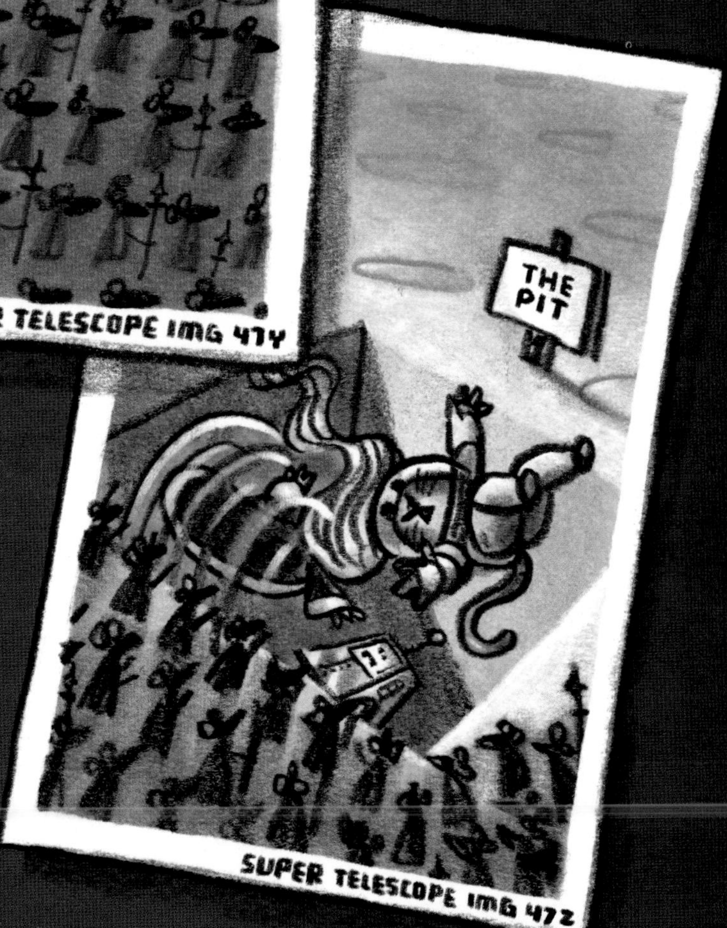
THE PIT
SUPER TELESCOPE IMG 47Z

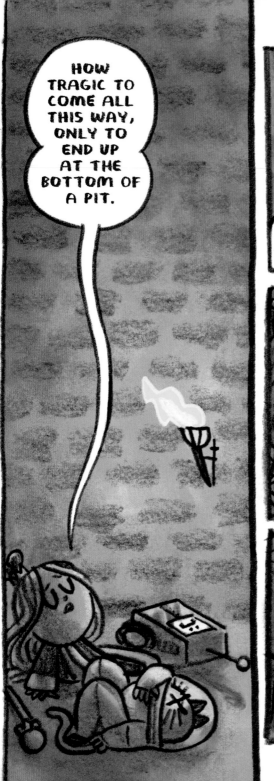

I LOVE THE MOON. THIS IS MY HOME.

GOODBYE, SWEET REALM. I'M SORRY.

SCOOP

TOUCH

PAFFFFFF

YOUR MAJESTY! WE MUST HAVE HOPE!

OUR SITUATION IS HOPELESS.

WE'VE HIT ROCK BOTTOM.

HA.

OUR PLIGHT AMUSES YOU, TOENAIL ROBOT?

I DID NOT LAUGH.

THEN WHO DID?

251

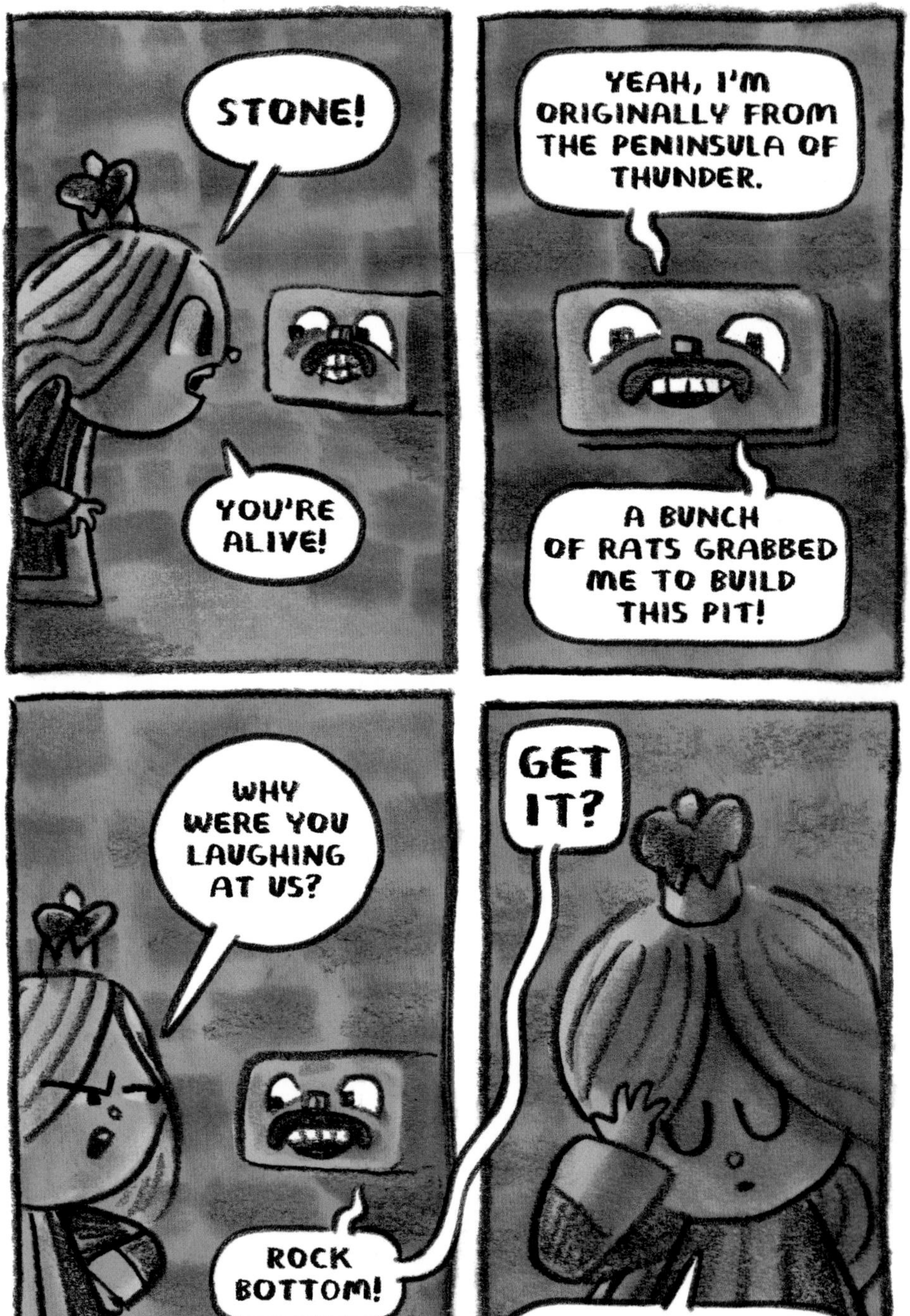
STONE!
YOU'RE ALIVE!
YEAH, I'M ORIGINALLY FROM THE PENINSULA OF THUNDER.
A BUNCH OF RATS GRABBED ME TO BUILD THIS PIT!
WHY WERE YOU LAUGHING AT US?
ROCK BOTTOM!
GET IT?
OH YEAH, I GET IT.

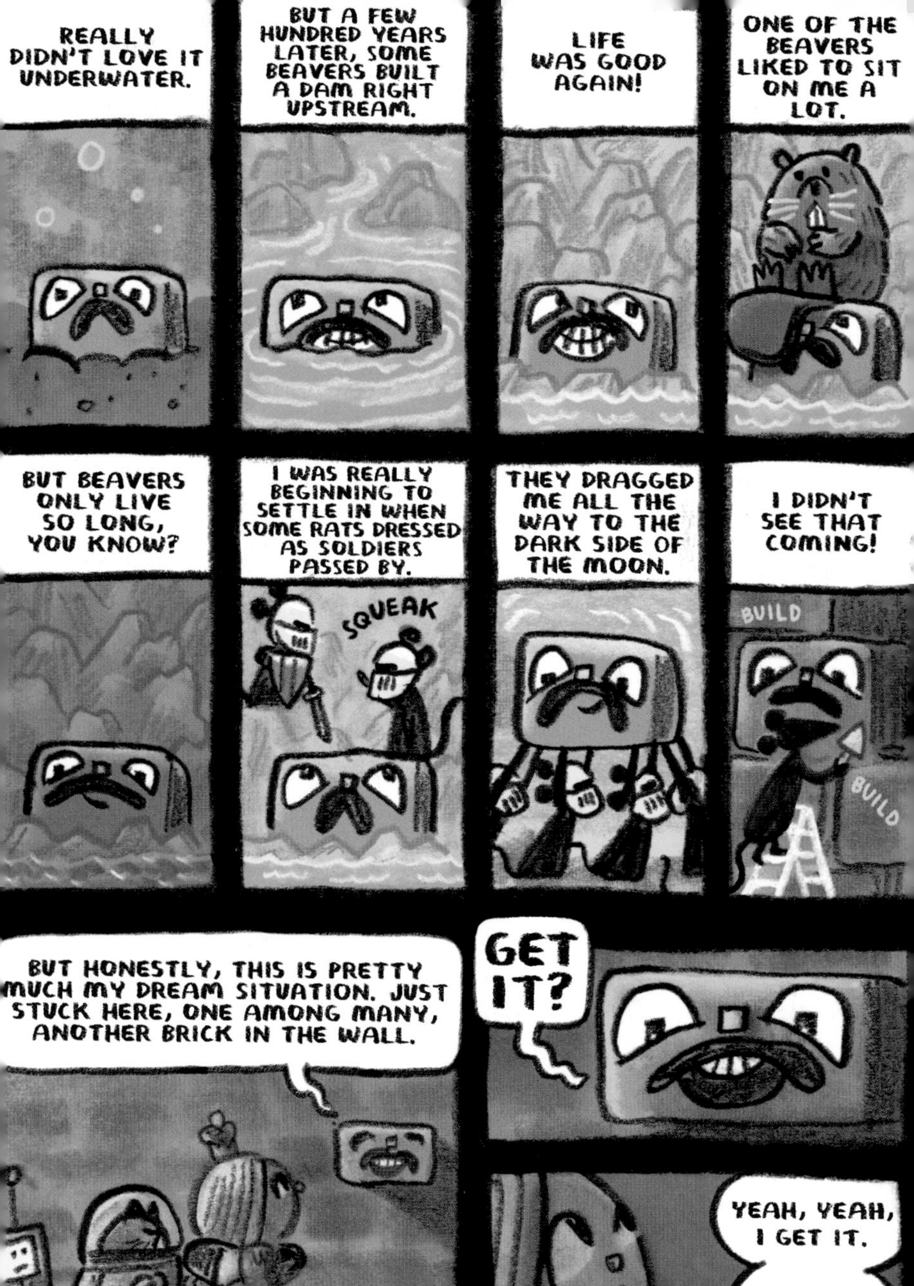
REALLY DIDN'T LOVE IT UNDERWATER.
BUT A FEW HUNDRED YEARS LATER, SOME BEAVERS BUILT A DAM RIGHT UPSTREAM.
LIFE WAS GOOD AGAIN!
ONE OF THE BEAVERS LIKED TO SIT ON ME A LOT.
BUT BEAVERS ONLY LIVE SO LONG, YOU KNOW?
I WAS REALLY BEGINNING TO SETTLE IN WHEN SOME RATS DRESSED AS SOLDIERS PASSED BY.
SQUEAK
THEY DRAGGED ME ALL THE WAY TO THE DARK SIDE OF THE MOON.
I DIDN'T SEE THAT COMING!
BUILD
BUILD
BUT HONESTLY, THIS IS PRETTY MUCH MY DREAM SITUATION. JUST STUCK HERE, ONE AMONG MANY, ANOTHER BRICK IN THE WALL.
GET IT?
YEAH, YEAH, I GET IT.
STONE, I HAVE TO SAY...

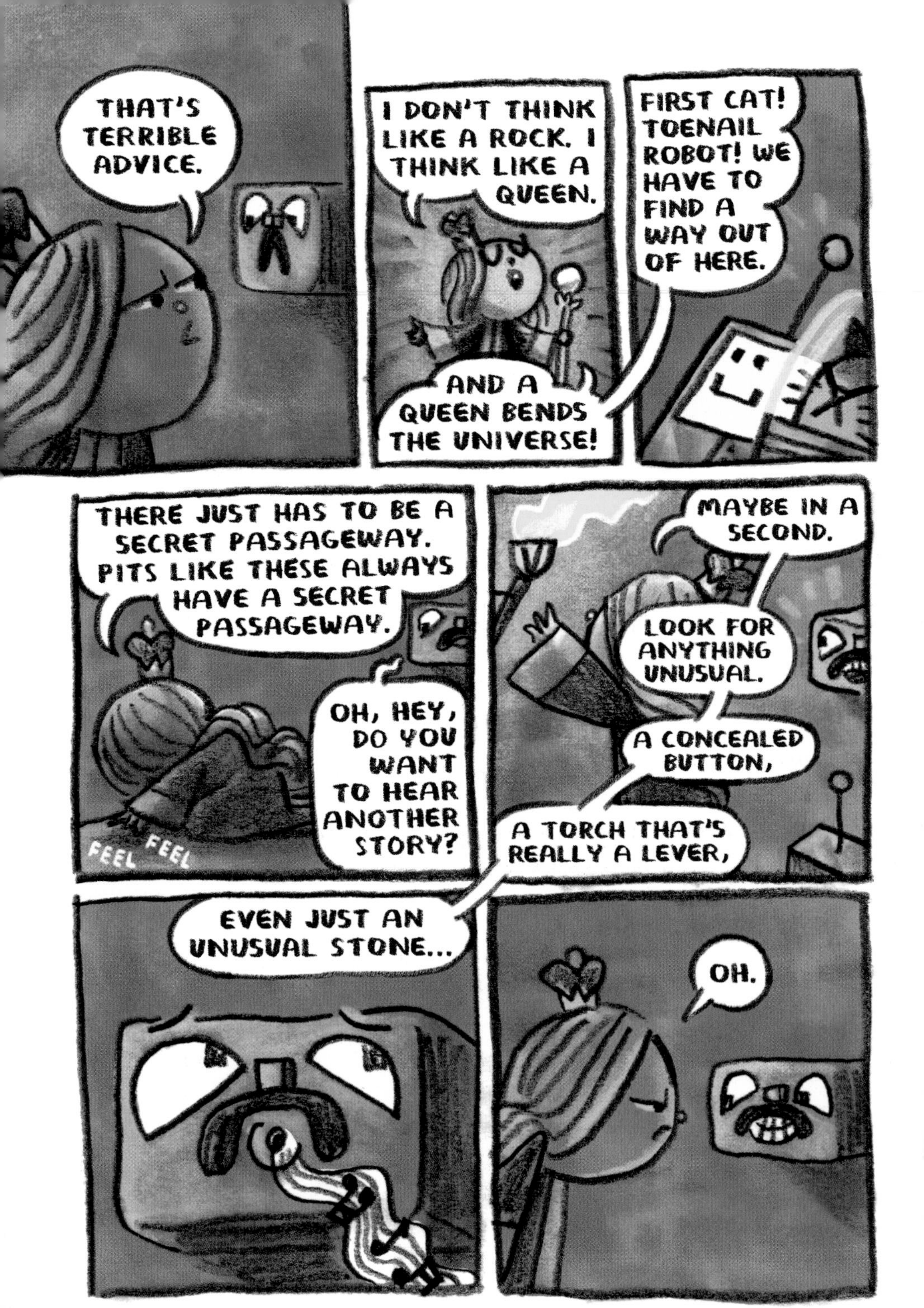
THAT'S TERRIBLE ADVICE.
I DON'T THINK LIKE A ROCK. I THINK LIKE A QUEEN.
AND A QUEEN BENDS THE UNIVERSE!
FIRST CAT! TOENAIL ROBOT! WE HAVE TO FIND A WAY OUT OF HERE.
THERE JUST HAS TO BE A SECRET PASSAGEWAY. PITS LIKE THESE ALWAYS HAVE A SECRET PASSAGEWAY.
OH, HEY, DO YOU WANT TO HEAR ANOTHER STORY?
FEEL FEEL
MAYBE IN A SECOND.
LOOK FOR ANYTHING UNUSUAL.
A CONCEALED BUTTON,
A TORCH THAT'S REALLY A LEVER,
EVEN JUST AN UNUSUAL STONE...
OH.

IF YOU STAY HERE, I'LL TELL YOU ABOUT THIS BEAR THAT USED TO SIT ON ME!

SORRY.

NO, NO,

FINGERS ALWAYS SMUDGE MY FACE!

PUUUUUSH

GETTING PUSHED CHAFES MY SIDES!

CLICK

MMFFFMM MFFMFMM

SLIDE

RAT TUNNELS!

WHICH WAY TO THE FORTRESS?

SNIFF SNIFF

MEOW.

LET'S MOVE!

CHAPTER 20
FINAL COUNTDOWN

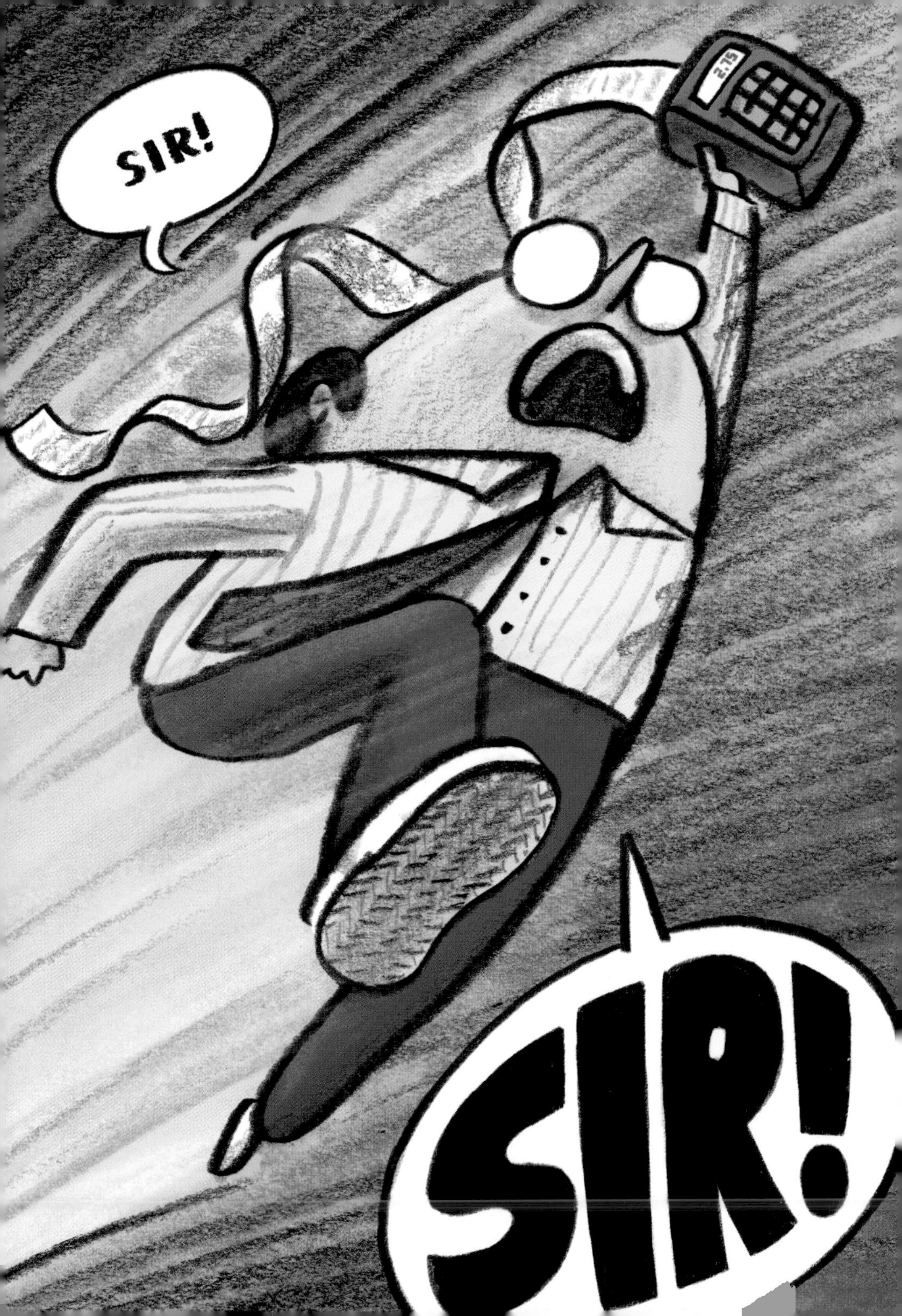
SIR!
SIR!

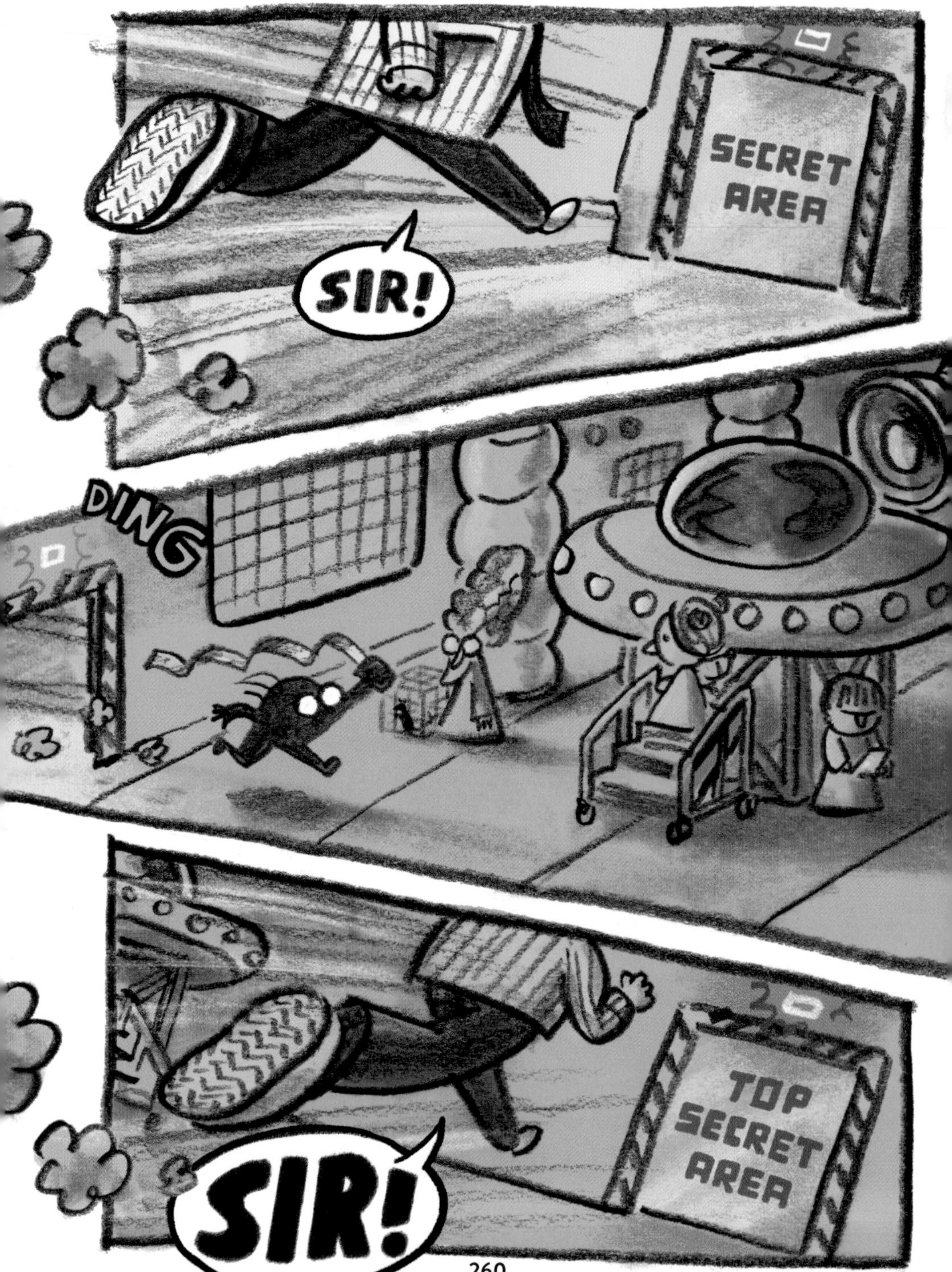
SECRET AREA
SIR!
DING
SIR!
TOP SECRET AREA

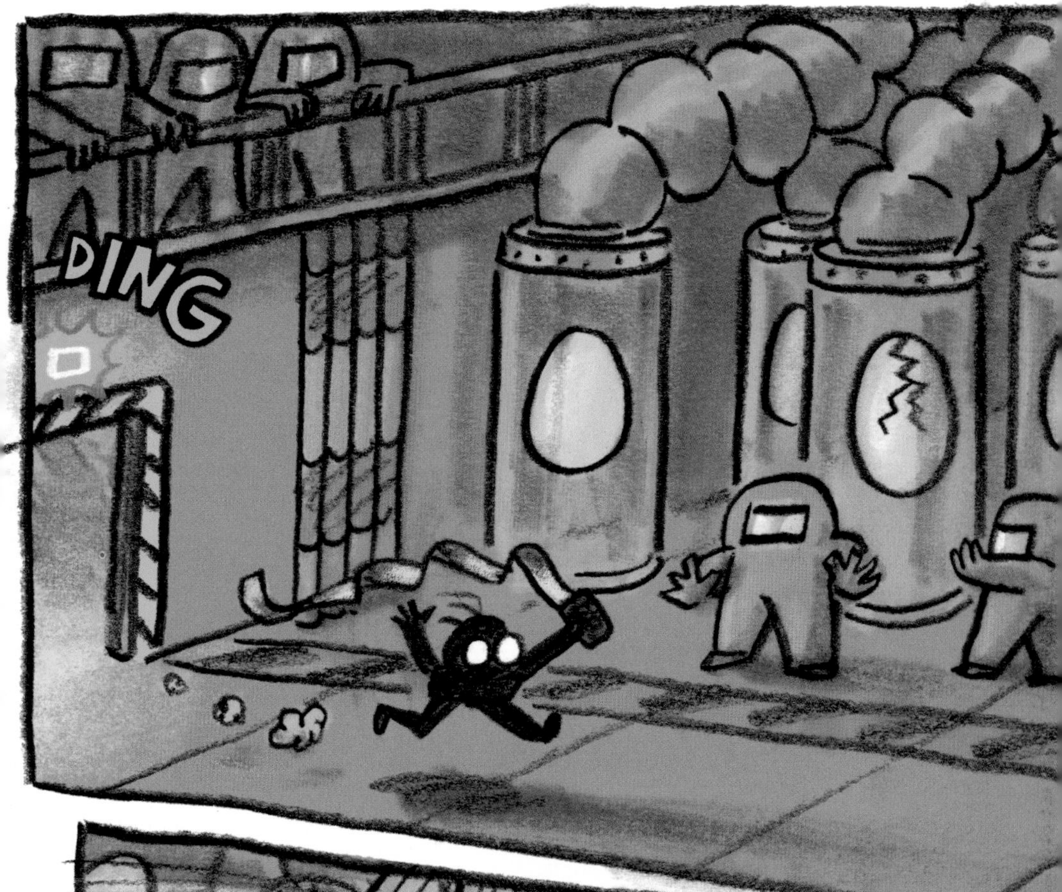
DING

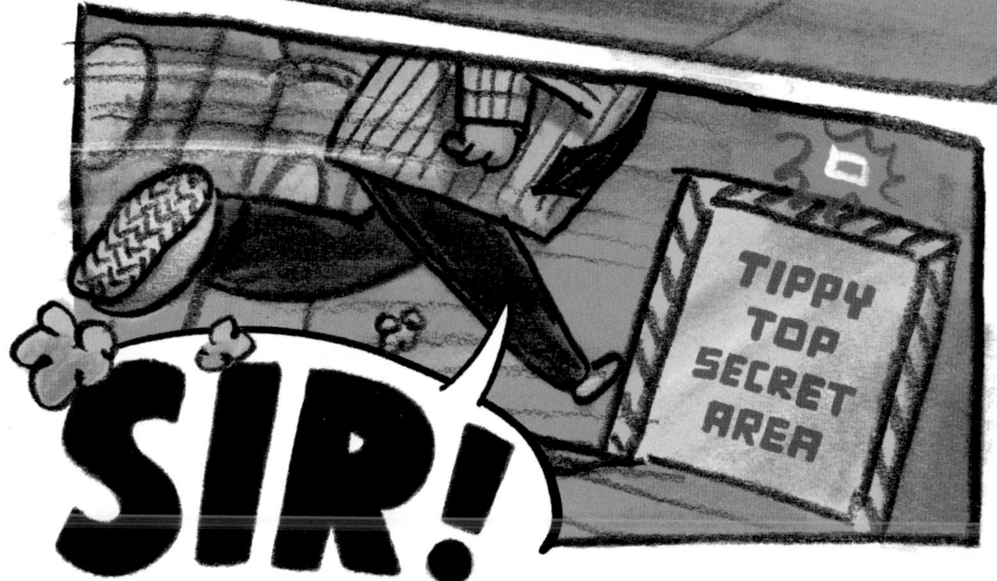
TIPPY TOP SECRET AREA
SIR!

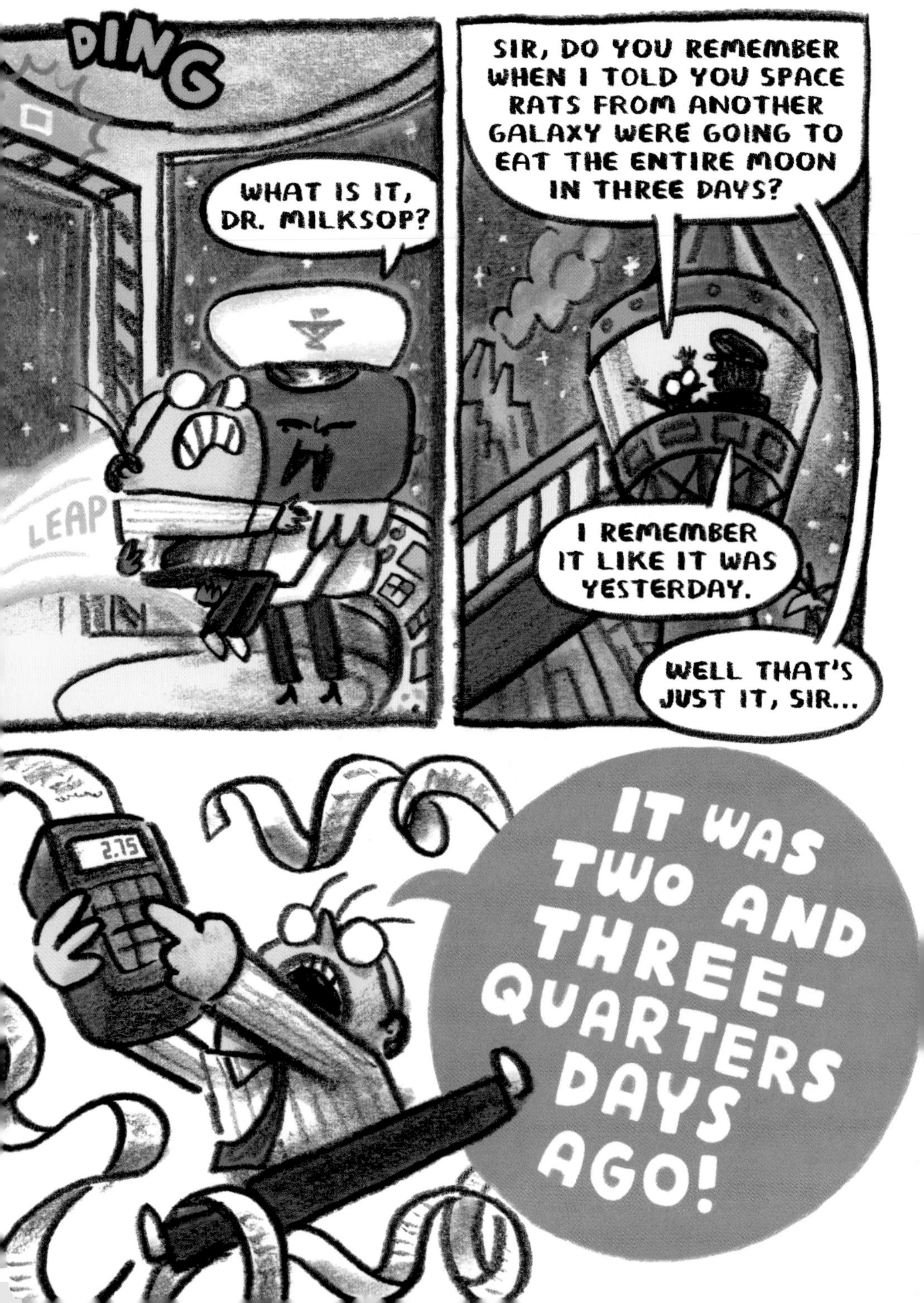
DING
WHAT IS IT, DR. MILKSOP?
LEAP
SIR, DO YOU REMEMBER WHEN I TOLD YOU SPACE RATS FROM ANOTHER GALAXY WERE GOING TO EAT THE ENTIRE MOON IN THREE DAYS?
I REMEMBER IT LIKE IT WAS YESTERDAY.
WELL THAT'S JUST IT, SIR...
2.75
IT WAS TWO AND THREE-QUARTERS DAYS AGO!

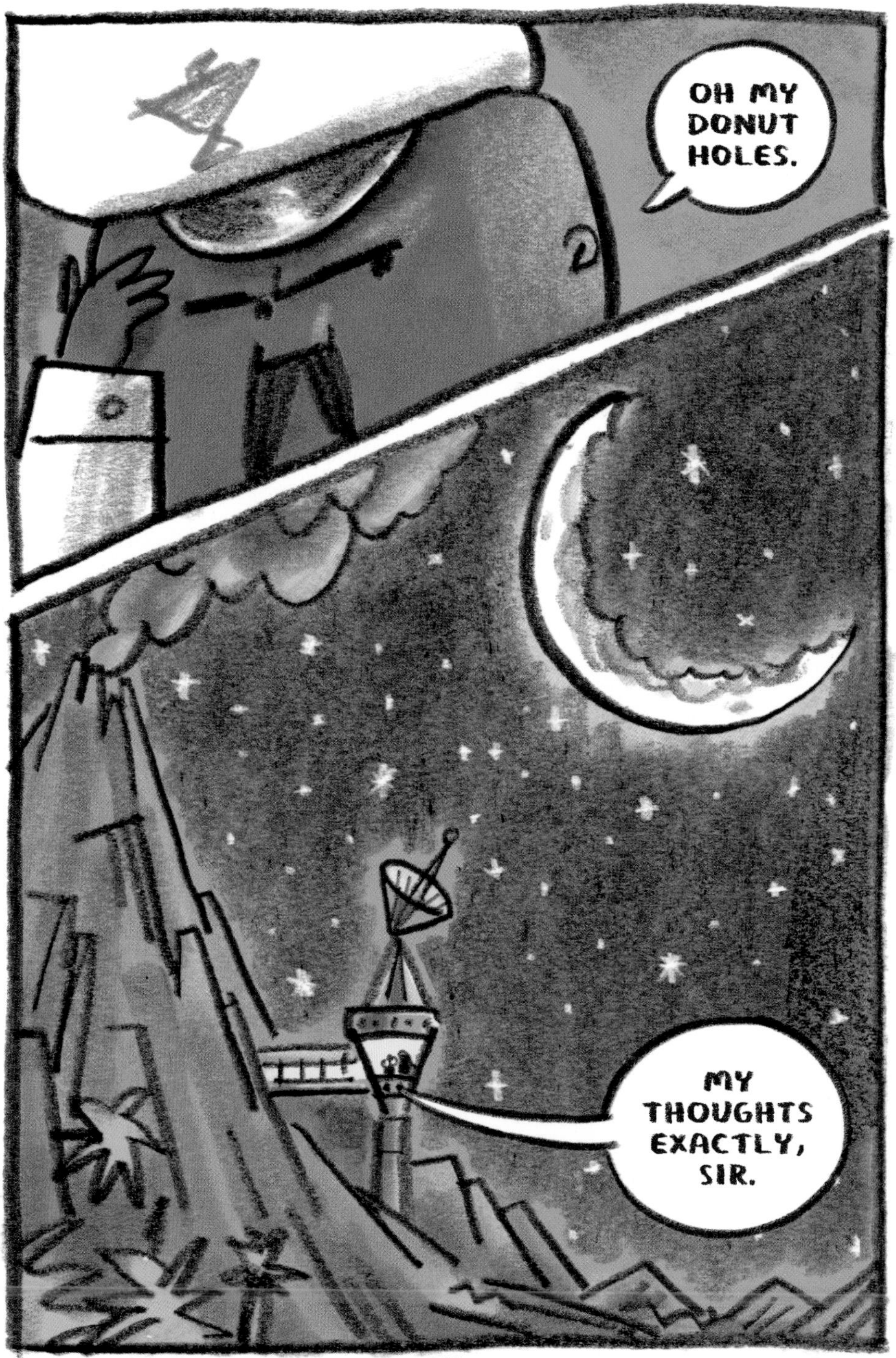
OH MY DONUT HOLES.
MY THOUGHTS EXACTLY, SIR.

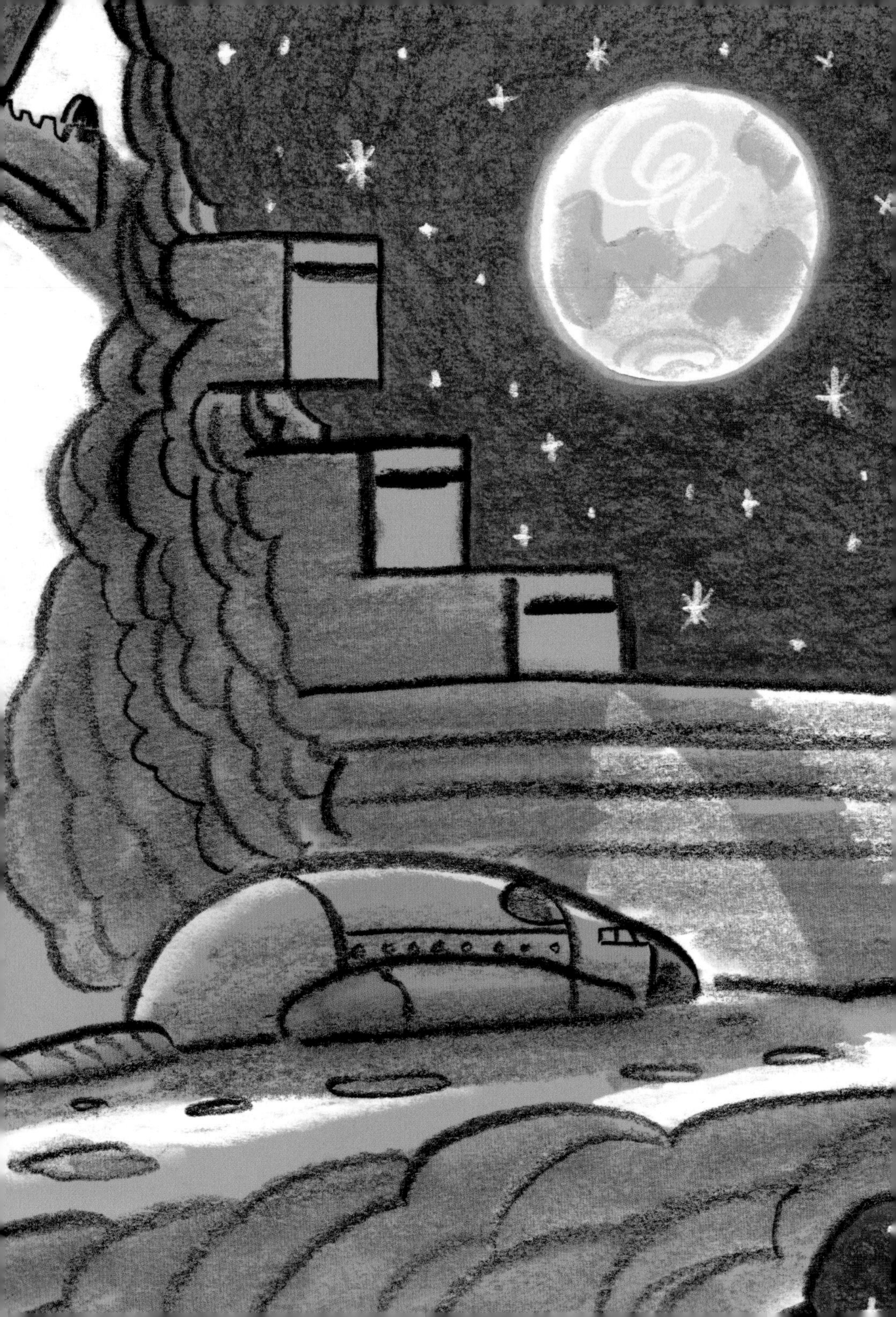

CHAPTER 21

THE RAT KING'S FORTRESS

267

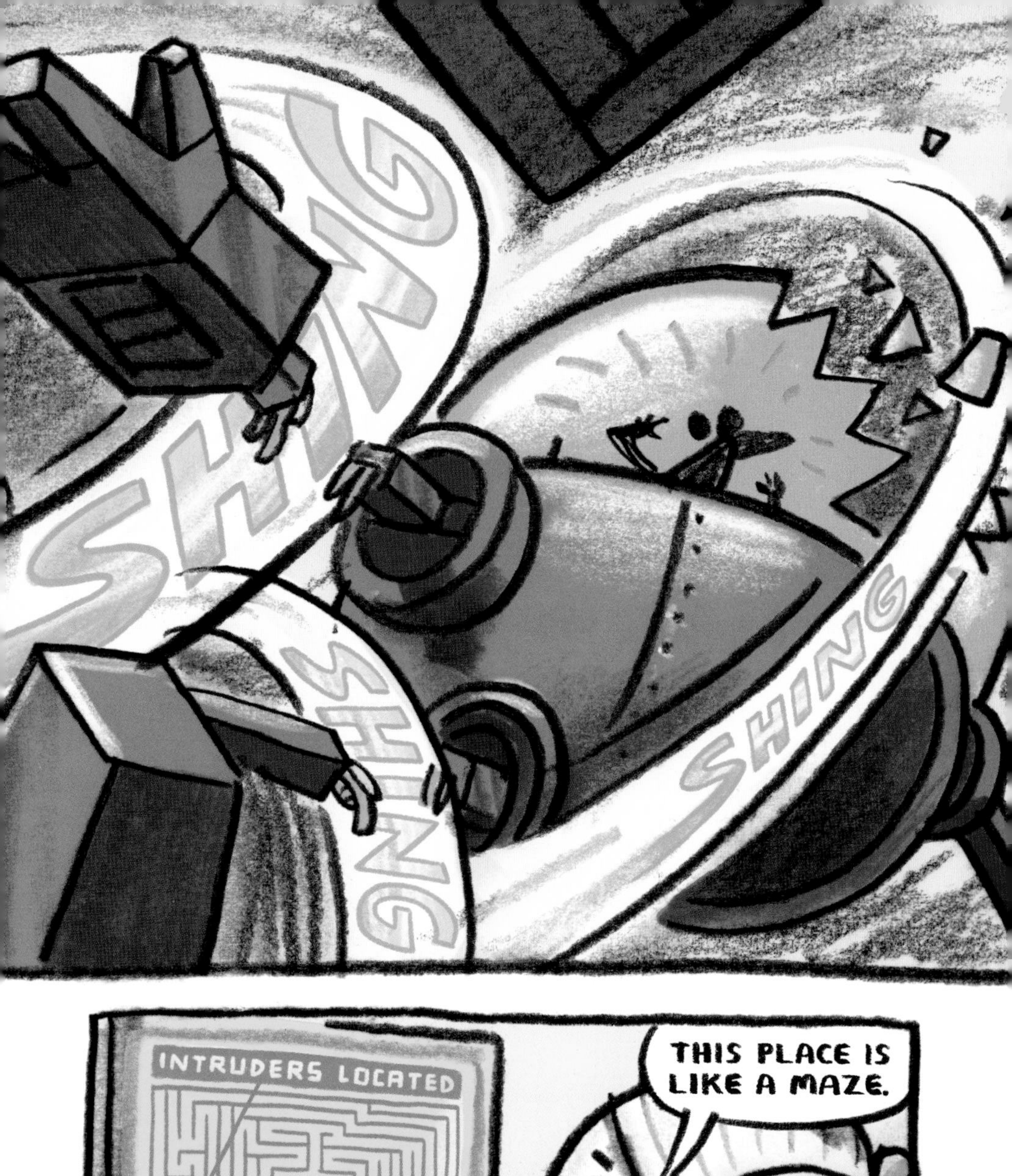
SHING
SHING
SHING
SHING

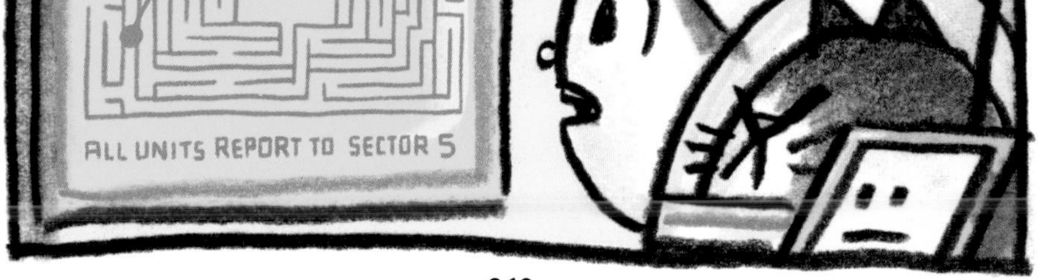
INTRUDERS LOCATED
ALL UNITS REPORT TO SECTOR 5
THIS PLACE IS LIKE A MAZE.

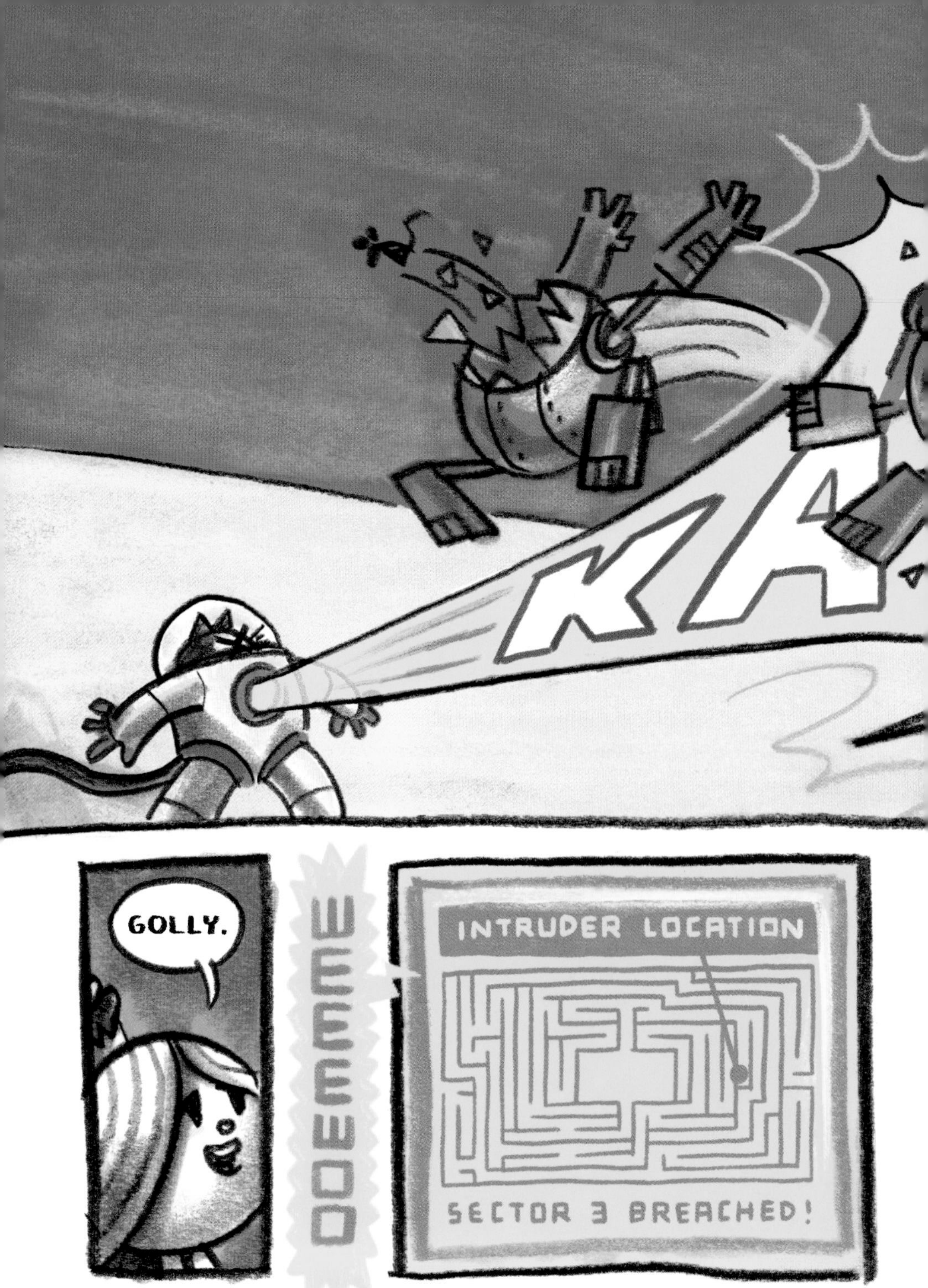

KA
GOLLY.
WEEEWOO
INTRUDER LOCATION
SECTOR 3 BREACHED!

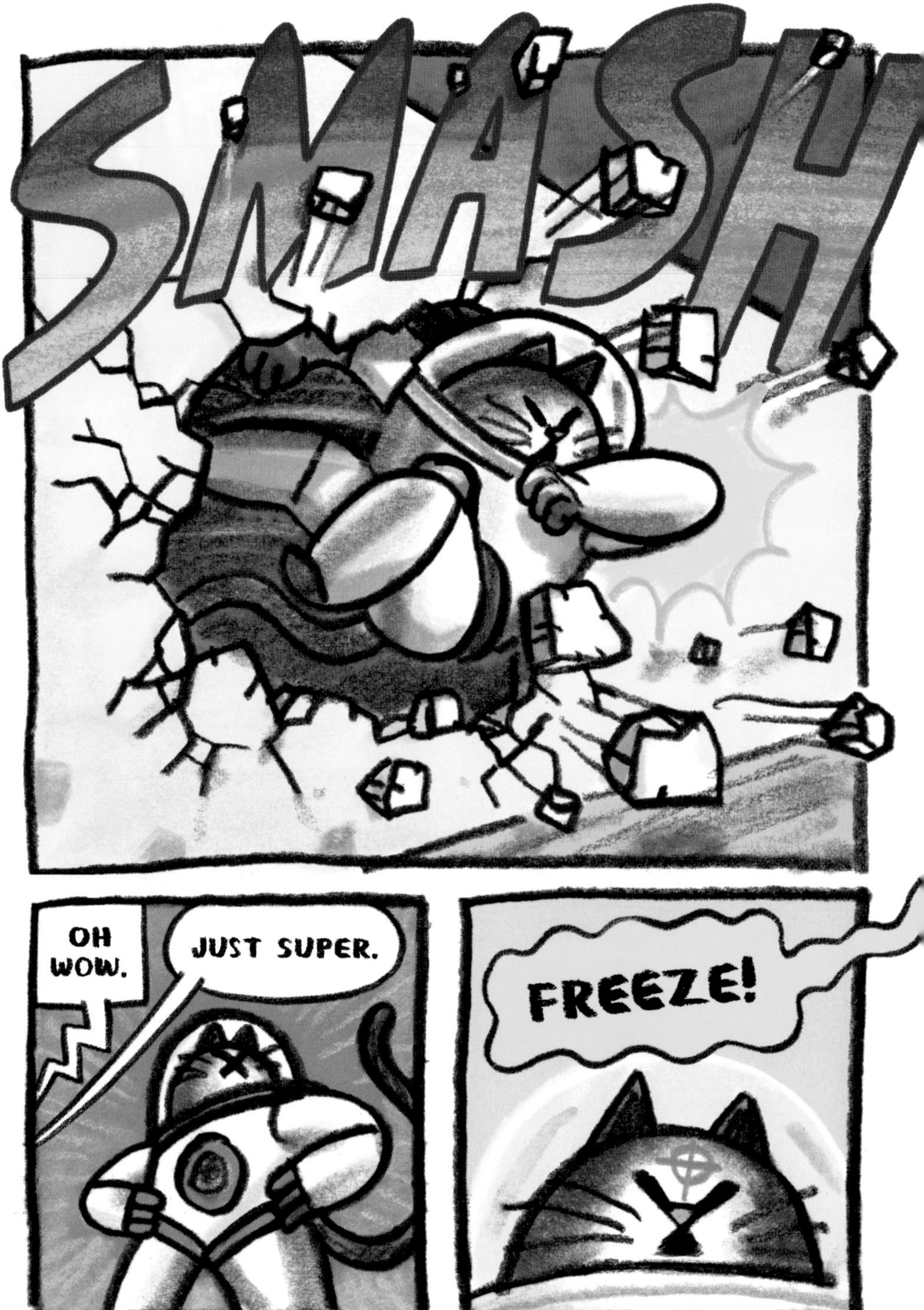
SMASH
OH WOW.
JUST SUPER.
FREEZE!

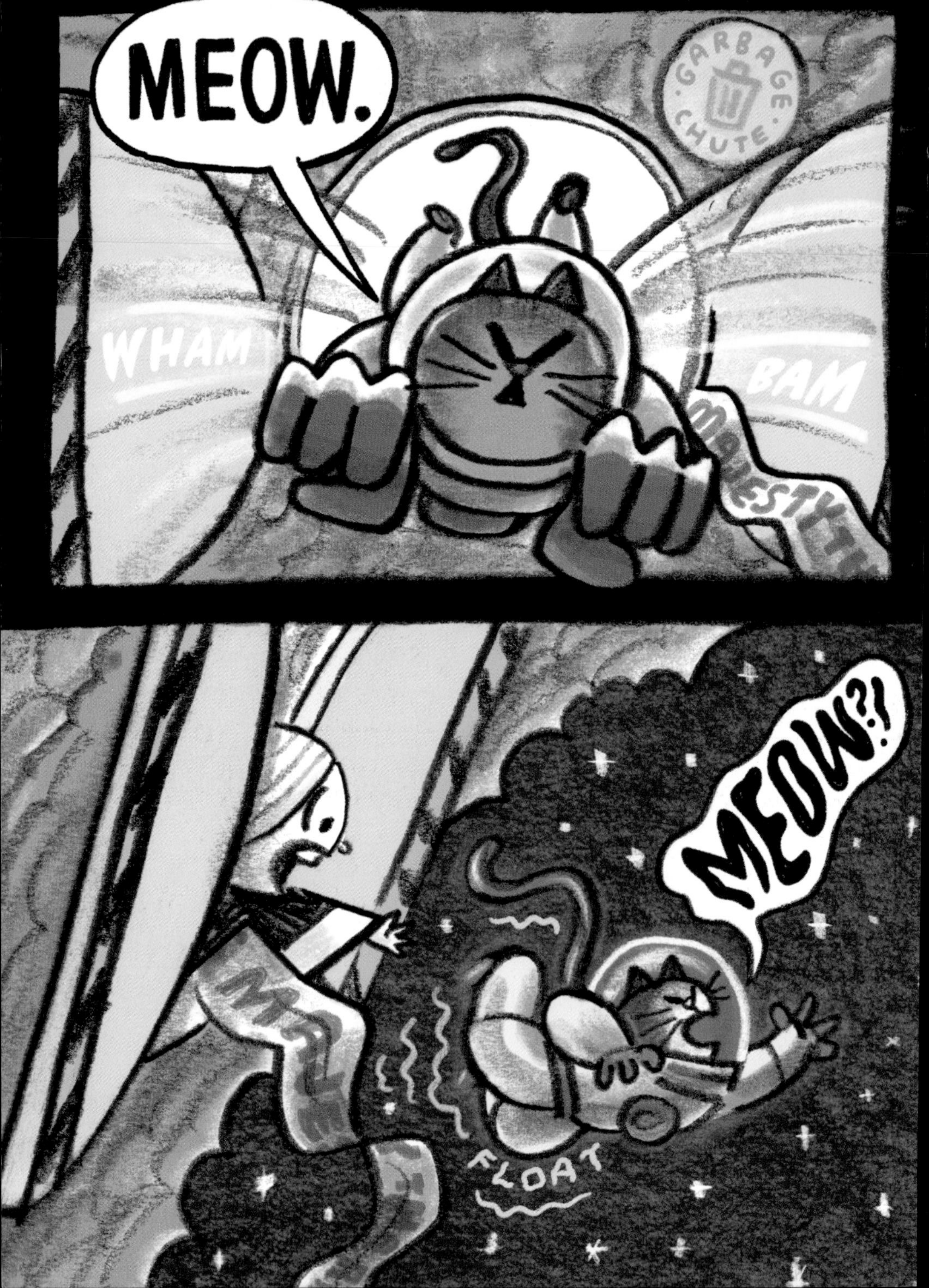
MEOW.
GARBAGE CHUTE
WHAM
BAM
MAJESTY
MEOW?!
FLOAT

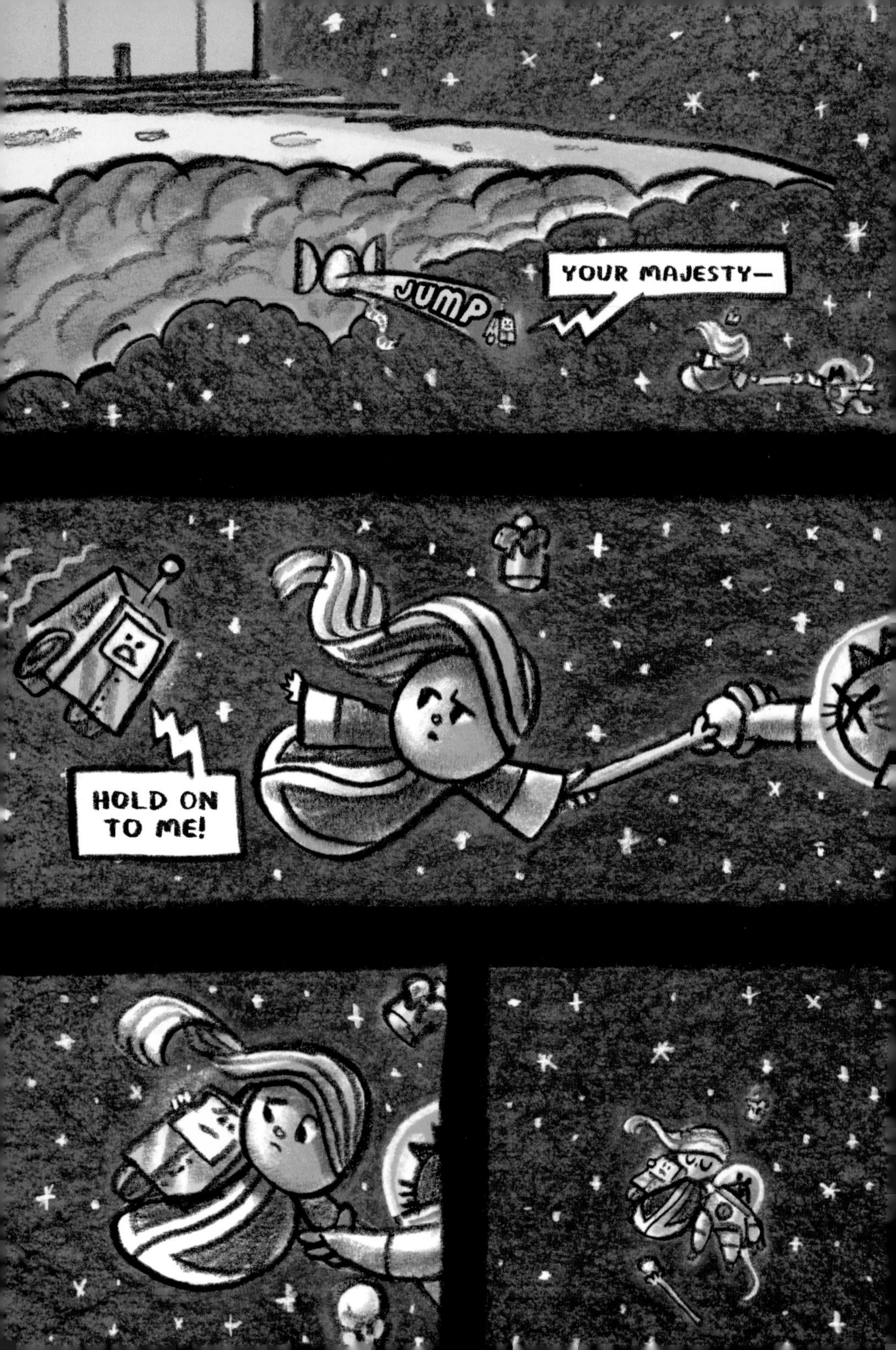
JUMP
YOUR MAJESTY—
HOLD ON
TO ME!

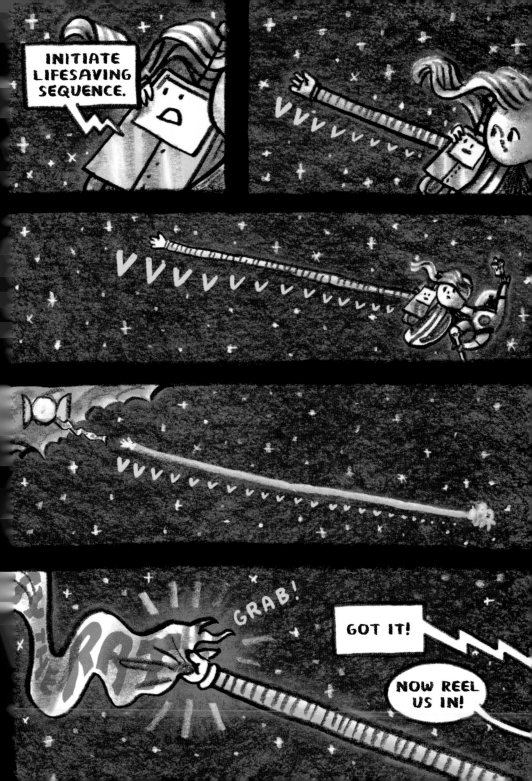

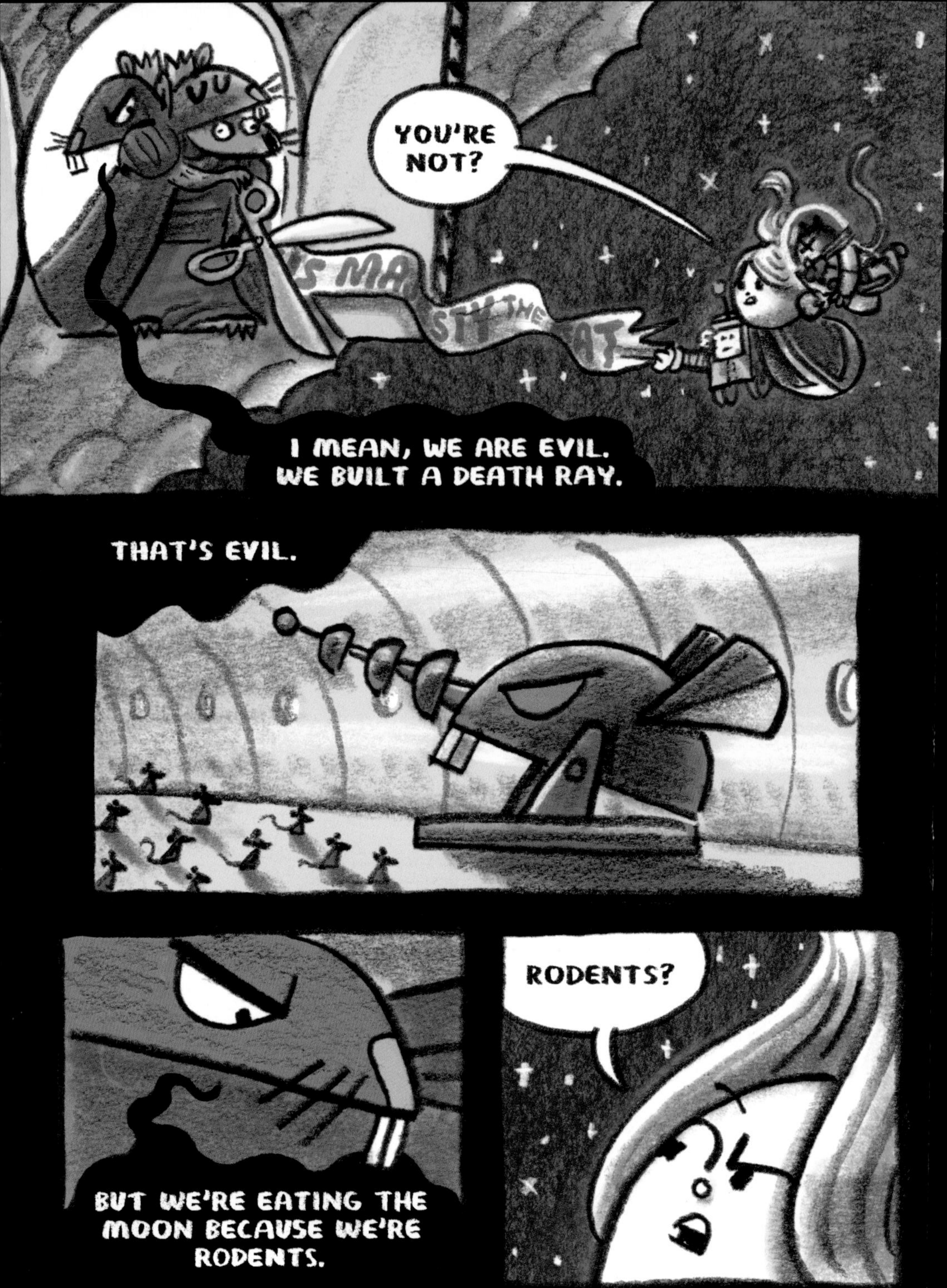
YOU'RE NOT?
I MEAN, WE ARE EVIL. WE BUILT A DEATH RAY.
THAT'S EVIL.
BUT WE'RE EATING THE MOON BECAUSE WE'RE RODENTS.
RODENTS?

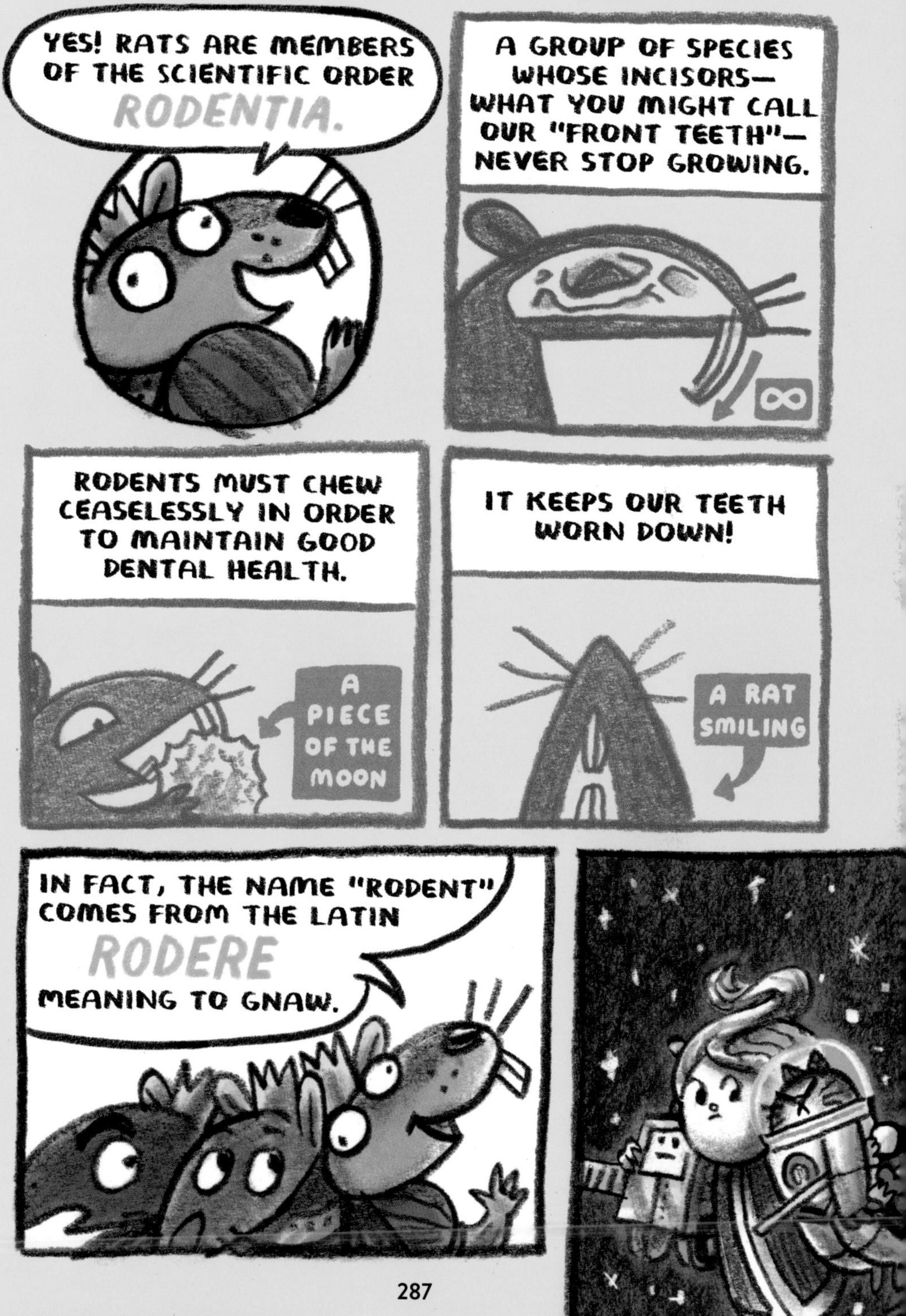
YES! RATS ARE MEMBERS OF THE SCIENTIFIC ORDER RODENTIA.
A GROUP OF SPECIES WHOSE INCISORS— WHAT YOU MIGHT CALL OUR "FRONT TEETH"— NEVER STOP GROWING.
∞
RODENTS MUST CHEW CEASELESSLY IN ORDER TO MAINTAIN GOOD DENTAL HEALTH.
A PIECE OF THE MOON
IT KEEPS OUR TEETH WORN DOWN!
A RAT SMILING
IN FACT, THE NAME "RODENT" COMES FROM THE LATIN RODERE MEANING TO GNAW.

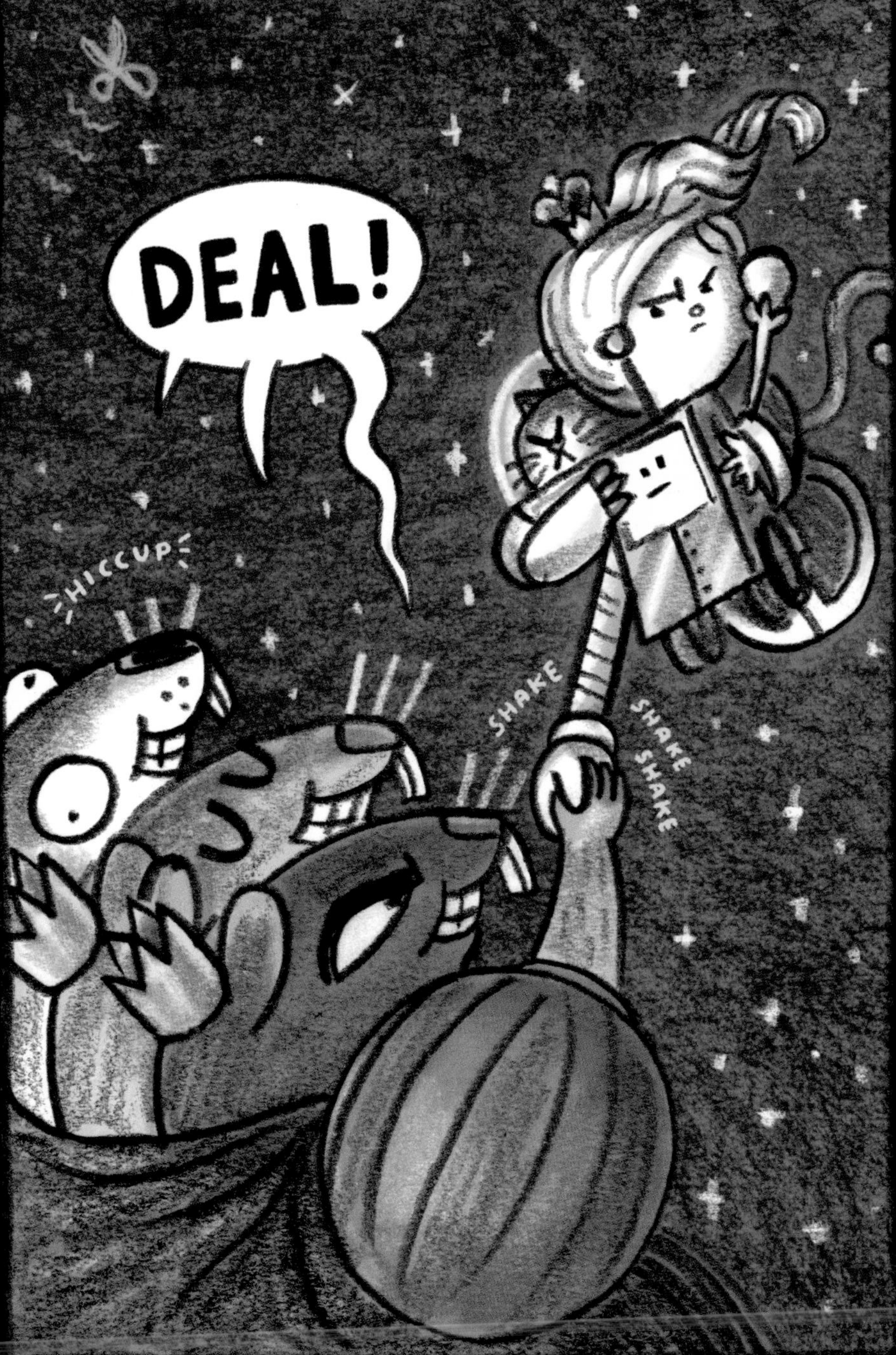
DEAL!
HICCUP
SHAKE
SHAKE
SHAKE

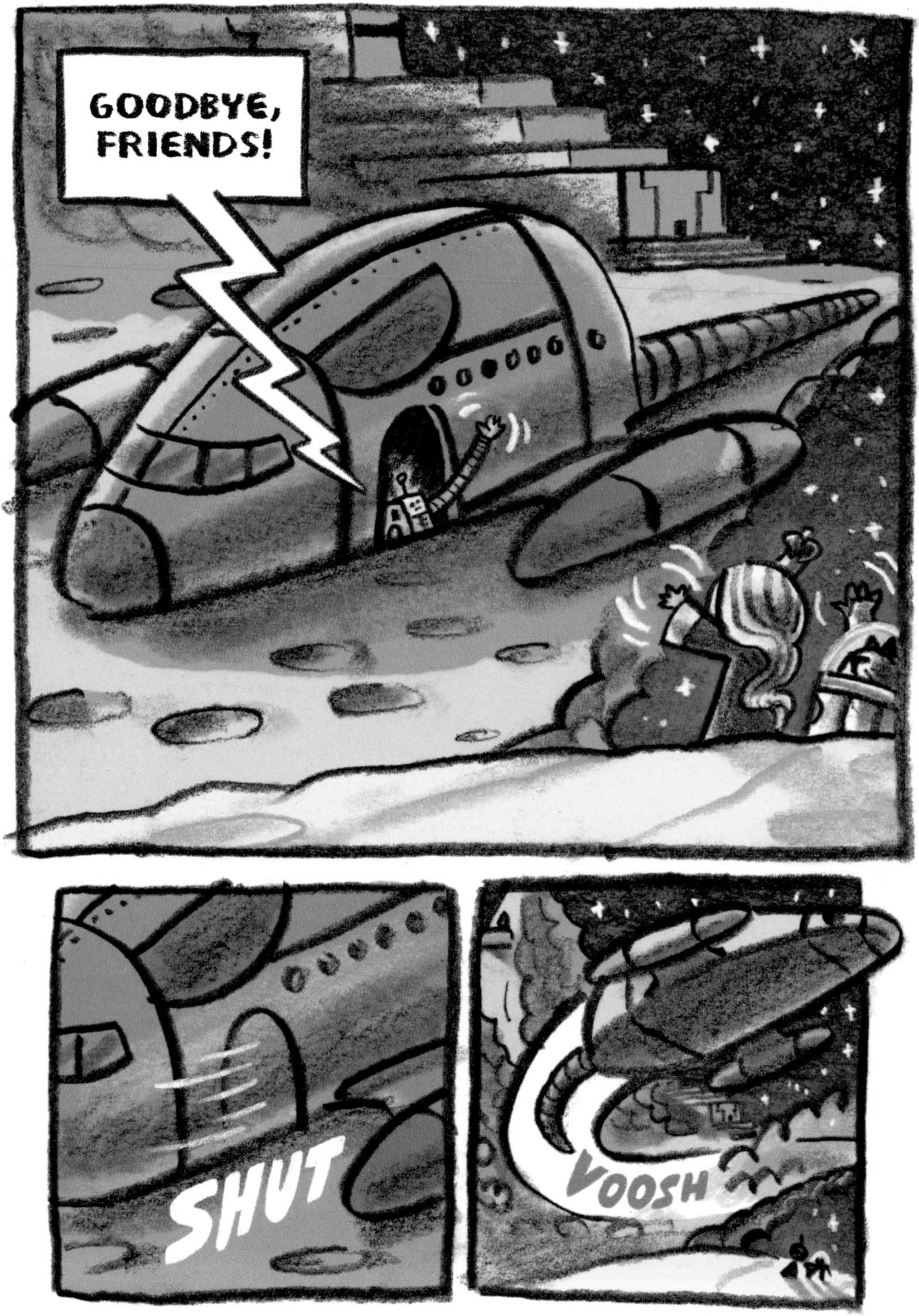
GOODBYE, FRIENDS!
SHUT
VOOSH

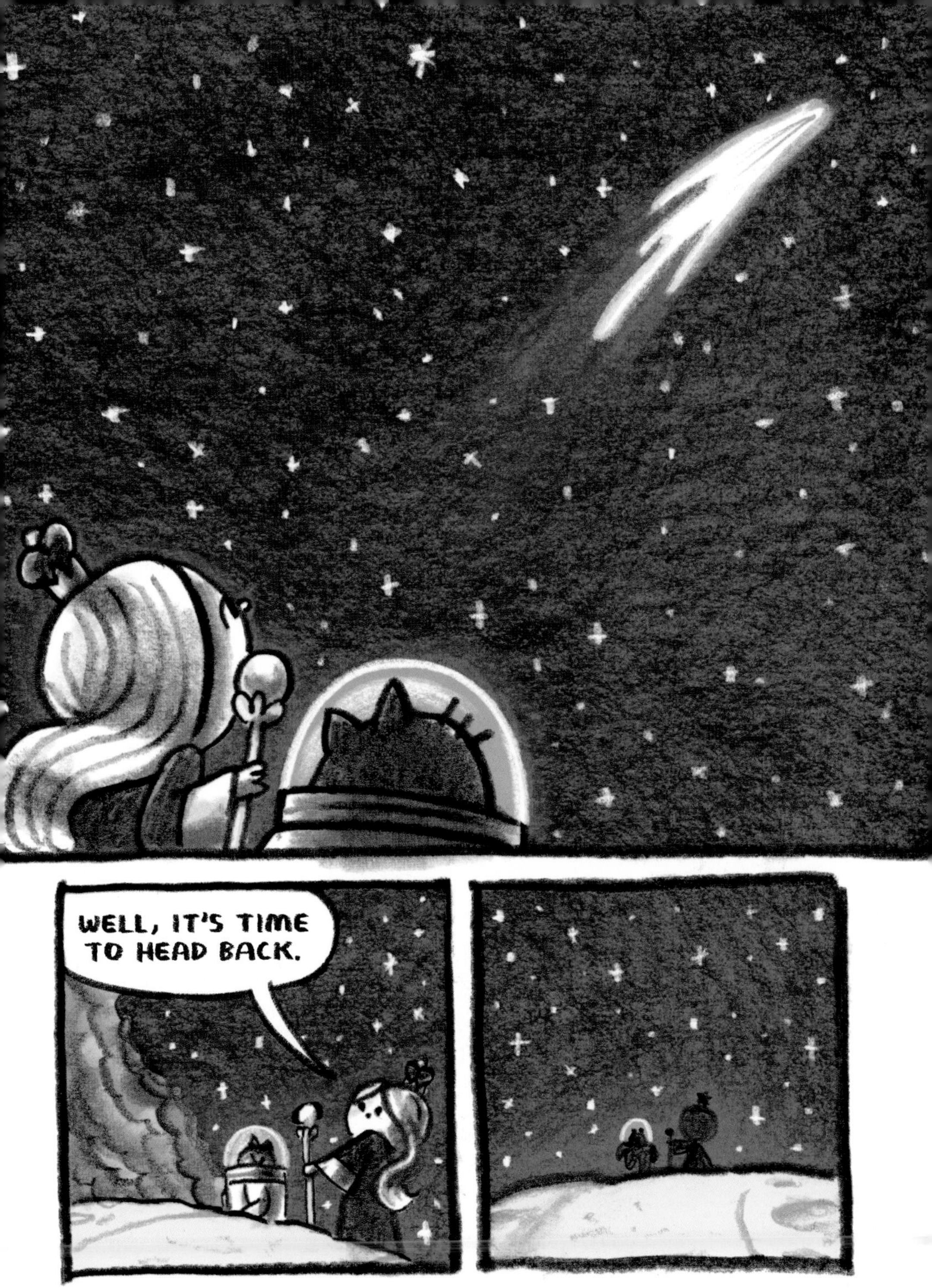
WELL, IT'S TIME TO HEAD BACK.

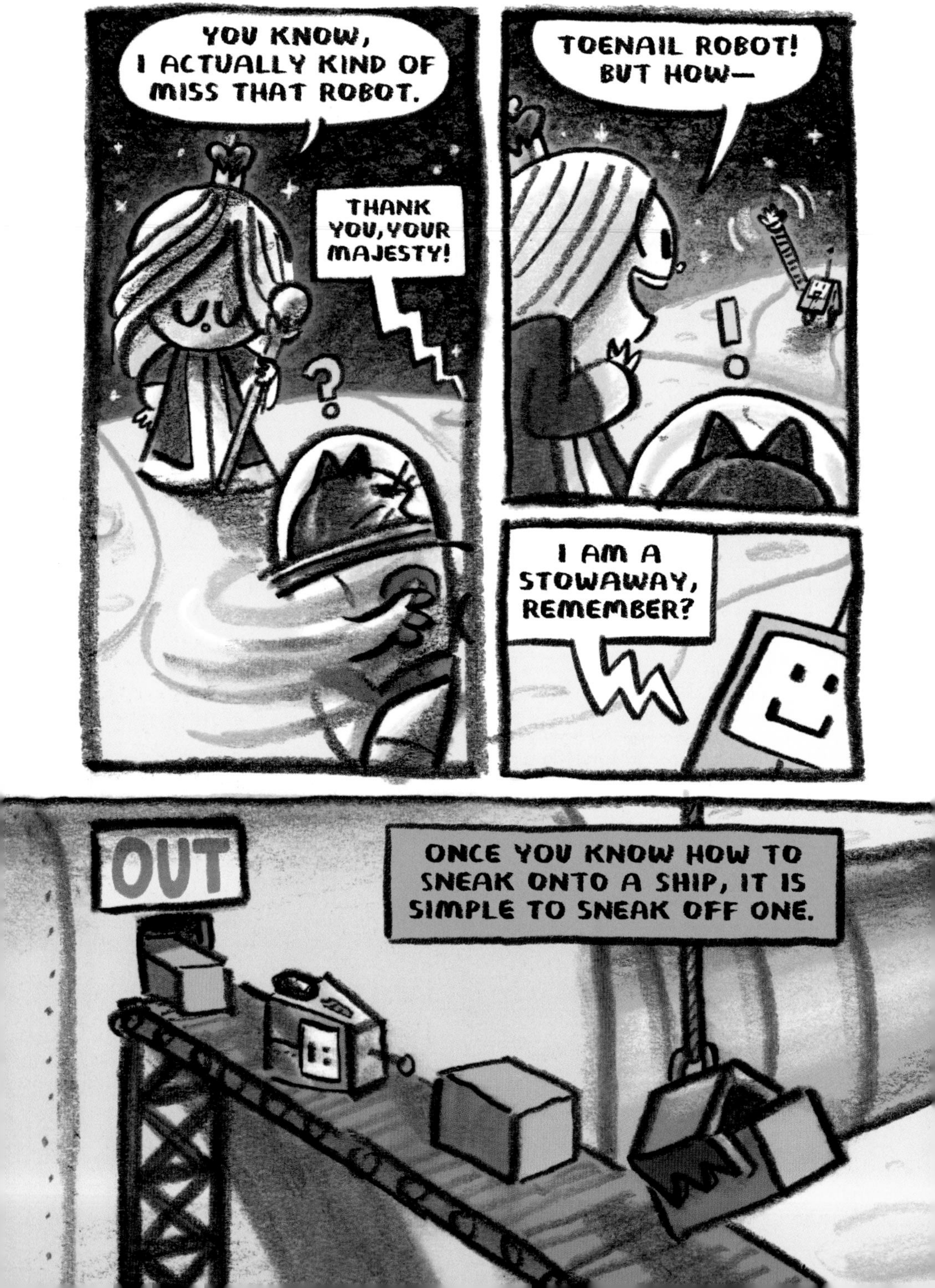
YOU KNOW, I ACTUALLY KIND OF MISS THAT ROBOT.
THANK YOU, YOUR MAJESTY!
?
TOENAIL ROBOT! BUT HOW—
!
I AM A STOWAWAY, REMEMBER?
OUT
ONCE YOU KNOW HOW TO SNEAK ONTO A SHIP, IT IS SIMPLE TO SNEAK OFF ONE.

IN THE BEGINNING, I WAS SURE MY PURPOSE IN THIS VAST UNIVERSE WOULD INVOLVE CLIPPING.

BUT OVER THE COURSE OF OUR JOURNEY, I REALIZED I AM CALLED TO A HIGHER PURPOSE:

TO BE A HERO.

TO BE COURAGEOUS! TO BE HONORABLE! TO BE LOYAL TO MY FRIENDS!

OK, OK, I GET IT. I FORGOT HOW MUCH THIS TOENAIL ROBOT TALKS!

MEOW?

THAT'S TRUE! WHAT WILL HAPPEN WHEN THE RAT KING DISCOVERS YOU ARE MISSING?

OH, I WOULD NOT WORRY ABOUT THAT.

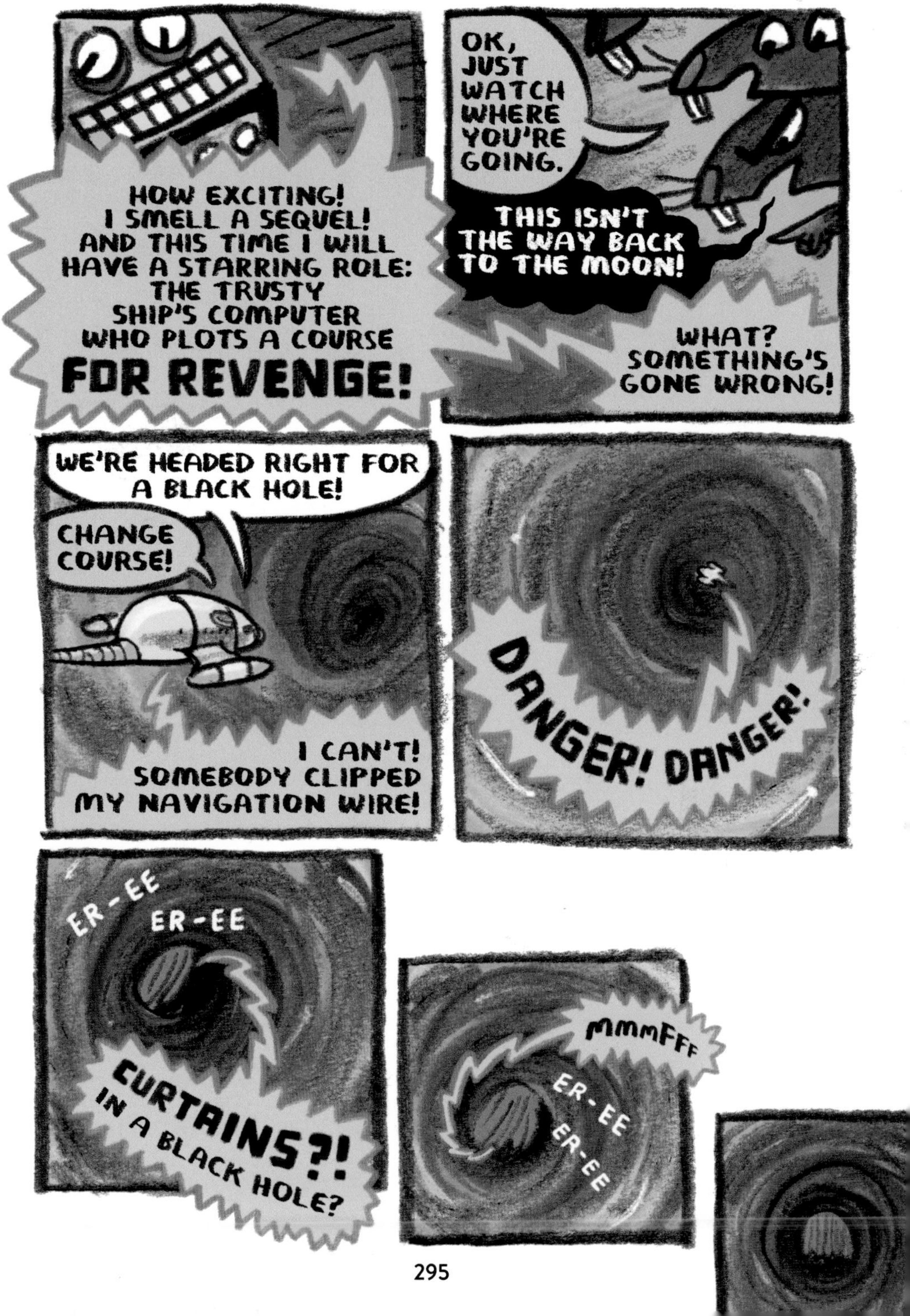
HOW EXCITING! I SMELL A SEQUEL! AND THIS TIME I WILL HAVE A STARRING ROLE: THE TRUSTY SHIP'S COMPUTER WHO PLOTS A COURSE FOR REVENGE!
OK, JUST WATCH WHERE YOU'RE GOING.
THIS ISN'T THE WAY BACK TO THE MOON!
WHAT? SOMETHING'S GONE WRONG!
WE'RE HEADED RIGHT FOR A BLACK HOLE!
CHANGE COURSE!
I CAN'T! SOMEBODY CLIPPED MY NAVIGATION WIRE!
DANGER! DANGER!
ER-EE
ER-EE
CURTAINS?! IN A BLACK HOLE?
MmmFFF
ER-EE
ER-EE

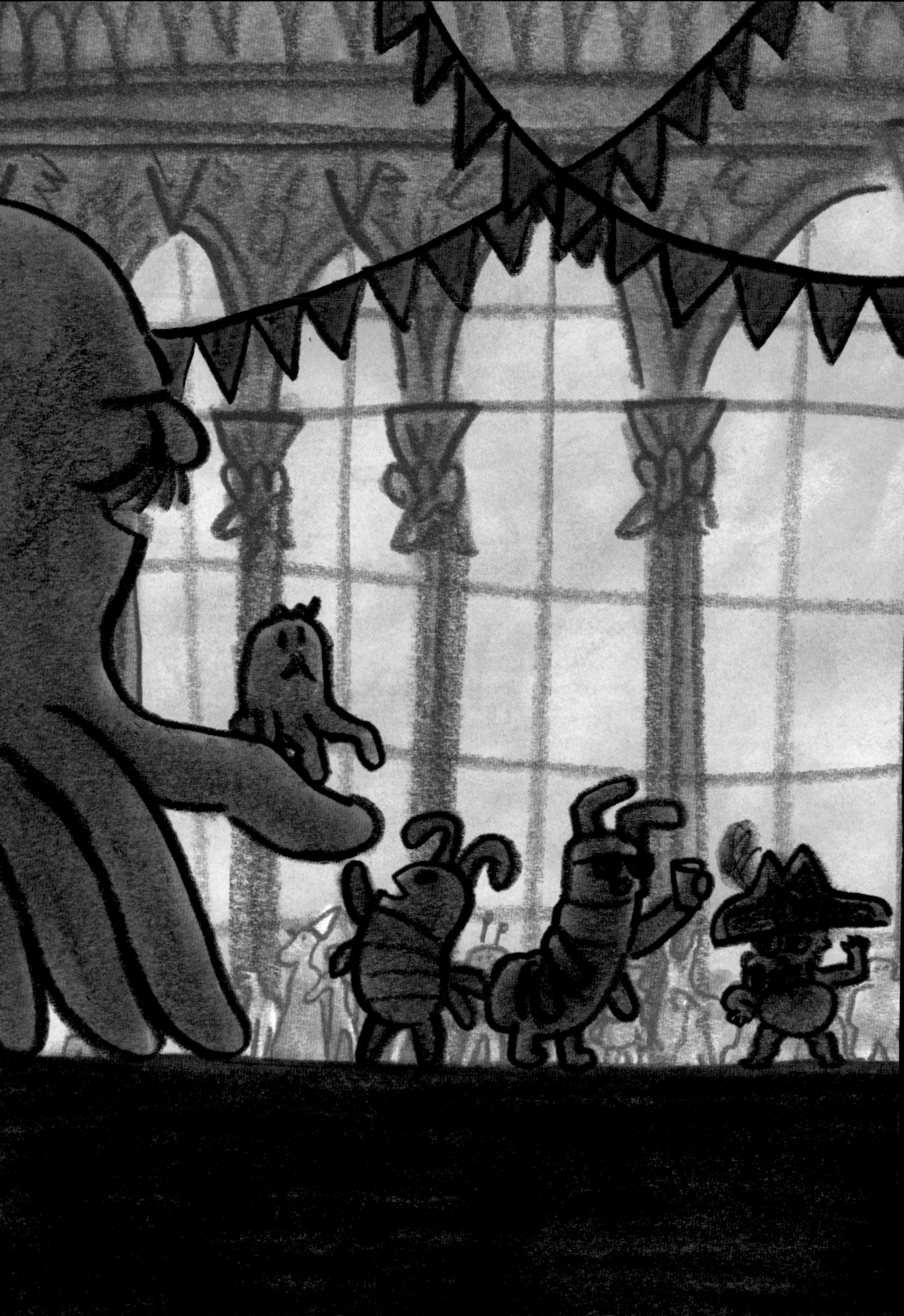

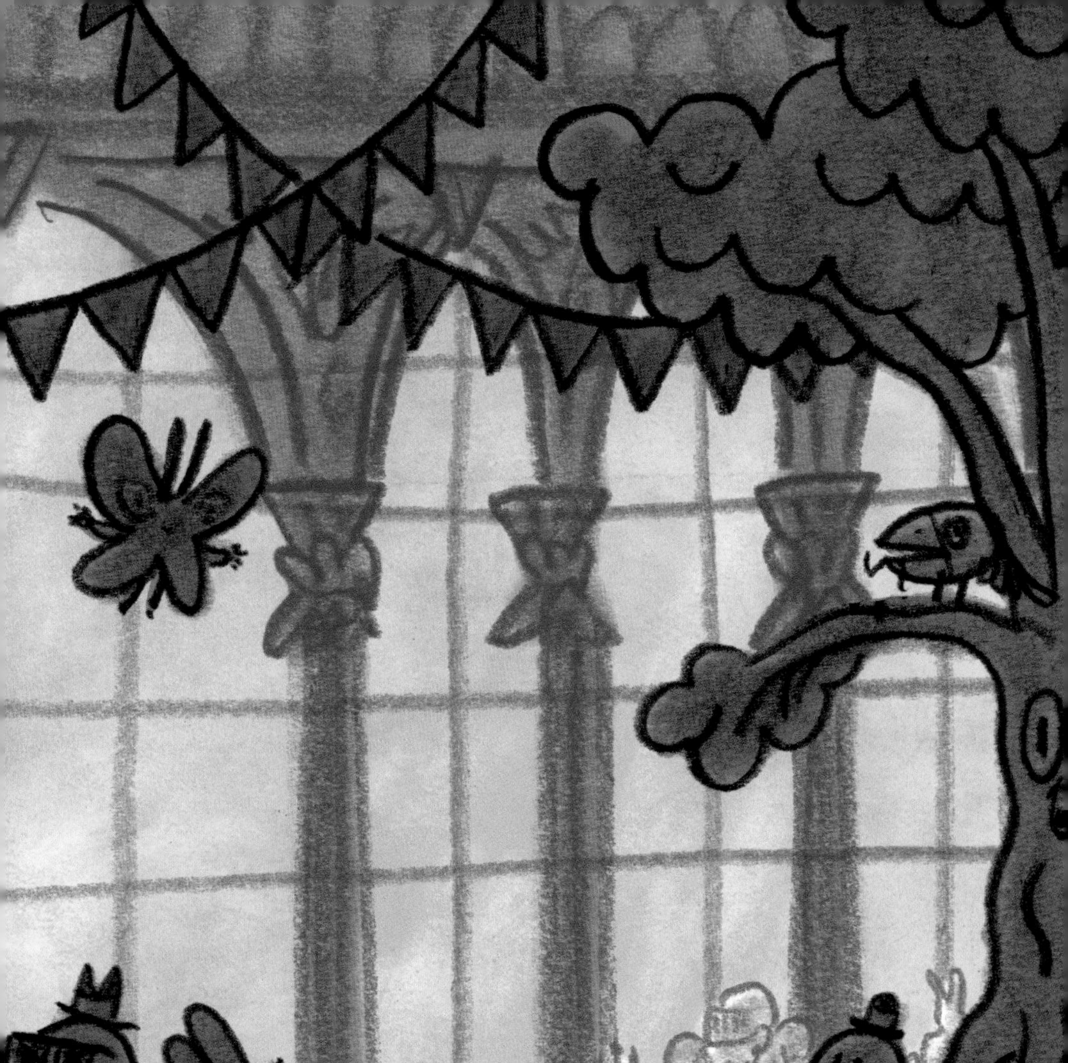

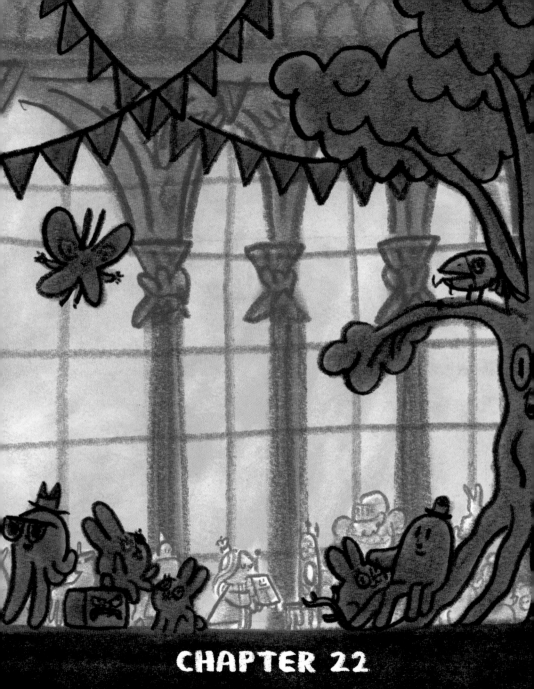

CHAPTER 22

FANCY FEAST

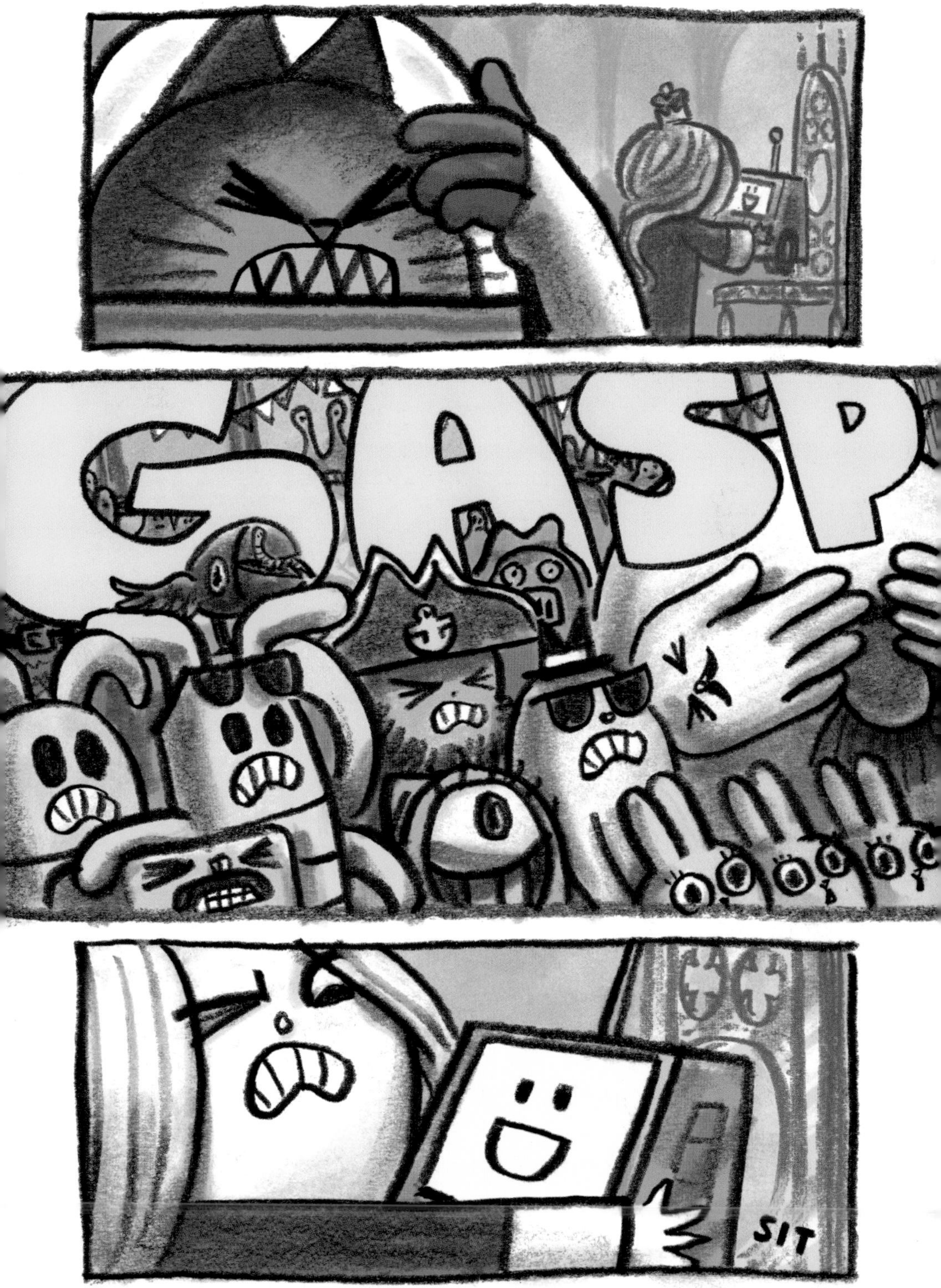
GASP
SIT

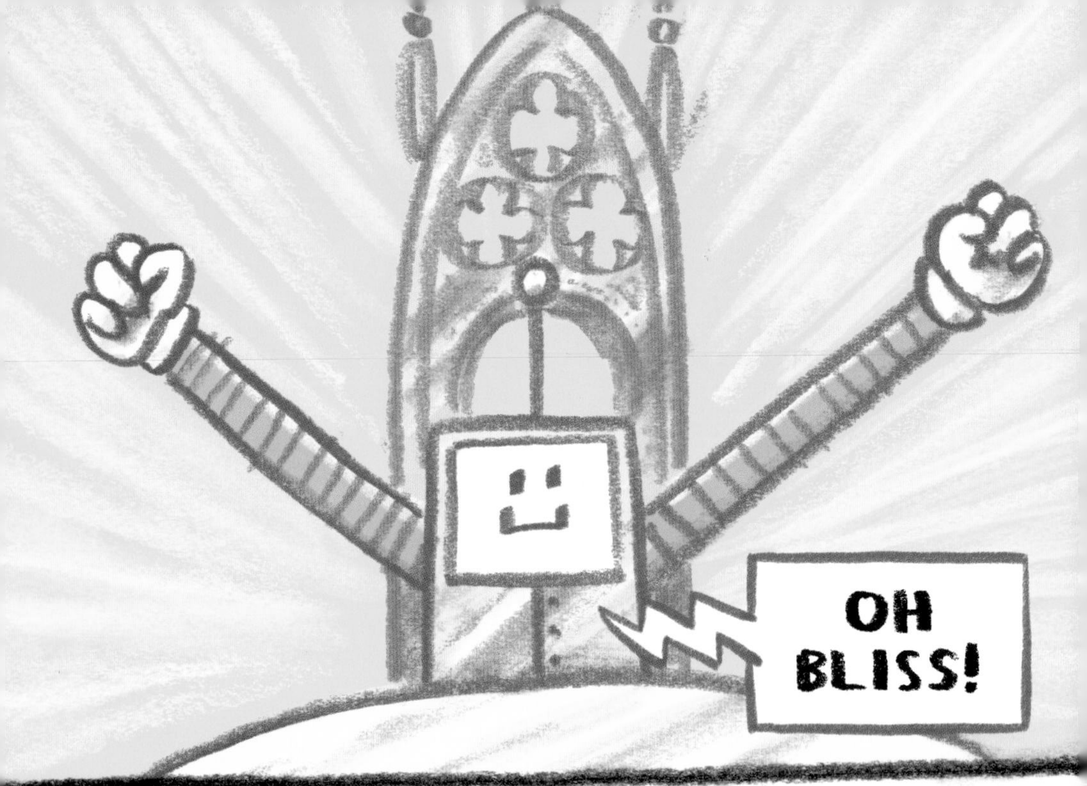
OH BLISS!

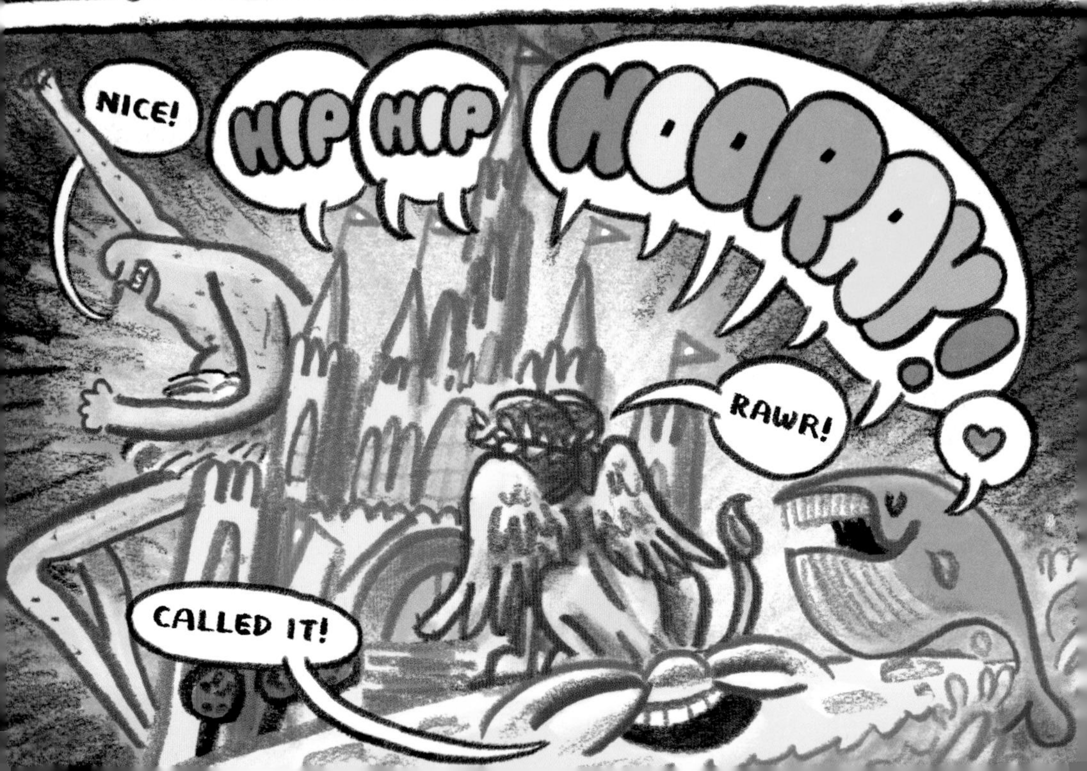
NICE!
HIP HIP
HOORAY!!
RAWR!
CALLED IT!

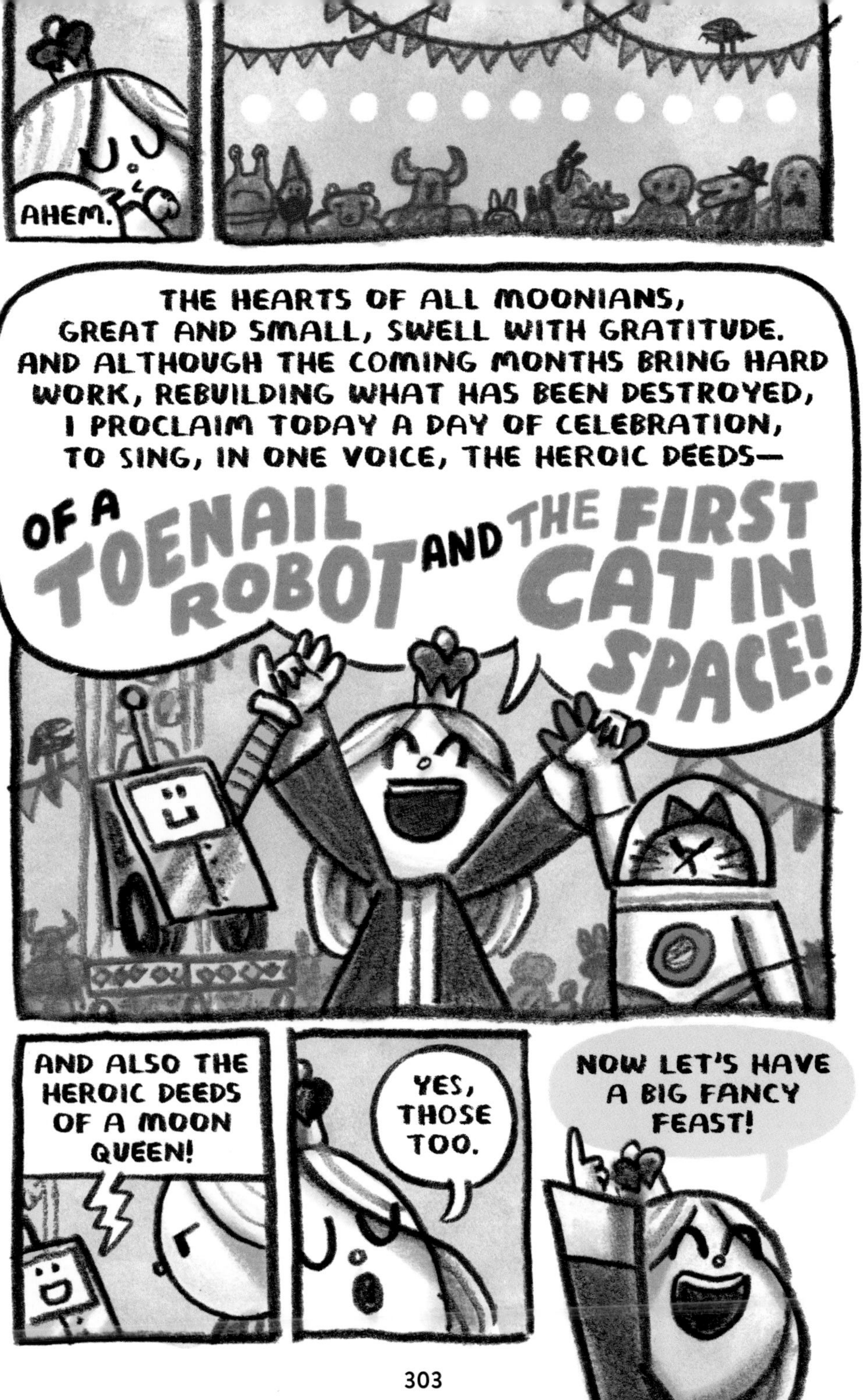
AHEM.
THE HEARTS OF ALL MOONIANS, GREAT AND SMALL, SWELL WITH GRATITUDE. AND ALTHOUGH THE COMING MONTHS BRING HARD WORK, REBUILDING WHAT HAS BEEN DESTROYED, I PROCLAIM TODAY A DAY OF CELEBRATION, TO SING, IN ONE VOICE, THE HEROIC DEEDS—
OF A TOENAIL ROBOT AND THE FIRST CAT IN SPACE!
AND ALSO THE HEROIC DEEDS OF A MOON QUEEN!
YES, THOSE TOO.
NOW LET'S HAVE A BIG FANCY FEAST!

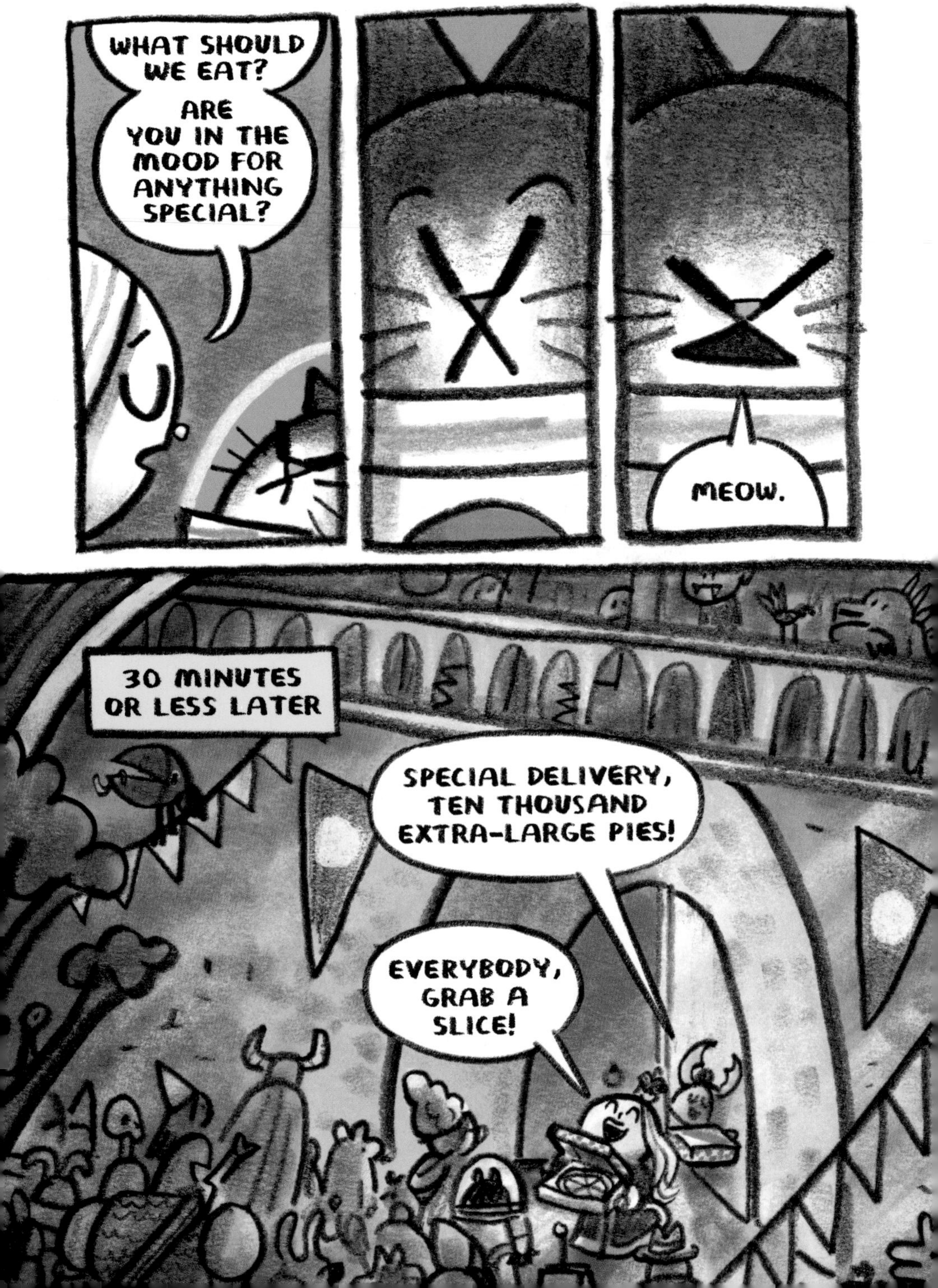
WHAT SHOULD WE EAT?
ARE YOU IN THE MOOD FOR ANYTHING SPECIAL?
MEOW.
30 MINUTES OR LESS LATER
SPECIAL DELIVERY, TEN THOUSAND EXTRA-LARGE PIES!
EVERYBODY, GRAB A SLICE!

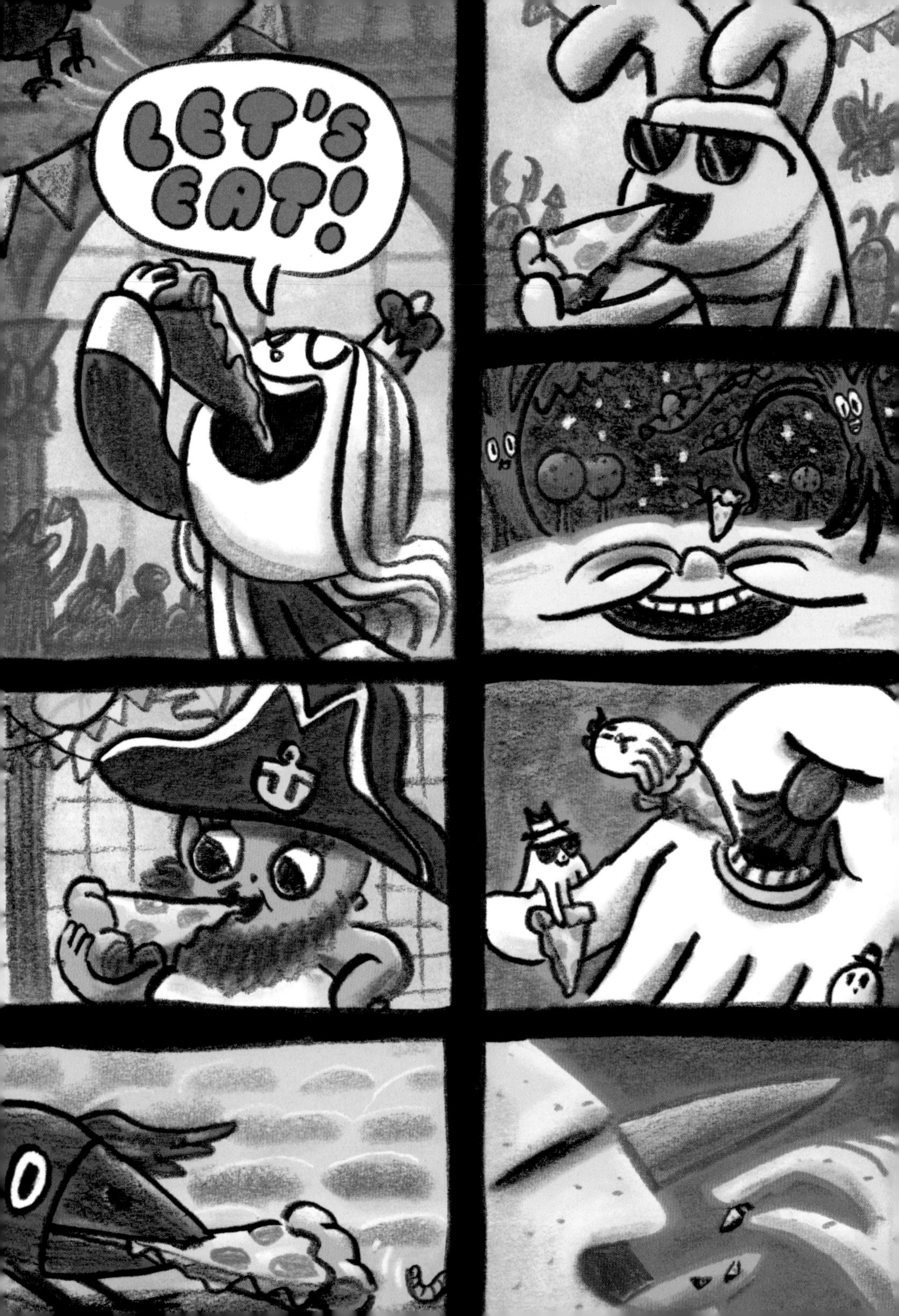
LET'S EAT!

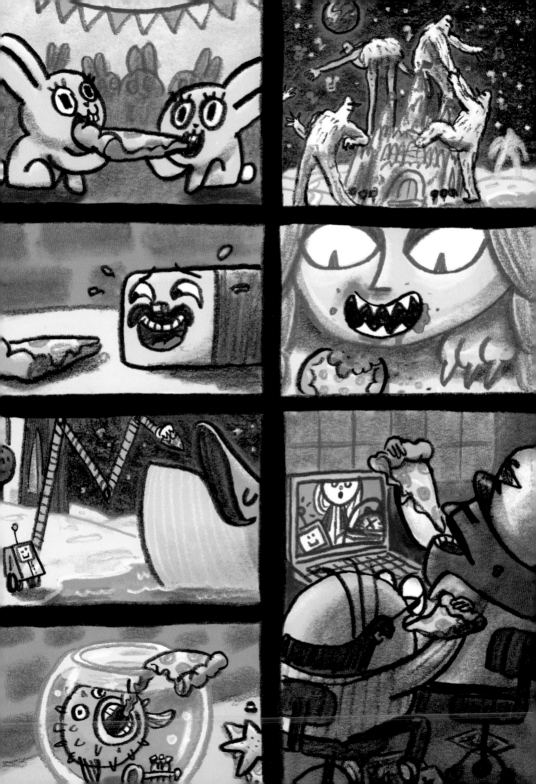

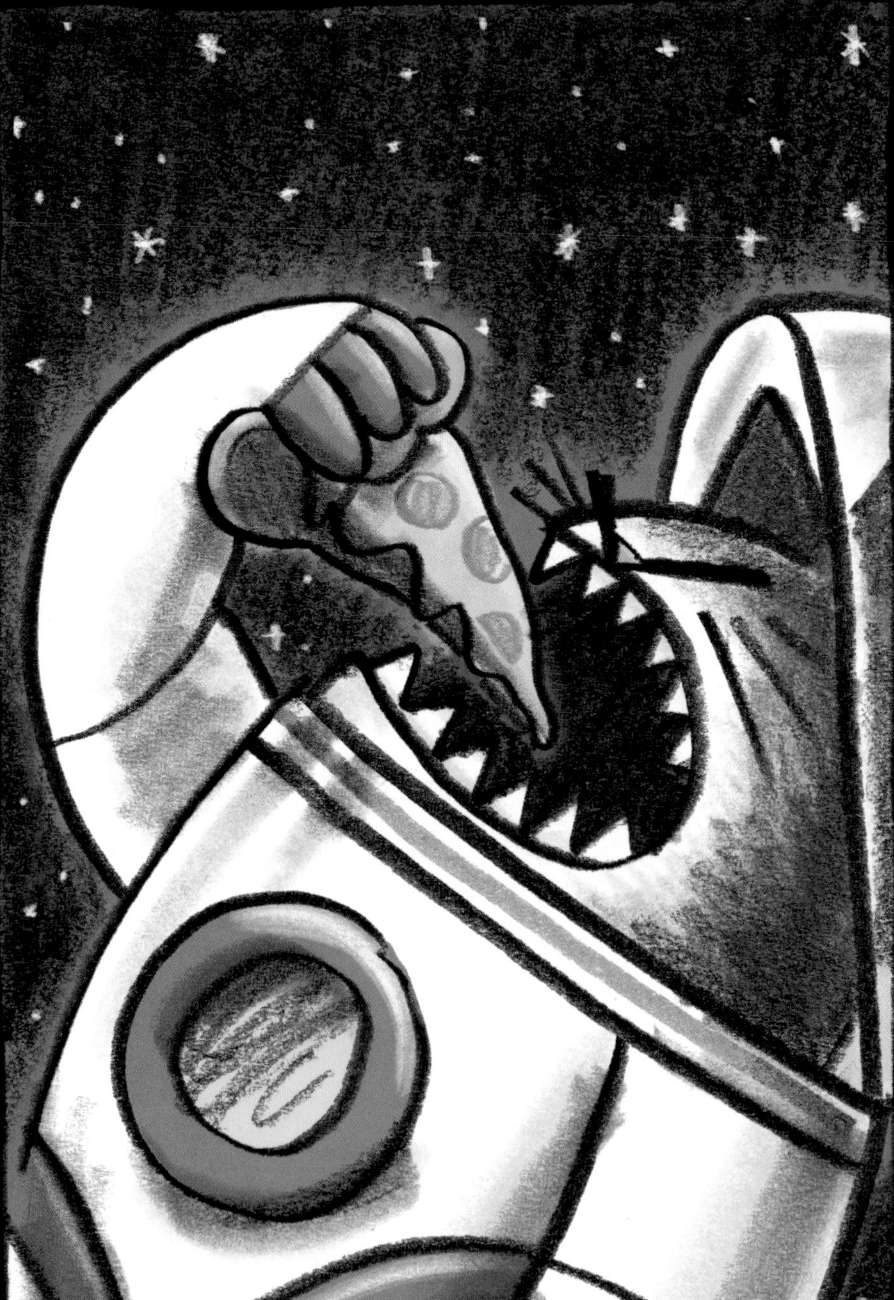

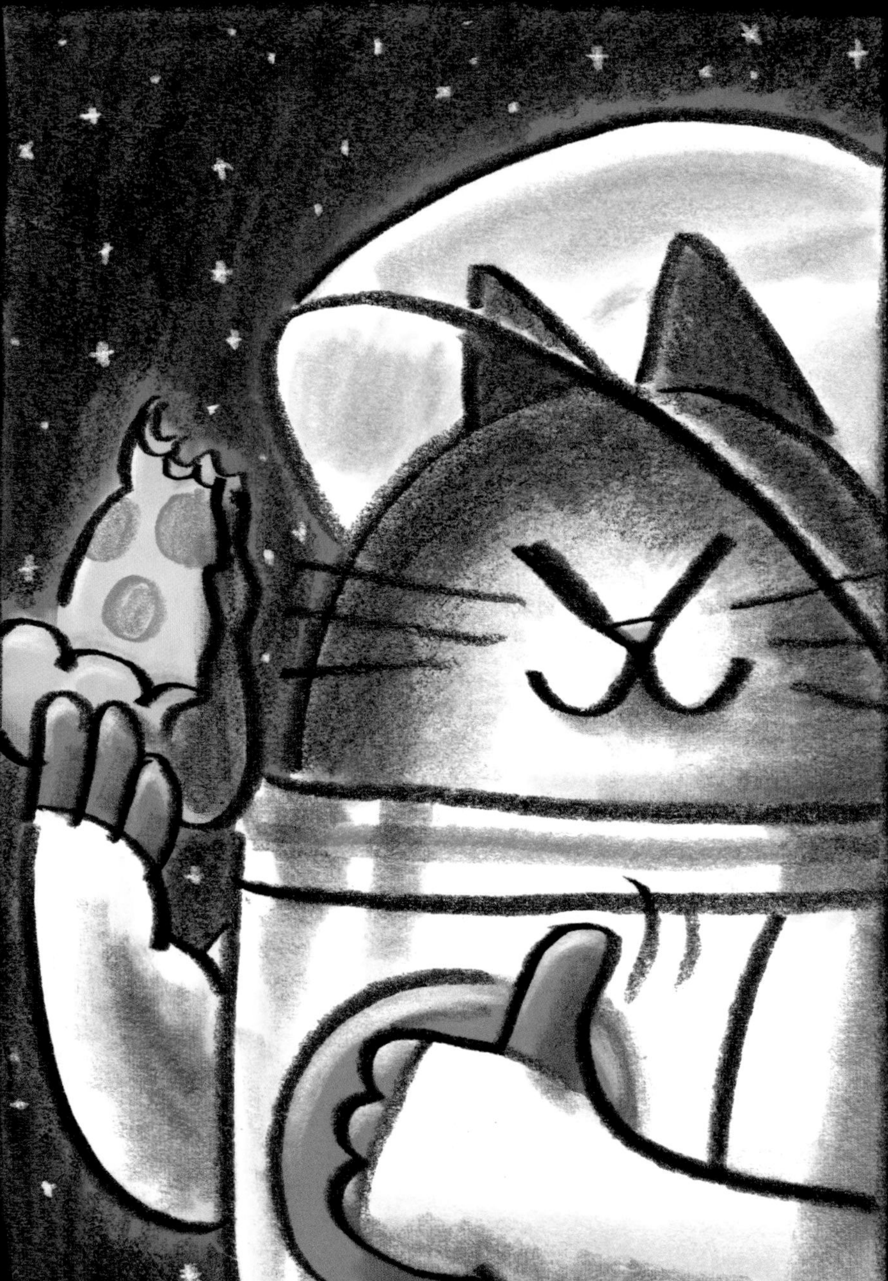

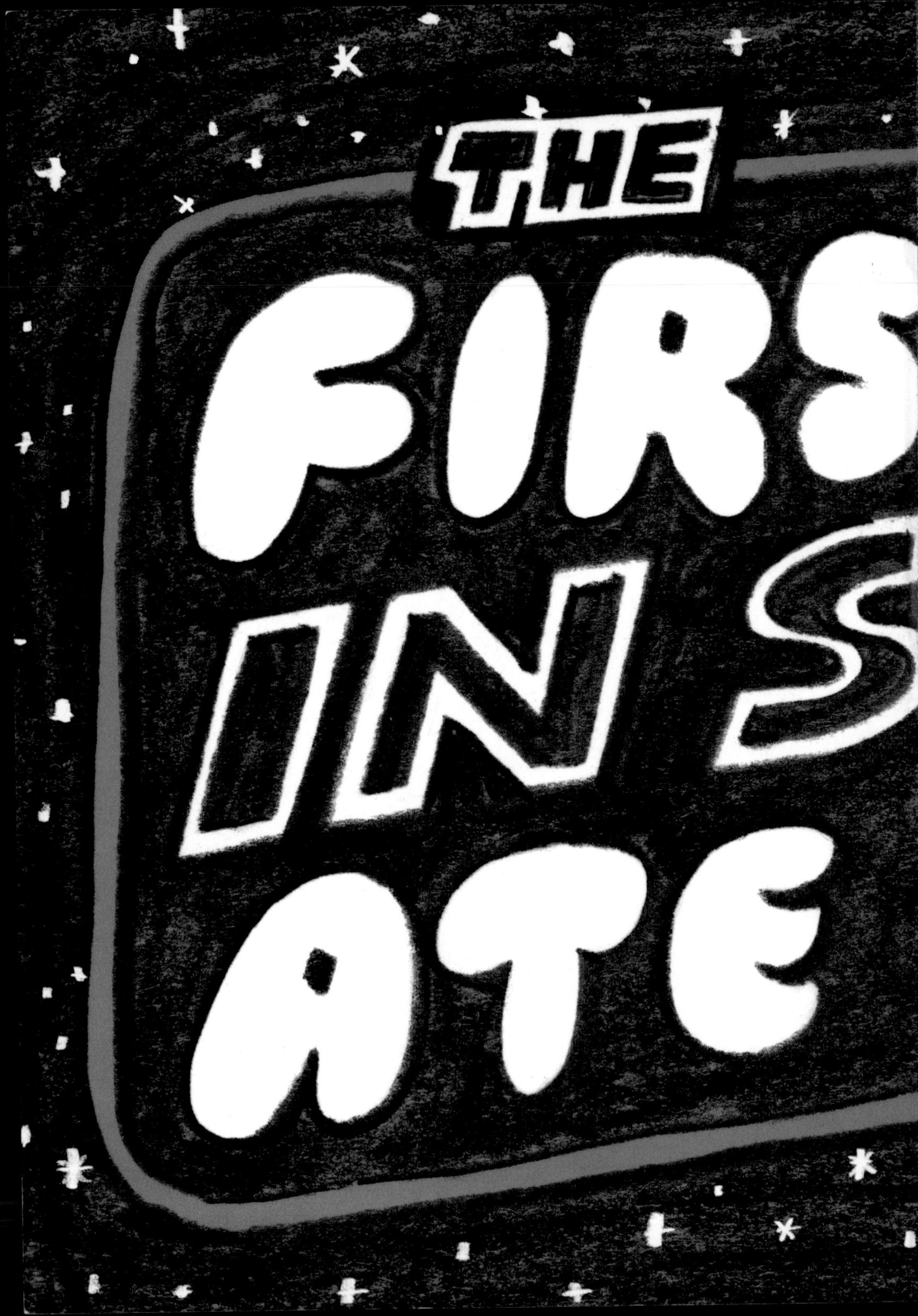
THE
FIRS
IN S
ATE

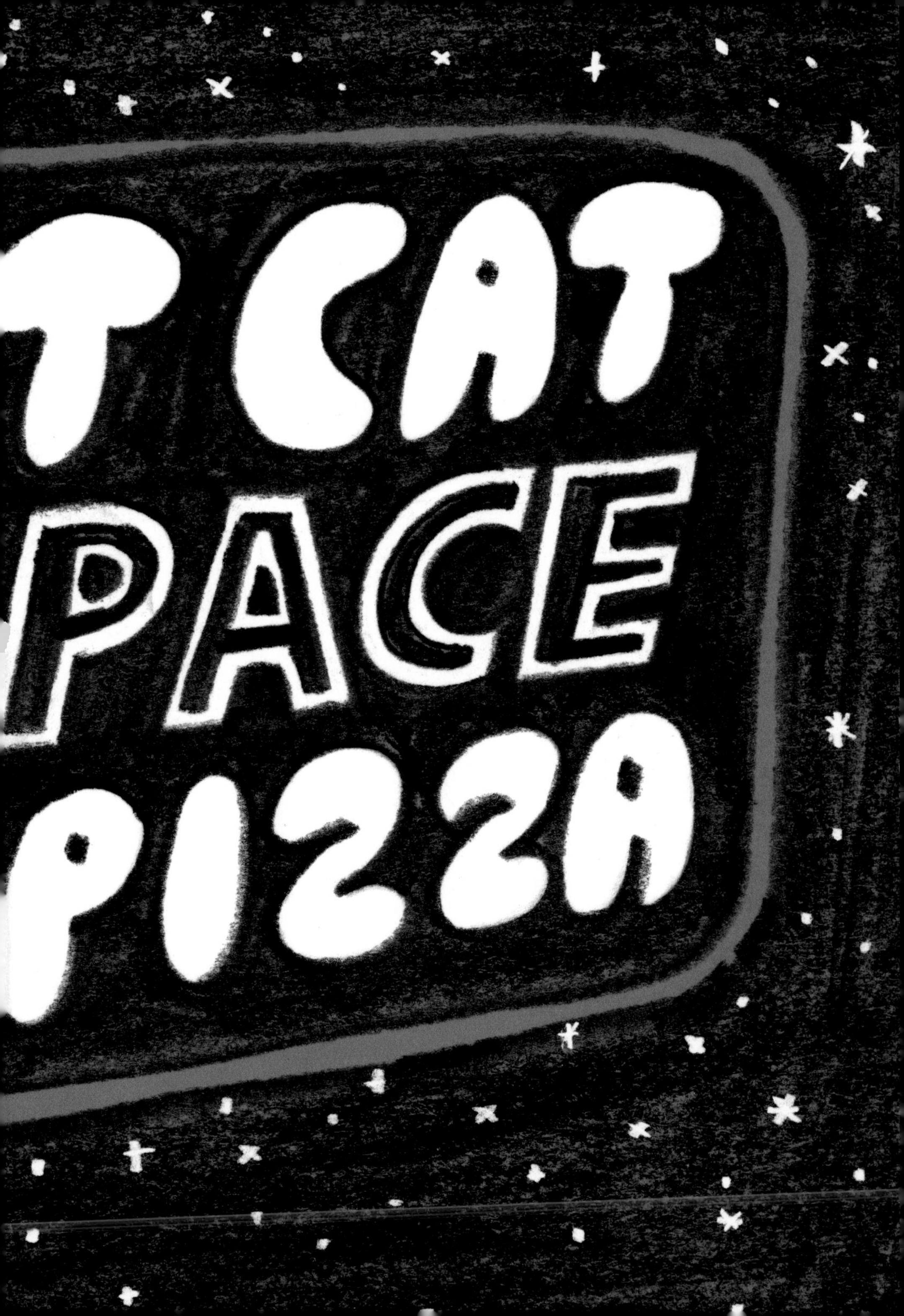
T CAT
PACE
PIZZA

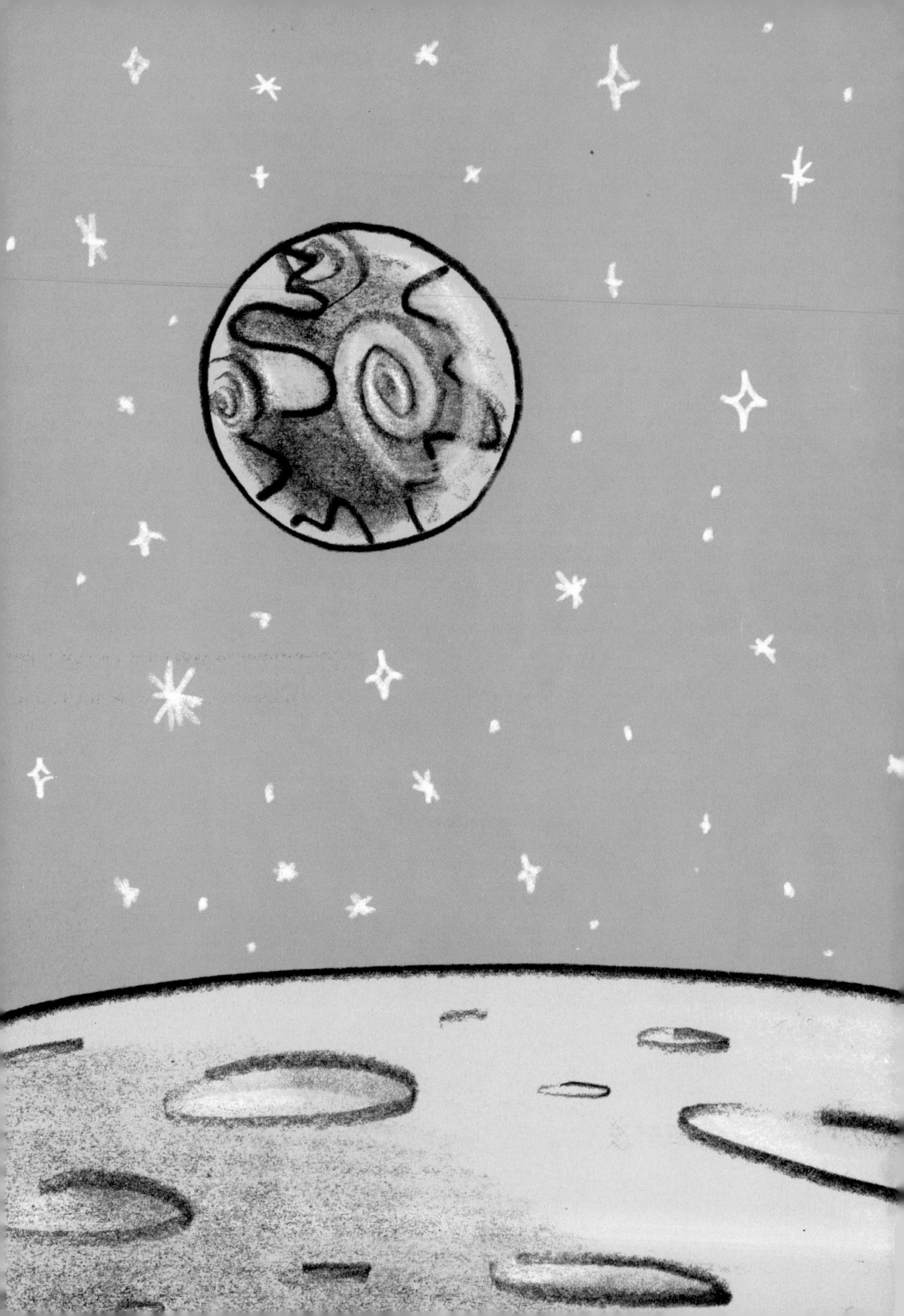